THE DUEL

It has been [illegible] es its terror have a [illegible]

The ladder le[illegible] ...ty feet in length by tw[illegible] ...ad been painted white, and willi[illegible] transformed it into a modern, brightl[illegible] ...hop. A heavy bench, fitted with a vice, stood agains[illegible] one wall, on either side were shelves lined with a magnificent selection of tools – all stolen from British army camps – detonators, coils of wire, insulating tape, detonator cord, batteries, an assortment of watches 'commandeered' from jewellers' shops throughout the island, an ammeter and all the paraphernalia of the modern Guy Fawkes.

'This will be your bomb factory,' said Nicos. He was bursting with pride. 'I furnished it myself.'

'It's magnificent,' Elvides told him. He looked at the boy killer with very different eyes: this was a strictly professional job of work. 'I congratulate you. Really.' They shook hands warmly.

'I haven't finished yet,' said Nicos.

By the same Author

THE BOMB THAT COULD LIP-READ
THE DEFECTOR
THE TERROR SYNDICATE
THE COMMITTEE

Donald Seaman

The Duel

Futura Publications Limited

A Futura Book

First published in Great Britain by
Hamish Hamilton Limited in 1979

First Futura Publications Edition 1980

ISBN 0 7088 1816 1

Reproduced, printed and bound in Great Britain
by Hazell Watson & Viney Ltd
Aylesbury, Bucks

Futura Publications Limited
110 Warner Road
Camberwell, London SE5

This book is for George and Peter, and all who have seen into the mouth of the dragon

FOREWORD

The duel originated in France centuries ago and to most minds, the word epitomises the affair of honour: a contest fought man to man with sword or pistol and with all things equal except the inner qualities of the contestants themselves. Over the years, that image has become a little tarnished. Some of those legendary Wild West gunfight duels were plain murder. Many a German student prized the duelling scars far above the nobility of the encounter. Then, with the advance of technology, the whole character of the duel altered. Fighter pilots travelling faster than sound fight duels, and while their courage may be unsurpassed the outcome too often hinges on the speed and manoeuvrability of the machine they fly in rather than the human element. Likewise, the duel has become largely impersonal: a chance encounter.

In this book I describe a new type of duel, unique to the times we live in. It is a duel in which not only may the two principals never meet face to face, it is one in which only one contestant tries to kill his adversary. The other merely defends: officially, anyway. It is a duel none the less – between terrorist bomb-maker, and the bomb disposal expert. The seed from which the book springs was planted many years ago by a good friend, a man of honour who has defused many, many bombs. 'Provided you live long enough' he said, 'in this game you learn eventually to identify the work of a particular bomb-maker, in much the same way an art expert learns to recognise the work of a great painter, say, by his brushwork. No matter how sophisticated or new the explosive device may be the signs of authorship will be there – and unmistakable.' His words painted a picture which has haunted my imagination since, a picture of two men who may never meet at all, perhaps never even know each other's names, yet grow to feel they know each other intimately as they meet, time and again over the years, to fight a lonely, blind and utterly deadly duel with the bombs and booby-traps of each successive terrorist campaign. So that this duel may be fought to a finish, I have brought my two contestants together: otherwise I believe the picture to be true to life.

The book itself is a work of fiction from start to finish. All the characters I have portrayed are invented, with one notable exception. Part of the scene is set in Cyprus, where I spent much time during Eoka days as a reporter, and no one could write realistically about terrorist bombing in that context without introducing the Eoka leader, the late General Grivas. But in this book even Grivas is fictitious – Grivas as I always personally imagined him to be. The people I have named as his Eoka lieutenants are fictitious, and none of the incidents as described in this book ever happened.

Many good friends helped me in the considerable research involved. Among them are a number of my former colleagues on the *Daily Express*, including – James Nicoll, deputy foreign editor, Cyril Aynsley, former chief reporter, John King, one of the first *Daily Express* reporters resident in Cyprus during Eoka days and now based in Bristol, Bernard Hall former reporter and Ted Brisland, our former chief librarian. I would also like to thank ex-Flight Lieutenant Lewis Parry of the R.A.F. now serving as engineer officer with DanAir, Norman Jeffery, Philip Dunn Snr., Peter Hill and Dr Bill Hunt M.D., F.R.C. Path., the Home Office pathologist. The other good friends who helped me so willingly prefer not to be named, but they know I am grateful.

Lastly, in case any reader should challenge the efficiency of the bullet proof vest described in this novel I wish to place on record that there is a British firm, Lightweight Body Armour Limited, suppliers of equipment to various police, military and security authorities. Their model '2Z' vest is specifically designed to withstand a burst of sub-machine-gun fire at a range of one metre upwards, and has been successfully tested.

Joe Miller awoke shortly before five in the morning and immediately switched off the alarm before it could ring and disturb his family. He held the luminous dial close to his face to check that he had a few minutes in hand and lay back with a sigh, reluctant to step down from the plane of sleep, savouring every moment of the bed's drowsy peace before surrendering to the demands of another Monday morning.

Dead on the hour, the rumble of the first Underground train emerging mole-like from its tunnel 100 yards from the bedroom window galvanised him into action. He leapt out and began to dress hurriedly, cursing the shift work that condemned him to be at the airport by seven in the morning. He was a fitter and from this moment on his day was charted to the minute. The same train and the same bus would carry him to Heathrow. By noon, the plane waiting in Hangar One would be ready for flight, A-1 Okay from the stators and thrust reversers in her four Pratt and Whitney turbofan engines up front down to the auxiliary power unit lying in wait behind the tail fin. She would take off during his lunch break, to head for the green coast of Ireland and gird her metal loins for battle with the headwinds that always lay in ambush above the big sea beyond. Then it was back at work on the next plane and the next, until the two o'clock hooter heralded the arrival of his relief shift: whereupon he would down tools, and follow an unvarying routine home to arrive indoors at exactly 4.15. Dinner would be set on the table at half past five, no matter what. While Mrs Miller put the kids to bed at nine he would stroll across the road to the Red Lion for a couple of pints and a game of darts, and return home at 10.45. The routine never altered.

Twenty minutes later he would be back in bed, snoring: a clockwork man turning on a spring wound for life.

His was a familiar and easily recognisable figure to the policemen guarding the hangars of Atlantic Airways, the American airline operating out of Heathrow: a big, handsome fellow with a mop of black curly hair, thick Groucho Marx moustaches and a swarthy complexion, like a gypsy. Once in a while if there was a security flap on, some officious sod might ask to see his airport pass. Nine times out of ten he could expect to be waved through without a second glance. But lost time cost money, and it was as well to be prepared.

He was due to start work this morning with a new maintenance crew. As he gobbled his breakfast he wondered what his new mates would be like and how many he could expect to know, at least by sight. Probably none: they were mostly Micks or nig-nogs these days, and that meant there were sure to be security problems.

Immediately, he checked his wallet to make sure he had the all-important pass with him. He had. Then he examined the contents of the brown plastic briefcase his wife had filled overnight with sandwiches, a thermos flask of tea, a Cox's Pippin, and the company-issue canvas shoes he was obliged to wear for occasional work on fuselage surfaces. All present and correct. A glance at the kitchen clock warned him it was time to go. Joe Miller snapped the locks of his briefcase shut, pulled on a hat and raincoat, and hurried to the door.

All the houses in the street where he lived were terraced, so that none boasted a garage. As a result cars were parked nose to tail both sides night and day, and he paid them no heed now as he set off for work. The two people waiting in the black saloon opposite his house watched intently as his front door opened to spill light briefly on to the all-embracing suburban gloom. They made no attempt to follow him until he had reached the shops on the corner and turned right, to head down the hill. For a second or two they saw him in the full glare of the street lamps, shoulders hunched against the rain, a thick-set, powerful figure.

'That him?' asked the driver.

'That's Miller.' The woman in the back was partly hidden by shadows. There was enough light to show a suitcase by her side, and as she leaned forward there came a glimpse of fur coat and nylon stockings. 'Don't rush things,' she warned.

Joe Miller was less than a quarter of a mile from the railway station when he suddenly became aware that a car had drawn into the kerb beside him, and pulled up with its engine still running.

'Excuse me,' called the driver loudly. Miller made no acknowledgment, and he tried again. 'Just a minute, sir, please.'

This time his head poked through the window, and Joe caught sight of a peaked chauffeur's cap. He stopped reluctantly, grudging every second of the delay. 'You speaking to me?' he asked. The impatience in his voice was unconcealed. 'Because don't be long, mate, I've got a bleedin' train to catch.'

'I'm looking for the South Circular,' the chauffeur replied. As if in apology for picking on someone in so great a hurry, he added swiftly, 'I'm trying to get to the airport, chum. My passenger here's got a plane leaving at seven.'

The rain was pelting down and Joe smelled the chance of a warm, dry ride to work. 'You want Heathrow?'

'That's right.' The chauffeur leaned out a little further, aimed a gloved thumb aft and lowered his voice confidentially. 'The lady here's getting a bit worried. I'm only a relief driver, see, and don't know my way round this neck of the woods.'

Joe's eyes took in the fur coat and the suitcase, and returned to the peaked cap. Talk about luck, he told himself. Aloud he said, 'You've fallen right on your feet this time, old son. I'm going to Heathrow myself as a matter of fact – I work there. And I've got to clock in by seven, too. If you want to give me a lift, I'll take you right to the doorstep.'

'That all right with you, lady?' The chauffeur formally sought his fare's permission, although his tone left her in no doubt of what the answer should be.

'Yes, of course.' Joe thought he could detect a slight foreign accent in her voice. 'Do whatever you wish – so long as I catch my plane.'

Joe Miller had the door open and was settled in beside the chauffeur before she had finished her sentence. 'Keep on down the hill,' he boomed in his cheerful Cockney voice. 'Straight across at the lights. Take the left fork when the road divides, then keep bearing left till you get to the Common. I'll direct you from there. It's a short cut.'

'Ta.' The saloon shot away, with its windscreen wipers pushing away the rain. But the lights turned against them and they were forced to brake at the bottom of the hill. There was the faintest hint of perfume in the car. The chauffeur and his fare-payng passenger sat in feudal silence, the delay seemed endless. Joe Miller began to fidget, and checked his watch.

As he slid his hands back into the warmth of his raincoat, his fingers encountered a packet of tobacco. He was an addict, and reminded now of his craving, he fidgeted even more. He looked round the front seat and noted the crumpled ends in the driver's ash-tray.

'All right if I smoke?' he asked.

'Sure.' The chauffeur tilted his head back in the direction of his fare. 'She doesn't mind.'

Joe rolled his smokes by hand. With tobacco too expensive to waste, he bent his head to concentrate on the task in hand. His neck gleamed pink and exposed in the glare of the traffic light, and the woman behind him seized her chance immediately. She opened her handbag and took out a syringe already fitted with a glittering, hypodermic needle. Her arm came up and remained poised over the target for a moment, fur-clad and menacing as the limb of a tarantula: then she plunged the needle down, and drove the point home into a vein pulsing in Joe Miller's neck. It burned him, like the sting of a wasp, and instinctively he leaned his head to one side and slapped at the wound. If he had not been taken so completely by surprise, he might have escaped: a single, downward turn of the handle at his side would have been enough to open the door and topple him into the road, in full view of the other traffic halted there. But he was dumbfounded by the very circumstances of the attack. Even when his fingers identified both the syringe and the jewelled fingers holding it fast in his neck, he was still unable to comprehend what was happening to *him* – to poor, ordinary, law-abiding, clock-watching Joe Miller.

For a few dazed moments he felt convinced he was dreaming, having a nightmare, and would soon awake to find his wife beside him, as warm and soft and comforting as always. His kidnappers had reckoned on this and watched him die without a struggle, exactly as the woman had predicted. The chauffeur laid down the cosh he had gripped as a standby, and waited for the lights to change. As the scoline entered his bloodstream, Joe Miller soon became paralysed. First the muscles in his neck refused to respond to the orders coming from his brain. The muscles in his arms and legs, and finally the whole of his body, quickly followed suit. The effect was purely muscular, so that while his sight and hearing remained unimpaired, he was powerless to call for help, or to pluck out the needle, or lift a finger to save himself. As his head fell on the dashboard he saw the packet of Golden Virginia open on the floor, with the precious tobacco spilling all over his shoes. What a bloody waste of money, he thought stupidly. From the corner of his right eye he caught a glimpse of the chauffeur's blue serge trousers, and watched his legs move as he slipped into gear and the car drove on. Joe could hear him and the woman talking about him, and understand every word they uttered. Yet there was nothing he could do about it, not a single damned thing: not even cry.

'Is he dead yet?' asked the chauffeur suddenly.

Dead? You bloody fool, what do you mean – am I dead yet? In his mind Joe Miller shouted the question, but no one could hear him: by now, the muscles of his mouth and throat and belly had all seized up, so that no sound emerged.

'Not yet,' said the woman. 'But it won't take long.'

If he was not dreaming, then he had to be mad. Joe could hear every word she said, even feel her soft fingers explore his pulse.

'Give it another minute,' she went on. 'It can't be long, he's suffocating very quickly now. But keep driving as fast as you can, we don't have any time to spare.'

God, *please* God, let it be a nightmare, Joe begged. As he prayed so came the pain, and with it panic, as he realised his lungs could no longer pump air. In all his thirty-eight years it had never once occurred to him before how good life was, and how much he wanted to go on living. Now it all came tumbling through his mind, together with pictures of his gentle, happy wife, his three beautiful children, and the terraced house by the railway line where they lay sleeping still, his job and his mates and the police – Christ! *the police*, what the hell were they doing, didn't they realise he was being murdered by two total strangers, two lunatics he'd never even clapped eyes on before? *Police!* he screamed silently. *Help, police! These people are suffocating me, I can't breathe!*

Joe Miller felt his head slip from the dashboard and bump against the chauffeur's legs. Instead of helping him, the callous bastard just grabbed a handful of black, curly hair and slammed the head back against the door of the car, and its protruding metal handle: and by God, that *hurt*! Oh, he could feel pain all right, especially this terrible pain in his chest that seemed to come from a red-hot iron band being clamped tighter and tighter with every second that passed, crushing the life out of him. And in the voice that no one could hear except himself, he began to beg and plead for mercy. There was no response. In a last desperate effort to live he ordered his body to fight its way free from the invisible bonds that bound it, but in vain: he was unable to flicker so much as an eyelid. Finally he died like a fish out of water, eyes bulging and mouth wide open, conscious throughout his agony of the unknown woman leaning over him, smelling faintly of perfume, feeling his pulse and impatient for him to be gone. A last protest shone in Joe Miller's eyes and then they became sightless.

'You can pull in now as soon as you like,' said the woman.

'Right.'

They stopped on the far side of the Common, when she came round to the front of the car to help search the body. But big Joe remained obstinately cumbersome in death, and they were forced to drag him out and lay him on a park bench to go through his pockets. The woman gasped at his dead weight as she held on to his ankles and stumbled after the chauffeur. Then they worked swiftly to strip off the overalls and ransack his pockets, clutching at the mop of hair and still warm flesh from time to time to prevent the corpse from sliding off its narrow bier. When they were finished the chauffeur heaved Joe's body over his shoulders and staggered with it to the boot of the car, where he dumped it inside like a sack of potatoes. He was forced to push and pull at the lifeless form before the lid would close, and sweat was running down his face when he climbed back behind the wheel.

'We're behind schedule,' said the woman as she checked her watch. 'Let's *move*!' As the car swung away she used a torch to check the contents of Joe's wallet, nodding her head in satisfaction when she found the airport pass they must have. She took his canvas shoes from the briefcase and threw them on the back seat. Then she sat back, watching the road.

The chauffeur had driven over the route a dozen times at this same hour of the morning: he knew every inch of the way, and what chances he could afford to take. Now he drove fast but never recklessly, keeping constant watch for any police trap, cornering hard, overtaking whenever a gap appeared in the line of traffic ahead. He pulled into the station yard at Hounslow with minutes in hand, and dowsed the lights. At once another man stepped out from the shadows and called softly to them through the open window.

'Everything go all right?'

'As planned,' said the woman. She passed over the canvas shoes and the wallet. 'The airport pass is in there. I've checked.'

At that moment, the airport bus arrived. As it backed into position its headlights rested briefly on the newcomer, and the two in the car murmured approval of what they saw. It was as if Joe Miller himself had come to life again, and climbed out of the boot to stand before them. There was the same black, curly hair and thick moustaches. This man had the same swarthy facial colouring without any need of cosmetic aid. He wore Joe Miller clothes. Platform soles to his shoes gave him the additional height he needed: in all other respects his build was strikingly similar to that of the man they had murdered.

'Fantastic,' declared the woman. '*Wunderbar.*'

She had picked Miller as their victim weeks before from a total of more than 300 Atlantic Airways maintenance staff. As soon as the choice had been approved, Joe Miller had been shadowed incessantly: followed to work each morning and home again every afternoon, with each stage of his journey timed by stopwatch. He had been photographed from every conceivable angle. He had been watched at work, mostly through binoculars. And he had been followed into the bar of the Red Lion each night, so that his Cockney accent could be taped and his mannerisms noted without once arousing any suspicion. If the Englishman had made it easy for his killers by his mania for clock-watching, the end result still spelled brilliant staff work, and augured well for the success of the operation.

The man impersonating Joe Miller looked keenly about him as it began to grow light. The train could only be a few minutes away now. 'You know where to dump the cargo?' He nodded his head at the boot of the car. His voice had a curious dry timbre.

'Yes.'

'After that, just wait for my call.'

'Don't worry, Paul. We'll be right by the phone every minute.'

'All right. I'll take the case now, Gudrun.'

She turned and lifted the suitcase from the back seat, balancing it on her knees. She snapped the locks open and took out a plastic briefcase, identical in size and shape and colour to the one used by the late Joe Miller although much heavier: this one weighed nearly six pounds. She tried not to allow her hands to shake as she passed it through the window. Somehow, while it remained locked in a suitcase she could shut her mind to it, but the moment she touched it, her limbs turned to jelly.

'Here, take it.'

The train rumbled in. All three of them watched as the first disembarking passengers ran past and scrambled on to the airport bus. As it pulled away from the station yard, the man impersonating Joe Miller tucked the briefcase casually under his arm and leapt aboard to join them.

Part One:
RAMAGE

The holiday had begun badly, even before the Ramages reached the strike-bound airport. The train for London had run dangerously late, an occurrence that generated an almost unbearable tension as time for take-off loomed closer and closer with all means of communication or movement denied them. When the train finally did arrive they were then obliged to join a vast queue, chafing with impatience as they awaited a taxi to take them direct to Heathrow. As they made to climb aboard, the driver refused to carry them – unless they first agreed to pay double fare against the distance involved, and the remote possibility he would have to return empty. Ramage was a man who knew when he was at the wrong end of a gun, and remained poker-faced as the cabbie laid down his terms: the main objective was to catch the plane, and time was running out fast. But even he was shaken once they had paid off their driver, and hurried into the terminal building laden with suitcases, hand baggage, passports and tickets. For here was bedlam.

Like everyone else in Britain about to travel by air, the Ramages were acutely aware that a group of trade union militants were staging a go-slow at Heathrow, to try to force their employers into meeting a new wage demand. What no one could possibly have foreseen was its total and dramatic effect: it was as if the very sinews of the world's busiest airport had suddenly been stricken by a paralysis, with almost all traffic brought to a standstill overnight. Hundreds of passengers had been left stranded, to find sleep where they could in the brightly lit, noisy, overheated lounges. Many flights had been cancelled altogether, and all the rest were subject to maddening and unpredictable delays. So far, no one had actually come to blows: although it seemed to Ramage that physical violence could not be far away. Frustrated men and women from every corner of the earth milled around them, giving vent to their feelings in a babble of angry tongues: Sikhs, Bengalis, Arabs, Japanese and Filipinos, African blacks and South African whites, Americans and Argentinians, all bitterly resentful of this shabby treatment they had no choice but to endure, some carrying children, all tired and heavy laden and impatient to remove themselves as far and as fast as possible from this hateful, grey, insular, strike-prone land.

Gordon Ramage set down his own luggage and stared about him in disbelief. Normally he was a man who was fiercely proud of his country, and the scenes he witnessed now angered and distressed him. Not for the first time since his retirement he found himself regretting that he had given up a disciplined life in the Services for one in this other, civilian world of devil-take-the-hindmost: and it irked him greatly that he was completely powerless to help his suffering fellow travellers. He stood there, frowning, like a rock in the middle of a storm-tossed sea, a big man with wide shoulders and large, capable hands that clenched and unclenched slowly in disapproval of the shambles in the hall. A frosty blue eye stared out from a face that might have been carved from stone: where the right eye had once been was a black patch, with the scar tissue below reaching back to the temple. He was hatless, and in the bright lights of the airport building his blond hair shone like wheat in a sunlit field. The other passengers took one look at the tall, imposing figure and went round him, leaving well alone.

A glance at the Departures Board showed that every service was grounded, with more than a dozen flights awaiting permission to take off, but he said nothing of this to Laura: the droop of her shoulders told him she was miserable enough as it was. Then he caught sight of the signboard that read 'Atlantic Airways', over on the far side of the hall. 'We're almost there, darling,' he said gently. 'Stay close.' He picked up the heavy cases as if they were toys, and began to shoulder a path for his wife through the crowd.

To mark the twentieth anniversary of its birth as an international airline, Atlantic Airways had earlier offered cheap tickets to every honeymoon couple flying to New York on the commemorative day. At first no great response was anticipated for what was essentially a publicity gimmick, and the offer rated no more than a line in most newspapers. Then the newly elected American President referred to it in his inaugural speech, an occasion he used to stress the importance of the 'special relationship' Britain and America had so long enjoyed. At once the idea of this Magic Carpet flight for newly-weds caught the public imagination, and snowballed. A hotel chain joined the scheme and offered them suites at a peppercorn rate of a dollar a day. A car hire firm allotted a fleet of Cadillacs to carry them free of charge on all local journeys. A Manhattan store promised a man-made fur coat 'impossible to tell from ranch mink' to every blushing British bride who cared to call in. A tailoring firm in the Garment District offered their husbands a free custom-made suit, to be measured on arrival and delivered in time for the trip home. TV sponsors tempted the honeymooners with more free gifts than any passenger could hope to get through the Customs without grave embarrassment. Suddenly, everybody wanted to be in on the act and by the time the closing date for applications arrived, 120 couples from all parts of Britain had arranged their weddings to coincide with the flight of the Honeymoon Jumbo, and thereby reap the benefit of an unforgettable holiday in America.

Even the men on go-slow had somehow been prevailed upon to permit this one plane to leave on schedule: so that as Ramage arrived the Atlantic Airways booking desk appeared as an oasis of calm in the desert of strife that plagued the rest of the terminal building. Each arrival was greeted with smiles, flowers, flashlight bulbs and a minimum of the tiresome pre-flight formalities before being whisked away to a champagne reception in the Alcock and Brown suite. The Honeymoon Jumbo that waited for them had been specially furbished in their honour. Curtains and seat covers showed Cupid aiming his darts. There were ornate souvenir menus listing a wedding breakfast prepared, boasted the airline, by the Savoy Hotel chefs regardless of expense. A taped recording of the Wedding March had been installed to provide background music at take-off and landing. And lastly, the plane itself had been granted an appropriate call-sign of R (for Romeo) J (for Juliet) Two Four Zero (for the 120 newly married couples flying in her).

If there had been no go-slow, then Atlantic Airways would obviously have reserved the commemorative flight for them alone. But as the rest of the fleet was grounded, so a stealthy transfer of stranded passengers began to take place without the knowledge of the strikers. Orders were quietly given to seat all the honeymooners together, thus filling the two main economy class bays to capacity. The newsmen accompanying them were put in first class. And an extra 170 fare-paying passengers, who would otherwise have been left cooling their heels on the ground, were brought in to fill the third economy class compartment and bring the overall complement on board to 448 men, women and children, including crew. No public announcement could be made for obvious reasons, but the girl at the booking counter smiled the good news at Ramage as he advanced determinedly on the desk.

'Your luck's in,' she said brightly as she studied the tickets he handed over. 'It so happens we have a few seats to spare on our Honeymoon Jumbo, sir. It looks like being the only aircraft that will leave Heathrow on schedule today – and you'll be able to tell the family afterwards that you flew to America with 240 honeymooners as your fellow passengers. Won't that be lovely?'

Ramage held his tongue, reasoning that this was no time to look a gift horse in the mouth.

'It will be a flight you'll never forget,' the girl promised. 'Beginning with a champagne reception after takeoff, and followed by a banquet in place of the normal in-flight meal, with a choice from more than a dozen main dishes. All drinks on the house, incidentally: there are no hidden charges of any kind on the commemorative flight.'

Ramage's face brightened considerably at that.

'Individual gifts for each passenger,' she continued, 'to mark the company's twentieth birthday. And – live entertainment throughout the journey, from *Frank Gadsby*.' Gadsby was a young American singer whose records were selling by the million. He had been on tour of Europe for the past month, and was returning home in triumph. 'You'll love every moment,' the girl vowed.

Ramage himself had little ear for music. His own choice would have been to read and sleep during the long journey, and inwardly he quailed at the prospect of Frank Gadsby or anyone else crooning at him from Cork to Cape Cod. On the other hand the young woman who held the prerogative of flight transfer was clearly a Gadsby fan, and Ramage was determined that nothing was going to stop him from leaving this Tower of Babel on the one plane of the day likely to get away on time. A quick glance at his wife warned her to remain silent as he told the white lie.

'Nothing we'd like better,' he declared staunchly.

'Fine,' said the girl. 'In that case, sir, please report to the embarkation lounge as soon as we've weighed in your luggage, and stand by for your call.'

She watched him, fascinated, as he felt in his pockets for the passports. I know that face, she thought, as she surveyed the high cheekbones, the black patch and the fearful scar: from the newspapers, surely. She flicked through the pages of his passport as she checked his American visa, to see if she could find any clue to nudge her memory. He was forty-eight years old. Under the word 'occupation' it read, simply: 'Army officer, retd.' The name Gordon Ramage sounded vaguely familiar, but she could not place it. She looked up and saw a line of others behind him, hoping to join the flight. She clipped a baggage voucher to his airline ticket and handed back his documents with a smile.

'Goodbye, sir,' she said. 'I hope you enjoy the flight.' She nodded politely to Laura. 'Good-bye, ma'am.' Then they were gone, and she returned to the business in hand.

The tiny group of Special Branch officers strategically positioned outside the final departure lounge was the only outward sign of authority on the alert in the entire public area. But appearances were deceptive: no nervous bride or groom waiting to board Romeo Juliet 240 could even remotely guess at the extent of the security precautions being taken to safeguard them – indeed, to safeguard the lives of every passenger passing through Heathrow.

The 2,800 acres of land that together make up the world's biggest international airport form a kind of fortress, prepared for almost every imaginable contingency. They contain, for instance, a Disaster Control Centre, which is maintained in a state of permanent readiness. Its function is to cope with every kind of airborne catastrophe resulting in heavy casualties. It has mortuary areas, designated for instant use with unlimited supplies of 'dead bags' to hold the victims and a multitude of blank cards held ready to match identifiable fragments of skin and bone with names, addresses, and telephone numbers of next-of-kin. They also maintain a London Airport Police Force, an independent police unit under its own Commander: kept on permanent patrol against every conceivable kind of crime, ranging from handbag snatching to terrorism. The Commander heads a small army of three hundred constables, forty sergeants, and a corps of senior officers as well as a Special Branch unit, an anti-hijack squad and fourteen dogs. It has its own armoury, with guns and ammunition available if the Commander believes the situation warrants their use. His is a fully composite Force, and a big one by comparative British standards. Full scale exercises are held occasionally in conjunction with the Army, who practise schemes to seal off the airport with troops, tanks and armoured cars in the event, say of a terrorist attack on incoming planes with SAM missiles.

The 2,800 acres form an enclave within the Home Counties. Its administrators handle air traffic that lands and leaves at the rate of one plane a minute – strikes permitting, of course – a grand total of twenty-five million passengers each year (the number is growing) and an export-import trade exceeding that carried by seaborne traffic sailing up the Thames to the ancient Port of London. Full-time security within the enclave requires an enormous amount of intelligent planning and forethought, and is maintained only by a constant, grinding routine. It begins with the Customs men. There are always Customs officers on the prowl, armed with sheaves of cargo manifests and the powers to order a spot-check search of every plane, hangar or warehouse container. The passenger passing through Heathrow sees only the man on the baggage counter, asking 'Have you anything to declare?' But the Customs target is far more ambitious than the petty smuggler with his extra bottle of spirits, or hidden Swiss watch: the real war is fought against the heroin smugglers, the currency racketeers, and the gun-runners who are always seeking new ways to breach the enclave's defences.

No plane ever receives a clean bill of health for the asking, and the Honeymoon Jumbo had been through the full security mill that morning. Customs men searched her holds from end to end as she made ready for flight. Behind them in the loading bay, security men using 'Inspectors' – portable radiographic machines, cameras really, fitted with X-ray eyes – scanned the contents of every cargo container before they were manhandled on to trolleys, and wheeled away to the waiting aircraft. (This was a lesson learned from the attack years earlier by Japanese Red Army terrorists at Lod airport, in Israel. On touch-down, the three terrorists took out weapons they had previously hidden in freight baggage, and opened fire on unarmed passengers standing round them in the Customs shed. More than 100 people were killed and wounded before the terrorists were overwhelmed). Behind the 'Inspectors' came the dogs.

A dog-handler led a brace of eager, snuffling Alsatians down the huge line of suitcases and other baggage waiting to be loaded into the freight hold. On the word of command, they lowered their black muzzles to the leather-and-plastic trail and began to analyse the infinite variety of scents placed before them. They took their time and worked in silence: both dogs were old hands at the security game, and were trained to halt and bark only if they recognised the bitter-almonds tang of nitro-glycerine, the hallmark of the aerial bomber.

Like the screening of all passengers by metal-detector to prevent hand-guns and knives being smuggled aboard, all this was routine in the context of modern air travel. So, too, was the scene inside the silver hull of the Jumbo, where a 'Presentation Crew' – eight cleaners led by a supervisor specially trained in security techniques – worked their way briskly from stem to stern. They were not merely hoovering and shampooing the carpets, folding and smoothing the hundreds of blankets and pillows, or cleaning the seats, windows, four hundred ashtrays, six galleys and twelve toilets on board, although that was their principal task. They also peered inside every locker and probed every inch of cabin space to make doubly sure no package or box or briefcase had found its way aboard by accident – or terrorist design. Together, cleaners and supervisor in the presentation crew formed a combination of Mrs Mopp and Sherlock Holmes that missed nothing as they went their rounds.

Shortly after the Ramages walked into the Duty Free shop to buy their presents of liquor and perfume, the Honeymoon Jumbo was finally pronounced 'clean' in all security respects and the order to commence embarkation was given immediately. With a full passenger load, the airline staff knew it would be a race against time to get their vaunted commemorative flight airborne on schedule, regardless of the possible reaction of the strikers and all other problems that might arise, and the pressure mounted dramatically as their deadline drew near. Company headquarters in New York had demanded a three-way telephone hook-up between the airport, the Haymarket office of Atlantic Airways and themselves so that they could be given a blow-by-blow account of proceedings until Romeo Juliet 240 actually left the ground. This was in addition to the batteries of telex machines already chattering away, and was purely a panic-stations order. The first such telephone report merely confirmed what Manhattan already knew, that the captain of the aircraft had been on board for almost an hour with his flight deck crew doing all that could be done to ensure that the Big Bird took off on schedule.

They had tested the controls and studied the weather charts. They had fed last minute alterations to the computerised flight plan into their black box navigational system, officially known as the INS: a technological marvel that was wedded to the auto-pilots to give robot-controlled flight at the touch of a button. (Jumbo crews swear that the INS can do just about anything except mix a dry martini.) It will pilot the plane for them on request, by continuing to feed the captain's instructions automatically to the plane's various control surfaces. At any given moment in flight it will tell its human colleagues where they are in the sky, their true compass bearing, the strength of the winds they are encountering, how far they are from the nearest way-point – like a weather ship, for instance – and from their final destination: and exactly how long it will take them to reach both. Inside the Honeymoon Jumbo, Captain Brdwzynski and his men gave the INS a dry run, patted its push-button control panel by way of thank-you, and then settled back to wait for the other pieces in the preflight jigsaw to drop into place.

Down in the bowels of the aircraft, the chief steward and his cabin crew of fourteen, four male pursers and ten stewardesses, worked like beavers to complete embarkation and loading in the fastest possible time. But no matter how hard everyone worked, or how often London and New York exchanged facts and figures by telex and telephone, three vital factors affecting the time of takeoff remained outside the crew's control.

First was the union go-slow. Admittedly, an undertaking

had been given, but the airline was practising a deliberate deceit: and it was doubtful if the promise would be kept if the truth about the passenger load became known. Then there was the question of the missing honeymooners. One couple had failed to turn up at Heathrow, and now the airline executives had to decide – how much leeway should they be given to join this unique flight, named in their honour? Finally, and potentially most serious of all, was a mystery electrical fault that was plaguing the Jumbo somewhere along the 100 miles of internal wiring that served her delicate controls. It was like a virus, striking at different points at infrequent intervals: one of the fitters had spotted it during routine maintenance that morning, and efforts were still being made to pinpoint and eliminate it finally.

As a precaution, the night-flight Jumbo was rolled out early and placed on stand-by, but no one in Atlantic Airways wanted to see it used unless flight cancellation was the only alternative. In the time that was left to them now there could be no question of duplicating Romeo Juliet 240's magnificent furnishings, and even the sumptuous wedding breakfast might be threatened. So the ground staff toiled desperately, inside the plane and out, to get the Honeymoon Jumbo airworthy on time. These fitters were easily identifiable in their bright red company overalls and special issue canvas shoes. At first, to comply with the strict security precautions in force, they were stopped and searched each time they boarded Romeo Juliet 240, while the contents of their tool kits were likewise examined. But as time went on, and the same fitters passed the same guards every ten or fifteen minutes, the regulations were relaxed by unspoken agreement and the fitters waved through with a smile and a nod of recognition, to save precious minutes.

Whatever his innermost feelings may have been as he surveyed the ant-like activity going on around him, the Captain of the commemorative flight allowed none to show on his face as he sat there, high on the flight deck. He answered all queries and gave orders to his crew in the same, even, cheerful tone throughout. His only concession to the hideous SNAFU out there on the ground was to reach out once in a while, and touch the lucky mascot he always carried with him. It was a miniature ivory figure of Buddha, hand-carved, sitting cross-legged in a tamarind cup, eternally at prayer. Say one for us while you're at it, little Buddha, he would say to himself each time he touched the lip of the bowl: and at the same time, grin sheepishly at his own foolishness. Now he spoke to Control, for the fiftieth time.

'Hello, Control, this is Romeo Juliet Two Four Zero. I ask you again, is there any sign of those two missing lovebirds, over?'

'Control to Romeo, mo mo.' There was a brief pause and then the clipped British voice came back. 'Sorry, old man, it doesn't seem to be your day today. The orders are to proceed with embarkation, and stand by.'

'Thank you. Over and out.'

Suddenly, miraculously, it all began to fit together. One of the ground staff made his way personally up to the flight deck to report, but the grin on his face told its own story before he ever opened his mouth. 'All stations go,' he said to the Captain. 'We fixed that bleedin' electrical fault at last. We'll have you all ready for takeoff in another five minutes.' He squatted on his haunches as he spoke to them, a big handsome man with curly black hair and Groucho Marx moustaches. His face was as brown as a gypsy's. The bulky tool-kit rested between his open knees, and he clutched a sandwich in one, oil-smeared hand.

'A trying old day and no mistake,' he declared. The Cockney accent was very marked, his voice dry and harsh-sounding. 'But I told you we'd get you away on time, didn't I?'

'You sure did, friend.' Captain Brdwzynski took the hint and passed over a carton of duty-free cigarettes. 'Here, have these, compliments of Atlantic Airways.'

'Ta, I'll share 'em out among the lads.' He slipped the carton inside his capacious tool-kit and gazed round the flight deck with brown, intelligent eyes. 'Well, that's it, I'll be off then.' He gripped the heavy bag easily in one hand and began to descend the spiral stairway that led down to the first class section. 'Don't worry, I'll let meself out,' he quipped as his dark, curly hair disappeared from sight.

'Okay, pal. Thanks a million,' they called after him, thankful that he would be gone before the extra 170 passengers started trooping onboard.

The fitter paused at the foot of the stairway and peered inside the first class compartment. It was empty, awaiting the arrival of the media: they were still at work outside, recording the final moments on the ground, and would be the last to take their seats. The whole cabin was untidy with equipment, portable typewriters, grips, briefcases, and photographers' satchels spilling open to show spare cameras, lenses, and yellow cardboard mounds of film. It was the work of a moment to open his tool-kit, lift out the brown plastic briefcase, and slide it out of sight beneath a window seat halfway down the aisle. He snapped the tool-kit shut and left the plane immediately, running down the steps to join his mates on the runway. Minutes later they were all in their van, and on their way back to the hangar.

'Control,' said Brdwzynski joyfully, 'this is Romeo Juliet Two Four Zero, and we're in business again. All repairs and maintenance finally completed, at twelve seven pip emma. My cabin crew will have embarkation completed in another ten minutes, except for that missing couple. So I can have this flying bedroom airborne just as soon as you guys give me clearance, over.' It was the happiest speech he had made all morning.

'Control to Romeo. We'll see what we can do for you, over and out.'

Brdwzynski rubbed his chin thoughtfully and spoke to his First Officer. 'Joe, I have a feeling that Schumacher will put punctuality before romance, and order us to leave on the button if we get clearance. Just the same, I want you to go aft and tell Fats to keep one entry-port open until the last possible moment – and until I give the order personally to close down, you got that?'

'Okay, Lucky.'

'Have a word with those sheriffs yourself, you hear me? I want you to make absolutely certain they know exactly what's happening on the ground. Above all, I don't want any of them to jump to the wrong conclusions if they see two kids pushing their way onboard at the last minute, okay?'

'Roger.' The First Officer grinned as he climbed out of his seat. 'Hell, that would be some story for the Press boys, two of our honeymooners shot dead for arriving late.'

Captain and First Officer were in deadly earnest behind the banter. 'FLY ATLANTIC, FLY SAFE' was the inscription that stared out from every hoarding carrying the company name, and from the red cardboard cover of every passenger ticket it sold. The four words were not intended simply as a tribute to the skills of the airline crews, or the technical excellence of the machines they flew, although both were freely acknowledged throughout the world of aviation. More than anything else they spelled security, and with Atlantic Airways that extended far beyond any catchy slogan: it represented a creed.

It was often said that Louis D. Grossman, the airline president and a former four-star Army Air Force general, was security-minded to the point of obsession. Those who knew him by repute only attributed that to his Services background, and of course it played some part. Like all senior American commanders he loathed and distrusted all Communists, and blamed them for almost everything that went wrong, in civilian life as much as in the Forces. Anyone who tried, say, to hijack one of his planes was automatically dubbed 'a Commie bastard' no matter what their intention or background. But there was more to his passion for security than military prejudice, as his close associates were quick to learn.

He was a widower who had married great wealth, and like so many rich men born poor, remained careful with money all his life. For every dollar invested, he looked for two to come back. He never tipped: it was not in his nature to give anything for nothing, certainly not money and most certainly never under duress, for as well as being tight-fisted he was as obstinate as a mule. Over the years his fellow directors had come to accept that their president would rather bleed to death slowly than pay ransom to any hijacker, for example, as some of his rivals had felt compelled to do. In fact there were those who insisted that it was this recurrent nightmare of what terrorism might cost him, rather than concern for the well-being of any of his passengers, that goaded him into demanding watertight security at all times for his fleet of Jumbos spanning the world.

Atlantic Airways had been the first to fly armed teams on every plane as a precaution against terrorist attack. They were called Sky Sheriffs, sharpshooters who were specially trained to enforce a new kind of frontier law five miles high: and the General introduced them to the world in typical fashion at a time when hijack was almost a daily occurrence. 'We're going to meet these Commie bastards head on,' he declared. 'My sheriffs have orders to kill every goddam son-of-a-bitch who tries to take us on.' In the years that followed all attempts to hijack Atlantic Airways' planes had failed, and the Sheriffs had built up a fearsome reputation in the process: so that now Captain Brdwzynski wanted to make certain there were no misunderstandings as the Honeymoon Jumbo prepared for flight.

Overall responsibilty for maintaining the company's reputation for top security was now in the hands of Byron Schumacher, the General's son-in-law and executive vice-president. On his instructions, all flight crews had to attend regular briefings on the latest anti-terrorist procedures. All ground staff likewise, no matter in which country they served, compulsorily attended lectures given by security experts. Unlike his father-in-law, who expected blind obedience to all orders, Schumacher was worldly enough to accept that attending lectures would produce little more than lip-service from the average workforce. So he introduced a stick-and-carrot system as well, one that was guaranteed to keep the airline employees security-conscious at all times. The carrot came in the form of a $1,000 bonus, payable in cash, to any non-executive who could produce an original and practicable idea for improving existing company precautions. The stick was wielded by a team of supervisors, roving hatchet men with powers of instant dismissal for anyone found guilty of neglect or laxity even, in observing standard security measures. There was no appeal against their verdict. As a result, their descent on any airport and the inevitable snooping which followed, was not only resented but greatly feared: precisely as Byron Schumacher had intended when he recruited them.

He was a dapper and clean-cut fifty-year-old who took great care to preserve a youthful image, for the General liked to have young men about him. He was a man with few pleasures: for him, business efficiency transcended all other requirements. Below the bland exterior, he was a humourless man. The Schumacher smile was rarely more than a practised facial exercise, and the eyes behind the gold-rimmed glasses would remain as cold as perma-frost. He was consumed by ambition: he had aspired to the General's wealth and power from the beginning. The first requirement, to create an opportunity wherein he could impress the older man with his powers of leadership and executive flair, had arrived fortuitously early on in his career with Atlantic. That led to the second, an invitation to the General's home. Schumacher saw to it that the second led to the third, and penultimate step, of marrying the General's daughter and only child, Myra. It had called for endurance, more than three years of formal but assiduous courtship: once that was achieved, he felt he could wait for the rest to come to him naturally, like windfall apples, and took great care to do nothing that would incur his father-in-law's displeasure.

As soon as he arrived at Heathrow he proceeded to drive everyone in authority close to distraction with his demands, for he was determined not to fail with the Honeymoon Jumbo assignment. He badgered the Airport Controller, and through him his Head of Security and the Commander of the police force, with incessant queries and demands concerning pre-flight security. Later, as the go-slow began to bite and he saw all his hard work threatened by industrial unrest, he turned his attentions away from the security chiefs and towards the union leaders: lobbying, cajoling, bribing. What precise deals he made were never disclosed, but in the end he emerged with the one thing he had to have to ensure success – an undertaking from the strike leader that his men would do nothing to hinder the departure of Romeo Juliet 240.

That was only the start of the Schumacher blitz.

He also hand-picked the crew, awarding command to Captain Walter Brdwzynski. Brdwzynski was not a man he liked overmuch: on the few occasions they had met in the past Schumacher had come away with the curious impression that the pilot saw through him, and despised what he saw. However, there was no denying the man's flying record and ability: what was more, he had been hired by the General personally when he first applied to Atlantic for a job. With his own reputation at stake, he believed the choice of Brdwzynski as pilot gave him the best of both worlds.

He named Carl Ohlsen as chief steward, with Lindy Parsons as the senior air hostess. Carl 'Fats' Ohlsen had been with the airline since its formation and had served as chief steward on Flight One, the company's maiden voyage. Nowadays, he mostly flew as a kind of airborne Jeeves to tend to the General's needs, on business or vacation. He was a big man, a white-haired six footer who had seen it all in his time: fire, fog, engine failure, turbulence so severe it seemed no aircraft could survive, one hijack bid and a crash-landing. But he had never lost a passenger yet, and was automatic choice as head of the cabin crew for the commemorative flight.

Melinda Parsons was from Selma, Alabama. Her first twelve months with Atlantic Airways had been spent on her knees, as a cleaner. One morning she plucked up courage to walk into an office she had been dusting only an hour before, and in a shy, diffident voice asked the occupant for another job with the company, as an air hostess. Vacancies were being advertised in the paper that day, and she was determined to be first in the queue. The office happened to be Schumacher's: he was newly joined then, a minor executive. He opened his mouth to order her out when by chance the General walked in, to talk sales promotion with this new young executive and size him up. He allowed Melinda to finish her piece and made no attempt to intervene. Instead he took a seat by the window in silence and waved at the two of them to carry on.

Byron Schumacher felt as uncomfortable as a cat on a hot tin roof. The world of the 1960s was far less enlightened than it is today. Here was the opportunity he had sought to impress the president with his sagacity – but which way was he supposed to jump? Desperately he ran through his mind to see if he could recall any utterance by the General on the delicate subject of coloured aircrew. He found none, and glanced covertly at the old man's face. There was no clue to be found there, either: it remained inscrutable. Goddam you, you black bitch, said Schumacher to himself – how dare you put me on the spot like this? His fingers drummed importantly on his desk, and he gave the girl his humourless smile. Then inspiration came to him, like a lifebelt to a drowning man.

'Only one thing counts in this airline,' he told her. 'And that is – are you good enough for the job?' He looked at her resentfully, and saw not a wide-eyed, skinny, apprehensive coloured girl determined to lift herself out of the ghetto, but an intruder and distinct embarrassment: he sweated at the realisation that his own future with the company might well hinge on the decision he made. He forced himself to repeat the question, and it was all he could do to keep his tone paternal and kindly. 'Tell me, uh, Melinda,' he said, 'the truth, now: do you honestly think you're good enough for such an important job?'

She looked from one white face to the other. Somehow she

sensed that the old man by the window wanted the final answer to come not from her, but from her inquisitor. 'Try me,' she replied, and passed the ball straight back to Schumacher.

Still without any help from the General, Schumacher sent up a silent prayer and pressed a key on his inter-office communicator. 'Fats,' he said brusquely, 'this is Byron Schumacher. I have a young woman here, asking for a job as air hostess: name of Parsons. I'm sending her along for a month's trial. But don't get any wrong ideas, and don't hire her – unless you think she's up to it. That's an order.' He waved aside her thanks and waited until she had left the office. Then he turned to face the General. 'And now, sir,' he said, 'how may I be of service to you?'

That was ten years ago. He had no hesitation now in naming Lindy as chief hostess on the commemorative flight. Apart from proven experience, she owed him a favour: and that made her doubly dependable.

There were two clocks on his desk, side by side, set to remind him constantly of the time difference between New York and London. It was 7.15 a.m. in the General's home on Long Island, and Schumacher could picture the scene as if he were present. The old man would have shaved and breakfasted long since. Right now he would be smoking the first cigar of the day in his study, his 'command bunker' as he half-jokingly called it. In the background a telex machine would be chattering snippets of information from a dozen countries where his planes were refuelling. The male secretary who lived in would have pinned together each separate report arriving overnight from London, and placed them on the breakfast table much earlier: they concerned a prestige flight, and took priority over all else. Old as he was, General Grossman showed no sign of wanting to hand over the reins of command to any successor: not even to his son-in-law.

As he acknowledged that unpalatable fact, Schumacher chafed at another thought never far removed from his mind, that the old man might even choose someone else to succeed him at Atlantic. In which case – all other considerations apart – the years spent with Myra would have been wasted, and nothing in the world could compensate for that. What a relief it was to be 3,000 miles from that strident voice and the orders it never ceased to bark. She was accustomed to wealth and to being obeyed, and was too old, too rich, and too set in her ways to allow anything, even marriage, to change her way of life. It was Byron who had had to bend, and to his dismay he found that by accommodating her he was perhaps damaging his own claims to the seat of power. Myra Grossman was used to wintering in Acapulco or Florida, and to enjoying at least one European tour each summer. When Byron first protested that such constant perambulation might harm his professional advancement, she laughed and spoke to the General. 'Daddy, I want my husband to be with me some of the time, not chained to a desk all year round: you understand, don't you?'

She got her way, but Byron felt he could almost hear the General's growl of disapproval. And he hated the long periods of inactivity, the round of boring and hugely expensive hotels, the games of bridge and the inane chatter that followed in Myra's wake. His own interest in women had always been lukewarm: he found them an intrusion on far more important and meaningful matters. For him, power was the spur: even more than the acquisition of money, although he recognised that wealth and power walked hand in hand. He felt there was nothing he might not achieve, that there was no limit to his horizon, on the death of his father-in-law. A late entry into politics, for instance: high office even, a post close to the White House itself – and the seat of ultimate power. He wriggled deliciously on his chair at the very thought of it. Myra had told him weeks ago that the General's private physician had urged her father, at seventy-eight years of age, to take things a little easier. It was impossible to tell yet how he would react, although Byron personally regarded the assignment in London as a possible straw in the wind.

'Every time I pick up a newspaper, Byron, I read about a new strike in Britain. Now I see they've got one at London airport. I want you to get over there and make sure it doesn't screw up our commemorative flight.'

'Yes, sir.'

The shrewd old eyes appraised him carefully. 'Reckon you can handle it, Byron?'

'I know I can, General.'

'Well.' Sniff. 'All right, it's your baby. I'll advise the Board to that effect.' His forefinger poked at Byron like the barrel of a gun. 'I'll be here if you really need me. But don't come whining everytime some Commie bastard farts in your face. Because I won't want to know.'

'Leave it to me, General.'

'I'll let Rogers handle this end.' Rogers was ten years younger than Byron, a whizz-kid from Pan-Am who had joined the Atlantic board two years earlier at the General's invitation. Schumacher regarded him as his most serious rival for the throne, and his eyes glittered as the old man spoke the name.

'Yes, sir.'

'I'll be here to keep an eye on him, of course. But you'll be on your own, Byron. It's one hell of a responsibility.'

'And I welcome it, General. I'll make arrangements to get away tonight.' At first he had been elated: it seemed his big chance to score over Rogers. Eight days later he was a little less sure. It was hard to know at times if the General had picked him on trust – or placed him on public trial. By the briefing he had given, Schumacher was allowed to contact him only in emergency, yet the problems that arose were endless and varied. For instance, like this goddam fault in the Honeymoon Jumbo's wiring system. It had called for a knife-edged decision this morning, whether to change planes while there was still time. Schumacher had ruled against it, but the hours that had ticked by had proved increasingly nail-biting and tense: and still he did not know the outcome. As if in answer to his thoughts there was a knock at the door and Johnson, his London manager, walked in.

'The ground staff have finally traced and corrected that electrical fault, sir.'

'They sure cut it fine.'

'They did, indeed. But things are looking up elsewhere, sir. We'll have embarkation completed by 12.20. That's firm.'

'Excellent. So Brdwzynski can be airborne on schedule.'

'I hope so, sir.' The Englishman hesitated to commit himself. 'There's still a very awkward industrial situation out there. The strikers have been demonstrating again this morning – for one awful moment I thought they'd heard about our passenger list.'

'They're not going to touch the Honeymoon Jumbo. I've told you that repeatedly.' What did they want him to do, spell out the word 'bribery' in capital letters?

'Yes, sir.' Johnson filled his pipe without further comment.

'And what about the two missing passengers?'

'Still no word?'

'None. I've just checked.'

'Then there's no problem. Tell Brdwzynski I want to see his plane airborne at 12.30 *precisely*.'

'You wouldn't consider holding on a little longer, sir?' asked the Englishman. 'I mean, the fact they haven't phoned could mean they're somewhere close, and hoping to make it. And Brdwzynski shouldn't have any trouble in making up lost time, once he's under way.'

Schumacher stared at him coldly. 'Let's just concentrate on getting this show on the road, Johnson. The General will be watching our performance very closely: so you make sure nothing happens to louse things up, okay?'

'Yes, sir.'

'Don't feel sorry for those kids, Johnson. Feel pleased for us: it's a great story. We'll find them stranded some place, with their car broken down maybe. So we play Father Christmas, find them a hotel room, fill it with flowers, serve them a meal like the one on the plane – and have the newspapers photographing every minute of it. If they miss the plane by only five minutes, it's an even better story. *We* can't miss.'

'Quite.' Johnson got to his feet. 'I'll get things organised as soon as we hear from them, sir.'

'Do that.' Schumacher dismissed him with a wave of his hand and settled back to watch the departure of Romeo Juliet 240 on closed circuit television. Sometimes he wondered why these English guys didn't ask you to pee for them while they were at it.

Out on the runway, all was done. On receipt of the Captain's order, the last entry port slammed shut and the steps were wheeled away. Red warning signs shone in all compartments, NO SMOKING and FASTEN SEAT BELTS, as the hugely excited honeymooners tried to settle down. Fats Ohlsen read the official message of welcome and then added a few words of his own.

'This is a great day for all of us in Atlantic Airways,' he said. 'It's our twentieth birthday in international aviation, and you're all invited to the party, folks. We'll start serving the champagne as soon as we're airborne, and I promise you a flight you'll never forget. So make sure those lap straps are fastened and sit back to enjoy yourselves. Here we go.'

The four turbofan engines, each weighing around four tons and capable of producing an incredible 87,000 horse-power thrust, whined impatiently as the plane taxied towards the end of the runway. Dark clouds scudded overhead, the rain was teeming down. To hell with the rain, thought Brdwzynski, looking out from his lofty perch and rejoicing in the power at his finger-tips. *Flying*: this was what a man lived for.

'Romeo Juliet Two Four Zero to Control,' he said briskly into his headset. 'We made it on time. How about you guys, over?'

A little time elapsed before the answer came.

'Control to Romeo, you have clearance for take-off.' The speaker tried without success to keep the surprise out of his voice. 'We wish you a very happy anniversary flight, and safe landings. Over and out.'

Brdwzynski gave a triumphal thumbs-up salute and said to his flight deck crew, 'Let's go!' No other plane had succeeded in beating the strike to leave London on schedule for days past: it seemed a good omen. The Captain checked his chronometer, reached out briefly to touch the ivory Buddha with his left hand, and then sent the 350-ton aircraft hurtling down the ribbon of concrete like some enormous greyhound sprung from the trap. Faster and faster it went, 120, 130, 140, 150, 160 m.p.h. Plumes of spray flared out from the undercarriage. The roar of her engines sounded over Heathrow like a rumble of thunder. Suddenly the nose lifted, and Romeo Juliet 240, the Honeymoon Jumbo, was airborne.

Byron Schumacher called Long Island immediately.

'Good morning, General. It's my honour and pleasure to report the commemorative flight under way.' He ogled himself in the mirror on his desk as he spoke, like a bird preening its feathers. 'Romeo Juliet Two Four Zero took off with a total of 448 souls on board under the command of Captain Brdwzynski at 12,30 today local time.' Pause for effect. 'Twenty years to the minute after Atlantic One left on her maiden voyage.'

'Nice work, Byron.' Credit where credit was due, thought the General. 'I guess you had your share of problems, at that.'

'None I couldn't handle,' replied his son-in-law modestly. 'But yes, sir, there were problems. Right until Brdwzynski was airborne.'

'I have an AP flash coming off the tapes now.' The old man peered at the slip of paper his secretary handed to him. 'It says two of those honeymoon kids failed to make the flight by minutes after surviving a car crash, and stood weeping in the lounge as our Jumbo took off. What happened there?'

'Like the man says, they checked in too late, General.' Schumacher frowned as he listened to his father-in-law's comments. 'No, sir, they weren't hurt, that's typical newspaper exaggeration, just shaken up a little. And you can't blame Brdwzynski for wanting to get away on time: these people hadn't booked in when he gave the order to close up for take-off. But we won't lose by it, I'm taking care of that, sir.'

'I'm not sure I follow you, Byron.'

'Hell, there's no such thing as *bad* publicity, General! I intend to hand these kids over for TV interviews at the same moment Brdwzynski touches down in New York. That way we'll get the best of both worlds, simultaneous live coverage in England and America. Sir, you couldn't buy a script like that for a million dollars.'

'I guess you know what you're doing.' The General decided to keep well out of it. 'I'll be leaving for Manhattan shortly. Keep me informed of any untoward development. I'll talk to Brdwzynski myself later in the day.'

'Yes, sir. Good-bye for now.'

Schumacher yawned, and ordered coffee to be brought in. Then he lay back in his swivel chair, pushed his glasses high on his forehead, and rubbed his eyes with his knuckles. God, but he was tired: these few days in London had really bushed him. Quickly, he reminded himself it was only to be expected. He had driven himself hard, done everything required of him – and more. His greatest success had undoubtedly been to find a way round the go-slow, this sly technique the British employed to draw their wages while still contriving to withhold a service from the fare-paying customer. Admittedly, his own answer to it had been unorthodox: but the bribe had paid off, and results were all that mattered in the Big League. He had survived unprecedented pressures since he arrived in England, from the General, the unions, the media, the run of last-minute crises beginning with the electrical fault and ending with the appearance of those two weeping kids in his office – and he had won through. Schumacher doubted if the General himself could have handled the situation more efficiently. The only matter now requiring his attention was to arrange the interviews tonight, and book an onward flight for the stranded honeymooners. A novel idea occurred to him – why should he not escort them personally to New York? 'Airline chief helps stranded kids.' He could almost see the headlines already, and rang for Johnson to set the wheels in motion.

'Mr Johnson has gone to the hospitality lounge, sir' said his secretary. 'To thank the Airport Controller and all concerned for their help in getting our Jumbo away on time. Shall I call him for you?'

'No. I'll go down and join them myself,' he told her. 'It's a time for celebration, when all is said and done, eh? Personal calls only while I'm there, okay?'

'Yes, sir.'

It was a little after one o'clock when he walked into the lounge. Johnson hurried across to him at once. 'Ah, Mr Schumacher. I think you know everyone here, sir.'

Schumacher's eyes lit on the Controller and his aides, and the groups of newsmen. He waved a greeting across the room, took a glass of champagne from a passing tray and walked over to speak to the Airport Controller. 'How nice to see you here at our little celebration, Gregory. Thank you once again for your splendid co-operation over these difficult past few days. The General's delighted at the outcome, needless to say. I've just spoken to him, in New York.'

'Congratulations.' The Controller raised his glass in reply. 'I still don't know how you won those strikers over, Schumacher, indeed, I'm not even sure I want to. But congratulations, none the less. We were all delighted to see your commemorative flight get away on time – even if the other airlines, British Airways included, haven't been so fortunate.'

'It's no secret,' said Schumacher blandly. 'Everyone's got a soft spot for honeymooners, unions included. I simply appealed to their sense of fair play. Of course, the fact that it's a non-profit making flight may have helped too. Ah, excuse me, gentlemen.' He turned to the hostess who had materialised at his elbow. 'You want me?'

'If you please, sir. Your secretary says there's a personal call for you. Will you take it here in the lounge?'

'Sure.' As he turned to follow her, he wondered who it might be. Not Myra, anyway: it was still not yet eight in the morning in New York. He took the telephone the girl held out for him, and nodded his thanks. 'Schumacher.'

'This is the Liberation Army, Schumacher.' He recognised the voice at once, like a harsh whisper, as dry and brittle as autumn leaves crushed underfoot. 'Listen carefully, because time is already running out. That Honeymoon Jumbo of yours took off with a bomb on board, and unless the airline pays a substantial contribution to Army funds everyone in the plane will be killed before it reaches New York.'

There were familiar sounds in the background, and the American tried desperately to identify them as the voice continued.

'The price of finding out where the bomb is hidden – and how to deal with it – will be five million pounds, Schumacher. Half a million to be paid here in London, the balance in Deutschmarks through your office in Frankfurt. I'll give you the details later: this call is to allow you time to make all the necessary arrangements to draw the money.'

Where the hell was that call coming from? What were those familiar noises he could hear?

'Don't attempt anything foolish, Schumacher, not if you value those lives on board. This bomb is triggered to an altimeter, which means it will explode automatically with the drop in atmospheric pressure if you order the pilot to divert and land. It is also fitted with a time device, set to go off before the plane arrives over New York. How do you like that, Schumacher? Your Honeymoon Jumbo can't turn back and land, and it's due to blow up a few hours from now anyway. Some bomb, eh?'

Of course! Those sounds he could hear were women's voices – airport voices, broadcasting messages above the pandemonium of the booking hall outside! At once he realised who was threatening him: you morons, you jerks, he thought contemptuously, did you really think you were going to scare Byron Schumacher with all that crazy bomb talk?

'Now you listen to me' he hissed into the mouthpiece: he remembered just in time where he was, and kept his voice low. 'You overlooked one important little detail, my friend. In Atlantic Airways we *never* pay blackmail – and we don't give a damn who's pointing the gun at us. Next time you call I'll have you put straight through to the police, d'you hear? Now go peddle your threats some place else.'

But he was too late: the line was dead, he had been speaking only to himself. No matter, he thought as he replaced the receiver and walked away. Whoever made the call would have hung up by now anyway, and disappeared among the crowds thronging the hall: all that really mattered was to know who was behind it. The Liberation Army, indeed! Even Schumacher was compelled to pay grudging respect to the audacity of the airport strikers. Oh, the call had come from the go-slow boys, he had no doubt about that: no one else would have dared, or perhaps even had the opportunity, to trace his movements and ring him from within the airport itself. Yet it was a bold choice. There could be very few people in the western world who had not heard of the Liberation Army, or 'A.L.' as they were sometimes known.

A.L. was a German terrorist group apparently based somewhere in the Rhineland, and rapidly amassing a tally of kidnap and murder that made even the Baader-Meinhof gang seem cherubic by comparison. It first came into prominence less than a year before the commemorative flight took place, when the police in Dusseldorf arrested a girl student in connection with the abduction and murder of a local banker. The girl, who came from a good middle-class family, was sentenced to ten years' rigorous imprisonment for complicity. As she left the dock she gave a clenched fist salute and spoke for the first and only time throughout the trial: 'Guard yourself', she warned the judge. A week later he was killed when the court building where he sat was blown up. Responsibilty for his death was claimed by A.L. in a letter to a newspaper, in which the writer warned 'We will explode a bomb every week from now on until Gisele' – Gisele Mittel, the girl sentenced to ten years' jail – 'is released.'

There was a flutter of apprehension, but no widespread concern. Then in the five weeks that followed bombs went off in court buildings from Frankfurt to Bremen, killing twenty-seven people and injuring 118 more, including judges, lawyers, court officials and policemen. Public confidence in the forces of law and order took a sharp knock. Soon there was a marked reluctance throughout western Germany for many people to attend court at all, officials and witnesses alike. The impasse –

and the bombings – ended only when Mittel managed to escape from prison, midway through the sixth week of the bomb terror. She was never recaptured, and the authorities had still not succeeded in living down the rumours that followed: even though the Chancellor himself had issued a firm denial of any official complicity in the escape.

The kidnappings started almost as soon as the bombings ended. Soon new rumours began to sweep the country – not all of them untrue – of blackmail being paid by a number of prominent men to the new terrorist organisation, and before the year was out the man in the German street was asking his neighbour if he'd heard the one about the Federal tax collector who took less money from his clients than A.L. But it was no joke for the men in office, or the tycoons whose funds helped maintain their Parties in power. All such persons had to have round-the-clock protection. Ministers lived with armoured cars stationed in their suburban gardens. Within a year of Mittel's escape from prison, the Liberation Army became a household name throughout the western world, and Germany herself – rich, proud, efficient West Germany – was very nearly reduced to a State under siege.

However, even allowing for the gang's fearsome reputation, there were a number of logical reasons why Schumacher should refuse to take the telephone threat seriously. The Liberation Army had never operated beyond the German frontier: and while accepting that one day it might, there could be no possible reason to suppose its first foreign victim would be an American firm operating out of London. Atlantic Airways had no connection, real or imagined, with business interests in Germany other than normal air traffic rights. There was no sense to a threat from A.L. and Schumacher – always a practical man – rejected it entirely. On the other hand, he had been in confrontation with the trouble makers at Heathrow, and he had got his Jumbo airborne by a combination of double-dealing and trickery. What could be more predictable than a furious reaction from some of the militants – and an eleventh-hour bid to scotch the commemorative flight by the only means available after take-off, a hoax telephone call?

There had been earlier threatening calls, and Schumacher had ignored them all – also on common-sense grounds. They had come when the Honeymoon Jumbo was still on the ground, and passenger-less so that the only precautions which could have been ordered were in fact already in force, to his certain knowledge. He listed them once more in his methodical mind. The plane had been guarded night and day by his own security force as well as the airport police. No ground staff had been allowed on board unless they held official passes – passes which were issued only after the people concerned had been given security clearance. The Jumbo had been searched from end to end immediately before take-off. All luggage and freight had been vetted by X-ray equipment, and all passengers submitted to metal detector scrutiny before embarkation. There was no way anyone could have smuggled a bomb aboard the Honeymoon Jumbo before it left that morning: of that, Schumacher felt positive.

None the less, his own position *vis-à-vis* the calls had undergone a subtle change. The plane was no longer grounded, and empty: it was airborne with nearly 450 souls on board, a fact which brought with it a shift of responsibility. Captain Brdwzynski was in charge of Romeo Juliet 240 now, and responsible for the safety of all therein. It was Schumacher's duty to report the anonymous call, and discuss with the authorities what course to take in alerting the pilot of the possible dangers involved. In normal circumstances, he would never have hesitated: in this case he was genuinely convinced he was dealing with a hoax call, aimed solely at disrupting the airline's commemorative flight, something he was determined he would not allow to happen. In the event, he decided to steer a middle course. A quick glance round the lounge showed him that the Controller had gone. Quietly, he button-holed the head of security, a former Wing Commander called John Messenger, and manoeuvred him out of earshot of the others.

'Wing Commander. Mind if we talk shop for a moment?'

'Course not, old boy. Fire away.'

'You're the man in charge of security here. In your considered opinion, is there the remotest chance some lunatic could have hidden a bomb in that Honeymoon Jumbo before it took off this morning?'

'Of course not.' Indignant blue eyes scanned Schumacher's face. 'What is this, some kind of joke?'

'I assure you it's nothing of the kind, Wing Commander. I've just taken an anonymous telephone call from a man who claims to have done exactly that.'

'Ah.' Messenger waited for him to continue.

'Let me say at once I consider the security precautions taken to safeguard this flight entirely adequate – watertight, even.' Schumacher removed his glasses and began to polish them with his handkerchief, frowning short-sightedly as he spoke. 'Uh, strictly between the two of us, Wing Commander. I heard background noises as the man spoke, and I'll swear they were voices coming over the tannoy system here in the airport.' He paused for a moment, and then said, 'Tell me, do you think my anonymous caller might have been one of those go-slow people, out to cause mischief?'

'It's entirely possible, I suppose.' Messenger stroked his chin thoughtfully. 'Everyone here seems to know you filled the Honeymoon Jumbo with passengers from your other flights . . . it's only a question of time before the strikers find out, and they're bound to feel aggrieved, I should think.'

'*Precisely*.'

'Right. I'll get my chaps to look into it right away. It shouldn't take too long to find out – we know who the militants are, don't worry.'

'Well, thank you for that, I'll stand by till I hear from you.'

'You'll send a warning message to your pilot, of course?'

'Well now, I've got problems there, Wing Commander. Look, I'm absolutely convinced this call came from one of those damned strikers – a hoax, pure and simple. But we've got nearly twenty newspapermen travelling on the aircraft. The minute Brdwzynski orders a plane search, those guys are going to burn up the air with bomb-scare stories, you know?'

'I accept that, but your first duty – '

'It *can't* be coincidence that the only plane to take off on schedule today gets a bomb warning half an hour later, goddammit! And I'm not thinking only of the airline now, Wing Commander. Look, the President of the United States has expressed a personal interest in the Honeymoon Jumbo flight – as you know – and they don't come much higher than that. Forgive me, but I have to say it: what's he going to think of security here if he reads a spate of bomb-scare stories, followed by an admission they were all based on a hoax call by some militant striker?'

The Wing Commander hesitated.

'Well, I'll get inquiries started immediately: as soon as we hear one way or the other, I'll contact you personally. What you tell your pilot meantime is for you and your people in America to decide. But I wouldn't wait too long if I were you. You know the old saying, better safe than sorry.'

'There's no question of anyone taking chances where the lives of our passengers are concerned. The point is, I'm *certain* this is a hoax call – moreover, a call made by troublemakers here at this airport. Let me ask you one final question, Wing Commander. How long will it take your men to trace and question these militants?'

'Hard to say for sure.' Messenger checked his watch. 'They won't have gone off duty yet. Fifteen minutes, perhaps. Half an hour at most.'

'Right. In that case, I'll await your report before informing my captain. And before alerting New York.'

It was twenty-eight minutes past one. Romeo Juliet 240 had just crossed the Irish coast and was entering the Western Approaches.

'Ready when you are, General.'

The door of the study swung open as Doctor Louk peered round with a cautious smile. He was senior medical adviser to Atlantic Airways, a post that carried few onerous duties and a generous salary. The appointment carried with it an unofficial role, of personal physician to General Grossman for which he received nothing but a hard time. The old man had always been a fire-eater and age had made him hugely cantankerous. Now that his health and strength were failing, Louk was never far from his side.

'I've been ready this past hour, dammit. Let's go!'

Doctor Louk beckoned Grimmett forward. Grimmett was a man of sixty-four, with a straight back and an air of stoic resignation: he had been the General's servant throughout his Service career, and still tended him. He helped the old man aboard his wheel chair, and folded the rug round his legs. As always, there was a last-minute flurry of excitement as the General left for the office. His secretary, Schuster, fussed round with advice and an assortment of papers as Grimmett pushed the chair down the hallway, through doors that parted electronically and which finally led out on to the porch. Mo Ryan, a former FBI man who was the General's personal bodyguard, spoke to the local police through a walkie-talkie as he followed behind. The police were informed whenever and wherever Grossman travelled, as a routine safety precaution. On the morning run to the office, two police motorcyclists met the little convoy on the turnpike and stayed with it until it crossed safely into Manhattan.

Thick mist enveloped the garden, deadening the call of the songbirds. Ryan took the front of the wheelchair and Grimmett the rear, and between them they carried the frail old man down a Niagara of steps to his limousine, with Louk bidding them be careful as he brought up the rear: courtiers in a royal procession. As soon as the General had been made comfortable the convoy set off, with Grimmett at the wheel of the first car, Ryan beside him and the old man already at work in the rear, giving orders for the day to a tape recorder. Louk's role then was to keep station fifty yards behind, so that the General would have alternative transport available in case of accident or any other emergency. The police escort appeared through the mist with a wail of sirens, and duly took over the lead. Then had been travelling only a few minutes more when the buzzer sounded on the General's car-phone.

'London for you, sir. Urgent call from Mr Schumacher.'

'Put him through.'

He pursed his lips impatiently and wondered what Byron could possibly want now. There had been a time when he had regarded him as an outstanding, even dynamic executive: young enough to be schooled as a suitable heir to the Atlantic Airways throne yet mature enough – and man enough – to be the right choice of husband for his beloved, but strong-willed and spoiled, daughter Myra. Most of that high regard had gradually been eroded over the years. Myra had him under her thumb, treated him like some damned pet poodle. At first the General believed Byron put up with it because he loved her, and that any doting father could have understood and forgiven: now he was not so sure. For some time he had had the growing impression Byron was capable of loving no one but himself, that his behaviour towards Myra was a disciplined one, calculated to keep the peace for entirely selfish motives. There were also marked similarities in his attitude towards the General:

never questioning his views but forever rubber-stamping them, meeting each and every demand with an obsequiousness dressed up as unswerving loyalty. There were times when the old man thought he could almost feel Byron Schumacher circling stealthily behind him, like the vulture stalking a meal that must surely soon be his. There was nothing he could do about it without arousing Myra's anger and resentment: she seemed to love Byron well enough, and he had no wish to hurt his daughter unjustly. He wanted to be sure of his ground before he made any irrevocable move, such as altering his will. This was one of the reasons why he had given him the Honeymoon Jumbo assignment, to let Byron stand on his own two feet while he was tested to breaking point.

There was no denying it had been a difficult time for the man in charge. A whole sheaf of newspaper clippings from London had kept the General informed of the chaotic state of industrial relations at Heathrow. Plane after plane had been grounded, financial losses had been very considerable. If ever there had been an obvious and tempting target for the trouble-makers then surely it must have been Atlantic's much-publicised honeymoon flight. Yet Byron had emerged apparently unscathed, and had even got the plane away on time: in all the circumstances, a fine piece of work. The General sighed – if only his son-in-law could have left it at that, and allowed events to speak for themselves . . .

'I didn't expect another call yet awhile, Byron,' he said pointedly. 'I'm still on my way to Manhattan. What's up?'

'Trouble, General, and it's looking bad. There's a threat to blow up the Honeymoon Jumbo. Some guy phoned in and claimed it took off with a bomb hidden aboard.'

'When was this?'

Byron hesitated. 'Well, sir, we took the actual call, uh, about half an hour after take-off: about one hour ago now. Naturally I checked it out at once with the head of security here. He took the view it was most likely a hoax call, made by one of the strikers. This was based on the very strict precautions taken against possible sabotage before the plane left London.'

The General forced himself to remain calm. 'Okay, so what's happened now – Brdwzynski's searched the aircraft and found a suspicious package on board, is that what you're trying to tell me?'

There was a marked pause before Schumacher answered this time. 'Well sir, uh, in view of the security chief's assurances, his repeated and firm assurances of the strict precautions against sabotage, and the, uh, general assumption it was a hoax call from this no-good bunch of strikers here at the airport . . . and in view of the large number of newspapermen on board . . . we, that is, I decided, uh, it would be better not to alert Brdwzynski until the phone call had been checked out. Unfortunately, that took a lot longer than – '

'Jesus, Byron! Are you telling me you allowed an aircraft of ours – a plane with nearly 450 people on board – to fly all this time after receiving a bomb threat without even giving the pilot a chance to take protective action?'

There was no reply.

'Answer me this question, then,' said the General savagely. 'Why the hell are you suddenly off-loading the responsibility now? What's happened to frighten *you?*'

'Sir – *please* – you have to believe me, we were genuinely satisfied the whole thing was a phoney, an eleventh-hour bid by the strikers to hit back at us after getting the Honeymoon Jumbo away on time! The British security men here were still questioning some of the militants when I received a second call, ten, fifteen minutes ago. This time the man said if I didn't believe they meant business, to take a look at a certain car in the parking lot. I got the airport police to check it out at once. They found the body of one of our fitters inside – he'd been murdered, General.' Schumacher's voice was hoarse with distress now. 'This was a man who was supposed to have been working on the Honeymoon Jumbo up till take-off, sir. But the police believe he's been dead for at least eight hours, and if that's right, someone else must have taken his place in the maintenance crew today – someone who would have had access to every nut and bolt in the aircraft, and all the time in the world to plant a bomb aboard if he wanted. I'm sorry as hell about this, General, but that's what threw me – the sudden realisation this threat could be real.'

'I thought it must be something like that,' said the old man grimly. 'And I'm sorry, too – about a whole lot of things, Byron. Most of all I'm sorry you're not on that plane yourself, to sweat it out with the rest of the kids up there. Now, get off the air so I can talk to Brdwzynski and give him the score. And while the aircraft is being searched, I'll have him divert to the nearest airport for a thorough check by bomb disposal teams.'

'Sir – don't do that!' Schumacher sounded close to breakdown. 'In his first call the man said the bomb was fitted with an altimeter device, which would automatically set it off if the plane was ordered down. General, please, hold on now, I keep telling you, I honestly did not believe the threat was genuine at the time . . . but in the light of this murder, I . . . I have to advise you very strongly against giving Brdwzynski orders to divert.'

If they had been in the same room, the General would have struck him. It was several seconds before he could bring himself to answer his son-in-law.

'Byron,' he growled, 'I don't have any idea what else you may be holding back from me, and I don't have time to drag it out of you right now. So here's what we're going to do. Two weeks ago I assigned responsibilty for this commemorative flight to you: and that's the way it's going to remain, you hear? I'm going to call Brdwzynski immediately, and instruct him to carry out an air search – and then, to report his findings to *you*. He's going to complete this flight – one way or another – on your executive orders alone, is that understood, Byron? Those 448 lives are going to remain your responsibility throughout the voyage, and maybe for the rest of your worthless life, d'you hear?' There was no immediate response, and the old man purpled with rage. 'Acknowledge!' he roared into the telephone. 'Acknowledge my orders, Byron, goddam you!'

'But General,' wailed his hapless son-in-law, 'you haven't given me a chance to tell you yet. These terrorists are holding us up for a five million pounds ransom – *nine million* American dollars, sir. How the hell am I going to play that one?'

'I thought all my executives knew the answer to that kind of problem,' declared the General brusquely. 'In this company we don't pay blackmail – we look for the way round it. And that's the way it's going to be with the Honeymoon Jumbo, okay? Now then, get off this line while I talk to Brdwzynski.'

Five miles up in the sky and nearly 400 miles over the ocean, the wedding breakfast was proceeding in great style. Captain Brdwzynski made his speech, as soon as he was clear of strikebound Heathrow. He then read messages of welcome from the

American President and his First Lady, as Fats and the cabin crew served more than a hundred bottles of Krug '64 to a popping of corks that sounded like drumfire. Then, as the honeymooners held hands and before the feasting began, Frank Gadsby performed the first half of his concert. Not for him were the animal sounds of punk, rock and all the rest of the modern scene: he was a crooner from that great school first ushered in by Crosby and continued by names like Sinatra, Como and Bennett. He sang his ballads 'live' in each of the two compartments set aside for the newlyweds, crossing from one to the other at intervals, while the broadcast continued throughout the rest of the aircraft – flight deck included.

Brdwzynski sat in his pilot's seat humming 'Carolina Moon' with his passengers, and watching an infinity of grey unfold above and below them as he guided the plane through the jet-stream. The headwinds were steadily mounting in ferocity. Ten-tenths cloud shut out all sight of the sea below. A layer of haze above blocked out the sunlight as completely, so that in between it was like flying through the steam from a giant kettle. Slap, slap, slap! went the windscreen wipers, to clear away the streaming mist. Bright green moons rose and fell on the radar screen. A myriad coloured lights flashed and twinkled in the constellation of switches and gauges that together made up the multi-million-dollar electronic brain of the Jumbo. And all the time the four mighty fan-jet engines thundered in the background, each one producing as much horsepower as twenty railroad diesel locomotives. As she climbed up to join the crew, senior stewardess Lindy Parsons gazed round at the familar, busy scene in the 'front office' of the world's biggest and roomiest aircraft – and reflected, not for the first time, how cramped and Lilliputian almost the crew's quarters seemed by comparison with the space allotted to passenger comfort.

'Coffee coming up,' she announced brightly. 'I deeply regret that the management won't allow me to serve you guys any of the Krug '64.'

Brdwzynski waved a thank-you: co-pilot and flight engineer glanced round with a smile, nodded their thanks, and went on with their various tasks. This was the command post: the whole atmosphere utterly different to the rest of the plane. Each man's eyes scanned a hundred dials incessantly: in here, the air was blue with tobacco smoke. As the headwinds buffeted them, the huge plane bucked and trembled, like a thoroughbred feeling the whip.

'How's everything back there, Lindy?' asked Brdwzynski.

'It sure is some party, Captain,' she told him. 'I don't think I ever saw such thirsty passengers in my whole life: it beats me where they put it all!'

'It's the occasion, Lindy,' chuckled the pilot. 'They just can't shake off the habit of saying "I will" whenever you appear with the drinks trolley, I guess. What the hell, we don't fly 240 newlyweds every day – let them enjoy themselves.'

'They're doing that all right,' she said. 'Just listen to them singing!' She looked out of the windscreen with an experienced eye as the plane suddenly lurched again, like a hiker tripping over an unseen stone. 'Which reminds me,' she added. 'Frank Gadsby wasn't looking too good, the last time I saw him. I'd better get back and see how he is.'

'Do that, Lindy. Thanks for the coffee. Warn Fats we may be late into Kennedy if the weather worsens.'

'Right, sir.' As she left with the empty tray, Brdwzynski heard the rasp of a well-remembered voice in his headset.

'Atlantic One calling Romeo Juliet Two Four Zero. You there, Lucky?'

'Top of the morning to you, General. And a whole heap of anniversary greetings from all of us on board the Honeymoon Jumbo.' They were staunch friends, these two, in spite of the considerable differences in age and status. General Grossman had been born in another century, before Orville Wright made aviation history in 1903 on Kill Devil Hill at Kitty Hawk, in North Carolina. Walter Brdwzynski had been abandoned as a foundling on the steps of a Roman Catholic church in Chicago in 1941, on the day that the Whittle jet was first airborne. But both were born to be aviators: they had dreamed the same dreams in boyhood, and they talked a common language as grown men. The fact that one was the airline president and the other his chief pilot was a matter solely for mutual respect and admiration.

Grossman was a World War Two bomber hero. Brdwzynski could remember reading as a kid the story of the General's famous 'Raid on the Ruhr', a disastrous daylight sortie in which he lost fourteen out of his total attacking force of twenty Flying Fortresses. They were caught in ambush by a swarm of

German fighters, and cut to ribbons. Grossman limped home in a plane crewed almost entirely by dead and wounded. He was then fifty-six years of age and, as an Allied commander of great seniority, under orders not to expose himself to 'undue risk.' '*Undue* risk?' he said, when he got back. 'There ain't no such thing.' Typically, he tore up the orders, organised another and bigger attack force and went back next day to bomb the target out of existence. By so doing, he became a living legend.

He met Brdwzynski for the first time when the young man applied for a job with Atlantic Airways while on leave from Vietnam. He asked him very little about his Air Force career, and his experience of big jets: he could get all that from the sheaf of papers in his hand. What he wanted to hear at first hand was about the raids on Hanoi, and this new kind of war that American pilots were fighting, the war of the B.52's and the Russian-built SAM's. Brdwzynski told him, and painted a sombre picture.

'Those Commie bastards,' said the General. 'They never give up.' He looked quizzically at the young man in front of him. 'That why you want to quit, son? Are you scared?'

'There have been times, General,' Brdwzynski admitted, 'when I've been shit scared. But that isn't why I want out. Any more than the next man, that is.' He rubbed his jaw as he groped for the right words. 'With respect, sir, the war you fought was different. Every American knew then that if we were beaten by the Japs and the Nazis, the lights would go out all over the free world. So, you fought till you won. Vietnam is something else, General. I'm not fighting for America – at least, not for any of the Americans I seem to have met on this leave. They hide their sons from the draft and demonstrate outside the White House, rather than allow their boys to fight alongside my pilots in Vietnam. They see the war as a political gamble and as a long, sad and costly mistake: and I'm afraid I agree with them, sir. That's why I'm getting out. Not because I'm a coward – but because my conscience bothers me.'

It was a marathon speech for the normally taciturn Brdwzynski. He sat back rubbing the ivory Buddha in his pocket, while the old man studied the photostat copy of a document he held in his hand. The citation that accompanied the award of the Air Force Cross said that 'Captain Walter Brdwzynski . . . led his squadron time and again with resolute determination against heavily defended enemy targets, and on each occasion personally remained over the objective until the mission had been accomplished and the crews under his command . . . could themselves return to base.' Except for the name of the recipient, the words might have been taken from his own citation for bravery years earlier. He stood up to indicate that the interview was over, and held out a hand.

'All right, son,' he said gruffly. 'There'll be a job waiting for you here just as soon as those discharge papers come through. I'm prepared to take you on as a Grade One pilot, commencing salary $40,000 a year. Sign the form my secretary hands you on the way out, if you find the terms acceptable, and we'll be in touch with formal contract details later. Good luck.'

As soon as he had signed and he found himself back in the corridor outside the Atlantic Airways office again, Brdwzynski took the ivory figurine from his pocket and solemnly kissed it. Now, as he sat in the Jumbo and heard the General warn him that there could be a terrorist bomb hidden aboard, his first, involuntary reaction was to reach out his left hand to the windscreen and grope along it until he encountered the Buddha. Then he rubbed it between his fingers for luck as he shook his head wonderingly, and asked himself 'Say, did I dream all that, or what?' He cast his mind back to the scene in London that morning, as the Boeing was made ready for flight: and in the mind's eye he watched the police patrol the runways, and the airline's own security teams search each compartment inch by inch.

'Goddammit,' he told himself, 'I *must* have been dreaming – those guys didn't miss a trick.' He gazed round at his own flight deck. First officer Joe Eckhardt was speaking on another channel to Gander, calling for an updated weather report. Flight engineer Bronson was bent over the instrument panel, checking the readings. The four engines ran smoothly, rumbling defiance at the winds outside. Everything was as it should be, routine and peaceful.

'Romeo Juliet Two Four Zero to Atlantic One,' he said distinctly. 'General, can I have that again – slowly, please? I think I must have misheard you in the static.'

The headset crackled into life immediately.

'I told you,' repeated the old man harshly, 'that Byron just called up to report a terrorist threat to your aircraft, Lucky.

A man has phoned in to say that there's a bomb hidden on the plane. Now, there's been a fair amount of confusion back in London, one way and another: at least that's how it looks to me. At first they thought it had to be a hoax call. Now they insist circumstances warrant an air search. Therefore I want you to carry out standard procedure, and report your findings back to London, affirmative or negative. Over.'

'Your message received and understood. Stand by, please.' Brdwzynski stabbed a finger down on the INS keyboard and read his position: 46 deg. North 40 West. He examined the chart briefly and spoke again to the General. 'How long has that stupid – I beg your pardon, sir, I mean how long have they been sitting on this bomb warning in London?'

'At least one hour.' In a few terse sentences the General explained how it took an additional telephone call – and the discovery of the body of a murdered fitter – to persuade his son-in-law to raise the alarm. 'On top of everything else, we now have a big ransom demand. It doesn't look good at all, Lucky.'

'Yeah.' Brdwzynski pored over the chart again, and reached a decision. 'Sir, in view of the amount of time lost, I think I'll just tell the passengers we have developed a minor engine malfunction – and head back to Shannon for a thorough search by bomb disposal teams. That will – '

'Negative.' The General spelled it out for him. 'These guys are claiming they put an altimeter switch on the bomb, and to my way of thinking, they could be telling the truth. In the circumstances, I'm afraid I'll have to order you not to divert, or attempt to land anywhere – unless you get clearance from London first. I want you to get an air search under way, Lucky – and make it fast. Report back to Byron with whatever you find, and take your orders from him. Meantime, I'll do everything I can from this end to help. Over.'

'Very good, General. Thank you, sir. Over and out.' The pilot turned the headset switch to intercom and called the after galley. 'I want the chief steward up here, on the double. Move it, will you?' Then he leaned across the cockpit and began to talk urgently to Eckhardt and Bronson.

Ohlsen's face was pink with effort by the time he hauled his bulk on to the flight deck to join them. 'I've just given instructions to start serving the Truffle Sauce Supreme to our passengers,' he said in a mock reproach. 'And that's a hell of a time to send for your chief steward, captain. With great respect.'

'Stow it, Fats. D'you have orders marked "Emergency procedure – bomb on board" back there?'

'Yes, sir.'

'Then let's do it. Fast.'

'Yes, sir.' The old man shinned down the spiral stairway and hurried aft. As he entered the rear section he saw Lindy serving dinner, and beckoned to her.

'Lindy, I want you!' He remembered in time to smile an apology to the passengers concerned. 'Excuse me, folks.' Then he repeated the order. 'As soon as you can make it, kid!'

'Coming.' With a single gesture of her finger she handed over the trolley to another hostess. Then she followed Ohlsen into the galley. 'What's up, Fats, we running out of champagne or something?'

'A bomb scare, kid. Lucky thinks we may have one on the plane.' They spoke in lowered voices, standing face to face with legs braced as the aircraft swayed and shuddered in the growing turbulence. 'Know what we have to do, Lindy?'

'Sure.' It was all in the book. 'Where do we start?'

'In there.' He nodded his head at the aftermost section. 'After that, we'll try the honeymoon kids. Last of all, the gentlemen of the Press in first class.' He could still find time to grin at the thought. 'And God help us all then. I reckon the Captain's got trouble enough as it is.' He patted her shoulder. 'Try not to upset anyone more than you have to, okay?'

'Sure, Fats. This your first bomb too?'

'Yeah. Let's go.'

They each took a card printed in red from the galley locker and studied them briefly. The cards showed a numbered list of instructions on how to cope with the emergency. Number One looked at first sight to be about as scientific – and useful – as sticking a pin into a list of runners to find the winner of a horse race. It said:

'On receipt of the emergency warning, cabin crew will proceed calmly along the rows of seats, inquiring of each group of passengers in turn "Please, is there a bomb disposal expert among you?" '

To ask such a question with a bomb about to explode, perhaps under your very feet, sounds so naive, so brazenly optimistic, that it never fails to raise a laugh among air crew in training. In Atlantic they called it the Rabbi's Prayer, and always added, sotto voce *'You should be so lucky!'* Even now Lindy had to fight down a nervous impulse to giggle as she made her way down the aisle, repeating the question over and over again. This was the compartment that held the 170 economy class passengers who had been secretly transferred to the Honeymoon Jumbo in London, and they sat in rows of eight: three abreast on the port side and five a side to starboard. Below the end four rows lay the entrance to the freight hold, and the last row of all was reserved for the use of cabin crew at take-off and landing. The two stewards worked from the galley end, working their way aft to the tail. Lindy took the starboard side.

Few people paid them any attention until it fell to their own turn to heed the loaded question. And even then their first reaction was to gape blankly, so unexpected was it and so completely out of character with the carnival air of the flight. By the time its full, sinister implication sunk home, Fats and Lindy had passed on: so that one by one a line of heads craned round after them registering shock, and incredulity, then horror and fear. And, as the dam burst, so their behaviour followed a pattern. Knives and forks and glasses were put down, as the taste of the banquet suddenly turned to bile. There would be silence for several seconds. Then the wretched passengers would turn back to each other, demanding reassurance from their neighbours, firing question after question shrilly and urgently.

What the hell did those two stewards think they were playing at? I mean, no one actually *said* there was a bomb alert, did they? Surely – *surely* – it was all a dreadful misunderstanding, it had to be some kind of drill, like boat drill on an ocean liner: well, didn't it? God in heaven, they didn't mean – they *couldn't* mean there was a bomb actually on this plane: could they? On this aircraft? On the Honeymoon Jumbo, for Christ's sake? Who would be insane or wicked enough to want to commit a crime like that?

Fats and Lindy shut their ears to the clamour behind them, and pressed on. Gordon and Laura Ramage sat in the innermost seats in Row M, starboard side, the last row but three. Both were drowsy from their long day and the surfeit of good food and drink and lay back, seats fully reclined, eyes closed, mouths smiling, drifting along in the timeless limbo of the seasoned air traveller, with the cares of strikebound Britain banished to the furthest recesses of their minds. They were on holiday, and – if no one minded them saying so – few families in the plane might consider they had earned one more. Books and newspapers lay unopened on their laps as they day-dreamed of the sunshine ahead. Dimly they became aware of a voice calling them from a million miles away. Gordon roused first, to find the dusky face of Melinda Parsons peering down, no longer smiling but tense, and troubled. Immediately he pressed the release button in the arm of his seat and glided upright, shaking his head like a swimmer coming up after a dive as he struggled to gather wits scrambled by sleep. There had been an ominously familiar ring about the words this girl had uttered, and it called for a genuine effort on his part to ask her to say them again.

'Hold on, miss.' He put out one of those big hands as she started to turn away. 'What was that you just said?'

Lindy took a deep breath. 'I'm trying,' she repeated doggedly, 'to find out if . . . if we have a bomb disposal expert aboard the plane.'

The momentary quaver in her voice betrayed the tension she felt and Ramage recognised the signs at once. I can't believe it, he told himself savagely – not again, not here! In the same moment he felt his wife stir at his side and knew that she was awake too, listening to every word that was said. He forced himself to return Lindy's question with a smile as bright and false as fool's gold, and ordered his voice to remain calm and steady.

'Bull's eye,' he said. 'What can I do for you?'

The smile made him look younger than he was, but there was no mistaking the air of quiet authority about him: Ramage wore it like a badge. It showed in the resolute set of the jaw, the measured tone, the calm acceptance of the challenge her question implied. Lindy thought of the hoary joke that went with the Rabbi's Prayer – *you should be so lucky!* – and smiled back in heartfelt relief.

'We have no idea what the problem is, sir,' she told him, 'but I sure am glad I found you! Would you come with me to the Captain, please?'

'Of course.' He turned to Laura and squeezed her hand, gently. 'I suppose you heard that?'

'Yes.' Her eyes were enormous with fear.

'Bet you any money you like they've had a hoax call, back in London.' He unfastened his safety belt and stood up. 'Not to worry. Airlines get them all the time.'

The right answer failed to come and she clung to his hand, terrified.

'Come on, now: chin up.' He bent down and kissed her on the cheek. 'I'll let you know the score as soon as I've spoken to the captain.'

Then he was gone, murmuring an apology to the other passengers in Row M as he squeezed past. He marched briskly behind Lindy through the length of the huge plane, no longer marvelling at its size but hating it, scouring it with a professional eye as he looked for possible hiding places for a bomb. The wedding breakfast was in full swing in the other compartments. The singing was over and the banqueting had begun, and no one paid them the slightest attention as they walked through. Finally Lindy led him on to the flight deck.

'Hey, we found a bomb disposal expert!' she announced triumphantly. Her voice made it sound as if their troubles were already over, and the three faces at the controls brightened immediately. 'Captain Brdwzynski, this is Mr Ramage.'

Brdwzynski leaned from his seat and shook hands. 'Boy, am I glad to meet *you*!' The strength of his grip matched the Englishman's as his eyes took in the black patch, and the scars. 'Okay, Lindy. You get back and tell Fats to belay the rest of that bomb drill until I give the order.'

'Yes, sir.' Her eyes stayed on Ramage's face as she backed down the stairway. 'Good luck, Mr Ramage!'

'Thanks' he said, and this time his smile was warm and genuine. He turned back to Brdwzynski. 'All right, Captain, what's your problem?'

'Problems, plural.' The pilot scratched his ear, as if wondering where to begin. 'We got a call from our airline president, oh, maybe ten minutes back, warning us that we may have a bomb on board.'

Ramage stared around him curiously as he waited for the pilot to continue. Needles flickered on a bewildering array of dials. Red and green lights blinked across the face of the instrument panel as the Jumbo rolled and swayed in the jet-stream like a heavyweight boxer riding a flurry of body blows. Now Eckhardt held her on manual, as his Captain and the bomb disposal man conferred together.

'Problem number one, we've wasted a dangerous amount of time already. London received an anonymous tip about the bomb soon after we took off, but failed to alert us because they thought it had to be a hoax. Then one of the ground staff was found murdered after a second call, and the police believe a terrorist may have taken his place to nobble the plane. Now on top of everything else, the airline has been socked for a big ransom demand. So they finally decided to let us in on it – one and a half hours later.'

Ramage looked at his watch. 'Jesus.'

'Yeah. Well, ordinarily in circumstances like that I'd head like a scalded cat for the nearest airport and offload my passengers while bomb disposal teams carry out a search for the weapon – if any. But we can't do that here.'

'Oh, why not?'

'Problem number two. London thinks those terrorists may have wired our bomb to an altimeter trigger. In which case the surest way to find out would be to attempt to land.'

'So – your people have been told to hand over the money to find out how to save us, right?'

'Right. There's only one fly in the ointment. Atlantic Airways don't pay ransom. Ever.'

'Ah.' Ramage gave him the ghost of a grin. 'And to think that stewardess told me your name was *Lucky*.'

'Yeah.' Brdwzynski found himself grinning back. At least the Englishman had a sense of humour. He wondered about the eye. 'You an Army bomb disposal man, sir?'

'I was.' It was a wry smile indeed now. 'Finished my time three weeks ago. This flight was to celebrate my retirement leave.'

Comment would have been superfluous. 'Well, you're the expert,' said Brdwzynski slowly. 'Where do we go from here?'

'Let's see. Can we get hold of the person in London who actually received these calls?'

'Sure, no problem.'

'In that case, that's where we start. Every scrap of information helps: the more we know in advance, the better our chances once we find the bomb.'

'Right, I'll get him. You want the crew to start searching the plane while you talk to London?'

Ramage pinched his nose between forefinger and thumb as he considered the offer. Finally he said, 'I think not, Captain. A few minutes either way shouldn't make any difference at this stage. And it might be better if I go round with the search team.'

'Whatever you say. Incidentally, you'll be talking on our company frequency, so don't bother your ass about radio procedure. This is like an open telephone line between us and them.'

'I follow.'

'The man you want is called Schumacher. Byron Schumacher.' Brdwzynski ran his tongue round his mouth as he weighed his next words. 'He's our airline president's son-in-law. And the biggest prick in the outfit.'

Ramage thought it might be wiser to steer a neutral course. 'I'll remember that' he said. He donned the headset Bronson handed to him and took the flight engineer's seat as the pilot called London.

'Byron Schumacher,' he heard a voice announce.

'Schumacher, this is Brdwzynski.' He wasted no time on formalities. 'Listen, we struck gold: found a bomb disposal man among our passengers, a Mr Ramage. He needs to talk to you before we begin our air search. Stand by.' He stabbed a finger continually at his own head-set, like a theatre prompt giving an actor his cue, until Ramage found the right switch and broke in.

'Mr Schumacher, this is Gordon Ramage. Sir, I'm trying to stitch together a picture of whatever we may be facing here, and I believe you may be able to help me. Now sir, I want you to try to recall the exact words the terrorists used in their calls today, and in particular, any reference they made to the bomb itself. Fire away.'

'Yes, well, uh, let me see now.' His clash with the General had shaken his son-in-law and Schumacher found it difficult to remember anything clearly. 'Yes. I had two calls this morning, both from the same person, incidentally: a man. I remember he began by telling me he was a member of A.L. – the German terrorist outfit, you know?'

'Yes.' Ramage's heart sank a little as he heard that.

'Then he said "Your Honeymoon Jumbo took off with a bomb on board this morning, Schumacher." He knew my name, d'you realise that? That's why I felt so sure he was someone from the airport here, one of the strikers, you know?'

'Yes, sir, I follow. But what did he *say*?'

'He said "Unless you pay a very substantial sum to the A.L. funds mighty soon, everyone is going to be killed before they get to New York." '

'What time was this?'

'Well, I'd say around 1.10, maybe 1.15, London time: something like that. Say, I'd like to explain – '

'Please, Mr Schumacher: just concentrate on what the man *said*. I already know about the delay.'

'Oh, you do?' He was on the defensive now. 'Well, then he went on about money. You need to know about that, Ramage?'

'No. Just the bomb. Everything he said about the bomb.'

'Well, then he said "I'll give you the details of how I want the money paid later. Meantime, don't try anything foolish if you value your passenger's lives. Our bomb . . ." just hold on. I'm trying to get it exactly right . . . "our bomb is triggered by an altimeter, and that means if you order the pilot to land, it will explode automatically from the drop in atmospheric pressure . . ." '

'You're absolutely certain about that, Mr Schumacher? About him saying that the *fall in atmospheric pressure* would trigger off an explosion?'

'Well.' He had to think hard: Schumacher had been so anxious to identify the background noises he had barely listened to what the man had said. 'Yes. That's exactly what he said. I'm certain of it.'

'Good, that's a big help. Anything else you can remember?'

'He also said it contained a time bomb, set to explode before you reached New York anyway. That's what made me feel it had to be a hoax call, I mean, two bombs in one, crap like that, you know? "How do like *that*, Schumacher," he said, "your plane can't turn back to land, yet it's going to be blown to pieces before it gets to New York – unless you hand over the money." '

'I see.' Ramage noted each point carefully. 'And did he give you any idea what the time limit was?'

'No, only that it would be before you arrived at Kennedy. The rest was all about money. Then, when he called the second time and I told him we wouldn't give in to blackmail, he started to get very angry. That's when he said to look in the car – '

'Yes, sir, I know about the body in the car. Tell me, what did your people in New York say after it was found?'

'I don't think I follow you.'

'I was wondering what was decided about the ransom.'

'How's that again, Ramage?'

'I'm asking about the money – has your company agreed to pay the ransom, dammit?'

'Now see here, Ramage, I won't be – '

'Mr Schumacher: it looks as if we have a time bomb on the plane, and thanks to you people on the ground we've already lost more than an hour in searching for it. No, sir, *you* will listen to *me*! I'm a bomb disposal officer, not a bloody magician – and while we're searching for this device I expect your airline to do everything in its power to try to persuade these terrorists to tell us where the bomb is hidden, and what steps we have to take to render it harmless. Christ Almighty, man, we don't have *time* to argue with them!'

'And I keep trying to tell you,' groaned Schumacher, 'I don't have that authority, Ramage! None of us here have, only the General can make a deal like that, that's why I spoke to him before I called Brdwzynski – '

'Then I suggest you try him again,' ordered Ramage. 'And this time, make sure he listens – we've got nearly 450 lives at risk here, and possibly only a few hours left in which to save them! What the hell is the matter with you people down there?' His face was scarlet as he tugged off the headset. 'Sorry about that,' he said to the pilot. 'Once upon a time I used to think we had a monopoly of fools in the Services. How wrong can you be!' He blew his nose violently. 'Well, we'd better press on with the air search, captain.'

'Ready when you are,' said Brdwzynski.

'Right. Then if it's not already standard drill, here's what I want done. All passengers to remain in their seats. I want them to collect every item of personal baggage – hats, coats, booze, books, the lot – and sit with it on their laps until I come round. And only those things they can identify as their own, mind. They're to leave the rest for me to check.'

'Right.'

'Under no circumstances must they try to examine any unidentified parcel or package.'

'I'll see to it.'

'Galleys and toilets will have to be checked by the crew. The same rules apply to them – if in doubt, leave well alone.'

'Whatever you say. Do we look for anything in particular?'

'Not really. If there is a bomb on this plane – and we don't know that yet – the two-way device you heard Schumacher describe would be fairly small, and compact. My guess would be around four to five pounds in weight at most, and inside a harmless looking cover – most likely a phoney gift parcel, or a briefcase. Something like that.'

'I see.'

'And if we draw a blank in the passenger accommodation, I'll take a search party down in the hold.'

'Okay, Ramage. If you'll join Fats and Lindy to organise the search teams, I'll have a word with the passengers.'

Brdwzynski estimated that if the headwinds remained constant, six hours more flying time would put them over New York. He climbed back into his seat and motioned to his First Officer to keep the controls. His first act was to press the button that lit the SEAT BELTS signs throughout the plane: then he allowed his passengers a minute or two to settle down, before he made the most difficult speech of his life. Oddly enough, it was no help at all that he was unable to see the faces of his audience.

'Ladies and gentlemen, this is your captain again.' He tried to keep his voice even, and relaxed. 'I guess I have an apology to make this time, because this is no way to treat honoured guests on the occasion of our company's twentieth birthday party.' He paused for a moment, wondering how to sweeten the pill, but decided there was none. 'However – and I have to tell you this – our office in London has just received a telephone call from some man who claims he hid a bomb on this plane before we left Heathrow this morning. JUST HOLD ON, AND HEAR ME OUT,' he added firmly. 'Calls such as this always, but always, cause us the maximum amount of inconvenience: but that doesn't necessarily mean that they amount to anything in the end. Every airline in the world today gets plagued by similar calls some time or another, mostly from screwballs who want to get rich quick but don't aim to work for their money, like the rest of us. Perhaps it will surprise you to learn such calls are so commonplace, we even have a drill worked out how to cope with them.'

In the tail compartment, where the passengers had already been questioned by Fats and Lindy, the Captain's announcement was received in silence: they were already frightened half to death. But in the remainder, especially in first class where the Press was gathered, there was consternation for a while. By this time the cabin crew and the Sheriffs were positioned throughout the aircraft, with orders to deal promptly and firmly with any signs of panic. They themselves tried to lead by example, all drawing on that quiet, inner strength that comes only from training and discipline.

Brdwzynski went on, 'Now folks, it's a matter of record that nine out of every ten calls like this turn out in the end to be a hoax, just plain, ornery bluff.' It was a lie, but none of them knew that. 'However, they scare everyone out of their wits every time, and they keep coming because the animals who make them are sick, and get their pleasure that way. They are also very smart, because they realise such claims are very difficult to disprove quickly, so that most airlines would rather feel safe than sorry – and pay up regardless.' He took a deep breath. 'I don't need to tell you that Atlantic Airways have already indicated that they're ready and willing to pay whatever is needed to find out the truth – just as soon as our mystery caller rings back to say how much, and when, and where.'

He was clearly a man who believed it was as well to be hanged for a sheep as a lamb.

'But that doesn't mean we can afford to sit on our butts up here and wait for every little thing to be done for us. Nor does it matter that this plane was searched from end to end by security experts at Heathrow only a few hours ago. In Atlantic Airways we believe in being doubly sure about passenger safety – so now I'm going to ask every one of you to assist the crew in carrying out a simple, routine check, okay? Right, here's what I want you all to do.'

He repeated Ramage's instructions slowly and carefully and gave them all time to settle down again, with their hand baggage piled on each lap. When he continued, it was in a bright and cheerful tone, like the hey presto! of the magician lifting a rabbit from the hat.

'Now for the good news.' They could almost hear him chuckling. 'Among the passengers on this plane today is Great Britain's top bomb disposal expert, Mr Gordon Ramage. I don't need to point out what a swell break that is – it means that we can draw on his expert advice in the air while the police are working for us down on the ground, trying to trap the man who made this call. Even if it should turn out to be one more hoax in the end – and the odds on that happening are very much in our favour – well, we're still mighty glad to have Mr Ramage to call on at such a time. He will be coming round with the stewards to every compartment in a few minutes time, to carry out a routine search. Now don't forget, and this is very important, if you see anything you don't recognise as your own, like a case or a package or indeed, anything at all, DO NOT pick it up and attempt to look inside. Simply leave it where it is and tell the stewards as they come round. Everyone quite clear on that?'

Brdwzynski's realistic yet deliberately homespun approach had hit exactly the right note, thought Ramage, as he looked at his fellow passengers. Long faces had replaced all the laughter, but they were as steady as soldiers on parade.

'I shall remain in constant touch with Heathrow until this whole thing is cleared up, one way or the other,' promised the pilot. 'And I'll keep coming back as often as I can to give you all the latest information, from our own people on the ground as well as from every section of the aircraft up here. The cabin crew will be right there with you to handle any personal problems that may arise. All of you will please remain seated for the time being. Meantime, unless and until I receive orders to the contrary, I intend to keep heading straight on for New York, folks: as scheduled. Thank you.'

Ohlsen's decision to start at the back of the plane and work forward was confirmed by Ramage and approved by Brdwzynski. The pilot's reasoning was entirely selfish: he intended to keep the newspapermen out of his hair for as long as possible. They would want to file stories in flight and they would demand permission to take photographs, especially of Ramage at work. There was a BBC reporter due to make a live broadcast soon, and if he was permitted to talk to London, everyone else would insist on the same rights. As of now, however, the journalists would all be compelled to remain in their seats until after Ramage had searched their compartment – which was last on his list. It was only one of the problems he had to consider, but one that could not be ignored: and he welcomed the respite, to give him time to think it over. But no sooner had he congratulated Fats on his cunning than a call came from the air hostess in first class, to report that her charges were becoming 'kinda restless'.

'Right, Joe, I'll take the ship,' said Brdwzynski. 'I want you to get down there and talk to the Press boys about this whole situation. Tell them I'll do my best to open a channel for restricted messages as soon as possible, but emphasise that in view of the emergency they must understand passenger safety has to over-ride all other considerations; blah blah. Hell, you know the drill Joe, just stall them. Tell them anything you like, just as long as you make sure they stay put in that compartment, got that?'

'Aye, sir.'

Eckhardt made his way down the spiral stairway into the first class section and at once knew how Daniel must have felt on entering the lions' den. Like so many people who have no real idea of what the media needs to carry out its essential function, Joe Eckhardt completely misinterpreted their reaction to the bomb scare. Hitherto, he had taken their presence for granted: like sea-lice on a fresh-run salmon. If he had thought about them at all, it would be on the lines that with a free trip to America, with all the food and drink they could guzzle provided free of charge, a captive subject and no more than a few hundred words to write at the end of it all, they were on to a good thing. They should be grateful: yet now, far from showing gratitude, they were displaying a disgraceful lack of understanding of a very serious situation indeed. Instead of piling their luggage on their laps and waiting dutifully for Ramage to come round, they were hammering away at their typewriters and shouting at the stewardess, insisting she find means of getting their messages away or take one of them to the Captain immediately. Instead of showing concern at their own plight, they were voicing in no uncertain terms their extreme displeasure at the lack of communications on what was jokingly called a *facility* trip. The photographers wanted permission to walk round the aircraft with Ramage and photograph the search in the honeymooners' compartments. The din was appalling. What in tarnation did they think this was, said Eckhardt to himself: a goddam circus?

'... evening newspaper ... last edition coming up ...'

'... I demand ... to be allowed to get in touch with my office ...'

'... how the hell can we do our job if you keep us ...'

'... pictures ... can never be repeated ...'

'... how can you justify your attitude when the captain himself said nine times out of ten this was a hoax ...'

'... world's biggest circulation ... and if your airline imagines ...'

'... Christ, you invited us to come on this trip and had the gall to call it a facility ...'

'... deadline ...'

'... surely, one photographer ...'

'GENTLEMEN!' The First Officer had to shout at the top of his voice to make himself heard. 'You heard the Captain just now! That means – now *hold on*! – that means you know as much as we do ourselves at the moment: we're still waiting for news from London. A telephone call has been received, and all we can do as a result is to search the aircraft – which we are about to do with the help of Mr Ramage. Captain Brdwzynski has asked me to tell you he will open a channel for you guys to send restricted messages – just as soon as the situation permits. Meantime, passenger safety takes priority over all other matters. That's it.'

'Just a moment, please.' The reporter who addressed him looked even younger than Eckhardt himself. 'How many words?'

The First Officer looked blank. 'I'm afraid I don't get you.'

'These restricted messages you mentioned. How long must they be? How many words in each take?'

Eckhardt said the first number that came into his head. 'One hundred.'

'Thank you, that's great.' His youthful looks were deceptive. This was an experienced journalist determined to coax every ounce of information out of the flier, so that he should not waste a single one of those hundred words. 'One other thing, Mr – er?'

'Eckhardt.'

'Mr Eckhardt. Can you tell us why the Captain has decided to push on to Kennedy rather than head back, say, to Shannon which is much nearer? Or doesn't he take the threat seriously?'

'Of course he does.' He knew why well enough, but wondered how much he should disclose. 'Uh, it's a command decision. The Captain's privilege.'

'During a bomb alert?' The reporter had him in a corner now. 'I always understood it was standard procedure to divert to the nearest international airport and offload one's passengers in the event of a bomb warning. Or has that been changed – and if so, can I quote you?'

All righty, you asked for it, thought Eckhardt: so I'll give it to you straight between the eyes. 'Okay,' he said. 'As long as you men promise not to scare the ass off our other passengers, I'll tell you why. That's right, diversion is normal procedure. Except this time.' He looked round the compartment as the journalists hung on his every word. 'Our unknown caller told the London office he'd put an altimeter bomb on the plane. Know what that means?'

'No.' In fact, they wanted Eckhardt to tell them, because his words made the story.

'Well: assuming he's not bluffing. That means a bomb which will explode automatically with the change of atmospheric pressure – the moment we reach a certain altitude in descent.'

They listened in complete silence.

'And since no one except the terrorists know what that altitude may be, Control in London fully endorses Captain Brdwzynski's decision to continue to Kennedy and buy time while the search for the bomb goes on.'

They were not so dedicated that they could hear their own death sentence read out without showing some emotion, and their faces paled. Eckhardt decided to give them full value for their money. 'This unknown caller also said our bomb is fitted with a timing device, which is set to explode anyway before we reach our destination. If he's telling the truth, that means we've got it both ways.'

'Is he offering your company a way out?'

'The usual thing. A ransom demand. I don't know how much.'

Or unless Ramage, your bomb disposal expert, can defuse it first, thought the reporters. They had enough material for a thousand words now: the race against time. Another hand shot up as Eckhardt turned to leave.

'Make it fast, please' said the First Officer. 'Every minute's gold dust.'

'I'm a photographer.' The voice was calm and matter-of-fact. 'Would you please ask the Captain if he will allow one of us – at least – to photograph Mr Ramage on a pool basis?' He hurried on as Eckhardt opened his mouth to say no. 'Look, if we land safely, everyone's going to want to know what went on up here. The demand for pictures will be fantastic, and your own airline will be looking for them, because they will add up to the best publicity your company could ever have. And if we don't land safely, it's not going to matter anyway.'

That made sense. Eckhardt found himself mildly surprised to discover that these loud-mouthed, free-loading, abrasive people wanted nothing but the facilities to carry out their own specialised job. 'Okay,' he said. 'You pick the man, and I'll ask the Captain when I go back up. No promises, mind. But I'll do what I can.'

'Thank you.'

Even before he had left the compartment they were at work composing their first one-hundred-word despatches, and drawing lots for the pool photographer's job. No one gave a thought to searching among the hand baggage for a possible bomb: First Officer Joe Eckhardt included. It was now seven minutes after three, London time.

Playing hunt the thimble for a bomb is always a bastard, no matter what the location. Ramage had lost count of the times he had jelly-legged his way into the stillness of a hastily deserted building, following an anonymous tip-off that there was a bomb hidden inside. It is one of the oldest terrorist techniques, this business of telephoning a bomb warning to an office block or a tenement building or a crowded multiple store to say that the men and women and children inside have got precisely twenty minutes – or ten, or maybe only five – in which to get out alive. Their screams on the exit stairs will guarantee a healthy respect for the power of the terrorists concerned for years to come from everyone in hearing distance: especially if they can hear the ones caught on the top floors. And the technique is just as effective even if no explosion takes place within the specified time limit. Only a fool will thereupon assume the call to have been a hoax: all must wait to find out, but the bomb disposal expert can only wait for so long. Then, if nothing has happened, he has no choice but to go in – and play hunt the thimble. Alone. Treading on a carpet of egg-shells with every step he takes, acutely aware of the risk involved, half-expecting death to lurk in ambush round every corner.

Nowadays in Britain, thanks to the genius of the handful of bomb disposal men who held the ring in Ulster during the first, worst years of the IRA campaign, you can sometimes send in a metal robot to search for you: while you lie flat behind a wall of sandbags and guide it via a television screen. Not always, of course. And not at all when Ramage first started: in those days, everyone did it the hard way.

Occasionally there would be an explosive device right in front of you, as soon as you went in: slap in the middle of the floor, impossible even for a blind man to miss. Ramage himself had actually seen some with the word 'BOMB' daubed on the outer casing, in bright red paint. If you happened to be sufficiently green and trusting and unschooled to attempt to dismantle such a device in the ordinary way, thinking to yourself 'What cocky bastards they are, painting the damned name on it like that – I'll show 'em!', then you would be asking for Trouble with a capital T. Because as soon as you set to work on 'BOMB' you set off another device: the killer bomb this time, the real McCoy, ten pounds of polar ammon gelignite hidden in the desk drawer behind your back, or inside that innocent-looking wastepaper-basket by your feet. There is no end to the tricks they like to play, these bomb-makers.

Sometimes you might encounter no bomb at all – but a sniper instead, lying in wait in a rented room across the street with the hairline cross of his telescopic sight trained on that parcel on the table he knows you have got to investigate sooner or later during your search. Or you might walk into a whole series of booby-traps, jigsawed together: there are endless variations to this most murderous version of hunt the thimble.

Some men bought it with the first job they went on, others successfully defused a hundred devices and went on to live for ever. But just to be the joker who searched for the bomb: never knowing where it might be hidden, never knowing what was required to set it off – a step on the wrong floorboard, a ring on the telephone, the flick of an electric light switch – ah! that really sorted out the men from the boys.

And while Ramage could honestly say he had forgotten how many times he had seen into the dragon's mouth, it was none the less true this was the first time he had been called upon to look for a bomb in an aircraft in flight. He found it an almost unbearable situation: to be asked to conduct the search for explosives against the clock and within full view and speaking distance of an audience, all of whom were aware that they would be the victims if the worst should happen. It was a degrading experience to crawl on one's hands and knees, and peer through a forest of human legs to see if there was a container, or a package, in some dark corner that held a live ticking bomb. And the fact that his fellow passengers were so patient and so kind – and so pathetically grateful for his puny efforts – only served to make it worse, somehow.

Hardest of all was to keep the Judas smile on his face, the smile of bluff reassurance held in readiness for all the frightened eyes he could not avoid: his own wife's included. What good that smile did, Gordon was unable to say. Some who watched it prayed silently, others prayed aloud for God to guide his hand. However, it was a fact on the Honeymoon Jumbo that many of the passengers displayed sterling courage. There were those who actually joked with him as he came by. Others shook him warmly by the hand, or kissed his fingers: most uttered quiet words of encouragement, and all gave him their thanks. A few offered him cigarettes, one or two a drink. No one allowed him to pass by without some acknowledgement, and on his rounds Gordon experienced the most curious sensation, almost one of humility, as his own anxiety steadily mounted. Matrons and young brides of only a few hours sat stoically in their seats, belts fastened, with little heaps of hand baggage piled awkwardly on their laps, forcing themselves to make brittle conversation as he searched desperately to locate the obscene device that threatened to snuff out every life on board – his own included – at a moment's notice.

'Thank you.' 'God bless you, sir.' 'Good luck.' 'We'll never forget you.' Their words followed him all through the plane, like a benediction. And all the while the aircraft bucked and swayed in turbulent headwinds as she stayed obstinately on course, five miles above the storm-tossed sea. It was a setting none of them would ever be able to forget until their dying day: whenever that might be.

Nor could Ramage fault the cabin crew. The way they addressed their Captain, some of the expressions they used jarred on his British ears. But their discipline was magnificent: there was no other word to describe it. They joined in the search with him willingly. They soothed frightened passengers with a word here, a smile and a gesture there. They led women and children and pale honeymooners to toilets that had already been searched, they nursed and comforted them back to their seats again – seats that had become a temporary prison – as the search continued. Yet although they maintained strict discipline throughout, never once did they forget to treat their charges as human beings, with all the frailties and vagaries of the race. Rather than allow his passengers to sit and fret when the search had passed them by, for instance, Fats Ohlsen gave orders to resume in-flight service (tea and coffee only) to help soothe their frayed nerves, and perhaps in some minds to create an impression that things were gradually returning to normal. His pursers and stewardesses made little jokes and asides to lighten an atmosphere that otherwise might have tended to become claustrophobic. In its hour of crisis, Romeo Juliet 240 proved herself to be a well-found ship.

Human nature being what it is, even Lindy found her hopes rising as they quit the last of the economy class compartments without finding anything untoward. 'What do you think, Mister Ramage?' she asked him. 'You reckon those guys might have been bluffing, after all?' Neither the casual tone nor the smile on her face fooled him for a moment: she was as scared as any of her passengers, and seeking some kind of reassurance.

He racked his brains for an answer that would do just that, without committing him either way.

'I sure hope so, Lindy,' he said, gently. 'Just to look for these damned things scares me half to death, between you and me. How you can cope with all those passengers at the same time I'll never know.' Then they came to the first class section.

Ramage had met many Pressmen during his career, most frequently during the IRA campaign in Ulster: and like most British Servicemen, regarded them with mixed feelings. It was nice to have one's deeds – one's good deeds, that is – recorded in the newspapers for the folks back home to read. But journalists swarmed everywhere, like flies, even when their presence was not welcomed. And too often, they got their facts wrong. Admittedly they were working against the clock, and there were times when certain people deemed it wiser to withhold some of the facts from them. Even so, their stubborn refusal to accept whatever the Army told them necessarily as gospel, and their insistence on giving the other side of the coin – even when the dimmest mind could see that it was straight terrorist propaganda – was infuriating, sometimes even harmful, to the interests of the security services. However, there was no use shutting your eyes to the fact that the reaction of the media played a critical part in influencing public approval, or condemnation, of all military action today: especially in the kind of street war the British Army found itself forced to fight, say, in Ulster. So it behove the authorities not only to tolerate their activities, but much more: actually to invite them to observe and judge one's tactics and behaviour at first hand, and to take them into one's confidence even at the bleakest moments and on the most sensitive of subjects. To try to keep them in the dark on any matter almost always proved fatal, and over the years Ramage had come to accept that as a golden rule. He weighed that in his mind now, as he entered the noisy first class compartment.

There was noticeably less gratitude and warmth in evidence here than there had been in the other compartments he had searched. Instead, he was greeted by a barrage of questions, all of them forthright, perhaps even faintly hostile. Because he realised they were born of frustration, Ramage ignored them: behind him, Lindy clucked like an old hen at the outrage.

'When you've all finished,' he said placidly, and waited for the hubbub to die down. 'I know you chaps have got a job to do. But so have I, and you're not helping me or yourselves.'

He gestured at their equipment, scattered around the carpeted deck. 'Ten minutes ago the Captain asked *all* passengers to collect and identify every item of hand baggage, and keep it with them while we searched the plane. What's the matter with you fellows – d'you think the Press has some kind of magic of immunity from bombs, or what?' He relented as soon as he saw them cease typing and bend down to sort through their copious baggage. 'Listen, I've still got to check the flight deck and the freight hold after I'm through here. But as soon as I can, I'll be back to try to answer all your questions, how about that?'

That was fine, they said. There was only one question. 'Are you *the* Gordon Ramage?' asked one reporter. 'The George Cross colonel?'

'I'm Colonel Ramage,' he told them. 'Correction, I was: I'm finished with bomb disposal now. That is, I thought I had until I came on this trip with you chaps.' They all grinned at that and good humour was restored. 'All right then, let's get on with it. Everything accounted for?'

It took less than a minute to isolate the briefcase the terrorist had hidden beneath the window seat. Before Ramage could stop her, Lindy knelt down to retrieve it and held it aloft. 'Nobody want this one?' Twenty pairs of eyes examined the plastic grip in her hand, but no one answered. She tried once more. 'No one recognise this?' Still there was no reply.

'I'll take that, Lindy,' said Ramage quickly. His face remained expressionless as he hefted it, and estimated its weight: about four to five pounds. 'Ask the Captain if it's convenient for him to come down for a moment, would you please?' Brdwzynski came at once and he showed him the briefcase, holding it carefully in front of him.

'This belong to anyone on the flight deck, Captain?'

'No, sir.' The pilot shook his head vigorously. 'We've accounted for everything we brought on board with us, and I've searched the front office, personally. Clean on both counts.'

'I see.' Ramage lowered his arm, very gently. 'In that case, I'll need to open this up and take a look inside. Would you ask the crew to clear a working space for me, please – somewhere right at the back of the aircraft?'

'Sure. Lindy here will see to that for you. Go ahead and tell her what you want done.'

'Thank you.' He remembered Laura, alone in Row M. 'I'd like the tail section evacuated, let's see, everyone out of the last four rows of seats: can you do that? Thank you, Lindy, make sure they take all their belongings with them.'

'Yes, sir.'

'Double check there's no one left in the toilets. Then have your girls barricade off the area with pillows, blankets, life jackets – anything they can find to stop possible blast.' He smiled at her, to try to make the words sound a little less terrible. 'As fast as you can, please.'

'Yes, *sir*.' She hurried away and Ramage turned back to Brdwzynski. 'Captain, I'll also need a set of tools.'

'Bronson's got so many tools up there I sometimes wonder how we get off the ground. Hold on.' He ran up the stairway and shouted for his engineer. 'Bronson! On the double!' The big man came bounding down. All at once he caught sight of the briefcase in Ramage's hand, and froze in his tracks.

'Sir?'

'It may be nothing to worry about,' explained Ramage patiently. 'But I have to open it up to find out. And not by the normal means. I'm going to need pincers, pliers, a sharp knife – anything at all you think might be useful.'

'Okay,' said Bronson. 'Where do you intend to work?'

'Tail section. Lindy's clearing a space for me now.'

'Tools coming right up.' Bronson turned to climb back to the flight deck when something else occurred to him. 'Hey, I'm an engineer. You want someone to give you a hand back there, Mr Ramage?'

'Thanks.' It took guts to make an offer like that, and Ramage was grateful. 'But I'm afraid union rules won't allow it. Just those tools, please.'

'I'll have them with you in a minute or two.' Bronson disappeared and Ramage started to make his way aft, taking care not to jar the contents of the briefcase as the plane rolled and dipped. Brdwzynski climbed back into his command seat, checked his position on the chart, and called Ohlsen.

'Everyone out of those tail seats, Fats?'

'The last passenger's leaving now, captain. Toilet's cleared.'

'Okay, start throwing up that barricade, fast. You have my authority to take anything you need. I want all four of those pursers working on it right away.'

'Aye, sir. One moment, please.' Brdwzynski heard him repeat the instructions to someone in the background. Then Ohlsen said, 'Mr Ramage just got here, Captain. With the package.'

'I want one man to stay close with him – on this side of

the barricade. His job will be to make sure Ramage gets everything he needs without delay.'

'I'll take that duty, Lucky.'

'Right.'

'Shall we keep the service going, Captain? And liquor?'

Brdwzynski thought hard about that. 'Keep everything moving, but watch it, huh? We have troubles enough without any drunks fooling around.'

'You know us better than that, Captain.' There was reproach in his voice.

'I guess I do at that. My apologies, Fats. Okay then, get 'em singing back there. We're not dead yet, right?'

'No, *sir*.'

Brdwzynski flicked back to company frequency and called London again. 'Atlantic Two, this is Romeo Juliet Two Four Zero.'

'Come in, Romeo.'

'This is Brdwzynski. Hello, Johnson, I want to talk to Schumacher and the top security man in the airport. Over.'

'Hold on, please.' The pilot fretted impatiently as the seconds ticked by. Suddenly the headset crackled into life again. 'Byron Schumacher.'

'Our position is 46 20N 21 30W' said Brdwzynski as he read from the INS keyboard. 'We just found an unidentified briefcase among the personal effects in first-class, and have taken protective action accordingly. I have given orders to evacuate twenty-six passengers from the rear of the main economy class compartment, and have them brought forward. We are sealing off that section of the tail unit as a protection against possible blast, while our bomb disposal expert prepares to open up the suspect case and have a look.'

'That sounds bad. I'm sorry.'

'Yeah. We don't know what's in it yet, but if there *is* a bomb Ramage is going to need all the help you can give him. Have you heard from those terrorists again?'

'Negative, Lucky.'

'Don't horse-shit me, Schumacher. This time you *have* to pay. What's happening about the money?'

'I can't tell you,' insisted Schumacher. 'We're all set here to make the first payment in sterling, if it comes to that. But the bulk of the cash has to come in Deutschmarks, and that has to have the General's clearance. Hell, you know that. As soon as word comes through, we pay up.'

'Schumacher, if you're stalling – '

'Lucky, I'm telling you, *we can't raise the General.*' Schumacher sounded desperate. 'We know he's in his car and somewhere between the house and the office. But his car-phone's not answering. I have reported a breakdown to the American operators at White Plains who are treating it as an emergency case. I have also warned our New York office to alert the police, in case the General's been involved in an accident. I tell you, I just don't know what's going on. He couldn't be out of touch at a worse time.'

'It stinks' said Brdwzynski. 'I don't believe it.'

'Well you'd better believe it,' replied Schumacher succinctly. 'No one – but no one – can sanction that payment in Deutschmarks other than the General himself, unless or until the company lawyers receive official notification of his death or other incapacity to sign papers. Without him, we can't move.'

'Okay.' Brdwzynski was filled with doubt, but time was running out fast. 'I still don't like it, but let's examine what we got left if he doesn't show.' He looked once more at the charts. 'We're approaching C.P.'

On the Atlantic crossing, there is no such thing as the 'Point of no return' for an aircraft with the Jumbo's range. 'C.P.', or 'Critical Point' is the position from which it is as quick for the pilot to continue to his destination as it would be to return to base.

'Check.' Schumacher was studying identical charts in London as they spoke.

'Nearest weather ship, CHARLIE.'

'Check.'

Because of the cost of maintaining them, only four weather ships are now stationed permanently in the North Atlantic. They are code-named MIKE, for the joint Norwegian-Netherlands vessel, LIMA, British, ROMEO, French, and the Russian, CHARLIE.

'I can make CHARLIE inside the hour' Brdwzynski went on. 'Maybe even quicker than that, using this gale as tail wind. You want me to circle CHARLIE while you try and strike a deal with those terrorists?'

'Negative,' said Schumacher, unhappily. In his heart of hearts he was convinced that the General would never make a straight deal with the Liberation Army. Instead he would wriggle, he would procrastinate, he would huff and puff over the terms without ever giving a direct no – until it was too late to reach *any* agreement. And if that turned out to be the case – given the Jumbo's inability to descend – it made little difference as far as Schumacher could see whether it was over a rescue ship or not when the time-bomb exploded. Even so, it was his duty to try to keep some hope alive.

'We have a better idea, Lucky. Why not make for Colorado Springs?' The runways at Colorado Springs lie more than 6,000 feet above sea level. If the Jumbo could make them in time, then there was a chance – an outside chance, but still a chance – they might prove high enough to defeat the altimeter device.

'We're over a barrel there, Schumacher. Problem is these goddam headwinds: they're eating up the fuel, while I daren't economise. I have to maintain maximum speed because of the time-bomb, and I can't go below the jet-stream in case I set off the altimeter trigger.'

To descend below the core of the jet-stream, in the face of excessive headwinds, is standard drill: even a non-flier like Schumacher knew that. 'Then climb above it,' he suggested.

'It would still create problems. Look, we're at 35,000 feet now.' Brdwzynski spelt it out for him. 'By taking her up to 40,000 or even more, I could burn enough juice to put Colorado Springs way out of range. I'll have to work on it, and let you know.'

Schumacher reeled off a number of alternative airfields sited across the North American mainland. Brdwzynski rejected them all in turn, either as too low or out of range. While he was still talking to London, Fats Ohlsen appeared on the flight deck and silently handed him a note. The pilot read it quickly, nodded an acknowledgment, and carried on speaking into his headset.

'Well' he said, 'that's one thing settled, anyway. Those terrorists aren't bluffing, Schumacher: Ramage just sent word he's found a bomb in the briefcase.'

'Oh my *God*!'

'You'll need to bring your sights down lower than that,' said Brdwzynski, brutally. 'The first thing you have to do is raise the General – fast – and talk him into making some kind of deal with this gang.' He listened in disgust to the stumbling, tortuous answer. 'And I don't give a damn how tough he can be, you just do it, you hear? You think you're the only one with problems, uh? Over – and out!' He shook his head, and climbed out of his seat, swallowing hard.

'Guess I ought to talk to Ramage,' he said to Eckhardt. 'Moral support, you know?'

'Sure, Lucky.'

'What does Gander say about the weather?'

'Worsening. Winds freshening from the west.'

'Okay.' Brdwzynski decided to take a gamble. 'Take her up out of the jet-stream, Joe. Then set course for Colorado Springs.'

'Colorado Springs. Aye, sir.'

Laura Ramage had just settled in the new seat they had found for her, forward in the compartment, when her husband came through with the briefcase in his hand. She knew at once what it had to contain, and her first, natural reaction was to tremble with fear, at the same time she felt a terrible sadness for him, coupled with a sense of injustice. It seemed to her monstrously cruel that having survived so many dangers as a serving Army officer, he should immediately be faced with another on his retirement: and somehow, the fact that he was on holiday to celebrate that retirement when the crisis arose made it even harder to stomach. On the day he had left the Forces, and arrived home as Lt. Colonel Ramage, rtd., she had gone down on her knees to thank God for his safe deliverance. Now there were no more prayers left in her: she felt she had used them all up, over the years. All she could do now was to sit quite quite still, share the fears that were all about her and wait, as each minute took an eternity to tick past into the next.

Her first thoughts then were for her two children, left behind in England. It made no difference whatever that they were no longer helpless infants. Betty Ramage at nineteen was a woman already, with the scalps of at least two lovers adorning her belt to Laura's certain knowledge. John was only twelve, but blessed with a sturdy sense of independence ingrained in his character by the school he attended. But in their mother's mind they would always be children, and she was miserably aware that there was no one else to look after them once she and Gordon were gone.

She could not explain why but from the moment she had woken this morning she had been dogged by a feeling – a premonition, almost – that trouble awaited them on this long-awaited holiday. Gordon had laughed at her when she tried to mention it, and brushed it aside as nonsense. But there was no denying the chain of misfortune that had followed them from the moment they set out, the train, the taxi, the strike: and she was inclined to think now they were omens, warnings that they ought not to have left home at all. She found it positively agonising to watch the cabin crew as they seized pillows and blankets from the racks overhead, and hurried to strengthen the frail barricade they were putting up behind her. If only they could put the clock back! Suddenly Gordon entered the compartment carrying the briefcase, and she saw him turn his head to look for her. She realised that he would be too far away to talk to her as he passed, and she was grateful for that at least. With a tremendous effort she painted a smile on her face as their eyes met, even raised a hand of encouragement. 'Take care,' she said silently, mouthing the words: and he nodded his blond head to show that he understood.

They were the same foolish words that she had called after him for so many years: the paradox being that it was Gordon who always appeared to survive mentally unscathed, while she died a thousand deaths waiting for him to return, waiting to hear the sound of his voice again. And she had found it grew harder to carry the burden as the years went by: as a bomb disposal officer, he had spent twenty years of his life in the ante-room of eternity. Yet while she had suffered so much she had never once known him weaken, or seen him afraid. On the contrary, he despised his enemies as cowards, and it was Laura who always experienced the fear.

Once he had passed by, she forced herself to take up a book and pretended to read, ignoring the whispers and the glances from the other passengers. This was the hardest part, the waiting: and it was cold comfort to know she had had so much experience.

As soon as he stepped behind the barricade, Ramage laid out the tool kit Bronson had provided and whistled his admiration. You had to hand it to the Yanks, they never spoiled the ship for a ha'p'orth of tar. Every tool there was made from the finest chrome vanadium steel, and together the whole collection must have been worth many hundreds of pounds: tweezers, ammeters, pliers, pincers, a Stanley knife with an assortment of gleaming new blades, callipers of every description, a whole range of screwdrivers, spanners and wrenches, a magnifying glass, torches, clamps, rolls of masking tape – Ramage had never seen such a magnificent set before, far less worked with one during the whole of his Army career. That thought brought a wry grin on to his face, even now. He could remember a time in Belfast when he had arrived with nothing; and on locating the device he flagged down a passing bus and borrowed a few tools from the driver. There had been no need to explain, on that grey, wet Irish afternoon, why he needed them: the handful of infantrymen in the road, the curious manner in which all of them flattened their bodies into every available dip in the ground, and the tell-tale insignia on Ramage's sleeve – a tiny, flaming grenade sewn six inches above the cuff – told the horrified driver the whole story at a glance. He drove off like a bat out of hell, while Ramage set to work and defused a hundred-pound bomb.

This one in the plane was a mere stripling by comparison, weighing only a few pounds: but still powerful enough to reduce the tailfin of the Jumbo, and the whole after-section he had cordoned off, to a puff of dust drifting through the sky. Ramage blew on his hands as he set to work, suddenly aware that he felt chilled to the bone. It was an odd thing, that: no matter where a man found himself, in the gentle rains of Ireland or the blast furnace that was summertime Cyprus, as soon as he began to work on a bomb so he would feel cold; as cold as any mourner at the graveside, and just as alone. And he experienced exactly the same sensation now, even in a plane filled with people. With a sigh he took up the Stanley knife, wedged the briefcase firmly and started to cut into the bottom right-hand corner.

He cut delicately through the plastic skin, easing the pressure as he began each downward thrust, acutely aware that if his hand should slip to send the blade plunging clumsily through, it would spell instant death for all on board. As soon as the aperture was large enough he inserted a finger, and peeled away a strip of the soft, shiny covering. Then he leaned down and put his nose to the cavity, like an old-time physician sniffing a wound for gangrene, and was immediately rewarded by the bitter smell of almonds.

Ramage continued to pick gently at the aperture, working it wider and still wider with his nails until he was able to look inside and count the sticks of explosive wired together there. *Nine*. He could only see their base as yet, but that was enough to tell him they formed a main charge weighing four-and-a-half pounds. All were wrapped in the shiny, ugly, waxed brown paper he had seen so often before, and he recognised them instantly as sticks of polar ammon gelignite. They would weigh exactly eight ounces each – explosives need to be measured precisely, for obvious reasons – while their waxed paper wrapping was to absorb any 'sweat' leaking from the dangerously volatile nitro-glycerine content. It was the nitro-glycerine that gave off the tell-tale smell. And although he could identify them, Ramage had no way of telling how old the sticks might be, or how unstable. He put down his knife and scribbled a warning note to Brdwzynski.

'Ramage to Captain,' he wrote. 'Inform London bomb confirmed. Main charge consists of 4½ pounds gelignite. Still investigating.' He timed the message, and called for his runner.

'You there, Fats?'

'Right here, sir. Something I can do for you?'

'Message for the skipper.' Their eyes met through the makeshift barricade. 'I'm afraid it's a bomb all right, Fats.'

'The hell it is.' His hand came through to take the note. 'So, take it easy in there, okay?'

'Will do.' Ramage's face was thoughtful as he set to work once more. At least he had unearthed one clue for the police at home to work on, in their hunt for the terrorist gang. Polar ammon gelignite comes from one source only in Britain, from Ardeer in Scotland, north of Stranraer – and the manufacturers were sure to keep a tally of customers. Once the police checked on all recent thefts and started asking questions, someone might recall a car parked in suspicious circumstances or some other incident on the day of the robbery that could lead to an arrest. It was a small enough clue: but men had been caught before from leads just as slender and – delightful thought – hanged as a result. Thus encouraged, Ramage worked away with renewed energy, always keeping the blade well away from the press stud that would open the briefcase for him at a touch. He had a hunch it would do much more than that. The terrorists may have told Schumacher their bomb was fitted with two devices only, a clock and an altimeter, but Ramage took that information with a large pinch of salt. He would be very surprised if a bomb-maker as skilled as the one he was fighting here had omitted to fit an anti-handling trap too: for auld lang syne.

'Hi, there.' Brdwzynski's voice was calling him through the gap in the barricade. 'Got time to talk for a moment, Ramage?'

'Of course, skipper.' He stood up and looked out. 'I think it might be wiser if you stayed on your side, though. Kind of crowded in here.'

'Sure.' Brdwzynski handed him a cup of tea. 'Compliments of the staff. Just say the word if you want anything stronger.'

'Tea will be fine.' Ramage sipped it gratefully.

'Smoke?' The pilot held up a carton of cigarettes.

Ramage hungered inexpressibly for tobacco at that moment, but kept his hands deep in his pockets. 'I'll take you up on that when I'm through. Along with the drink you offered me.'

Smoking on the job is the worst crime in the book for a bomb disposal officer. On the ground, the drill is to establish a funk-hole as near to the bomb as safely possible for storing the kit – radiography equipment, sensors of every kind, exploder, wire, string, tape, everything – and to have tea and a smoke sent up from the vehicle laager each time you come back. The unwritten but rigidly observed rules forbid more than one man with the device, but allow two in the funk-hole. (Ramage knew one man who made military history in Ireland by having fish and chips sent up: and eating them, with appetite unimpaired.) In the tail section of the plane, there was no place for a funk-hole. So Brdwzynski had to stay on his side of the flimsy barricade, while Ramage had to go without his tobacco.

Brdwzynski nodded in understanding, and kept his own cigarette unlit. 'How's it going?'

Ramage pointed at the hole he had cut in the briefcase. 'The gelignite's in there. Somewhere on top I expect to locate our altimeter and the time-switch. Then as soon as I've analysed the-make-up, I'll start to take her to pieces.'

'Uh huh,' said the pilot, just as casually. 'Any idea how long that might take?'

'It's something you daren't rush. Pull the wrong plug, and – zap!' He watched the pilot's face. 'Why, something special in mind?'

'Yes. I've given orders to set course for Colorado Springs. The runways there are more than 6,000 feet up.'

'Ah.'

'Which means we're going to need a lot more flying time. And we aren't going to get it unless you can put that time-bomb part out of action first.'

'Even if I do' cautioned Ramage, 'you could still come unstuck with the altimeter device. If it works on radar, that is.'

'It's a chance we'll just have to take. Along with everything else.' If the terrorist who called Schumacher was telling the truth when he claimed the bomb would be detonated by atmospheric pressure, there was a chance the Jumbo could land safely at 6,000 feet: at least it was that much higher than the runways at Kennedy. But if he had lied and the bomb was wired to a *radar* altimeter – one that registered height above ground level by sonar – then they would be killed on the approach to any runway, no matter what its altitude.

'I've got no means of telling you yet which sort we've got here,' said Ramage. 'And that's something I can't rush. Sorry.'

'And I've got no choice,' replied Brdwzynski. 'Schumacher is now saying no one can raise the General, and he's the only man who can authorise payment of that ransom. He could be stalling, I don't know. But that's what he says.'

'I see.' Ramage played the pilot's game and permitted none of his inner thoughts to show in his face. 'In that case, the sooner I get on with defusing this thing, the better.'

At that moment the chief steward hurried up to Brdwzynski.

'Excuse me, Captain. Joe wants you back on deck as soon as convenient, sir.'

'I'm on my way.' He reached through the barricade and touched Ramage's shoulder in salute. 'Good luck, pal.'

'And you, skipper.'

Ramage rubbed his hands together as the pilot walked away. Then he turned back to the bomb, shaking his head almost in despair.

There really was no way you could hurry the job, no way at all, no matter how desperately Brdwzynski needed to know the answer to the riddle of the altimeter. Ramage sighed, and concentrated fiercely on the job in hand. He cut through another section of the plastic casing and pulled it back cleanly, as if he were peeling a banana. Suddenly, he found that his brain had begun to transmit messages independently to his hands: almost as if he was talking to another person.

'Take it easy, hands: whoever put this thing together is clearly a pro, and therefore certain to think like one. So, before you do anything irrevocable, I have to put myself inside his mind to see what *he* was thinking as he built it . . .

'He claims to have fitted an altimeter switch as well as a timing device. All right, we'll accept that and look out for both – after all, he was putting maximum pressure on his victim at the time, and these are things that could easily be challenged if he was thought to be bluffing. You and I also suspect he has included an anti-handling device, but for very different reasons: that was his insurance policy against premature discovery of the bomb. by one of the ground staff, say, or an over-inquisitive passenger.

'Above all, we have to remember he built this thing to make money – by blackmail. And if he fails to do so with a sophisticated weapon of this calibre, there can only be one answer: he will have been outwitted by a bomb disposal *expert*, someone experienced enough to call on every trick in the book to render it harmless. Which means, therefore, that as well as money there are two reputations at stake here – his own as much as his adversary's – and he's going to safeguard his own accordingly. This briefcase you're holding is going to be choc-a-bloc with snakes and ladders, hands: be quite certain of that if you want us to live through this . . .

'Now then, think – where are his traps most likely to lie? I have a hunch we will find the first in the physical make-up of the bomb itself: I don't know why, I just feel it in our bones. Ten to one it will turn out to be ridiculously simple and straightforward, say a metal spring tightened to hair-trigger sensitivity and waiting to be released by something really heavy, like the weight of a fly's legs on the press-stud there below the handle. Nothing fancy, that's for certain: its only merit lies in surprise, and we've already decided that it's intended for outsiders who get too nosey, not for experts like us. He *expects* us to spot that one, he'd be disappointed in us if we didn't. I'd think he's put something really special inside for you and me, hands . . . so proceed with the utmost caution, and remember: the name of the game is *staying alive*.'

At that particular moment in time Ramage would cheerfully have traded every penny he possessed to know the identity of the bomb-maker he was up against. Nor was it idle curiosity. He belonged to the world's most exclusive club, one in which membership may be counted on the fingers of a single hand: where admittance is gained only when candidates can safely dismantle the most sophisticated device, quite possibly one that has never been seen before, yet stand up at the end and say positively who made it. By the nature of his work, the sophisticated bomb-maker cannot be a novice. By the same token only the true expert will be able to recognise his workmanship, and identity it as surely as your art dealer knows the masterpiece by its brushwork and technique.

He will identify the bomber by the unique manner in which he crimps each wire, by the type of component he favours, by the technique he uses – this one may favour the clutter mechanism, that one the collapsing circuit: and from a compound of such tell-tale clues, the expert will be able to walk into court and swear on a Bible that 'X' and none other made this particular bomb. Others in the investigative team may find fingerprints later to confirm his judgment, but they will be superfluous: the disposal expert *knows*. Bomb-making at such a level is the one art-form in the world where there can never be a perfect forgery: only a fair likeness. In the same way, bomb disposal is the one trade above all others where to be accurately forewarned is to be forearmed as never before. Know your adversary, and you may expect to know what to look for round the next corner – and the one after that, whereas Ramage was acutely conscious he had barely begun to examine this device. He worked away cautiously, losing all count of time, probing deeper and deeper into the entrails of the bomb. All at once he saw the altimeter.

Removed from an instrument panel, altimeters look rather like miniature travelling alarm clocks and weigh perhaps no more than three or four ounces each. Ramage sucked in his breath at the sight of this one: a spider's web of wires, red and thin and fine as gossamer, all of them less than a sixty-fourth of an inch in diameter, fed into its circular steel body. The face was turned away from him, so that he was unable to read the height recorded by its hands. Even so, to reach it at all represented a significant advance. He stopped work for a moment to flex his fingers, and gazed on his find as rapturously as a jeweller assessing a rare, uncut stone: beautiful!

All that was needed now – in theory, anyway – was for him to snip through a single strand of wire with Bronson's pincers: the device would then be disconnected, and rendered harmless. A less experienced man, or a tired one, or merely one working against the clock, might have been tempted to do so, but not Ramage. He continued to rub his hands and flex his fingers, and while he shifted in his seat he forced himself to think calmly about the situation. He came to the conclusion there might be a trap waiting for him here, one of the traps he feared. If there was, he reckoned, it would come in the shape of a solenoid – a form of switch, built into the circuit – which would automatically detonate the bomb as soon as that circuit was broken. This was the technique known to the trade as 'the collapsing circuit' and it had killed too many men already during Ramage's career. So instead of cutting through the wire he continued to probe patiently, like a detective spying the ground for clues, until his caution was rewarded and he found the solenoid.

It was like a tiny electro-magnet: taped to the body of the 4½ volt battery that armed the whole device. In its turn the solenoid was linked by a network of wires as fine as capillaries to the other master switches that could separately detonate the bomb, to the anti-handling switch he had already anticipated as well as to the dial of the altimeter. Its circuitry was beautifully fashioned, so that in the midst of his own torment Ramage was compelled to give it grudging approval. He came to the conclusion that among the ranks of all the most powerful terrorist organisations in the world – Arab, German, Irish, Italian and Japanese – there would at the very most be a dozen bomb-makers capable of putting together an explosive device as sophisticated as this.

He had done well to progress this far. In terms of bomb disposal ability, he supposed that to defuse such a bomb successfully might be considered akin to scaling Everest. But there was a long way to go yet, before that happy moment came about, if ever it did: even as he picked up his tools and bent over the briefcase again, an inner voice cautioned him 'The detonator – you haven't located the detonator yet!' And in the same moment another thought occurred to him, this time one so obvious and elementary Ramage could have wept with shame to think he had overlooked it so far. He had forgotten about the timing device! While he had been congratulating himself on finding that solenoid and tracing its capillaries to the other master switches, he had overlooked the timer – the killer-device that at this moment worried Brdwzynski even more than the altimeter.

He shook his big yellow head in disbelief. All he had done so far was to look inside the briefcase – as far as he was able – and to smell the damned thing. Of course! He should have been *listening*, too, listening for the tick of a clock. He had no need to remind himself why he had failed to do so. It was the fashion these days for bomb-makers to use a clock without working parts, such as one fitted with a quartz crystal mechanism, so that no give-away tick could be picked up by the stethoscope. But what terrorist would bother to take that kind of precaution with a bomb he was going to hide in an *aeroplane*?

With the reasoning came a flush of shame, as Ramage rebuked himself for his carelessness. Perhaps this was what the act of retirement did to a man, even in the brief space of time that had elapsed since he left the Army. As soon as the mind switched off the whole body slowed down, you overlooked the obvious, and that fine cutting edge quickly became blunted. Well, if that was true, then they would all be dead soon, himself and Laura included. He got up for a moment and moved round in the tiny compartment, forcing his limbs to function normally, and clearing his mind ruthlessly of the doubts and fears that came crowding in: this was no time to weaken.

He went back to the briefcase and knelt beside it, then laid his head upon it as tenderly as if he were a doctor looking for life in a sickly child, shut his eye tight – and listened. He willed himself to shut out all other sounds from the aircraft, the drone of the engines, the creaking movement of the hull, the hum of frightened small-talk from passengers nearest to the barricade, and concentrated solely on the thing beneath his head. For a long while he could hear nothing. For one brief moment he thought perhaps he could hear a faint, internal rhythmic movement but the next it had gone. Patiently

Ramage lifted his head into the air, shook it to clear the cobwebs, and placed it back on its murderous pillow. He concentrated with every fibre in his being, and this time he reaped his reward – his ear detected the muted but unmistakable ticking of a clock. Ramage felt so elated, he could have burst into song.

When Ohlsen first brought the summons that took him back to the flight deck, Brdwzynski felt elated, too: he hoped he would find a message waiting to say the General had been contacted and was ready to pay for the information Ramage so urgently wanted. Instead, he found long faces and an aircrew dismayed by new fears. 'What goes on here?' he demanded.

'We're not sure, sir,' said Eckhardt unhappily. 'But something screwy's happening. We've started to lose height and we can't correct it.'

Brdwzynski climbed into his seat and glanced at the altimeter. They were below 34,000 feet. 'I'll take her,' he ordered. He began to pull up, slowly and easily, in an attempt to bring the nose back to level flight. There was no response, and the needle continued to flicker back. Next he turned the wheel and kicked the rudder bar – not hard, so not to alarm his passengers – and the plane answered immediately with wheel and yaw. Now he pulled back on the stick a second time, and more firmly: but again there was no response. 'What's doing it, Sam?' he shouted.

'Sure beats me, Lucky,' replied the engineer. 'According to the book, this is something that can't happen – but it is, and right under our goddam noses! I don't get it, Captain: the pitch channel suddenly started to feed nose-down information, and the plane responded. I can't cure it, because I can't disengage.'

'Have you monitored our rate of descent?'

'Yes, sir. Pretty slow, thank God: around 100 feet a minute.'

'And what time did this malfunction begin?'

'I'd say, twelve minutes back. When Joe first attempted to climb.'

Brdwzynski rubbed his chin furiously. 'D'you suppose those guys who dressed up as fitters to sneak the bomb aboard could have spooked the auto-pilot, Sam? With another timing device, maybe?'

'They were crawling all over the aircraft for long enough.' Bronson shrugged his shoulders. 'They had the time, all right – and the opportunity. I'm not so sure about the knowledge: this is a hell of a complicated piece of machinery, Lucky.'

'Any obvious signs of tampering?'

'None. But I guess anything has to be possible with people like that.'

Brdwzynski bit hard on his bottom lip: he had to act, and soon. Continued loss of height at the present rate of 6,000 feet an hour would take them below the minimum altitude required to land at Colorado Springs – if it went unchecked. And there were attendant problems. As the plane descended, its airspeed would decrease with the rise in outside temperature, so that in any case he would need more fuel – or even more flying time – to get there anyway.

'Joe. I want you to go aft, and explain the situation to Ramage. Tell him about the loss in height, and say it gives me no option but to change course again and head for Kennedy. You can say we're working on it – but that it's beginning to look now as if it's all up to him. Sam, keep on trying to locate this fault while I talk to London.'

'Aye, sir.'

They were back in the core of the jet-stream now and the Big Bird was bumping badly, and lurching from side to side with the impact like a Scot at Hogmanay. Brdwzynski realised that his poor passengers were in for a desperately uncomfortable thirty minutes and maybe more on top of all their other problems, and there was not one damned thing in the world he could do about it. He took a deep breath and vowed that, if he lived he would pay these terrorists back one hundred fold for their satanic behaviour.

Schumacher's office at Heathrow was packed with officials, the air thick with tobacco smoke. The Air Controller was present, and Messenger, his Head of Security, as well as the Commander of the airport police force. There was also a senior officer from the Special Branch, and two communications experts from Scotland Yard. The open line to Romeo Juliet 240 was manned by Johnson, Atlantic's London manager. At this moment in time there was no contact with Brdwzynski: instead, all the extension phones were linked to Schumacher's own, awaiting the next call from the Liberation Army. A company engineer moved from desk to desk, checking the apparatus installed to tape all incoming calls, from whatever source. Thus, if Brdwzynski should call while efforts were being made by the police and GPO to trace the vital call from A.L., the pilot's demands would automatically be recorded for action minutes later. In the outer office, a team of secretaries maintained constant contact with New York, awaiting news of the General. He had been out of touch now for nearly thirty minutes.

'Let's run through it again while we're waiting, Mr Schumacher,' said the police Commander easily. He was a burly, solid, unflappable man. 'When these terrorists call, you're to tell them the ransom *will* be paid – whether you've heard from General Grossman or not by then, and irrespective of anything he may have said to you himself, is that understood, sir?'

'There'll be hell to pay when he finds out.'

'We're just going through the motions, sir, to try to save those 450 people in the plane: there's no financial risk to your company involved. Now then. You have that half-million in sterling bundled ready at the Haymarket office?'

'Yes.' And by God, they had had to twist his arm to make him agree to that, too. 'In small denomination notes, all unmarked.'

'Good, good. And you've briefed the airline executives in Frankfurt on what to do?'

'I have, but I might as well tell you, they're none too happy about it. The Liberation Army appears to have a particularly fearsome reputation in Germany, Commander – and I'm afraid my staff there don't share your faith in the abilty of the local police to protect them.'

'Mr Schumacher, please: I keep reassuring you that members of your staff will be in no way involved. Police drivers here and in Frankfurt will keep both appointments.'

Schumacher chewed his lip anxiously and thought 'But the terrorists know where to find us afterwards': he said nothing with Johnson present, and prayed that everything would go according to plan.

'There's no way they can get away with it,' said the commander cheerfully. 'I've positioned two squad cars, both crewed by armed marksmen, near your office in the Haymarket. The Germans have got their crack anti-terrorist squad on the job over there. You see sir, we'll nab the lot – and save your plane in the process.'

'I most sincerely hope so.'

'Just leave everything to us, Mr Schumacher. All you have to do is set the ball rolling by handing over those unmarked notes in London – in case they're standing by to send back a signal to Germany. We'll take over after that. You'll get every penny back as soon as we've rounded them up.'

'The General still won't like it.'

The Commander ignored that. 'Keep the caller talking as long as you can, sir. The usual drill. There's always a chance we can trace him.'

As if on cue, the red light on Schumacher's desk lit up. 'Stand by,' ordered the Commander, and the room fell silent. He motioned to Schumacher to pick up his own telephone, and four other hands lifted an extension instrument in the same split second, like a ballet movement.

'Ahem! This is Byron Schumacher.'

'This is the Liberation Army. Is the money ready?'

'Yes.' He hesitated only for the fraction of a second.

'If you're lying, if you've informed the police, you're dead: I swear it. Now then, here's what you do. I want the sterling packed in suitcases and locked in the boot of an Atlantic staff car. Then tell your driver to park it in the underground garage at the Globe Hotel in Park Lane and hand the keys in to reception. To await Mr Miller, Room 505.'

'Please. I'm writing this down, so there'll be no mistake. Globe Hotel. Room 505. Mr Miller, you said?'

'Yes. Don't try to keep me on the phone too long, Schumacher. Or I might get the wrong idea.'

Schumacher shook like a jelly and held his tongue.

'The money in Frankfurt is also ready? Small denomination notes, fifties and under?'

'Every pfennig.'

'You will follow exactly the same routine there, except that they'll need two cars to move that lot. See that both drivers are instructed to lock the cars in the car park and hand the keys to reception at the Vir Jahren hotel. Same room number, same name. To await Herr Miller's arrival. We shall have someone there, watching – and listening.'

'I understand.'

'It is now 1600 hours precisely.' The voice sounded insufferably confident, even jaunty. 'See to it that all three cars are in position with the keys handed over by 16.30.'

Schumacher looked round the room for guidance. The Commander caught his eye, and nodded. 'Yes,' said Schumacher. 'Ahem. 16.30, yes, yes, I understand.'

'Let me warn you again against trickery. If any attempt is made to follow those cars or to intercept them, you personally are dead from that moment on.'

'There will be no tricks.' He shuddered as he said that, and had to expel each word from his throat.

'Good. As soon as we receive word the money has been handed over safely, I'll call you again, and tell you how to save your passengers and your plane. It will be a very fine safety margin, Schumacher. See to it you don't waste any time.'

'I – ' There was a click, and the line went dead. Immediately the room was plunged into a hive of activity as messages passed between the airport, the operations room at Scotland Yard, and the German Federal authorities. The GPO reported that there was no hope of tracing the call, nor of identifying any background noises. And all the time Brdwzynski fumed, as he was forced to wait for Schumacher to call him back.

At last, they were all done and he was put through to the pilot. 'This is Byron Schumacher. Sorry to have kept you, but I was just talking to New York. There's still no news of the General.'

At the urgent request of the German police there was to be no mention of the plan to intercept the Liberation Army terrorists at this stage – not even to the Captain of the threatened aircraft, because of the number of journalists he had aboard.

'Jesus,' said the pilot, disgustedly. 'Does that mean you're just going to sit there on your fat ass and do *nothing* till he shows up?'

'We're doing everything we possibly can,' groaned Schumacher. 'I realise it must be tough for all of you up there, but you've got to take my word for it – we're working flat out to help you.' He felt he was sailing close to breaking-point, from strain and self-pity. It was all so monstrously unfair:

whatever happened now, he could not win. If the bomb went off and killed everyone on board, the General would blame him for failing to raise the alarm quickly enough. If by some miracle the plane was saved, he would still be condemned for not acting correctly from the outset. The fact that the General's own 'disappearance' at the height of the crisis was no more than a ploy to avoid payment of the ransom was neither here nor there: Schumacher would never dare to accuse him of such tactics, far less be able to prove them. But that was only part of it – even worse than the self-pity he felt was the fear that threatened to engulf him, fear that the terrorists might try to kill him once they discovered he had tricked them, or worse, kidnap and torture him while they held *him* to ransom. With an effort, he forced himself to listen to what the pilot was saying.

'... in those circumstances, we could not make Colorado Springs anyway. I have therefore re-set course for Kennedy, ETA, 14.15 hours local time.'

'Confirmed,' said Schumacher. At least it relieved him of all responsibility: finally.

'In the meantime I want you guys to talk to Boeing and see if they can suggest any logical explanation for the pitch failure. Make it top priority, will you?'

'I'll get Johnson on to it right away.' He beckoned across the room to his London manager. If the same problem had arisen earlier to threaten the commemorative flight he would have been on to it like a terrier after a rat, driving the makers berserk with his calls. Now all he could think about was his own plight.

'Progress with the bomb is slow. Ramage has the briefcase opened up far enough to see the explosives. Right now he's trying to trace the electrical system: his problem is, it may be booby-trapped,' said Brdwzynski.

'I see.' Johnson pushed an old newspaper cutting across the desk, and Schumacher glanced at it cursorily. 'Well, that's certainly the best man in the business working for you up there.' Only he could make it sound as if he was conferring a favour on the luckless 400-odd souls on board. 'I have an old newspaper clipping in front of me right now. Ramage has got more medals than MacArthur, you know that?'

'He's great,' said Brdwzynski shortly: he was not going to

allow Schumacher to side-track him for any reason. 'But you and I are talking about problems outside his control, right now. Let me know the instant you hear from Boeing and the General, okay? I'm running out of time up here – fast. Over, and out.'

All the time he had been speaking to London his subconscious mind had been trying to tell the pilot that something physical was happening around him – something affecting the flight of the plane. He sat utterly still, strapped in his seat, both hands clasping the wheel that refused to answer, as he tried urgently to identify whatever it might be. He had so many problems on his mind that his brain felt sluggish. His eyes roved across the panorama of gauges spread out in front of him, his ears checked the pitch of the engine, his mind turned the pages of a book of experience written in 5,000 flying hours. Then he realised what it was he could feel – something so obvious he tapped his forehead in mock disgust, and turned to his first officer.

'Hey, Joe.' The altimeter read 31,000. 'Feel anything?'

'Right.' Realisation came to Joe Eckhardt in the same instant. 'She's coming out of the jet-stream.'

That was good news and bad news. The good news was that the dreadful bumping would soon come to an end, bringing comfort and some much-needed cheer to their terrified passengers. The bad news was registering on the altimeter: already they were 3,000 feet closer to that unknown height at which the bomb in the briefcase would be exploded by the drop in atmospheric pressure. Brdwzynski shut his mind resolutely to that.

'Joe. Send Fats up here, will you? And listen, take his place on the barricade till he gets back: I'm going to put the cabin crew to work.'

'Aye, sir.'

A few minutes later, Ohlsen climbed on to the flight deck.

'You sent for me, Lucky?'

'I did. Feel how smooth she's riding now?'

'Yes, sir.' The old chief tried not to show his astonishment at being called to the flight deck to answer such an obvious question. 'So?'

'So it's time our passengers were cheered up a little.'

'Sir?'

'I want that concert going again, Fats. Have a word with the singer – what's his name, right, Frank Gadsby – and tell him

Captain's compliments, and can we please have 'Carolina Moon' and the other numbers all over again.'

Ohlsen had seen Frank Gadsby only once since the bomb announcement was made. He had been pale and distraught and in need of cosseting by both manager and Press agent: Fats doubted if he could open his mouth to croak, far less sing. 'But Captain, he ain't feeling so good, he – '

'Just do it, Fats. I don't care if you have to break his arm to get him to perform. Atlantic Airways paid him $10,000 to travel with us and sing to those kids, and by God he's going to earn it!'

'Yes, sir.'

'I'll give you five minutes to get everything organised. Meantime I'll talk to our passengers, and give them the score.'

'Yes, *sir*.' When Fats had gone, Brdwzynski switched the headset to 'All compartments.' 'Ladies and gentlemen, this is the Captain again. I guess everyone will have noticed how much smoother the ride is now.' He tried to sound as casual as possible without being patronising. 'It was too bumpy up there in the jet-stream, so I brought her down: for your personal comfort, of course, but also to allow my cabin crew to resume normal in-flight service – correction! our Honeymoon Jumbo *special* service – of food and refreshments and whatever else you may require. But please observe I have left the seat belt signs *on*. This is normal flight procedure, in case we encounter further turbulence en route to New York.'

It was also a necessary precaution in case Fats and his stewards had to quell any outbreak of panic and hysteria.

'However, I ask all of you to remain seated as far as possible at least until we have solved this bomb scare mystery once and for all,' he continued. His motto was if you have to tell a lie, make it a good one. 'London tell me they haven't heard again from the unknown man who called them earlier. Meanwhile Colonel Ramage, the bomb disposal expert who has so kindly volunteered to help us, still has a number of unidentified pieces of baggage to sort through at the rear of the plane: some of you may have seen the little cubby-hole we rigged up for him. We think every piece was shipped aboard in error at Heathrow because of a mix-up due to the strike – but we're not sure and as you will all appreciate, it's a slow and laborious business to open each piece of baggage separately and examine the contents. However, until that's done, neither we nor London can say for certain if our mystery caller was bluffing or not.'

Brdwzynski scratched his head, and prayed for inspiration. What could anyone find to say to comfort a plane-load of frightened people at such a time?

'So there it is, folks. Until we do know, I have no choice but to instruct my stewards to escort all of you who need to leave your seats, at all times. Just press the call sign above your heads and they'll come just as fast as they can. And in case that sounds like raising your hand and saying "Please teacher" – well, ladies and gentlemen, I'm deeply sorry, but the order stands until I give the all clear.'

Joe Eckhardt pointed to the altimeter. It read 28,000 feet now.

'We're on course for New York, as originally planned' continued Brdwzynski stubbornly. 'Although we lost a little time in the weather back there, I still expect to land on schedule. I'm also happy to tell you that our famous celebrity guest star Mr Frank Gadsby has volunteered to carry on with the concert we were all enjoying so much at lunch-time. He won't be able to move around among you, of course, as he did earlier, but the compartments are all linked on sound, so that we can join in with him.'

It was all he could do to keep his eyes averted from the altimeter, but his voice remained cheerful and confident.

'Once I'm through this time, folks, I promise not to interrupt again for any reason, except to tell you when we're about to land in New York. However, there is something I would like to say to you all first. It's something I have already said to the authorities back home in England – and that is, we in the crew of the Honeymoon Jumbo are very, very proud of you for the magnificent way you have all behaved in such very difficult circumstances. On behalf of my crew and the airline we serve – thank you for making our own job so much easier.'

The moment the Captain had finished speaking, Fats Ohlsen gave orders to the cabin crew to pile their trolleys high with food and drink, and to keep them rolling. In the galley forward of the mid-section passenger compartment, Lindy took the towel from Frank Gadsby's limp hands and fluttered around him, holding a mirror. Frightened though he was, vanity prevailed: he combed his hair into place, and straightened his tie. The two brandies she had given him had restored the colour to his cheeks. Before he could change his mind she led him back to his place in the front row of seats, and sat him down between his manager Lew Franklin and his agent, Manny Sloan. 'He's looking great,' she said and reached for the microphone.

'I feel lousy,' countered the crooner, unhappily.

'It's not fair on my boy,' protested his manager, not entirely without justification. He was careful to keep his voice down, as befitted the guardian of such a star reputation. Lew Franklin was a pro who had seen it all, from the jerks who couldn't sing a note but earned a fortune on the strength of their sexual reputation, to the prima donnas who would walk out of a show on opening night because they felt their dressing-rooms were insultingly small. But even he had to admit that to ask anyone to sing like a nightingale with a bomb ticking away backstage – man, that was rugged.

'Lew's right,' echoed Manny Sloan loyally. 'Frankie needs inspiration, you know?'

As Lindy hesitated, a passenger in the next row of seats joined in. 'Inspiration is something all of us need right now,' he said.

She recognised him at once, one of the twenty-six who had been uprooted to make a working space for Gordon Ramage. He looked tired, with deep pouches below his eyes and lines running down from cheek to chin: Lindy put his age at more than sixty. He was ordinarily dressed. Only his voice was remarkable. It was rich and deep, vibrato as the chime of a bell.

'There's one thing we've all forgotten, the source of all inspiration.' He smiled at the famous star and his advisers. 'Prayer.' Then he turned to Lindy. 'Would you allow an old man to invite everyone to join him in a prayer?'

'Well,' said Lindy doubtfully. She wondered what Brdwzynski would say about that. One thing he would not tolerate would be any suggestion of last rites: the whole tone of his address to the passengers right from the beginning had been one of calm unflagging confidence. And yet to pray, and perhaps invite others to join a man in prayer, did not seem so unreasonable a request to make in all the circumstances. 'I don't know about that, sir.'

'Please.' He held out his hand for the microphone, and at the same time stared round the compartment, including all those who could hear him in the conversation. 'I sense the need, young lady.'

Fats appeared at her side as if by magic. He had feared the worst when the Captain's words had been followed by silence, and had left his post in case Frank Gadsby needed further persuasion. Now he straddled his legs and took over. 'Anything wrong, Lindy?'

'No, sir. Nothing wrong.' She gave him a grateful side glance. 'This gentleman here thinks the passengers might like to join him in a prayer before listening to Mr Gadsby.'

'On the contrary.' The smile never left the old man's face. 'What I said was that a prayer *first* would give Mr Gadsby – and the rest of us – the inspiration we need.'

'Would you mind stepping this way for a moment, sir?' Fats gestured him out of his seat with every courtesy, but it was no less an order for that. Then he took his arm gently but firmly and led him into the galley Lindy and the singer had just vacated, watching him all the time with thoughtful blue eyes. 'Your name sir, please?'

'Izard. The Reverend John D. Izard. From Deer Creek, Deschutes, Oregon.'

'And your passport, please.' The chief steward checked the details inside and handed it back with a taut smile. 'Thank you, Reverend.'

The tired looking man just stood there, waiting for him to say what was in his mind. 'See, we have a kind of difficult situation here, Reverend, and I hope what I'm going to say won't cause offence. But there's a world of difference between a man sending up a prayer when he's in trouble – and someone calling a prayer meeting to say "Prepare to meet thy Doom." ' Fats held up a massive hand to cut off all theological debate. 'Right now, we have a whole lot of badly frightened people out there. Oh sure, they all seem cool and disciplined enough: but they're scared all right, scared out of their minds, and one wrong word – just one – could start the stampede. My job is to see that doesn't happen.'

The tired looking man said nothing, but waited for him to finish.

'Now, as long as you and I understand each other, I'll do a

deal with you. I'll allow you to say your few words, and invite the other passengers to join you in a prayer.'

'Thank you.'

'Provided I have your word you won't scare these good people any more than they're scared already.'

'I'm not sure – '

'You know *exactly* what I'm driving at, Reverend. None of that oh-death-where-is-thy-sting routine, okay? I guess I don't have to spell it out to a man of the cloth.'

'How dare – '

'Do I have your word, or don't I?' Fats towered over the little man. 'Listen, I may as well tell you, Reverend, it's the only way you'll ever get to use a microphone on this aircraft. Make up your mind.'

'You leave me with very little choice.' The minister smiled gently up at the Chief Steward. 'As it says in the Good Book, "Weigh thy words in a balance, and make a door and bar for thy mouth", eh? Very well – I swear I will say nothing to alarm anyone out there, as God is my witness. Will that suffice?'

'Sure.' Fats nodded to Lindy when they got back. 'It's all settled, kid. This here is the Reverend Izard, and he's going to introduce our resumed concert starring Mr Gadsby here' – he smiled encouragingly at the young singer, and held his shoulder firmly – 'with a word of prayer. You can hand him that microphone as soon as you like.'

'It's a pleasure, Reverend.' Lindy returned to her station by the galley. Fats remained where he was, leaning against the bulkhead with arms akimbo.

'Ladies and gentlemen,' the old man said, 'I'd like to introduce myself to y'all. I'm the Reverend John D. Izard from Deer Creek in Oregon, but please, don't anyone worry on that account, I'm not speaking to you now for what some might think is the obvious reason: in fact, I just gave the crew a promise I won't even mention the Hereafter in my little address, in case anyone started to get the wrong impression.'

That brought a faint smile to one or two faces.

'I'll only take up a few moments of your time in any case, because I know how you're all waiting to hear Frank Gadsby sing again: and with a voice like that, I don't blame you. However, speaking as a minister, I felt it only right and proper to send word to The Man at this time – all things considered: and to invite you all to join me, should you feel so inclined. I'm not going to pray for my own skin, let me hasten to add – I wouldn't be so darned presumptuous. No, I'm thinking of all the good people on this plane working so hard to try to help me, like Colonel Ramage back there behind his wall of pillows and blankets at the rear of the aircraft, all on his own. He sounds like a mighty fine person to me. I don't know about you folk, but I regard his presence among us today as nothing short of miraculous, and oh yes! my friends, I'm going to say a prayer for him. "Father, we ask you please to watch over this brave man, and to guide his hands." '

The man from Deer Creek may have been small physically, but vocally he was a giant. The calm, resonant tone of his voice sounded oddly comforting: somehow, it exuded a quiet confidence, a belief that all would be well no matter what danger threatened. Fats looked round the compartment for reactions. A few sat back with their eyes shut and hands clasped together. Others smiled now and again as they listened, and nodded agreement with the words that were said. Where there had been tension earlier in so many faces, now there was peace.

'Then there's the Captain. He tells us not to worry, but just think for a moment of his own position: so much responsibility to carry, and all in the unique loneliness of command. I'm going to pray for him too, and in my heart I know he won't mind. "Please, Lord, add your skills to his, for we have a long way still to go." '

No one stirred as he spoke.

'Turn your thoughts next to the members of the crew, these young men and women who have spent every moment of the journey tending to our physical needs as well as our fears. That calls for a very special kind of devotion and courage in all the circumstances, as I think you'll agree: so let's pray for them too. "Oh Lord, please tend to their secret needs, as they have so unselfishly seen to ours." '

The turbulence had abated now, and the Jumbo flew as steady as a rock.

'Lastly, my friends, spare a thought for all those unknown people on the ground working so hard to help us, every bit as hard as the crew of this plane. Think of the policemen, searching through the streets of London for the wicked man whose telephone call began the nightmare for us all. Think of the officials of the airline, whom our Captain has said are willing to make any sacrifice so that our lives shall be spared. And lastly, let us remember the families and friends we have left behind us: they must know of our plight by this time, and perhaps even more than us will need His strength to sustain them through the long journey. Let us pray for all of them.'

Throughout the giant plane there was silence, as both passengers and crew hung on every word.

'For myself I ask nothing at all,' continued the minister. 'Like I said, I wouldn't be so presumptuous. I've lacked for nothing in my life so far, and if the Scriptures are right this is only an apprenticeship for better times to come, anyway. That being the case – and my firm belief – I shall content myself with the words of a psalm: more of a declaration of faith, you might say, than any appeal for help. Join in, if you want to: might even do y'all a power of good.'

Slowly, he began:

' "The Lord is my shepherd, therefore can I lack nothing. He shall feed me in a green pasture, and lead me forth beside the waters of comfort. He shall convert my soul and bring me forth in the paths of righteousness, for his Name's sake. Yea, though I walk through the valley of death I will fear no evil, for Thou art with me: Thy rod and Thy staff comfort me. Thou shalt prepare a table before me against them that trouble me: Thou hast anointed my head with oil, and my cup shall be full. But Thy loving kindness and mercy shall follow me all the days of my life, and I will dwell in the house of the Lord for ever. Amen.'

Almost all the passengers, and many of the crew, spoke the familiar words with the minister. Ramage listened as he sat hunched over the bomb: it took him back to Tremeneth, the Cornish village where he was born, and the days when his parents were alive – the Twenty-third Psalm had been his father's favourite. Lindy listened, close to tears. Selma lies in the Bible Belt, and her own childhood had been a compound of religion and grinding poverty. The chief steward listened closest of all. While the minister had kept his word, at the same time he had succeeded in snapping his fingers at the restrictions placed upon him: what was more, in so doing he had bolstered morale, not harmed it. Fats recognised the hand of a professional, and approved entirely. Even the newspapermen were impressed. It was tempting to dismiss the whole thing as *schmaltz*, but there was no gainsaying either the aptness of his timing or impact of the old man's delivery. Up on the flight deck, the officers listened in silence. Nobody spoke for a while, after the minister had finished. Finally, Brdwzynski turned to his engineer.

'Making any progress with that malfunction, Sam?'

'Negative, Captain.' He gave a wry grin. 'Maybe we should ask the Reverend to say one for the auto-pilot.'

'Yeah.'

Joe Eckhardt brought the pilot down to earth. 'Hey, what about those newsmen, Lucky? We promised them they could file stories sometime, remember?'

'So we did. Okay Joe, go down and see what they've got. You can also tell them I'll allow one man to take pictures of Ramage at work – just as soon as he gives permission. But interviews with the passengers will have to wait. No one moves around without an escort till Ramage is through. That's an order.'

'Aye, sir.'

The pilot called London again as his First Officer went below. This time he had to wait even longer than usual to speak to Byron Schumacher.

The two nation police trap to catch the commandos of the Liberation Army might conceivably have borne fruit but for one thing: the daylight-saving hour's time difference between Britain and West Germany. Somehow this elementary but all-important factor became overlooked in the flow of urgent messages between Whitehall and Bonn. Afterwards, neither Force would admit to blame: but the fact remained that as Scotland Yard cars rammed the ransom vehicle in London – after it had dropped off the money at a rendezvous – the police in Frankfurt were still taking up positions round the Vir Jahren hotel. Then man who had telephoned Schumacher did not wait to collect any of the half million left as bait at the rendezvous. From a flat across the road, he watched police marksmen take up their positions: then he walked down into the street, climbed into his own car, and drove off with his woman accomplice. A mile further on they stopped briefly to ring a colleague in central London, who in turn called Germany and gave the alarm. Then they went to ground in their various apartments, and waited.

At five o'clock Schumacher's telephone rang again. He was as nervous as a chicken who knows there is a fox in the run. 'Atlantic Airways,' he said, and then corrected himself. 'Byron Schumacher.' A room full of ears eavesdropped on the extensions.

'I warned you,' said the harsh voice, 'but you didn't listen. Now you're going to pay the penalty, my friend.'

Schumacher was too frightened to speak.

'The deal is off. Those passengers on your plane are as good as dead already. Nothing can save them now. Or you.'

That loosened his tongue. 'I was acting under orders, there was nothing – '

'And what have you achieved? The British police picked up one man – a driver hired for the job. There was ample time to warn our commandos in Frankfurt. You simpleton, didn't you think we were prepared for treachery?'

'I keep telling you, I wasn't to blame – '

'We shall take reprisals, Schumacher. First we shall bomb your whole fleet of Jumbos out of the skies. And when the last one has crashed, we'll come for you.'

'Listen, please, if it's money you want – '

Before Schumacher could finish, his caller rang off. All eyes in the room viewed the vice-president of Atlantic Airways with something close to contempt as he put the phone down. Few doubted the terrorists would seek revenge for the loss of the money. Most disliked Schumacher sufficiently to find a morbid pleasure in his present plight. But terrorist threats did not always and inevitably translate into deeds, and there had to be a better way to face up to them than to crawl.

In the end the police Commander took pity on him, and spoke up. 'Don't worry, we're not beaten yet,' he declared. 'We'll turn the screws on that driver, and have Identikit pictures of the whole gang circulating by nightfall. They won't find it easy to get away, sir.'

Schumacher regarded him with loathing. This was the same policeman who had got him sentenced to death by A.L. – and now he was telling him not to worry about it unduly! Before he could frame a suitable answer the door swung open and his secretary looked in. 'I'm sorry to disturb you, gentlemen.' Her eyes found Schumacher. 'Sir, you weren't answering your phone. We have New York on the line, Mr Rogers: he says it's very urgent.'

He felt numbed, indifferent to Manhattan's requests and demands. He felt past caring now – if the truth were known – to what happened even to the 400-odd passengers trapped on the plane. All he could think of was that harsh, menacing voice sentencing him to death. But the girl was insistent and his London manager pushed a receiver into his hands. 'Schumacher.'

'Bad news, Byron,' said a strong, alert voice from 3,000 miles away. 'The General's been badly hurt in a road accident. He's trapped under a pile of wreckage and the police here say that the chances of getting him out alive are remote.'

'Oh.'

'I just got word, from Doctor Louk. He was following in his own car and saw it happen. Seems one of those king-sized trucks had a series of blow-outs and came right across the freeway.'

Schumacher listened in silence.

'Grimmett's dead. And Mo Ryan. It's going to take a considerable time to cut the General clear, dead or alive. What do you want us to do, Byron?'

'How's that?' Did they really expect him to sort out every problem from London when he had a bomb-scare – and a personal death threat – on his hands?

Rogers was baffled by Schumacher's slow, almost palsied response to the news. Like every other executive in the company he was fully aware, embarrassingly so at times, of General Grossman's hardline attitude to all terrorist demands, no matter what the penalty. It was not for him to say if it was right or not. But a situation had arisen now that offered at least an opportunity for a more flexible approach, perhaps an eleventh-hour chance to buy back those 450 lives. Yet all Schumacher did was to grunt monosyllables, and drag his heels.

'Byron, don't you think we should call an emergency session of the Board to discuss this new situation? I've got everyone here: they've been standing by ever since you sent the first bomb warning. And realistically speaking – look, I'm sorry to have to say this to you – I don't think there can be much hope for your father-in-law from what Louk said. So if you wanted to take another look at that ransom demand – '

'It's too late.' Schumacher glared across the room at the Commander. 'The police tried to intercept the terrorists and failed. Now they've called to say the whole deal is off.'

'All the more reason to try a new approach.'

'You don't seem to understand, Rogers, this whole thing is escalating. Now they're threatening to kill *me*.'

'That's terrible. I'm sorry to hear that, Byron, and I know it must be hard to take. But we still have to deal with first things first. Where does this leave Brdwzynski and those 450 passengers of ours?'

'And I keep telling you, the deal's off. We've burned our boats.'

'Maybe not. Look, the General's incapacitated, even if he survives. That means the Board is in a position now to find the money – to do a deal of some kind – if you'll give us the lead. You could still appeal to those people on radio and TV, and offer to meet any terms they lay down.'

'Well – '

'Byron. It has to be worth a try. We can't stand aside and wash our hands of all responsibilities.'

It might work, thought Byron: and at least it was better – anything was better – than waiting for the Liberation Army to take its revenge and kill him. As well as saving the passengers, payment of the ransom would almost certainly get him off the hook too. However, he wanted no one to think afterwards this was Rogers' idea.

'You don't have to remind *me* of our duty to those passengers. I've been advising a settlement ever since we established this was a genuine bomb threat. That's on the record, here and in New York, Rogers. But you know the General as well as I do, and I intend no disloyalty when I say that.'

'Byron, please. We have to move fast if we hope to save that Jumbo.'

'Yes. Very well, you call the Board meeting and get Louk to sign a statement saying the General is physically incapable of reaching an executive decision. Then take a show of hands on the ransom payment, and let me know the result at once. Meantime, I'll talk to the authorities here about the broadcast.'

'Fine. Good luck, Byron. I'll call you right back.'

Schumacher put the suggestion to the Commander, who shied away from a positive answer. 'Look, sir, we don't have any powers to stop you going on the air and appealing to this gang direct. And like you, the police are willing to consider any scheme to save lives. So don't misunderstand me – please – if I point out the drawbacks in this one. We happen to have one of the gang under arrest and in custody, and my guess is those terrorists are sure to demand his release as part of any deal. They may also want a plane, safe conduct guarantees – you name it – before they're prepared to tell you what you need to know to deal successfully with the bomb. I don't say anything's impossible, Mr Schumacher. But that kind of thing will need ministerial sanction – and it takes time. You've only got a few hours left.'

Schumacher was not the kind of man to abandon a place in the lifeboat without a fight. 'For God's sake, Commander – forget about the problems, think about the lives at stake! At least, will you put my idea forward?'

'Of course, sir.' He would promise nothing, just the same. 'But I still think your Jumbo will be over New York before we get an answer.' He paused at the door. 'I'll keep you informed.'

As soon as the policeman had gone, Schumacher took the call from Brdwzynski. 'Good news and bad news, I'm afraid. I'll be as brief as I can.' Quickly, he told the pilot about the General's accident. 'In one way, it might help. Now that the General is physically incapable of making policy decisions, the Board is empowered to act independently: we can order payment of the ransom money, for instance. I've already discussed this with Rogers and we're going ahead. I've also made a request to the authorities here for permission to speak direct to the terrorists on radio and television, to say I'm willing to negotiate.'

'Now you're talking!'

'Yes.' He deliberately made no mention of the abortive police action. 'But it's still going to take time, Lucky: how long can you give us?'

'I wish I knew. Ramage is still working on the bomb, and we can't arrest this loss of height. Any word from the manufacturers?'

'Not so far. They have every available man working on it.'

'Hell.' Brdwzynski looked at the instruments. 'I can remain

airborne for four and a half hours – altimeter bomb permitting. That's the absolute maximum.'

'We'll be doing everything humanly possible to help down here.' This time he meant it. 'Try to hold on, Lucky.'

Laura Ramage felt calmer now but still could not bring herself to join in the singing going on so determinedly all around her. While the minister's words and the steadfast behaviour of her fellow passengers had made a profound impression upon her, the realisation that her husband was locked in combat with a bomb only a few feet away made it impossible for her to relax, even for a moment: and she knew that the only answer was to find something to keep her physically occupied. At home she would have baked a cake or knitted a pair of gloves. But what on earth could she do now? As soon as she came to a decision, she took out the compact she carried in her handbag and spent some time in repairing her make-up. When she was finally satisfied she reached up and pressed the call-sign above her head, and asked the stewardess to take her to Lindy.

'Hi there, Mrs Ramage. Something I can do for you, ma'am?'

'Yes please.' She came into the galley. 'I'd like you to give me a job to do.'

It was the first time in all her years in aircrew that Lindy had heard a passenger make such a request. For a moment, she hesitated. 'I don't think I quite understand, Mrs Ramage.'

'I want to do something – wash dishes, pour cups of tea, serve drinks – *anything* except sit on my own back there, and worry about my husband.' It was costing her an effort to maintain that bright, seemingly unruffled exterior. 'Please. Another minute in that seat with a strap round my waist and I'll go stark, raving mad.'

Lindy thought of the big man with the eye-patch crouched over the bomb. In a moment of compassion she realised that there must have been many, many moments such as this for the pale and slender woman opposite, and her heart went out to her.

'Sure.' She reached up and found a clean white apron. 'Here, this goes with the job: you can handle a tea-trolley with me, okay?'

'Thank you, I'd like that very much.' Laura tied the apron round her waist and smoothed it flat. It was costing her a tremendous effort to control her true feelings, but she managed to smile at Lindy. 'Right. Ready when you are.'

Ramage had to cut away almost all of the top outer skin to find the anti-handling switch he was seeking. It consisted of two lengths of red detonator wire tied in a blood knot – a fisherman's knot – and leaving two bare ends. That was all, the most elementary form of switch. Press the stud, slide the lock, and as the jaws of the case gaped open so the wires would slide into contact, complete the circuit – and detonate the bomb. It was exactly the kind of booby-trap favoured by the expert: one with classic simplicity of operation, so little work involved for the bomb-maker yet allowing for no possibility of failure if the briefcase was opened normally. As he had foreseen, it was included to thwart the curious passenger rather than the professional investigator: but the fact that he had guessed correctly in no way diminished his fears. Everything about this Jumbo bomb had the stamp of the pro.

It took him only seconds to snip through the blood-knot; one hurdle crossed. He resisted the urge to look at his watch, consoling himself with the thought that there was no point in hurrying to a funeral. The whole of the interior now lay open to him. There was a striped cloth crammed in the bottom to act as a cradle for the device: by the look of it a man's shirt. That might be of interest to the forensic scientists who followed him in the investigation. The circuitry that made up its electronic skeleton was held in place by the sides of the briefcase and the cradle below: the wires that ran down from the anti-handling switch, through the altimeter and timing device, led to the detonator hidden somewhere in the gelignite entrails of the device.

Ramage could see the alarm clock quite clearly now, as well as hear it. Fortunately, like the altimeter, it faced away from him: he preferred not to know how little time he had left in which to finish his task. He picked up the magnifying glass and examined the clock carefully. Its fine red wiring led through the metal casing to make-and-break points below: he traced each strand back until he was satisfied they contained no more hidden traps. As soon as he was sure of that he left the clock in the same way that he had left the altimeter alone, and pressed on with his search for the detonator. Neutralise *that*, and the Honeymoon Jumbo was saved.

He found it in the end, a slim, pencil-thin metal tube measuring two-and-a-half inches in length, buried in the centre of the gelignite bundle. Using his hands only now, he grasped the sticks and slowly prised them apart until he located the tiny pen battery that armed the detonator, and constituted the beating heart of the bomb. He teased its filament-thin wires with a finger nail to raise them clear, then took a pair of Sam Bronson's vanadium steel pincers in his free hand and snipped them through.

It was all over. After the almost unbearable tension of the quest the sense of anti-climax was stunning. Ramage sat quite motionless for a while, as if unable to grasp that he had won. Finally, he got to his feet and walked unsteadily to the barricade, like a man getting out of bed after a long illness.

'Hey, Fats' he croaked.

The old chief steward hauled himself upright: it had been a long journey for him too. 'Sir?'

At first Ramage attempted to scribble a note, but his fingers were so stiff and cramped he found he was unable to grasp the pencil. So he said, 'Please give the Captain my compliments, and tell him the bomb's been rendered safe,' instead. Then he realised how pompous and stilted that must sound, and beamed: a joyous, ecstatic blissful grin that spread from ear to ear.

'We've done it, Fats,' he declared. '*She's safe!*'

'Boy oh boy!' Ohlsen reached inside the barricade to seize Ramage's hand, and began to pump it up and down in sheer delight. 'That's great, Mr Ramage: congratulations!' The years seemed to peel off him like clothes in a heatwave. 'Hallelujah!'

'Thank you, Fats.' Ramage disengaged gently but firmly. 'Better let the Captain know as soon as possible, eh?'

'Yes, *sir*!' He hurried through the compartment, still chuckling.

Brdwzynski himself carried back the champagne, after making a triumphant announcement to his passengers. Frank Gadsby led them in singing 'For he's a jolly good fellow' and the roar of their voices followed the pilot as he made his way aft. He pulled aside some of the pillows and blankets and climbed through, stepping carefully among the debris.

'That song is for you,' he said slowly, and gazed about him in wonder as he stood with the bottle in one hand and two glasses in the other. 'Holy cow.' He handed one glass to the Englishman and kept the other himself as he filled both to the brim.

'Pilots who drink on the job are fired immediately,' he said. 'It's an automatic, inviolate rule of the air. Cheers.' He put the glass to his mouth and drained it at a gulp, then wiped his lips with the back of his hand. 'What the hell, I was going to quit after this flight anyway. My nerves can't take anymore.'

'I didn't see a thing,' Ramage assured him. He sipped his own drink slowly and luxuriously. 'By God, that tastes good.'

Brdwzynski looked down at the dismembered bomb with a rare expression on his face. 'I have to know,' he said. 'The height on the altimeter. And the time on that clock.'

'I plucked up courage to have a look just before you arrived,' Ramage told him. 'The altimeter was set at 5,000 feet – and it *was* an atmospheric pressure device. The time bomb was fitted with a delay mechanism, which would have given us another five hours flying time still. From which we can deduce they must have intended to direct us to Colorado Springs – or some other airport at more than 5,000 feet above sea level – as soon as the money was handed over.'

Brdwzynski nodded. 'So they were bluffing when they said we'd all be killed before we reached Kennedy?'

'Oh no.' Ramage held up the altimeter. 'We'd have gone up in smoke the moment you began your final approach, seven or eight miles out to sea.'

'Then why spook the auto-pilot?'

'I'm not sure they did,' said Ramage. 'All right, they're terrorists, but they have to have credibility, whether it's in carrying out their threat to murder people or in keeping their word to let them go once the ransom is paid. I think they were confident your airline would pay up, eventually. That's why they fitted a delay mechanism – not only to allow us time to land safely after the money was paid, but also to give themselves ample time to get clear with the loot first, My own guess is your auto-pilot had other mechanical problems.'

'Could be.' Brdwzynski nodded agreement. 'Bronson's been talking to the makers, and they suggested the auto-pilot may have been damaged accidentally when the terrorists were fooling around with the plane in London – trying to "trace" that phoney electrical fault. Anyhow, we'll know for sure as soon as we land at Kennedy.'

'It's all rather academic now.' Ramage poured himself another glass of champagne. 'You want the other half, Lucky?'

'No more till I'm back on terra firma.' He stood up and straightened his tunic, a lanky, string-bean figure of a man. 'Then I'll make up for lost time.' He gestured at the debris scattered over the deck. 'What do we do with all this?'

'It's up to you, really,' said Ramage. 'I can dismantle it further, if you like, no problem: or we can leave it for Bomb Disposal in New York. Whichever you want.'

'Does it make any difference to passenger safety?'

'Not a bit. You can never be a hundred per cent certain with explosives, of course, but the fact is, I don't have the right gear to tidy up properly anyhow. No acetone solvent to dissolve whatever leaks of nitro-glycerine there may have been: things like that. We're as safe as we're going to be until the plane has had a thorough spring-clean.'

'Fine, then we'll let someone else do the dirty work for a change.' Brdwzynski inspected his empty glass. 'I'll keep this – as a souvenir of my dangerous, peacetime flying career,' he joked. Then he turned to Ramage again. 'Listen, no heroics, but we'd all have been in one hell of a mess without you on this trip, buddy. If ever you need help – any time, now – you know where to come.'

'I'll remember that.' They grinned at each other: comrades in arms. 'Now, there are one or two things I've got to do in here before I go forward and rejoin my wife. Incidentally, if I may make a suggestion – it might be a good idea to have this section screened off until you land, even to leave one of the crew on guard, perhaps. There's a fair bit of gelignite lying around.'

'I'll see to it.' A thought suddenly occurred to the pilot. 'Say, we forgot the Press. Can I turn those photographers loose before you clear away in here?'

'As long as they shoot through the barrier' said Ramage. 'No closer, in case of accidents. Five minutes for pictures, an interview with the reporters afterwards, then I'm through: I'm supposed to be on holiday, remember?'

The cameramen swarmed round.

'Gentlemen. I can give you five minutes, that's all.'

One man came back after the others had left to photograph the honeymooners, and persuaded Ramage to allow him through the barrier. His was a classic study of the bomb disposal man at work, in all his unenviable solitude. He showed Ramage bent over the briefcase, knife in hand, alone among the empty seats. The cabin lights crowned the mane of yellow hair as if with a halo. The photographer told him exactly where to sit, how to hold the knife, where to turn the one good eye: and when at length Ramage had it right, he slipped an airline ticket into his breast pocket, with the words 'FLY ATLANTIC, FLY SAFE' clearly visible.

'That's got it,' he said, satisfied at last. 'One more time, Colonel. Fine, all through now. Like me to send you a print when I get back home?'

'I'd like that very much,' said Ramage. 'Thanks.' He gave the man his address, and went back to work. It took him perhaps ten more minutes to assemble everything for the American bomb disposal team, and he was just about to quit the tail section when something called him back to the device, as surely as if his name had been sounded aloud. On instinct he knelt over the briefcase again, and studied it intently.

Experience told him there was something familiar about this bomb in the plane, and it made no difference that it was the first of its kind he had ever defused. The same sixth sense also told him that the clues were here, right under his nose: but where? Ramage was aware that he was desperately tired, physically and mentally. His head ached abominably. He pushed the patch high on his forehead and rubbed the empty, puckered flesh below: the strain placed upon his one good eye by this demanding, close-quarter work had been one of the main reasons for his decision to quit the Army recently. But there was no escape now – patiently, he took up the magnifying glass and examined the circuitry for the thousandth time. Almost immediately he found the answer he was seeking – *there*, in the crimping!

The glass revealed a mark that the bomber had left on the neo-prene plug, the moisture seal. He saw the imprint on one of the flat surfaces of the crimp: too small to be picked up by the naked eye, but plain as the spoor of a wild animal in mud, under glass. Whoever had left that mark had done it *so* – Ramage went through the motions with his strong, sensitive hands – and again, *so*, to make doubly sure of the hold. In the process he had left a minuscule but clearly recognisable vee on the metal surface. At once, Ramage used the glass to check back along the rest of the circuit and by the time he had done knew, without any possibility of error, who had made this bomb. It was Paul Elvides – a terrorist he had first encountered in Cyprus twenty years before and last heard of reported missing, believed dead, in Ireland. The crimp carried his hallmark, unique and unmistakable: and the other features – above all his use of the collapsing circuit – combined to identify him to Ramage as surely as the handwriting in a letter provides evidence for the calligrapher. Elvides, by God!

It was a discovery of the first importance. The bomb had been placed aboard the aircraft only a few hours back. Some of the gang were in London at this moment, trying to extort money from the airline: and it was a near-certainty that Elvides himself, one of the world's leading terrorist figures and most experienced bomb-makers, would be among them. Therefore the chance was there still for the police to move in and arrest him, before he could get out of the country. It was Ramage's duty to alert them as fast as possible.

After a word to Fats to keep watch on the tail section, he hurried forward and spoke to Brdwzynski. Minutes later, he was talking to the Commander at Heathrow. 'There's no doubt about it,' he said firmly. 'This device was put together by a man called Paul Elvides, and I'm prepared to swear to that on oath. As soon as we put down in New York, I'll ask the police there to check for fingerprints, but don't wait for them, go out and grab him while you can. That driver you're holding ought to be able to give you a spot-on physical description, I should think.'

'I'll pass word on to the Yard right away, sir. And by the way, allow me to congratulate you – on a really wonderful job of work all round.'

Next, Ramage spoke to New York.

'Mr Rogers, you can tell that bomb disposal team I've made the thing safe: all they have to do is take pictures, and clean up.' He listed all the technical detail they would need to know, and added, 'And would you please ask the police to have a fingerprint squad standing by?' He told him why, explaining in a few sentences how he had been able to identify Elvides as the bomb-maker.

'The lieutenant of police is here with me now,' said Rogers. 'He says, consider it done. Meantime, I'd like to thank you on behalf of the company, Colonel, for your magnificent achievement in saving the lives of everyone aboard our commemorative flight. Atlantic Airways owes you a big debt of gratitude, and I greatly look forward to the pleasure of welcoming you and Mrs Ramage personally in a little while.'

It was the gentlest of reminders that there was much to be done before the plane landed. Ramage thanked him and handed back his headset, while Brdwzynski took over the call.

'How's the General?'

'Not so good. The accident caused a stroke, and it's left him partly paralysed – and unable to speak. Which means a change of command, temporarily anyhow. Byron flies back tonight to take over.'

Ramage stepped down at New York to a hero's welcome. The plight of the Honeymoon Jumbo had been followed hourly by every television network in the country, and the Mayor himself was there to greet the passengers as they landed.

'Ladies and gentlemen, when the President of the United States spoke some weeks ago of the reception that would await you here he was referring, of course, to the warm bond of affection that has always existed between our two countries: the Special Relationship. Today however, before I welcome those young couples for whom this anniversary flight was originally named, it is my duty and pleasure to pay tribute to the man whose skill and courage alone made it possible for their aircraft to land safely. I am referring, of course, to Colonel Gordon Ramage, the British bomb disposal officer and our honoured guest. Please step forward, sir.'

Big crowds had flocked to the airport as the drama of the bomb on the plane reached its climax, and there was a round of applause as the Mayor and the Englishman shook hands. Ramage gave no sign of the fatigue he felt: he stood very straight and still, an impressive figure with that powerful frame, the blaze of yellow hair and the black, forbidding patch.

'I bid you welcome, Colonel, in the name of all the citizens of this great city.' The voice droned on and on, paying fulsome tribute to Ramage's achievement in saving so many hundreds of lives. The Mayor finally ended by saying, 'I have a message here for you from the White House, which I propose to read aloud if you will permit me. It says "By your courage today, you have won the admiration of all Americans. As the elected leader of a nation which likewise will never surrender to threats of force, no matter whence they come, I salute you." It is signed by the President – and it echoes precisely the thoughts of us all.'

The Mayor's address was only the beginning. Atlantic Airways' officials succeeded the civic dignitaries, Ramage was called on to reply, Laura was greeted with a bouquet of flowers. Even when the speeches ended, there was no respite: Ramage was hustled away to face a Press conference, while the honeymooners left for their gala reception.

'Colonel, will you please tell us how you were able to name the terrorist Paul Elvides as the man who made the bomb on the Honeymoon Jumbo?'

That came as a blockbuster. It was only two hours or so since he had identified Elvides to the police in London. How on earth had word spread so quickly?

'News travels fast in this part of the world,' he parried cautiously. 'I didn't know the name would be known to you Press people yet awhile.'

'It's on the tapes, sir.' This was another reporter. 'They're saying Scotland Yard had already prepared a number of Identikit drawings from the statement made by the driver they arrested earlier. When you radioed London, they immediately issued Elvides' picture to all the TV channels – and as a result of the phone calls that came in, they cornered the gang in a London apartment. They're under siege right at this moment, Colonel.'

'Good,' said Ramage. His jaw jutted out as he stared round at the newsmen. 'Unfortunately, none of them will get the punishment they deserve. We've done away with the death penalty in my country, as you probably know.'

'But the point still stands, sir,' persisted his first questioner. 'These people still face long terms of imprisonment – and you've put the finger on Elvides as the one who made the bomb. What makes you so certain it was him?'

'In any device as sophisticated as this was,' said Ramage

deliberately, 'you would expect to find certain clues in the layout and construction. Some terrorists favour one technique, others a quite different kind. They all like to lay little traps here and there.' He scowled. 'You get to know them all eventually – if you live that long.'

'And you found signs pointing to Elvides in the Jumbo bomb?'

'Yes.'

'You don't need fingerprints to back up these findings?'

'No. My evidence would count as expert opinion in a court of law,' said Ramage. 'Now it so happens I have asked the New York police to examine this device for fingerprints, but that's because of the unique circumstances involved. This bomb was hidden on the plane in London, defused in mid-air, and has now been impounded by a disposal team working 3,000 miles away.' He gave the reporter a bleak smile. 'I intend to make sure Mr Elvides doesn't get off on some legal technicality.'

'What's so special about Elvides, Colonel?'

'His skills.' The black, sightless patch turned in the direction of this new speaker. 'He's one of the world's most experienced bomb-makers, maybe the best there is – and a professional killer. Take my word for it.'

'How many times have you come up against him personally, sir?'

Ramage let his mind wander down the years. 'Paul Elvides made bombs for Eoka in Cyprus, for the NLF in Aden, and on at least one occasion, for the IRA in Ulster: plus today's. These are all ones I know about *personally*.' Again there was that bleak smile. 'You could say we're old acquaintances.'

'You mean you've fought each other over a great many years?'

'In the sense that Elvides makes bombs, and I take them apart: yes. We've never met; to my knowledge.'

'Has he tried to kill you personally, Colonel?'

'Someone certainly has. On more than one occasion.' The empty socket ached at the thought, beneath the patch. 'In each case those attempts were made in areas where Elvides was known to be operating – and after I had successfully defused bombs made by him. I leave you to draw your own conclusions.'

'When was the first time?'

'More than twenty years ago.' The interview was moving into personal areas, ones he would have preferred to avoid: but reaction from the tension on the plane coupled with the knowledge that his enemy was trapped in a London flat combined to loosen his tongue.

'This is a timeless duel, Colonel?' They were fascinated by the thought of two men locked in combat over more than two decades.

'That's your phrase, not mine.' Ramage refused to dignify the contest. 'I'm saying there have been a number of attempts to murder me in that time. But perhaps that doesn't sound so good.'

'Aren't you afraid the other terrorists in the Liberation Army gang might try to seek revenge for what you've done today, Colonel?'

'I don't see why they should. I was a passenger on that plane quite by chance. Elvides wasn't out to get me this time, in fact there was no way he could have known I was on board. All he wanted was money – and whatever I did to thwart him was done in self-defence, as much as anything else. I can't see any terrorist gang getting too excited about that.'

'What happens if they don't see it your way, sir? And if their friends in that apartment are killed or captured?'

Round came the scarred blond head, slowly. The single blue eye gleamed for a moment. Then Ramage shrugged his shoulders. 'I'll cross that bridge when I get to it. I've retired from this game, I'm telling you. I no longer hunt terrorists, nor do I count myself as a target for any terrorist organisation. As far as A.L. is concerned and this bomb, we're just ships that passed in the night.'

He rose to his feet to indicate that the interview was over.

'Ladies and gentlemen, believe it or not I came to America for a holiday. With your permission, I'd like to rejoin Mrs Ramage and start that holiday – now. Good day to you all.' He marched out of the conference room, flanked by a bevy of airline officials.

The Ramages had hoped for a week's sight-seeing in New York before travelling down to Florida to join Laura's sister, who was married to a former American serviceman. But the interviews did not end with the press conference at the airport.

Magazines and newspapers – many from abroad – pursued them relentlessly by telephone, while American television came direct to their hotel to try to persuade them to appear on a dozen shows. By the end of the third day they suddenly realised that they had seen almost nothing of the bustling, exuberant city outside their hotel doors: instead they were prisoners of the media, for there was no end in sight to the London siege.

'This isn't a holiday,' said Laura finally, 'it's hard work. I don't think I can take much more.'

'I was just thinking the same thing,' Ramage agreed. 'Why don't we just disappear quietly and leave for Florida tomorrow?'

'Marvellous.' Laura pressed the button for the lift to take them up to their room. 'I'll call my sister right away.'

'You do that while I settle the bill and book seats on the plane.' The lift arrived, and the doors slid open. 'I'll join you later.'

A hand touched his shoulder as he settled with the cashier, and he turned to see Brdwzynski smiling at him. 'I've come to buy you that drink I owe you,' said the pilot. 'Is this a good time to call?'

'Of course. Good to see you, Lucky.' They walked to the bar.

'How's Mrs Ramage?'

'Gone to bed to dodge the Press. We're leaving first thing in the morning.' Ramage told him about their change of plans. 'We'll come back and do the sight-seeing when things have quietened down a little. And see more of you at the same time, I hope. Cheers.'

'I think you're right to get away.' Brdwzynski sipped his whisky. 'That siege in London is turning out to be quite a story, by all accounts. Now one of the networks here wants to get all of us – that's you and Mrs Ramage, Gadsby and the minister, all the honeymooners they can find plus me and the crew – to fly in a specially chartered Jumbo later this week and reconstruct the whole thing for the cameras. Can you beat that?'

Ramage shook his head in wonderment. 'What do they want, blood?'

'Don't worry, it won't happen. Our acting president Byron Schumacher has stepped in and said – no. None of the Jumbo crew is permitted to give any further interviews, or even be photographed by the media, without his permission. The official grounds are that the bomb story is bad publicity for Atlantic Airways.'

'He may have a point there.'

'Byron doesn't give a damn about the airline, Ramage: he's thinking about his own skin. He's terrified A.L. might carry out that threat they made in London to kill him. So he's given orders to play the story down, in the hope the terrorists will forget about him too.'

'You can't blame any man for that, Lucky.'

'Hell, they've forgotten him already: but you ought to see him! He's got more bodyguards round him than the Man in the White House,' said the pilot contemptuously. 'It's got so that no one can get into his office without being searched down to their underpants first. The night he flew back from London he had X-ray apparatus installed to scan all his mail – in case A.L. sent him a letter bomb. Now he keeps so many armed men on duty in our airline offices downtown they're scaring passengers away.'

Ramage signalled for more drinks, and said nothing.

'Threats on the telephone are bad enough,' said Brdwzynski slowly. 'Defusing bombs for a living is something else. How the hell did you manage to get into the business in the first place?'

'I think I must have had a rush of blood to the head.' Ramage grinned as he said it. 'They asked for volunteers a long time ago, when I was in Cyprus. And they were bloody choosy, too. Somehow, it made us all the keener to get in.'

'You come from an Army family, Ramage?'

'Christ, no.' He grinned at the idea. 'I was called up when I was eighteen: we used to have conscription in those days. But there was no work where I lived, so I stayed on. I suppose you could say it grew on me after a time.'

Thirty years of distinguished soldiering lay behind those casual words. He had been born in a hamlet called Tremeneth, in south Cornwall; the name means 'the place on the hill'. He was an only child, and in his home there was no money to spare. His father was a carpenter – no, far more than that, a magician who conjured superb furniture out of elm: enormous refectory tables with carvers and dining-room chairs, dressers, mantels, consoles and wardrobes. To this day, every big house for miles around possessed furniture hand-made by his father. Yet up to the year he died, he was lucky to earn £100 for three months' work.

'Will Ramage, furniturmaker' said the sign in the cottage window, and it was never spelled right as long as the old man lived. The front door stayed open and the world walked in, friends and strangers alike, just to watch his father at work – planing, shaping, gouging, and banging with his mallet loud enough to wake the dead in the churchyard at the end of the street. His mother was a gentle soul who said little and spent the whole of her time looking after the two men in her life. She would have laughed if anyone had told her her son would become a famous professional soldier.

A fire burned in the front room winter and summer, licking round a pot as black as a witch's cauldron. This held Will Ramage's glue. The whole house smelled woody and industrious. There was the sharp smell of turpentine mingling with the dull, clinging scent of freshly-planed wood and sawdust, and threading through it all the smell of glue, compounded of fishbones and horses' hooves: an unforgettable mixture. Ramage could have found his way home blindfold as a boy, simply by following his nose.

The woody smells were Ramage's most enduring memory of his childhood: those, and the singing. Tremeneth was a staunch Methodist stronghold, and his father sang hymns as naturally as other men today sing ballads. 'Rock of Ages' was his favourite, or 'When I survey the wondrous Cross', and he sang from sheer contentment in a voice that matched the elm he used – seasoned and mellow. Ramage smiled at Brdwzynski's question, and the memories it evoked. There never was a more unmilitary family than his own. And they never forgave the Army for taking their son away from Cornwall.

Every spare penny his parents earned was put aside to try to provide him with a better chance in life than they had had. It had been obvious for a long time that he lacked both the will and the skill to become a master carpenter, like his father and grandfather before him. When he won his scholarship, his mother took a job as cleaner to help him through college. When he left shortly before he was nineteen, Ramage still had no clear idea of what he wanted to do in life. Ideas stirred in his mind but he hesitated to put a name to them: the truth was that although he loved his family and his home, there were times when the smallness of everything in Tremeneth almost suffocated him. His father had never travelled beyond Plymouth in his life – a journey of less than sixty miles – and the boy was determined to do better than that before he was through. So that when the big, buff envelope marked 'O.H.M.S.' dropped through the letter box ordering him to report for his compulsory eighteen months' military service, he saw it as perhaps the only chance he might ever get to look at the world that existed beyond the Tamar, while his parents despaired.

'It isn't fair,' said his mother wearily. She thought of the hours she had spent scrubbing floors so that her son could become something better in life than a maker of elmwood tables, and could have wept: not for herself, but for her son. 'It isn't *right*. You haven't even started to live your life yet.' The year was 1948, and the memories of World War Two were still fresh in every mind. His father busied himself with cleaning his pipe, but the look on his face told its own story. And all the time Ramage wondered: how am I going to tell them?

The truth was that the letter lying on the kitchen table had come for him that morning like meat to a starving man. He knew that he wanted, desperately, to go into the the Army – not because he wanted to be a soldier, but because it offered a means of escape from a sleepy hamlet with a population of sixty-two. He forgot, now, all the arguments he used to try to reconcile his parents to the inevitable. He clearly remembered telling them, 'Don't worry, it won't be for long.'

That was thirty years ago. Now the two men talked on into the night, about bombs and terrorism. Brdwzynski told Ramage about Vietnam. Ramage spoke about Cyprus and Aden and Ireland.

'How about Mrs Ramage,' asked Brdwzynski. 'What did she think about the years in bomb disposal?'

'Hated it,' said Ramage evenly. 'I'm afraid she used to have all the nightmares in our family. In the end it got her down.'

'I'm not surprised.' Brdwzynski dropped the subject, just as easily. He looked at his watch. 'She's going to have every reason to hate me if I keep you talking any longer: time to go.' He insisted on paying the bill, and the two men shook hands warmly. 'Don't forget,' said the pilot. 'I owe you. Don't hesitate to send up smoke signals if ever you run into trouble.'

'I keep telling you,' grinned Ramage. 'I've retired. But thanks for the offer, just the same. Happy landings.'

It was just after midnight when the taxi left. The night porter stopped Ramage as he was about to take the lift to his room. 'There's a telephone call for you, sir: from the police in London. Maybe you'd rather take it down here?'

'Thank you.' Laura would be sound asleep by now. He stepped into a booth and took up the receiver. 'Ramage speaking.'

'My apologies if I've disturbed you, Colonel. I'm not sure what time it is in New York, but it must be late. My name is Evans – Commander Evans, New Scotland Yard.'

'I read your name in the papers this morning. The man in charge of the Kensington siege. What's happened now?'

'It's all over, sir. My men entered the apartment about an hour ago.' He paused for a moment. 'There are one or two things I'd like to discuss with you, if I may.'

'Go right ahead.' Ramage thought he could guess what was wanted: a written statement about the bomb in the plane, as the police prepared to bring Elvides to trial. Well, he could do that from Florida easily enough.

'Let me put you in the picture first,' said the Commander. 'I gave orders to my chaps to shoot their way into the flat, because the terrorists were threatening to kill the two hostages they'd grabbed; that young woman and her child, you know?'

'Yes. Did you manage to save them?'

'We saved the woman. There's still no news of the boy's whereabouts.'

It was then that the penny dropped. 'They got away with him,' said Ramage. He corrected himself immediately. '*Elvides* got away with him.'

'That's right, sir. And there was nothing we could do to stop him. We couldn't open fire without hurting the boy, perhaps killing him.'

'I understand. Were there many casualties?'

'Indeed. I lost a sergeant, killed as we went in. There were five terrorists in all, including two women: all armed. Our sharpshooters killed three of them. I doubt if the fourth will last through the night.'

'Has Elvides got transport?'

'Yes. He held a gun to the boy's head and forced one of our drivers out of a police car.' There was much left unsaid but Ramage could picture the manhunt now going on. 'He won't find it so easy to get out of the country, I promise you. Which is why I felt I should call you, Colonel.'

'Oh?'

'Principally to warn you that Elvides is at large. I believe you left your children behind in England?'

'Yes.' He refused to panic.

'Would you like us to put a police guard on them – at least until you get back?'

Ramage forced himself to think about it sensibly. He had recently retired from the Army and bought a house eighty miles from London. There was no way in which his address could appear in any public document, such as a telephone directory or on the electoral roll, for a considerable time to come: perhaps a year or more. Until that happened, Elvides would have nowhere even to begin to look for his family. Also, there was Laura to think about. If she thought for one moment the situation warranted a police guard on the children, nothing would persuade her to remain a minute longer in America. And Ramage felt it would be cruel to see her back in England, hesitant to leave the house and worrying continually about an attack which – almost certainly – would never come. No: he decided firmly against the offer.

'Perhaps we could reach a compromise,' he suggested as he explained his reasons for turning down a guard on the house itself. 'If you could have a quiet word, say, with the local police and ask them to keep an eye on the place from an occasional patrol car, how about that? I'd feel a lot happier while I'm away, I suspect you would – and the family won't even suspect what's going on.'

'I think that's very wise, Colonel. As long as this man remains at large.'

'There's only my daughter at home, incidentally: and she's at work during the day. My son's at boarding school. There's no way Elvides could possibly trace him.'

'I'll pass all the information on, sir. As it happens, I ordered a check on your Press cuttings when the siege first started – purely as a precautionary measure, you understand. I see they mention a house in Cornwall.'

'But not the name of the village. And in any case, we don't live there: it became our holiday cottage after my parents' death, many years ago.' He gave the Commander his new permanent address. 'I don't expect to be back in Cornwall before Christmas at the earliest.'

'Right, sir. That's all I wanted to know. As long as you're happy – '

'*Happy* is not the way I'd describe my reaction to the news of Elvides' escape. I'd have liked to see him locked away for fifty years, to be perfectly honest.' Ramage groped for the words he wanted to say. 'But I think the Press may have given a false impression – no, I don't mean that, let's say they've painted an exaggerated picture of my position *vis-à-vis* Paul Elvides. Because he was a bomb-maker and I was in bomb disposal at a time when both species were relatively thin on the ground, we've come up against each other many times over the years. And he's tried to kill me personally, there's no doubt whatever about that. But he's never *pursued* me from place to place: all his moves have been made when chance has placed us on opposing sides in the various campaigns. I never knew why he picked on me, none of us did. My own guess is that it could be a question of vanity, because I beat him too often, and the top bomb-makers are insanely jealous of their reputations. But that's over and done with, long since. There is no timeless duel as the papers like to make out, I've retired, I've quit the game. Elvides didn't know I was going to be on that Jumbo any more than I knew he was going to hide a bomb on board – as a matter of fact, I thought he was dead, murdered years ago in Ireland. And if I hadn't done what I did on the plane, I would almost certainly have been killed, along with everyone else. He knows that, as well as I do. And in my book he won't make it a new vendetta issue, any more than the Liberation Army will.'

'They've taken a hard knock today as a direct result of your intervention, sir, none the less.'

'Well, it happens sometimes, when you play that kind of game. But Elvides has got other fish to fry, he's not going to bother about me. He needs money, that much is obvious. There's no money to be had from a scrap with the Ramages – and he knows it. I doubt very much if I'll ever hear from him again.'

'I sincerely hope you're right, sir.' Messages about the man-hunt were piling up for the Commander. 'Thank you for your co-operation, and we'll have a word with your local police about keeping an eye on the house. Enjoy your holiday.'

'Goodbye – and good hunting.'

Ramage went up to bed in a pensive mood. As he lay awake in the dark, listening to the sounds of Laura breathing, so the memories of Cyprus came flooding back: to the time when the duel began.

He first heard about Elvides from a British director of intelligence. Ramage never knew the man's name, or saw him again. He had flown into Cyprus by Canberra bomber – the fastest means of transport available – to brief a hand-picked security services audience at the outset of the Eoka campaign.

'There can be no doubt,' he began, 'that this insurrection has been long planned and is being carefully orchestrated by sources outside the island, and I'm afraid we've collected a bit of a bloody nose in the process. We in London have given this question of outside help our urgent attention, and have reached a number of conclusions. Now, we do not attempt to dispute that the leader of the revolt is General Grivas – himself a Cypriot – or that he is unquestionably the man who has put such fire into the bellies of this peasant army. Nor is there any point in denying the obvious, that his efforts have met with a certain amount of success by tying down a British force of more than 20,000 men. None the less, Grivas remains to our minds essentially a figurehead. We are far more interested in whatever other fingers there may be in the Cyprus pie.'

He was a tall man in his middle fifties. His pale face and beautifully-cut suit made him odd man out in a room filled with hard sunburned figures in khaki drill.

'It follows from the parrot cry of *Enosis* that most of the outside help is Greek. We in British intelligence believe we know the people concerned there, and their degrees of importance in the main. However, we also suspect there are others involved as well – and for very different motives.' He paused. 'One Power can be counted on always to foment and exploit unrest in western bases overseas, namely, Soviet Russia. We say this holds true in the case of Cyprus notwithstanding the fact that Eoka gunmen have deliberately murdered several members of Akel – the Greek-Cypriot communist party. Naturally, all allegations of Russian influence will be hotly denied by Grivas and his crew, since he is a professed anti-communist. My answer is that he may well be genuinely unaware of what has happened. The Russian secret service tends to avoid any direct involvement with these nationalist movements, preferring to muddy the waters by acting through renegade middlemen. For some time we have argued that something on these lines has already taken place in Cyprus, and that the ranks of Eoka have been successfully infiltrated – possibly in no more than one or two instances – by puppet terrorists dancing to Russian strings.'

There was complete silence in the room as he continued.

'One of the reasons for my flight here today is to warn you that information has now reached us concerning one such person. We do not know what name he is operating under here. But his real name is Paul Elvides: he is Greek-born, a man somewhere in his early thirties – we have passed on such physical details as we have to Army intelligence – a trained saboteur and highly-skilled bomb maker. Let me make it plain here and now, gentlemen, that Mister Elvides will not be granted even so much as the formality of a trial if he is arrested. He is to be shot out of hand as soon as he has been positively identified, and his body disposed of. It is our considered opinion that he is too dangerous to be allowed to live.'

That caused a stir. Ramage himself could still remember the sense of shock – of outrage, almost – at hearing sentence of death passed on an unknown man so casually by this soft-spoken, well dressed stranger. Dear Christ, what a greenhorn he had been in those days.

'This man is a professional killer,' the director told them, 'and we anticipate he will have drawn up a varied selection of targets. The Governor and his military commanders will clearly be among them although none – we trust – will ever make themselves too easily available. Obviously, Elvides will go for the "soft" targets first – the civil servant tending his garden, the off-duty policeman, unarmed groups of Servicemen relaxing on some isolated beach: wherever the risk will be least and the kill ratio highest. Such murders will form the back-cloth to the overall terror campaign, and the more brutal a killing the greater impact it will have. And all the time Elvides will set traps for those he fears most of all, our intelligence agents, the Special Branch counter-insurgency officers, bomb disposal experts and the like.'

Ramage and his fellow officers grinned self-consciously as they heard that, for they were young then.

'Bomb disposal people can expect to be targets on two grounds,' he went on. 'First because Eoka want the sound of their bombs to echo round the world, while EOD men form the front line of defence against them. Secondly because of the detective role they play. As well as finding fingerprints in the bombs they defuse, they will guide us to the sources of supply for each component part. Now, if there is little a terrorist can do about infantry patrols except avoid them, it is equally true that the bomb disposal officer is infinitely more vulnerable and harder to replace.'

It was warm in the big room and sweat ran down his face as he spoke. As he peeled off his jacket and threw it over a chair, Ramage suddenly saw the gun he was wearing: butt forward, in a shoulder holster beneath the left armpit.

'The Greek half of this island is crawling with potential enemies, gentlemen,' he continued, 'and given the chance any one will betray you. A very few will do so because they regard you as colonial oppressors, the majority because they themselves are exposed to blackmail: but none of that will make any difference to their unfortunate victims. Remember, you will be fighting a new kind of war here in Cyprus: a war without front lines, against a ghost army, an enemy who will never be numerically strong enough to face you in the open. Instead there will be a thousand eyes spying on your every move, a thousand ears listening to every unguarded word spoken over the telephone or in a bar, all reporting back to Grivas and his hard-core team of killers. They in turn will set traps for your vehicles with electrically detonated mines, or wait in some alley to shoot you in the back and vanish as quickly into the shadows again. Selective assassination will follow as they grow bolder, and I would caution you all to be on your guard at every moment.'

The first bid to murder him came twenty-four hours after he blew up a bomb factory discovered inside the old walled city of Nicosia. The find ranked as a considerable success in the war against such an elusive enemy and the Army made the most of it in propaganda – by using the bombs to show that the terrorists were getting help from outside, yet without revealing how much they knew.

Lieutenant Ramage told a crowded press conference about the bomb factory unearthed near the Paphos Gate, and handed round photographs of the gelignite, detonators and equipment he had destroyed. 'We caught them on the hop,' he said. 'So much so that they left a number of unfinished devices on the bench.' He pointed to a line of boxes on the table in front of him. 'That one is designed to explode acoustically. This is light sensitive. In each case the circuitry is highly advanced and we are convinced no local terrorist would have the skill needed to put them together.' He looked round at the journalists. 'In our considered opinion, these devices prove that Grivas is getting outside help.'

Ramage's words – and his picture – appeared in the two English language local newspapers next morning. He went back to work as normal, and it was not until late evening that he left headquarters to drive home. He and Laura were living at the time in a bungalow in the northern suburbs of the city, about a half-hour's drive away. He rang to tell her what time he would be leaving: there was some interference on the line, but it was so commonplace that he paid it no attention.

The first of the Eoka execution squads had already made an appearance on the streets of the city, and no one driving alone took any chances. Drawing from a holster while at the wheel could prove a clumsy, time-wasting business: Ramage drew his .38, checked that it was loaded, and laid it on the empty seat beside him ready for use in any emergency. Then he bade goodnight to the M.P.s on duty and drove the pick-up swiftly through the outskirts of Nicosia down to the road-block guarding the approach to the Kyrenia road. It was after curfew, and only pass-holders were allowed out. Ramage stayed close behind a group of journalists driving back to their hotel. An ambulance from the General Hospital joined the little convoy as it neared the checkpoint: otherwise, the streets were completely deserted. Rolls of dannert wire concertinaed across the road to form the block, while an armoured car stood by in support. Armed soldiers questioned the leading car briefly, then waved all three vehicles through.

After the correspondents swung into the driveway leading

to their hotel Ramage had less than one and a half miles to travel before he, too, turned off for home. There were houses and a few shops dotted over the first 500 yards. Beyond that the tarmac road was unlit, with bare, rocky ground rising on both sides to the distant skyline, and a yellow rind of moon deputising for the street lamps. Ramage slowed down as he neared the turn-off, and waved the ambulance through. As it went by a man leaned out from the passenger seat, cradled the barrel of a pistol on his left arm and opened fire. The gun was fitted with a silencer and the faint, dry cough it uttered was lost in the sound of the engine. The first round shattered Ramage's windscreen, taking him completely by surprise. As he swerved violently the gunman fired again and again. Now one of the tyres burst and the pick-up skidded out of control to overturn in a ditch bordering the road.

Splinters of glass gouged the tarmac. The wheels spun crazily in the air. Ramage's face slammed into the dashboard and for a few seconds he lay there, stunned. Blood trickled from his nose, star-shells exploded inside his skull. Then from a hundred miles away he heard the squeal of tyres, and the sound of a vehicle reversing. Frantically, his left hand explored the seat next to him for the .38, but it had disappeared among the wreckage. Ramage shouldered the nearside door open, threw himself out and started to crawl along the ditch. Suddenly he heard the ambulance stop again. He froze at once, hugging the dirt, straining to hear above the crazy pounding of his heart.

The whispers told him there were two men out there: but the whispers were in Greek, which he could not understand. Soon they ceased altogether. Cautiously, he raised his head until he could see above the side of the ditch. In the half-light he could make out the figure of one man, crouched behind the ambulance: he would be the back stop. The other terrorist was a blur on the road, advancing stealthily on the pick-up, uncertain if the Englishman inside was hurt or playing possum.

It was only a matter of time before they both realised what had happened and strolled back to pick him off as he slunk along the ditch. His one chance of escape was to run for it – now. Slowly, not daring to breathe lest the sound betrayed him, he inched his way on to the parapet and rose to his feet. For that one second he felt utterly naked. Then he turned and ran like the wind, up the incline and away from the road.

He had covered only fifteen or twenty feet before they saw him, but by then he was bent double and zig-zagging over broken ground. For a few seconds they kept up a murderous cross-fire. The only sounds came from the muted cough of the guns and the sigh of an occasional ricochet, as a bullet winged off some rock like an angry bee. Ramage's plan was to keep below the skyline as he tried to work his way back to the shops and the street lights – and the Army patrols just beyond. As if they could read his mind, the terrorists split up. One man kept after him, the other climbed back into the ambulance and drove it a quarter of a mile down the road. Then he leapt out and jogged back up the slope, to cut off Ramage's line of retreat.

The noise of the engine starting and stopping told him what was happening: it also told him he was one against one – for a while, anyhow – and he reacted immediately. Somehow he increased his pace, flogging his body to the very limits of endurance as he charged up the rise, widening the gap between himself and his lone pursuer. His legs buckled, his lungs clamoured for oxygen as he sucked breath through an open mouth and that bloody, broken nose, but his brain remained clear and calculating. He halted as soon as he found what he wanted, and melted into the shadows behind a great boulder. Quickly, he scrabbled in the dirt for a weapon and came up with a stone as big as a grapefruit, with jagged, spiteful edges. Then Ramage clenched it firmly in his massive fist, and settled back to wait for his enemy to appear.

He heard him first: the faint, tell-tale scrape of leather sandals on shale. Then he smelled him, smelled the stench of sweat and cordite that clung to his clothes like some noxious scent on that sweltering night. Finally, he saw him: when he had crept to an arm's length away. He was like an ape, a towering, deep-chested figure with arms that hung down to his knees. Hair sprouting thickly from hands and forearms shone like fur in the moonlight. He was blown by the climb: the pot belly rose and fell sharply as he stared about him in the gloaming. The Luger in his palm looked as big as a cannon.

Ramage hit him with everything he had. Had he been an inch closer, the stone must have split the terrorist's skull open. Instead it landed on the mouth, breaking his teeth and sending him reeling back. In the same second the Luger came up in a reflex action, and he fired. The bullet passed so close it ruffled Ramage's hair before it whined away into the night. The Eoka man pulled the trigger again, but the magazine had been emptied in the chase. Without hesitation he hurled the gun at his opponent's face and came barnstorming in, head down, arms flailing. As the Luger clattered away down the slope Ramage hooked him, in the throat. The terrorist choked and countered with a roundhouse swing that landed flush on Ramage's broken nose. Tears ran down his cheeks: more blows hammered down as Ramage backed away, catching him on the nose, the mouth, the jaw. He felt the boulder behind him and recovered in time to side-step a knee in the groin. And then, as his assailant stumbled off balance, Ramage grabbed hold of his shirt and heaved with all his might, dragging the Cypriot head-first into the rock. There was a sharp clicking sound, like a stick breaking. As the man dropped Ramage dived on to him, straddling his back, throttling him from behind. His big hands dug in deep and he urged them together with every ounce of strength left in his body. It was some time before he realised that the Eoka man was already dead, that his neck had been broken as he hurtled into the boulder. Even then he was reluctant to let go. He gave one last vicious squeeze, and then searched the body.

Ironically, he found one spare magazine – but no sign of the Luger. All he could do was gather more stones, drag the dead man out of the moonlight, and prepare himself for another hand-to-hand encounter. The minutes dragged by, but nothing moved on the escarpment. No trucks drove past, no patrols appeared. After an hour Ramage heard a voice calling softly, from the direction of the road. He stayed motionless behind the boulder, and waited. A little while later the voice called again, louder and more urgently and closer still: he had to be moving along the ditch. After that there was only silence. Ramage's nose was grotesquely swollen. His body ached, he was hungry and thirsty – but he was alive, and he took consolation from the knowledge that the pain and discomfort kept him awake through the longest night he had ever known.

The helicopters found him soon after dawn. They called up the infantry to recover the wrecked pick-up, the abandoned, stolen ambulance, and to search the ground. Then they landed, to airlift Ramage and the dead man back to base.

While there was no direct evidence to tie Elvides to the first assassination bid, the second bore all the hallmarks of the bomb-maker at work. It came ten days later. Ramage was back on duty with his nose in plaster but otherwise unharmed. The mail that morning included get-well letters from people in England he had never met, together with gifts of food and cigarettes which he shared with his section. One parcel he opened was heavier than the rest: it measured eight inches by six and was one inch deep. Ramage tore open the wrapping paper and saw an album below, tied round and across with string. It looked innocent enough, with a coiled spring serving as spine, threaded through the loose leaves inside.

'All right, Carter,' he said to his clerk, and handed him the cake and cigarettes. 'Share those out among the lads. We'll use the album here to keep a record of all official photographs and our Press cuttings.'

He picked up the half-opened parcel again as the orderly left, and examined it casually. There were standing orders in bomb disposal to write and thank all who wrote to them, and Ramage looked now for the sender's address on the wrapping paper. Surprisingly, there was none. The postmark was so blurred as to be illegible. Even the stamps that should have accompanied it appeared to have come off in transit. While the parcel-bomb was not new – Jewish terrorists had posted them to targets in Britain years before, during the Palestine campaign – it was enough of a rarity to deceive the unwary recipient. Ramage himself had never encountered one before, nor did he have any of the X-ray apparatus that was later to become standard Army equipment. All he had was instinct, that sixth sense essential to survival in the early days of bomb disposal. He weighed the parcel in his hand, placed it gently back on the desk and looked at it again. This time the sight of the string *inside* the wrapping paper told him what to look for and set the alarm bells ringing in his mind.

First he shouted for a sentry to stand guard so that no one could enter the office without warning. Then he bent over the parcel and sniffed at it cautiously through his taped and swollen nose. It seemed to him to give off the faintest scent of almonds, and he nodded as if in approval. He cut the wrapping paper away and bound down the cardboard covers of the album with strips of adhesive tape as tightly as an undertaker screwing down the lid of a coffin. Then he gripped its metal spine with a pair of pliers and started to draw it, very slowly, through the hinge. Each second took a year to tick by. He forgot to breathe. The temperature in the room hovered in the high nineties, sweat from his brow fell like rain on to the covers, and all the time he felt as cold as a swimmer breaking the ice on Christmas Day.

When it was free at last Ramage turned to the loose leaves and teased them out, one by one. A third of the way down he came to the first page with a cut-away centre: then another, and another. He bent down and sniffed round the discoloured edges, like a fox outside the hen coop. The smell of almonds was quite distinct now, and from the weight of the parcel he guessed the bomb to contain not less than four ounces of commercial gelignite. At arm's length, that was enough to blind and dismember the luckless recipient: and it was addressed to *him*.

Soon afterwards he found the detonator and defused the device. Then he peeled off the tape, untied the string, and opened the album. The front cover was spring-operated and connected to an anti-handling device. The act of untying the string would have sent it flying up like a Jack-in-the-Box and drawn together two bare ends of detonator wire, tied in a blood knot, to complete the circuit and explode the charge. It was deadly, simple, and expertly made. An exceedingly thoughtful Ramage carried the bits and pieces down to his commanding officer to make a report.

As well as a set of finger-prints to match those found earlier in the bomb factory, there was an inscription in Greek written on the fly-leaf: 'For Elli.' The name meant nothing to Ramage, or to the officer who translated them. The only unarguable fact to emerge was that young Lieutenant Ramage had somehow become a personal target for Paul Elvides, the most dangerous killer on the island.

One of the most baffling aspects of their duel to Ramage then was Elvides, ability to strike back so fast and so venomously after each reverse: it was like treading on a rattlesnake. It was not until much later, when Cyprus had won its independence, that he learned the answer – all the Eoka terrorists were being fed with top-secret information by members of the largely Greek Cypriot police force. Whether you thought of them then as traitors or patriots was a matter of individual choice. But at the time it made Elvides seem larger than life, invincible.

The arrival of the first parcel-bomb was given tremendous publicity, to warn the rest of the community of this new danger they faced. And predictably, it was followed almost at once by another attempt to assassinate him: this time during a combined police and army raid in the Troodos. By skilful detective work, Ramage had traced the gelignite used in a whole series of bombs to a single asbestos mine near Limassol. He led the subsequent raid, and even as suspects were being questioned and rounded up, Elvides slipped through the security cordon and planted a bomb in Ramage's truck. Only a chance, last-minute switch of vehicles saved his life, and Ramage began to feel that he was living on borrowed time.

'Why you, for God's sake?' asked his C.O.

'It beats me, sir. He's got to have me mixed up with somebody else.'

But there was no mistake. It happened again and again. By saving General Benchley's life, Ramage very nearly lost his own. The empty socket in his skull ached as he thought about it, even now.

The summons came late at night.

'There's a hell of a flap going on in H.A.T.O., Ramage. There's been a break-in. Get over there smartly and check it out for explosive devices.'

'Right, sir.'

The initials H.A.T.O. stood for head of anti-terrorist operations. The post had been awarded to a General Rupert Benchley, a man who had won his spurs against other terrorists years before in Malaya. On arrival in Cyprus he picked for his headquarters a villa on the north coast near Kyrenia, and promptly set about turning it into a fortress. A detachment of Royal Engineers bull-dozed down as many trees as were needed to make an all-round field of fire for the troops inside. They also put up an electrified fence around the grounds, and built a helipad on the roof. An armoured car stood on guard inside the main gates, while infantrymen and dogs patrolled the lawns by night. The villa had formerly been the holiday property of a Greek shipping tycoon. A handful of his servants had been retained, after long and careful vetting by the Intelligence staff: all the rest were dismissed out of hand, and replaced by British servicemen.

Ramage – who did not know about the servants – looked around him on arrival and thought the fortress impregnable. The General was waiting for him, and personally led him upstairs.

'Come and look at this, will you?' He marched ahead of the junior officer and went through his sleeping quarters into the bathroom. He pointed at the bowl of the toilet. 'There.'

Ramage looked down at the water and saw a pale grey scum floating on the surface. 'Looks like wool, sir.'

'Yes. My aide spotted it as he did his rounds tonight. Always checks my quarters before I turn in.'

Ramage waited for him to continue.

'It's not merely slovenly, it's out of character. My aide decided to ask for an explanation, and sent for the valet. He'd forgotten the valet was out: it's his night off. But he discovered some exceedingly interesting things in his room. Come and see for yourself.'

The valet's room was in the east wing. The door stood open to show a squad of military policemen hard at work, stripping and searching every cupboard and drawer systematically. A rucksack had been placed on the carpet in the centre of the room. Laid out in front of it were a pair of pliers, a bezel, strips of tin and mica, reels of tape – and a number of detonators.

'The valet is an old man' said the General. 'He's been in service all his life, and wouldn't know a detonator from a darning needle: I'll stake my reputation on that.'

'Yes, sir.' It sounded logical enough.

'My aide didn't find the ruck-sack or the bomb-making equipment, though: the M.P.s found all that. What caught his eye was that rope you see there, running from the window to the garden. And whoever used it tonight, it wasn't my valet: it was his official night off, and he booked out through the guard-room downstairs, in the normal way. All the servants do, as a safety precaution. However, we've searched the entire building and found nothing out of the ordinary, not a damned thing. That's why I've called you in.'

'Yes, sir.' Ramage gazed long and hard at the tools lying on the floor. He could think of only one man with the flair and audacity to break into a building as closely guarded as this and hide a bomb inside. 'That bezel, sir. It's the kind of tool a terrorist would use to drill through a clock-face, you know?

I most strongly advise an evacuation of the building until I've had a chance to check it through, General.'

'I'll be damned if I'll run away from my own headquarters. No!'

'As you wish, sir.' Lieutenants never argued with generals, no matter how ill-advised their decisions. 'In which case, I think I'd better start in your own sleeping quarters, if I may.'

Ramage found the bomb quickly enough, hidden in the General's bed. Fingerprints proved it had been made by Elvides: how he managed to break into the most tightly guarded building in Cyprus was never explained. It was a highly sophisticated device, wired to explode from the weight of General Benchley's head on the pillow. The main charge had been stitched into a hole cut in the mattress, and fitted so snugly it would not have been noticed as the General climbed into bed. Its presence had been betrayed by the flock, floating on the surface of the water. It seemed that Elvides must have been disturbed during the final stages of the bomb-laying, tipped off – perhaps by the valet – that the General was on his way back: and had tried to dispose of the surplus flock by the quickest means available. Without that warning, the new head of anti-terrorist operations would almost certainly have been blown to kingdom come before he had brought off a single arrest.

The story made headline news all round the world. By its sheer audacity, the attempted assassination bid made a laughing stock of British security. In an effort to save face, to salvage what they could from disaster averted, the authorities played up Ramage's role in finding – and beating – the bomb. He was decorated, for the second time in the campaign. Elvides was named the wanted man, and a price of £8,000 put on his head, dead or alive. It represented wealth beyond the dreams of Midas to the ordinary Cypriot peasant, and was second in size only to the £10,000 already on offer for the betrayal of Grivas himself. Once again there were no takers. But it made a man sweat, just the same.

Five days later, as General Benchley's first search-and-destroy anti-terrorist drive gathered momentum in the Kyrenia mountains, a police informer passed word to Eoka that Lieutenant

Ramage was bomb disposal officer on the sweep. Elvides promptly laid a culvert mine alongside one of the forestry roads snaking down the ridge, 100 pounds of gelignite wired to flares further up the escarpment, so that any vehicles caught in the ambush after dark would be silhouetted against their light and become sitting ducks for the Eoka gunmen. That was the bait. Then he set the trap. He built a hide among the cypress trees, 400 yards away across the valley, waited till late afternoon, and through the same informer tipped off the Army about the mine. By the time Ramage arrived Elvides was lying in the hide, watching the track through field-glasses. By his side was a captured Lee-Enfield .303, fitted with a telescopic sight.

The little convoy crawled up the slope, keeping to the speed of the slowest vehicle, with engines complaining like old men with bronchitis. The Ferret came round the bend first, with the Bren gun gleaming dully from its iron face. Ramage's pick-up followed. Next came his special effects truck, with the bomb disposal equipment he would need. Last of all came an open three-tonner carrying Ramage's infantry escort, guns at the ready. The Army had learned from the first attacks and now it watched over its EOD (Explosive Ordnance Disposal) men like an old mother hen fussing round day-old chicks. As the rest of the convoy rumbled to a halt the Ferret accelerated to the top of the rise and stood sentry, squinting down the barrel of the machine-gun at the valley below. The infantry escort leapt from the three-tonner, slammed one up the spout of each rifle and vanished into the pines. Ramage sited his vehicle laager under cover and went to work.

He was a recruiting-poster soldier in those days: young, tough, dashing, with two ribbons on his chest and a matchless record of successes over the Eoka rebels. He had defused so many mines between Lapithos and Bellapais he could do the bloody job with his eyes shut. He rendered this one safe in half an hour without even raising a sweat and strolled back to the funk-hole to smoke a fag with the tea waiting for him. The light was just beginning to fade when he put the mug down and moved out on to open ground to tackle the flares. The main charge was safe enough, but sometimes the bastards ran a booby from one of the flares and you had to make sure. Ramage traced the thin red wires to the base of a rock and was just climbing round to take a look when the world exploded into a fireball of dazzling colours. Brilliant reds and searing whites that were agony to behold flashed before his eyes. Then a giant top started spinning and he turned on it, whirling round faster and faster until he could hold on no longer and slid off, into oblivion.

It was weeks afterwards before he pieced together what must have happened. Elvides had been waiting for him, with the cross-hairs of his sight trained on the red wires leading under the rock. The approach of dusk worried him not at all: telescopic sights collect light like a miser hoarding pennies, and even then he would still have seen his quarry as sharply as if Ramage was pinned under a microscope. The dipping rays of the sun would have given his bare head a golden crown. All Elvides had to do was wait, with his cheek nestling against the butt of the Lee-Enfield, holding his breath as the gleaming blond head moved inexorably into the centre of the hairline cross and his own finger started to tighten slowly on the trigger.

Ramage learned the rest from the commander of his infantry escort and the evidence found by the doctors at the operating table. The nickel-plated bullet had missed his skull by an inch – at the end of a 400 yard journey – and ricocheted off the rock above his head into a second, smaller stone which it demolished. A long sliver from the rock stabbed into his face like a bayonet, gouging open the flesh from the corner of his eye down across the cheekbone, to embed itself finally below the ear. In the same moment that he turned his head and screamed, a cloud of particles from the ricochet no bigger than the points of needles struck the upper part of his face. None had enough weight or were whirling fast enough to penetrate deep, and kill him. Instead they peppered the forehead and the eyes, aiming for the tiny blood vessels and nerves clustered round the iris and the retina. Only his left eyelid closed in time. When the bandages came off, Ramage was blind in his right eye and hideously scarred.

Laura groaned in her sleep, and turned restlessly.

Ramage thought about her and the children, and took a silent vow. 'Come near us again, Elvides,' he swore, 'and I'll kill you with my own hands, you bastard.'

Part Two
ELVIDES

There was a garage ahead, built under the arches of a viaduct. Paul Elvides drove in without hesitation and left the boy whimpering in the car as he climbed out and slammed the wooden doors behind them. There were several hours of daylight still to run, and by now they must have doubled the search for him and the boy: he could hear a helicopter chuttering through the leaden sky even now. The clue they sought was the stolen police car, and he had to get rid of it as fast as possible. This seemed as good a place as any; he would decide afterwards what to do about the child. The plain truth was that he was an encumbrance, like the car, now that Elvides was free.

The doors fitted imperfectly so that enough light filtered through to allow him to look round with some care. By bricking up the far side of the arches and adding doors, the space below the viaduct had been turned into a kind of gloomy, high-ceilinged cave. Old bedsteads, rusted pots and pans, worn furniture, a fat-encrusted gas stove and a whole array of bric-à-brac filled the far side from ground to roof. Wooden shelves had been fitted to the near wall and were piled with nuts and bolts, scraps of metal, and tins of grease. Sacks of rag and cotton waste paraded below them in a dingy line, like drunken sailors back from shore leave. The whole place stank of rats, oil and jetsam. Elvides guessed the owner to be some kind of rag and bone man: there was no way of telling when he might be back. If he had scoured the streets of London, he could not have found a better place to dump the police car. The chances were that when the owner of this garage found it, he would strip it down for scrap rather than report it.

He knew himself to be somewhere in the suburbs of west London, and there were two courses open to him. He could hide up here with the car and wait until dark before setting out on foot. Or he could take his chance now among the citizens of London, relying on sheer numbers for cover. Whichever he chose he still had to make his way back into the heart of the city, to the apartment in Chelsea he had rented long ago against such an emergency. The flat where he had been cornered with the others – and so very nearly captured by the police, thanks to those fantastic sketches flashed on the television screen every few minutes – had been Gudrun's. He had been lax, there: spending nights with her after the watch on Joe Miller was over, never once realising the kind of reputation she had acquired during her eight weeks' stay in England. Once a tart, always a tart: he should have known. She had been a call-girl before she joined A.L. He had met her only twice before in Germany, and knew nothing about her background until she told him herself – in bed, the night they worked out the timetable for Miller's murder and the ransom demands. Elvides shuddered now to think how careless, how criminally careless, he had been on this operation. Wherever he went with Gudrun, tongues must have been wagging behind his back, fingers pointed at the pair of them. No wonder so many people were quick to remember Big Paul, her escort, and tell Scotland Yard where to look for them both. Christ, the police were on to them in *minutes* once those pictures appeared on the screen.

Yet it all seemed to have gone so well until today. Miller was the perfect victim, predictable, identifiable, and totally unsuspecting. The airline busybodies had been so proud of their security checks on passengers that they forgot all about employees. Because of that it had been easy to smuggle the bomb on board: and technically speaking, the device had been a little masterpiece, one of the best he had ever made. Oh, they would have paid all right, he had been almost counting the money when suddenly the radio announcer had said that Colonel Ramage – Ramage, of all people! – was a passenger on the Jumbo: and somehow, from that moment on, he had known in his heart that the operation would fail. Not because of anything he had overlooked, or done wrong, but because of the incredible luck that always followed the Englishman, like a pet dog. He felt sick with rage at the very thought of the bastard: if it took him ten years this time he would track him down and kill him, not just for the Jumbo shambles but to even the whole score. Especially for Elli. But all that would have to wait while he decided – what was he going to do *now*?

He was no stranger to pursuit and instinct told him to cut and run for it immediately, while the hunt was strung out over so many miles and the hounds were running blind in their search for the drag. Even Grivas, who loathed him – the feeling was mutual – had christened him 'The Fox' for the brilliant way he had drawn off those paratroops during the flight from Troodos and then doubled back again, to go to earth right under their noses. Time and again the net had seemed about to close in on him recently in Germany: yet he had always escaped it, always led everyone clear, simply by following his nose. The sound of the helicopter coming back, flying low to sweep down to the river, finally decided him. He would take his chances in daylight, while the rest of the city stirred so restlessly, and use the rush hour to help him sneak into the flat in Chelsea later.

As soon as his mind was made up, he took stock of the situation and tried to assess his chances. His hair was a give-away: something would have to be done about that. He examined his reflection in the wing mirror of the car and told himself he would have to find some way of hiding that hair, the tumbling mass of dark curls he had dyed and styled to match Joe Miller's. It would mean buying – or stealing – a hat, at least until he reached the apartment: then he could change its colour. His clothes were nondescript enough. He checked the gun: seven rounds in the magazine. Good, then he could be on his way. As he turned to go, he remembered the boy.

With a start, Elvides suddenly became aware that he was no longer sobbing. For one panic-stricken moment he wondered if the brat could possibly have escaped, for a weeping child on the streets would bring the police homing in like a swarm of angry bees. A glance at the heavy garage doors reassured him. He crept up to the car again and peered through the windows, to see what his hostage was up to.

The boy was asleep, that was all. He lay awkwardly across the back seat, still sprawled where Elvides had thrown him during the first few miles of the chase: arms by his sides, little fists clenched, his face hanging down over the edge of the seat. He could not be more than five years old, and he looked a sickly child. His cheeks were flushed, his breathing came fast and shallow. The terrorist had no means of knowing his mother had kept him home from school that day because he was suffering from a bout of asthma. The medicine she had given him only an hour before Elvides had dragged them both from the flat, screaming in fright, had now done its work and acted as a sedative. One sandal was missing, lost in the scuffle as he had been carried to the car. His fair hair was damp with sweat. Unfortunately he had now served his purpose, and Elvides wondered what the hell to do with him.

He had killed a great many people in his time, some of them soldiers, policemen and security guards, but mostly ordinary bystanders who by chance had placed themselves within range of his bombs. And inevitably they included children, sometimes babies only a few weeks old and still fragrant with the miracle of birth, although he did not see that necessarily as any cause for shame, or even regret. Terrorism was his business, and such things happened: all he did was to carry out orders. Whether his bombs exploded in an empty government office during the hours of darkness or in some crowded public place in daylight was all one to him: the timing was his employer's whim and privilege, and – as Elvides saw it – his responsibility entirely. This was not to say, however, that he considered himself devoid of feelings.

He had, for instance, killed many Jewish adults – and not a few children – during his years with the P.L.O. He had done so because his instructions had been quite clear, to wage a campaign of terror that would shake the morale of the whole population, from Sinai to Tiberias. Accordingly he had built bombs of every size and design, destined for cafés and restaurants, cinemas and theatres, even to be posted to private homes. His Arab bomb-layers had smuggled them into places of worship and public toilets, private bathrooms and hotel bedrooms, on to planes, coaches, and trains: and between them, they had staged an orgy of killing. Elvides looked back on that part of his life with genuine pride in achievement.

But there had been accidents sometimes, accidents that were apt to cause almost as many deaths and injuries among his friends as his enemies, and those he regretted sincerely: although, as he always consoled the mourners, a certain number of accidents were inevitable. Bombs were blind, they were unable to differentiate between white skins and brown, between grey hairs and napkins. How many times had a lorry load of Cypriot villagers or Palestinian field-hands been blown to smithereens by the very culvert mines he had sited so cleverly to ambush the heaviest tank, or armoured car? There had been accidents in his bomb factories too, as well as others when his bomb-layers had been delayed by traffic so long that they had been hoist by their own petard as they ran out of time. All such accidents he very much regretted, while never once condoning carelessness: the first lesson every apprentice had to learn was that there was no margin for error in a bomb pyramid.

Having said all that, Paul Elvides was a man who would regard the deliberate, cold-blooded murder of any child with something akin to horror – unless, that is, there was a sound reason for it. He certainly did not look upon himself as a child-killer, the blindness of his bombs notwithstanding: he personally was revolted by sex-fiends, for example, who sought and found gratification in child-murder. He knew himself to be capable, say, of kidnapping a child and killing it if his ransom demands were not met by the parents concerned but again, he would see the murder as a result of parental callousness rather than wickedness on his own part. And even then he would carry out such an execution reluctantly, and solely to demonstrate that he was a man of his word. So the present situation placed him in a dilemma. To kill this boy went against the grain. The point was, did he have any alternative?

To walk out and leave him could be asking for trouble. If he woke up too soon and called for help, his cries might bring an early rescue – and the police back on Elvides' own trail. To bind him and gag him would probably suffice, but look where you liked in the damned garage and there wasn't an inch of rope, or wire: only nuts and bolts and that stinking gas stove without a door. Also, Elvides was impatient to be on his way. It might be unfortunate, but the quickest and surest way of covering his tracks was to kill the child, to strangle him now while he slept. He would feel nothing, it would be over in a matter of seconds. He opened the door of the police car, very quietly, and reached down with hands extended.

In the same instant he heard a faint scuffling sound behind him. Without hesitation he drew his gun and fired as he swung round, in a single smooth movement. Then he walked across to the far wall and kicked away the fallen piece of sacking in disgust. He was furious with himself: while the dead rat on the floor spelled accurate snap-shooting, it also meant he had needlessly wasted one of his last seven rounds – and he would need every one he could find if the police caught up with him before he gained the sanctuary of his London flat. He made his way back to the open car door and looked in. The silencer had deadened the sound of the shooting, so that the boy slept on. And the incident had won him a reprieve. It was not that Elvides was reluctant to lay the gun down, place his hands round the puny neck, and choke the life out of it on purely humanitarian grounds. He could face the prospect of committing four hundred and fifty murders in an aeroplane with equanimity, and would not shrink from killing a single child: certainly not in the circumstances. It was simply that he had thought of a better idea. The boy might still be useful to him.

He leaned down and ripped the shirt off his back, ignoring the terrified screams. He tore the cloth into strips, and used them to bind and gag his victim securely. Then he let himself out into the street, wedged the garage doors tightly behind him to guard against casual discovery of the boy, and hurried away without a backward glance. Within the hour, he was safe inside his Chelsea apartment. He needed to get out of the country fast: soon there would be no safe hiding place. His picture was already in the evening papers, and by morning it would be published in every household in the land. In some ways, newspapers were more to be feared than television: their stories lasted longer. He unlocked a cupboard, lifted out a suitcase, and unlocked that in turn. From its false bottom he took out a manila envelope holding money and a variety of passports. There was no time anyway for an elaborate disguise, but he was a man who believed that a simple change of clothing and personality was sufficient. After momentary hesitation he decided to assume the identity of one Andreas Spiliotopoulis, retired watchmaker, born in Athens before the turn of the century, on 18 May 1899. He studied the passport photograph and printed physical description with great care: then poured dye into a wash basin and began to rinse his shock of hair until it turned ash grey. He dried it, combed it as straight as he could, and used a razor and scissors alternately until he had achieved a passable similarity to the short back-and-sides so popular in the late Mr Spiliotopoulis's day. A pair of plain-lens glasses, sober clothes and the limp of an old man fighting a losing battle with arthritis completed the transformation. He was pleased with the result shown by the mirror, and smiled his approval. Finally he took a tourist-class return ticket to Athens, issued in that country some time earlier by Olympic Airways, made sure that the forged entry in his passport was in order, and slipped it into his pocket with 2,000 dollars in cash and traveller's cheques. He made every movement slow and deliberate, already playing the role of the old watchmaker. From time to time he watched the TV screen, and monitored all the news flashes. Then he poured himself a whisky, picked up the phone and called Kurt.

'At your service,' said a voice, cautiously.

'This is a friend of Angela's,' replied Elvides, and waited. This was the code they had agreed if the bomb-plot went wrong, in case of any police trap. But there was no one with Kurt.

'Christ, I was getting worried about you! They're putting out a really good likeness every few minutes on television, have you seen it?'

'Yes. Look, I'm pulling out on the last Athens flight tonight, Kurt. I want you to pick me up here and relieve me of all my excess baggage first. Then I'll travel to Heathrow by tube: less conspicuous that way.'

'Why don't we leave together?' The constant bulletins were making him jittery. 'Don't tell me you're coming back, not after this lot?'

'I am.' Elvides emptied his glass. 'I've got some unfinished business to attend to. I want you to keep that apartment of yours paid up, store all the explosives and guns there, and keep an eye on the scene here for a day or two. Don't attempt to fly back to Bonn till the weekend at the earliest: when the heat's off.'

'Well, all right.' He sounded none too happy, though. 'Gudrun's dead, did you know that? They gave the news a few minutes ago. Apparently she died without regaining consciousness. What a *shambles*.'

'Lucky for her,' said Elvides. 'Otherwise I might have killed her myself, and not nearly so pleasantly. The stupid bitch blew the whole thing, do you realise that?'

'I guessed it. There was no other way they could have picked you all up at her flat so quickly.'

'That's right. Forget about her, Kurt. Now look, they obviously haven't found that kid yet – you know, the hostage. If they still haven't found him by the time my plane puts down in Athens, ring the police and tell them where he is. But if anything goes wrong and they grab me first, you may be able to use him to bargain with. I'll tell you where to find him when you pick me up.'

'Very good, Paul. I'll be round in a couple of hours.'

'*Wiedersehen.*'

He checked through the apartment meticulously, making sure he had left nothing behind that would give the police any clue to his assumed identity or destination. Fingerprints were another matter, of course. If you took a week to clean every room, there would still be no guarantee every print had been eliminated. He stowed the gelignite in cardboard boxes, and covered the sticks with newspaper: it was in good condition, and safe to move. As he worked he began to prepare in his mind the report he would submit to Angela when he finally arrived back in Bonn. There was bound to be one hell of a rumpus. He had been in sole charge of the London operation, it had been his idea in the beginning, and it had turned out to be a fiasco, A.L.'s first failure since its formation. The Liberation Army had nothing to show for its pains this time except four dead commandos, and two more on the run. The forces of law and order everywhere would be cock-a-hoop at that.

It would have counted as a Pyrrhic victory at least if Ramage had accidentally exploded the bomb in mid-air: that could have been written off as punishment for the airline's failure to pay up. However, he – Elvides – could not be held to blame in any way for Ramage's success in dismantling it. Ramage was acknowledged as the world's best bomb disposal expert, just as he himself was the leading bomb-maker, and there was no defeat in admitting that any bomb had been defused by a man of that calibre: not even one as sophisticated as the Jumbo bomb. Not could anyone have forseen that Ramage would be on board. It was sheer bad luck, a million to one chance. And while the operation itself had undeniably ended in defeat, the real disaster for the Liberation Army lay in the speed with which the police had been able to mount their counter-attack in London, and wipe out almost the entire commando. For that, Gudrun was the only one to blame. By behaving so stupidly she had put every one of her colleagues at risk, so that the moment his own name and description became known to the authorities, the police raid had been only a matter of time. If anyone was to share the blame with Gudrun, then it had to be Angela herself – who picked her for the assignment. But he would need to be careful how he made his point there. Not because he was afraid of Angela – the idea was laughable – but because the Russians would deal with him mercilessly if he split, or in any way weakened, the most successful terrorist organisation in Europe.

He poured himself another drink at the thought, and swallowed it greedily. He was fully aware that he was drinking more these days, not that it appeared to be affecting him in any way that he could tell. Mentally, he felt as quick and resourceful as ever. And physically? He looked at himself critically in the mirror, through the disguise that he wore. He was fifty-five years old, but beneath that old man's stoop he had affected there was not an ounce of spare fat on his frame. He held out his hands, turning them over as he examined them: hands that had built some of the most efficient bombs ever seen, and he was able to say in all honesty they were as steady now as they had been when he first learned the trade. He was as tough, and alert as he had ever been, while his technical efficiency was unquestioned.

He picked up the evening newspaper he had bought on his way from the garage, and studied it with some pride. Almost all of the front page was taken up with the Identikit drawing of himself, under the headline 'THE WORLD'S MOST WANTED MAN'. Then it said, 'Paul Elvides, the terrorist who hid the bomb on the Honeymoon Jumbo and early today escaped from the Kensington siege, was on the run somewhere in London tonight with his asthma-victim hostage, five-year-old John Pritchard – and the whole of the Metropolitan Force trying to hunt him down. Scotland Yard issued an Identikit likeness of Greek-born Elvides, a former Eoka gunman, with the following description: "aged about fifty-five, powerfully built, height five feet ten inches, swarthy complexion with thick wavy black and silver hair, possibly dyed black throughout. Last seen wearing a blue single-breasted suit, blue shirt, dark tie and black shoes." '

The paper went on to say that the huge search for the

missing boy had so far met with no success, and added, 'The Yard also issued this urgent warning to all members of the general public – "don't go near Elvides if you see him, but telephone the police and keep well away. He is armed, and exceedingly dangerous." Squads of specially trained police marksmen are standing by to answer any call which might lead to his arrest, and a spokesman confirmed that they have orders to shoot to kill if the need arises.'

The Identikit drawing was an uncomfortably good likeness: he would have to submit to the surgeon's knife and have his face rebuilt if he hoped to move about undisguised in future. The words that accompanied it were far from satisfactory: maybe he would have to teach this newspaper a lesson, one day. The word 'killer' was nothing more than a cheap journalistic jibe. Elvides knew himself to be far more than that. Killing might be his trade, but it was target killing, and called for courage and skills of the highest order. The truth was that he, Paul Elvides, was the most accomplished bomb-maker and certainly the most tactically aware the world had known since the Englishman, Guy Fawkes. As an organiser of the bomb pyramid, without which no significant terrorist campaign can ever hope to succeed, he had no equal.

The word 'killer' had a cowardly ring about it, too. That would be deliberate, of course, both on the part of the police who inspired it and the newspaper hacks who so faithfully printed it. In fact it was so far removed from the truth as to be laughable. He had demonstrated his courage far too often for anyone to label him coward: even that stuffy little shit Grivas had praised him for his bravery on more than one occasion, and it was not something he did lightly. Elvides poured himself another drink, a bigger one this time. How these British stuck in his craw, the army, the police, the politicians, the people, the newspapers, the climate, *Ramage* – agh, the whole poisonous shooting match! The joke was, he could give those journalists a story and a half, if he was so minded. No, not a story, much more than that: a saga, an *epic* story of hardship and courage and dedicated unflinching loyalty to the communist cause.

He had first come under Russian influence and training at an impressionable age, it was true, but it was he who had embraced the communist creed, not they who had indoctrinated him. He was tailor-made for revolution from the day he was spawned. His childhood in Salonika had been wholly without physical comfort, adequate food, or love of any kind. As a bastard, a foundling with no known parents, he had been shunted from one institution to the next until he was finally sent out in the world to earn his keep: from the age of ten, as gardener's assistant cum-slave cum-errand boy, on a millionaire tobacco importer's estate. It was there that the true gulf between rich and poor was forever engrained in his mind – the petty cruelties and humiliations and indignities were too numerous to dwell on. At fourteen, he was an expert thief. On the day 'Paul Elvides' was seventeen – the name was given to him by the Salonika authorities, after the street sweeper who first found him, wrapped in a newspaper – he was sentenced to four years' hard labour for assault in the course of house-breaking. Not for him were the glories of Greece in the early days of World War Two, when her soldiers whipped the Italians and the Albanians, only to be overwhelmed later by vastly superior German forces: he spent the whole time in a prison cell. He escaped from jail on the same night that the first German tanks rumbled into the city, and on the advice of more hardened criminals who broke out with him, volunteered for service in the German Labour Corps that was quickly recruited for work in the Fatherland. 'At least,' said the old lags, 'this way you get fed, and clothed. And the Germans have as good as won, anyway.'

Paul Elvides actually lived and ate better during the early forties than he had ever done in his life before. Work in the Todt Organisation took him first to the Ruhr, where he was employed as a surface worker in the mines, and later to Silesia, where he worked underground. It was there that he saw out the war, and there that he was captured by the advancing Russian armies in the snows of January 1945. But he and his friends had made their plans long before the Russians arrived to ensure their survival. They joined up with some Polish guerrillas in the autumn of 1944, and fought a number of skirmishes against the retreating German forces until they in turn were rounded up by the Russians.

Elvides' interrogation by an officer on Zhukov's staff not only saved his life – most of his Polish friends were shot – but it also resulted in his selection for special training back in Russia. That was because he was a Greek, and a bid by the Greek communists to seize power had already begun in Athens. That it was premature and doomed to failure under British pressure, was of no consequence to the Russians. Here was an opportunity to recruit, subvert, and employ at some more favourable moment in the future a Greek who was already fighting on the right side, albeit for purely selfish motives. Proper indoctrination would take care of all such minor blemishes in the man's makeup.

'Your name?' asked the Russian Colonel.

'Paul Elvides.'

'Say "sir" when you address me, pig's bladder. Age?'

'Twenty-two, sir.'

'Nationality?'

'Greek, sir. I was born in Salonika.'

'Ah. Another of the foreign scum working for the Nazis throughout the war.' To admit working voluntarily for the Germans was to ask for a place in line before the firing squad, and Elvides trembled in his shoes.

'No, sir.'

'How else does a Greek find himself on the Oder? Where were you working before you joined the partisans, Elvides: in the mines?'

'Yes, sir. But I was *forced* labour. They arrested me as soon as they entered Salonika and drafted me into the Labour Corps, excellency. It was work or be shot: we had no choice.'

'Why weren't you in the Greek Army at the time?'

'Ill health, sir. Tuberculosis. They wouldn't have me, even though I volunteered. It's all in my papers, sir.'

'We'll check it out. And you'd better not be lying.'

Salonika was a million miles away and just emerging from five years of German occupation. It was also in the grip of a bloody civil war. If the Russians could check prison records back to 1940, then they were a lot cleverer than they looked. Elvides was entirely happy to take that chance. He stood to attention and faced the Colonel boldly.

'I'm not lying, sir.'

'How long were you with the partisans, and what role did you play?'

'For the past five months I have been making booby-traps

to kill the Germans, sir,' said Elvides. The Russians would be able to check this out, and he needed to be very careful. 'I knew how to handle detonators from the mines, sir – and where they were kept. The partisans showed me how to build bombs, and then put me to work with the unit here.'

The Colonel thought about that. 'All right, Elvides. From this moment on you are forbidden to carry arms or explosives, under penalty of death. You will work as a labourer for us, clearing up the rubbish your German masters have left behind them – until we decide what to do with you. Dismiss.'

'Yes, sir.' Elvides hesitated to ask anything of him: the man was an ogre. 'Permission to make a request, please, sir?'

'Well?'

'You said you have ways of checking things in Salonika, sir. When you do, you'll find that my father was one of the leaders of the Communist Party there.' In for a penny, he thought: Elvides was a common enough name, there was bound to be at least one Party member among them. 'That's why he was shot, sir. And my mother too, so I heard. I never had the chance to find out about her for sure, and I didn't dare to own up who I was or they'd have shot me too. But that's why I joined the partisans here, to get revenge, sir.'

The Russian Colonel watched him carefully, but said nothing. He spoke no Greek. The whole of his interrogation was conducted in German which Elvides spoke inadequately, and he had to wait for the boy to show his hand.

'If there's any way of getting back to my own country, sir: perhaps to take up where my dear father left off – '

'Do you think I can't see through you, boy? You're afraid we shall shoot you if you stay here – for helping the Nazi war effort. And believe me, if my inquiries show that you have, that's precisely what will happen. Next.'

Colonel Kobolov had no time for Poles, partisans included: anyone who had remained alive outside a concentration camp by whatever means during the German occupation was of necessity politically suspect. However, all those he questioned gave Elvides a clean bill of health. He had killed enough of the enemy, they could vouch for that. And yes, he had spoken many times of his father as a leading communist in Salonika. *Mmmm,* thought Kobolov: I wonder. On the bottom of the interrogation form he wrote 'Has been working for the Germans in the Ruhr and Silesia since 1941. Five months with the partisans, good combat record. Claims he was forced labour (possibly correct) and that his father was a senior member of the Salonika C.P. Any use to Intelligence?'

It took months for the report to be studied and evaluated in Moscow, while the war moved to a climax. But eventually it dropped on the desk of a KGB man named Ivan Aleksandrovich Gruchev, deputy to the Chief of Department for Diversion and Terror (Balkans). His task at the time was to co-ordinate with the Political Wing, and together salvage what they could from the aftermath of the lost civil war in Greece. The politicos were instructed to send in as many agents as they could recruit, men and women prepared if necessary to spend years spreading the gospel of communism in the schools and universities, factories and dockyards, and especially among the Armed Forces. Gruchev's orders were simple, to keep the flames of civil war bitterness burning through strikes, intimidation and acts of industrial sabotage. Clearly, he could find work for an apprentice such as Paul Elvides.

No desk-bound Russian had any way of knowing for certain how much of his story under interrogation was truth or lies: Gruchev read the file closely, and suspected a sprinkling of both. However, he was enough of a realist to accept that there was only one way to find out: he therefore signed an order committing Paul Elvides to a special camp at Sverdlovsk for a 'rehabilitation course' of one year, to be followed by a period of training – unspecified – at the Departmental School of Guerrilla Warfare (Weaponry and Explosives Section) near Chkalov, in the Urals. The length of his stay there would be governed by two factors, the man's ability and the political situation prevailing in Greece at the time.

Elvides arrived in Russia as a cynic, ready to take whatever was handed out and thankful only that he had deceived one more tyrant. He would do whatever was asked of him, bide his time until he arrived back in his native Greece – and then promptly disappear. In the event, the two years he spent at Sverdlovsk and Chkalov had a profound effect upon him, one which influenced his whole way of life thereafter. He discovered among his young associates a patriotic fervour he had never experienced elsewhere: not even among the Poles, whose fighting Resistance sometimes seemed to him to stem from hatred of everything German as much as any feeling of patriotism. The Russians were markedly different. Their loathing of the Germans was every bit as fanatical, yet in their case it was transcended by a passionate love of country – and communism. Their burning Red faith seemed to be in the very air they breathed. Without exception they revered communism, gorged themselves on its teachings via the State-run newspapers and the State-run radio, and volunteered in endless queues to lay down their lives in its service. No one as young and unloved and rootless as Paul Elvides could fail to be impressed by such devotion. Communism was both mother and father to these people, almost literally since most had lost their families during the war years: and this more than anything helped to convert him from cynic to doubter, and from doubter to believer.

For the first time in his life he was encountering a society which wanted him, body and soul: one which was eager, greedy even, to relieve him of all personal responsibility and feelings of guilt. The Russian way of life was a crusade, a star to follow – and not just an idea to talk about but a reality, embodied in a strong and seemingly incorruptible central government which was happy to feed him, house him, pay him, clothe him, educate him, think for him, speak for him, to watch over every moment of his personal life while training him for a professional one, to select his friends with the same care as it hand-picked his tutors, to teach him all the beliefs it was necessary for a man to possess and yet, at the same time, to strip and unclutter his mind of all piddling non-essentials, such as individual thought and taste. And on top of all that, it offered Paul Elvides the most glittering prize that could ever be held out to a foundling: the promise of love, in a world of equality.

It was small wonder that he swallowed the bait of communism hook, line and sinker. From the day he left Chkalov he was obsessed with the desire to repay communism one hundred fold for all the blessings it had bestowed upon him. He was to find soon enough that there was no lack of opportunity ahead.

In 1949, the Department of Diversion and Terror dropped him in Thrace with discretionary orders to exacerbate tension between Greece and Turkey by acts of sabotage, de-railment and low-key assassination of frontier guards, police and Customs. He shone in the role and by 1952 had organised a network of contacts stretching from Alexandropoulis across country to Salonika, his home town, where no one recognised or remembered him but there were many sympathetic to the Cause. His men kept ancient hatreds simmering away where it would cause most damage, on the southernmost flank of the NATO alliance. At the same time, Elvides began to build himself something of a reputation as a bomb-maker, with his flair for creating small but sophisticated booby-traps. Very soon a number of minor officials began to exhibit reluctance to stand for office against communist opponents, and even fellow-travellers, in the areas where Elvides was operating. But it was no mindless campaign: he picked his targets with care, aiming at the corrupt and the bully as often as the dedicated Rightist, so that he won as much support from the uncommitted poor as he did from the more politically motivated.

And if that was no more than fruit from the seeds planted in Chkalov, it was still intelligent application: and his good work won notice back in Moscow. In particular, the considerable effect of one man's skilful use of the bomb as a weapon of political intimidation set in motion a whole new chain of thought in the Department of Diversion and Terror, where it was quickly appreciated that a single specialist like Elvides could promote as much discord as a whole band of guerrillas in former days – and thereby win publicity in the outside world even for the smallest and most unrepresentative minority. On Gruchev's instructions, Elvides was promoted, and given wider fields to conquer.

He was flown to Cairo after the coup that toppled Farouk to make contact with the Arabs. From Cairo he flew to Damascus, and from Damascus to Baghdad: all three seething with poverty and discontent. In each case the Russians worked to a pattern. First they stoked the fires of nationalism with propaganda beamed from Moscow. Then their diplomats on the spot sent paid agitators into the streets, to rouse the mobs. Last of all came the men like Elvides, to show them how to make bombs and lead the way into open rebellion. Yet with it all, the Western intelligence agencies would have been hard put to name Elvides as a Russian agent.

His funds came from local sources wherever he operated:

from the proceeds of bank robberies and kidnapping, or from the smuggling of drugs, and gold. The services he sold were practical, never political. He acted as instructor in the making of bombs, or as adviser on the organisation of the all important supply pyramid. Local figures led the insurrection: Paul Elvides merely rendered assistance. It was true that the general and continuing theme of his activities was anti-western. But the fact that they were anti-British in particular was seen by the more naive as no more than an accident of timing, since all occurred in an era of general British decline: an undeniable fact, but one which automatically made her possessions overseas targets for trouble in the changing, anti-colonialist post-war world. The trail that led back to Moscow was further obscured by a second undeniable fact, namely that Paul Elvides seemed equally happy to serve whoever footed the bill, on the Left or the Right. Cyprus appeared to be a perfect example of the man's political impartiality. No one could ever pretend that the Eoka rebellion was communist-inspired. It was a naked bid by firebrand Greek-Cypriots to impose union with their motherland on the whole community. Grivas himself was a noted anti-communist. Therefore it seemed that Elvides was what he claimed to be, a mercenary.

Constant secret lobbying went on behind the scenes in Athens while plans for the forthcoming insurrection in Cyprus were hatched. Arms and cash were desperately needed, as well as political support. At one meeting, offers were made to supply key men with experience of guerrilla warfare for service on the island if needed: and the name of Paul Elvides, bomb-maker and technical adviser, was accepted without question.

As far as Eoka was concerned, he was a soldier of fortune who had learned his trade in the war years, fighting underground against the Germans. Not even Grivas suspected him: he disliked him, but could not argue the value of his contribution to the struggle. Elvides flew into Nicosia in the summer of 1955 under the name of Parides, a Greek citizen and mining engineer from Salonika. The firm he claimed to represent – a Greek mining company, backed by American capital – had been persuaded to issue him with papers following discreet political pressure from Athens. They were genuinely considering possible investment in the Cyprus copper industry, and since anything that would reduce unemployment was seen as a first step to combating terrorism, mining engineer Parides was welcomed with open arms by the authorities. He was granted permission to carry out surveys in any part of the island considered necessary to prepare his report, and to stay indefinitely. His work permit was made out by the civilian authority. Details were lodged with the security forces as soon as the State of Emergency was proclaimed, and he was given a military escort – if requested – for survey work in dangerous areas. It was the perfect cover story.

In the same way that his two years in Russia changed him from displaced person and petty criminal into ardent communist and trained saboteur, so the years spent in Cyprus made a profound impression on Elvides too. He was a Greek, and no Greek could fail to absorb some of the passion and fury unleashed on the island by the bloody Eoka insurrection and harsh British counter-measures. His supply pyramid was soon under pressure, with one of his key men hanged.

A bleak little smile defrosted his face for a moment at the memory of Leonidas. A key man in the bomb pyramid certainly – he was the one who organised the first supplies of gelignite – but only a boy in reality: eighteen years and one day old for Christ's sake, when they hanged him! The story from Camp K was that the British had offered to trade him his life in return for information, but Leonidas simply spat into his interrogator's face. Elvides could picture him going to the scaffold, head held high to pretend he wasn't afraid, and swinging his game leg quickly in the hope that no one would notice the polio limp, and start to feel sorry for him.

He was one of the first Eoka men Elvides met. Leonidas was recommended for service in the bomb pyramid because the guerrillas rightly considered him physically unfit to fight in the mountains, and they sent him to Nicosia with a view to setting up the gelignite pipeline. It was a scorching hot morning, and Ledra Street shimmered in the sun. The rendezvous was outside the Ottoman Bank at noon, so that they could mingle unnoticed with the clerks as they left for lunch and siesta. Leonidas was twenty minutes late and Elvides hung about in that street of all streets – Murder Mile, as it became to be known – feeling as conspicuous as a fox loitering in full view of the hunt. Somehow he was expecting a grown man to arrive, and was hard put not to laugh when he eventually caught sight of Leonidas hurrying up to greet him. He was small and pathetically thin: drops of sweat sparkled in the hollows of his neck and soaked his shirt as he weaved and twisted on the tell-tale leg. 'You're Paul Elvides?' he asked politely, and held out his hand.

'The name is *Parides,*' hissed the bomb-maker. It was the kind of gaffe that could cost a man his life. 'Forget it one more time and I'll cut your fool tongue out, you hear me, boy?'

'I'm sorry.' Leonidas bit his lip and stared down at his sandals in shame. He looked as if he was ready to burst into tears.

Elvides surveyed this adolescent purveyor of explosives with feelings that were close to despair. And this is what I've got to work with, he thought: a real, live, Eoka guerrilla. Aloud, he said 'What kept you?'

'Soldiers.' Leonidas had walked eighteen miles to the rendezvous that morning, leaving home at first light. When he was 400 yards from his destination he had been grabbed by the hair, slammed against a wall and left to stand for an hour in the sun with his legs spread wide and his arms reaching up – agony for a cripple – to await body search, and questioning. But he was an Eoka recruit, and refused to complain. 'They've set up road blocks all round the old city. I think they're planning something.'

'In that case, let's keep on the move while we talk.' They strolled down the street as far as the camera shop and used the window to keep watch on the roadway behind. 'Nicos says you can supply me with commercial gelignite. Is that right?'

'All you want. With deliveries every Saturday, as soon as we get back from Amiandos.' Leonidas and his uncle delivered coffee and tobacco, sugar and spices, flour and raisins to the village on Thursdays, and stayed overnight with relatives. Amiandos was the home of the asbestos mines. And the miners, who idolised Grivas, smuggled out gelignite in a never-ending stream for the freedom forces, via their empty lunch-baskets.

'It's all set up? You can guarantee it?'

'I swear it on the grave of my mother.'

'Right. This way.'

The old city was like an enormous rabbit warren, with its network of teeming narrow streets and alleys all twisting and inter-linking inside the fortress wall. No refuse had been collected for days because of the troubles, and the reek of garbage fouled the air. It was siesta time, with the streets deserted and every window shuttered against the brutal sun. The flies in the meat market were so numerous they settled on the walls of the slaughterhouse like a living green coat, gorged on stinking scraps and as sleepy now as the humans of Nicosia. Elvides led the way down to the Mason-Dixon Line, the name given by the British troops to the rusting coils of dannert wire thrown up to keep Greek from Turk inside the warring capital. In the absence of any Army patrols he fairly raced along, with Leonidas limping after him in uncomplaining silence. The man Nicos had detailed to escort them on the final stage of their journey was waiting in the rubble of a burned-out house, as watchful and still as a scarecrow. He recognised Leonidas, and smiled a greeting. Then he moved off, keeping twenty yards ahead of the newcomers, doubling back towards the fortress wall.

This wall that rings old Nicosia, with the entry gates still standing, was built by the Venetians in the fifteenth century. Each one was positioned to correspond approximately with the geographical siting of the main towns on the island, the Kyrenia Gate, Famagusta Gate, and so on. The guerrillas had chosen an old house near the Paphos Gate for the bomb factory. It was ideal strategically, built on the rise and fronted by a long wooden balcony from which watch could be kept on the alley below. The alley provided the only way in for foot patrols and police jeeps, while there were a variety of escape routes for the occupants in an emergency – over the rooftops or out through a tunnel burrowed under the wall into the street behind.

'That's it' said their guide. 'They're expecting you.' He put his thumb and little finger into his mouth, whistled once into the drowsiness of the afternoon, and walked quickly away.

It looked innocent enough, dozing away with the paintwork flaking from its wooden façade like sunburned skin. The stairs were so hot they burned Elvides through the soles of his shoes as he climbed the stairs to the balcony. Floorboards creaked in protest as they walked along it. All at once, a door opened inwards and a hand beckoned. They stepped inside and were lost to sight in an instant. In contrast to the brilliant sunlight, it was so dark that several seconds passed before their eyes could adjust sufficiently to make out the faces of their reception committee.

A sentry stood guard inside the door, with a British Army Lee-Enfield slung from his shoulder. Next to him was Nicos. Already Nicos had won international fame as an assassin, as head of the city's most feared execution squad. Thus far he had personally accounted for six Britons, five servicemen and an unarmed civil servant, plus a Turkish Cypriot policeman by shooting them all in the back at point blank range as they passed through the old city. He was nineteen years old, not much older than Leonidas. But where Leonidas limped, Nicos swaggered: he was big time, a national hero who had made front-page headlines in Athens and London and New York. Now he bounced across the room, reaching out with both hands to greet Elvides, gushing with self-importance. 'My dear friend!' he exclaimed, and went to hug him. 'You're late, we were beginning to get worried about you.'

Elvides avoided his embrace and looked beyond him. In the corner of the room was a woman. She smiled as Elvides stared at her, and in the shadows the whiteness of her teeth seemed startling, unreal. He guessed her to be in her middle thirties, certainly older than himself and perhaps twice as old as these two Eoka boys. She was tall for a woman and slender, with dark hair scissored close to her head. Elvides disliked it: he thought it gave her a curious, school-marmish look. Her face was oval, and deeply tanned. There was a Sten gun on the table beside her. 'Hi there,' she said. The accent was unmistakably American.

'You're from the States?' asked Elvides, and was immediately furious with himself for asking such a naive question in front of the others.

'I'm Greek,' she corrected him. 'My father sent me to America for the war years, and I stayed on.'

'Elli's a doctor,' explained Nicos, 'with a practice here in the old city. That means a curfew pass from the security services, which is very convenient for all of us. She's here today because from now on she's going to work for you – on the orders of Dighenis. With that curfew pass, he considers she will be of most use to the bomb pyramid.'

'That's fine with me,' said Elvides. He saw nothing strange in women terrorists: one recruit in three at Chkalov had been a woman. Handling explosives stimulated the sexual appetite, too, he remembered fondly. 'It's nice to know you, Elli.'

Nicos swung round on Leonidas. 'When can we expect the first consignment?' he asked. He spoke brusquely, Elvides noticed: very much the seasoned commander to the rookie.

'Next Saturday, Nicos.' Leonidas stood to attention as he answered.

'Good. You wait here, then. I'll talk to you later, and tell you where my men will meet you to escort you in. You never come here alone, remember that.' He extended a hand of invitation to Elvides. 'Please. This way. I've got a surprise for you.'

Elvides followed him down a flight of stairs into the kitchen. There was an ancient stove in one corner. A hand pump and buckets provided water for all needs, toilets included. The stench was ripe. Nicos pulled back the pine table, took up the rug and pointed to a trap door. 'After me.' He was grinning with unconcealed pride.

The ladder led down into a cellar that measured twenty feet in length by twelve wide. The stone walls had been painted white, and willing Eoka hands had transformed it into a modern, brightly-lit workshop. A heavy bench, fitted with a vice, stood against one wall. On either side were shelves lined with a magnificent selection of tools – all stolen from British army camps – detonators, coils of wire, insulating tape, detonator cord, batteries, an assortment of watches 'commandeered' from jewellers' shops throughout the island, an ammeter and all the paraphernalia of the modern Guy Fawkes.

'This will be your bomb factory,' said Nicos. He was bursting with pride. 'I furnished it myself.'

'It's magnificent,' Elvides told him. He looked at the boy killer with very different eyes: this was a strictly professional job of work. 'I congratulate you. Really.' They shook hands warmly.

'I haven't finished yet,' said Nicos. He walked across the cellar and unlocked a cupboard. The wooden shelves were built into the rock and lined with books, some of them mossy with age. He took one from the bottom shelf, pressed against the wall with the flat of his hand and a stone block swung noiselessly open. 'In case of a surprise visit from the British,' he said, and shone a torch into the tunnel. The walls were just wide enough to take a man's shoulders. 'It goes a hell of a way down, into the old Jew's house in the next street. Go on, take a look.'

Elvides lowered himself in feet first. It was like sliding down a long, curving chimney. By the time he reached the bottom he was in total darkness. 'How do I get out?' he called. His voice was faint, as if it came from the bottom of a deep well.

Nicos leaned over. 'You'll find a groove in the corner on your right' he shouted. 'Push down hard with your heel. You'll have to come back through the street, though: the stone closes behind you as soon as you crawl out.'

'Right.' Elvides backed out on his hands and knees into a small and poorly furnished room. Enough light came through the curtains to show him an old man curled up in an armchair. He was Jakob the watchmaker, guardian of the Eoka escape route. It was impossible to tell if he was feigning sleep or genuinely unaware of the intrusion. Elvides took a good look at the wrinkled face, but left him undisturbed. The stone had already swung to, as silently as it had opened. He opened the street door and stepped out into the alley behind the bomb factory.

'Don't tell me you built the tunnel, too,' he said to Nicos when he got back to the house. 'Not in the few weeks I've been on the island.'

'No, that comes by courtesy of the ancient Venetians,' Nicos told him. 'Same people who built the city wall: we think they must have had security problems in their day, too.' It was the standard Eoka joke for everyone who inspected the tunnel for the first time, but there was no sign of laughter in his boyish face or dark, glittering eyes. 'My father planned to use that tunnel, once,' he said. 'Against the Germans, if ever they landed in Cyprus during the war.' He spat on the floor. 'The grateful British threw him in jail a month ago: he's an enemy now.'

They sat round the table in the room behind the balcony and drank ouzo with their sweet Turkish coffee. Leonidas took a cigarette out of his pocket but before he would light it, Nicos knocked it out of his hand. 'This house is more than 500 years old,' he said coldly, 'and dry as tinder from standing so long in the sun. I don't think you'd want to be anywhere inside our bomb factory if a fire broke out, my friend. Elvides here wouldn't even get out of the tunnel in one piece. For God's sake, man – think.' As Leonidas stammered his apologies, Nicos looked at his watch and stood up, silencing him. Now that siesta time was over the leader of Nicosia's dreaded street execution squad was due back at work – as a clerk in a council office. None of them saw any contradiction in that.

Nicos raised his glass in a final toast. 'To our brave leader, Dighenis.'

'Dighenis.' Elli said it as if it was a prayer. Leonidas joined her. Elvides emptied his glass and said nothing. Leonidas smiled at him uncertainly, bowed to Elli and limped out after Nicos. The bomb-maker and the doctor had to stay, until the sentry gave the all-clear. They drank more ouzo and sat in silence, immersed in their thoughts.

The sunshine dazzled them when they eventually stepped down into the street again. All the soldiers had gone now. Two policemen stood inside the Gate, lazily waving all traffic through: they were Greek Cypriots and wanted no trouble with Eoka. One of them saluted Elli as she walked by. 'Gracious lady,' he said, and smiled.

A few hundred yards further on she led the way into a narrow side street. 'This is where I live,' she said, and pointed to the house on the corner. 'You can come in if you want. There's no law against entertaining one's friends in Cyprus – yet.'

The house was a wooden shell leaning against the city wall. Half of the downstairs front had been a forge from the days of the first Turkish invasion, back in the sixteenth century: now it housed Elli's ramshackle Ford. The other half served as her consulting room-cum-dispensary. A naked bulb hung over the front door, above a board saying 'Doctor Elli Marvin, M.D. Hours, 8.30 a.m. to 10.30 a.m. Evenings, 5 p.m. to 6.30 p.m. No Saturdays or Sundays, except for wounded and emergencies.' A line had been drawn through the evening surgery hours and a typewritten card pinned on, which read 'IMPORTANT. Evening surgery must close ONE HOUR before curfew, by order of the Authorities.' Her living quarters were spread over the two floors above: they were tastefully furnished, gracious and cool. She led Elvides to the first floor, and a verandah overlooking the city. The narrow street leading down to the Paphos Gate gleamed like a bar of gold in the dying sun.

Elli put a plate of olives and a bottle of wine from the Troodos on the table, and told him about herself.

'Marvin's my married name,' she said. 'My American name. My father was Professor Vassilis, the Athens eye specialist, you know?' Elvides nodded his head to pretend he had heard of him. 'He knew the war was coming and sent Mother and me to America, in the summer of '39. I was ten years old at the time.' She sipped her wine thoughtfully. 'We never heard from him again after the German occupation. Mother was given leave to presume him dead in 1949, and married the American she had been living with all through the war, in Los Angeles. I'm afraid I didn't approve and said so: a silly, sentimental little girl who cherished a picture all through the war years of her brave father fighting the Germans. You fought the Germans, you can imagine how I felt. Maybe that was why I got married myself soon afterwards, I don't know.'

She frowned a little, and stared down into her wine.

'I was a medical student then, in my second year. Mel Marvin was sitting for his finals and was as lonely as I was: some weird family problem, I don't even recall what it was any more. Anyway, we got married the same week he was posted to Korea as a doctor in the Marines. He was killed in 1951, the year I qualified.' She looked steadily at Elvides. 'I don't mourn him, I don't even think a lot about him now. He was a nice enough boy, I guess, but we didn't know each other, not really. We were married for five whole days and then he went off for ever, you know? When they told me he was dead I suddenly realised I didn't want to stay in America one day longer. I wanted to go *home*. To Athens. Then three years ago I arrived here on a holiday.'

She refilled their glasses, and smiled. 'I think I'm getting just a little bit drunk. All that ouzo, I'm not used to it. So please forgive me if I talk your head off.'

'Please. Sometimes it does you good to talk.'

'Well, you're a Greek, you've come here to fight for us: you must know how I felt when I first came here. The minute I saw the people of Cyprus I knew what I had to do. There was so much poverty, so much ignorance, such a yearning for freedom. I decided to stay and I set up practice in this house, helping them in the only way I knew how, by healing the sick. I made a lot of friends in the process, and through them I discovered the true way to help Cyprus, by working for union with the Motherland; Enosis. I took the oath on the day that the armed struggle began, on the First of April – to fight for freedom, even if it cost me my own life, to obey our Leader's orders without question, and never to give up the struggle until Cyprus was liberated. Before you arrived my role was confined to helping the wounded, but I want to fight – like a man. Thanks to our beloved Dighenis, I've been given that chance at last. By working with *you*.'

She leaned over the table and kissed his hands.

'I will go where you tell me, do whatever you order me to do. I will even help you make the bombs, if you will show me how. Anything you ask.'

They were both a little drunk now. 'Come here,' he said and stood up, holding out his hands. She came obediently, smiling at him, lifting her mouth to his, crushing her body against him. Her arms slid round his neck as they kissed, and her legs began to tremble as his tongue sought hers. With a start she realised they were still on the balcony, in full view of anyone who looked up from the street.

'Not here,' she said, urgently. 'Inside.'

She stumbled as she backed into the room and slipped on to the floor. The hem of her dress flared back to expose her smooth brown legs. Elli made no attempt to cover them and sat there, hands on the floor behind her, smiling an invitation with her mouth and eyes. Elvides knelt down without a word, and parted her legs with his knees. He fumbled with his belt and tugged away his clothing as she unbuttoned her blouse. His mouth closed over hers as he took her, on the floor. She groaned and whimpered with the exquisite shock of flesh entering flesh, and rose to meet him. It was all over for both of them, quickly, far too quickly. Elli arched her back and screamed softly, shuddering as she reached the climax under the fierce, hungry thrusts of his muscular body. He held her thighs in his hard hands and gripped her tight, lifting her against him, grinning exultantly in the sheer lustful joy of release. The minutes stole by, and neither of them moved. Suddenly they heard the soft ringing of a bell: it was time to open the surgery. 'That was beautiful,' she said, and ran her hands through the shining black waves of his hair, kissing him again and again. 'I knew it would happen. The moment I saw you this afternoon.'

She went into the bathroom and washed quickly. Elvides dressed, stretching like a huge, sleek cat. She reminded him of the German *fraus* in Silesia who had queued up for his services, desperate for a man after so many months and years alone. Although on second thoughts it was not really like that, not with Elli. This one hero-worshipped him, she gave herself to him because she saw him like a knight in shining armour come to slay the British dragon: a saviour, a deliverer from evil. He smiled at the thought. At that second she came in through the door. He looked up and to his astonishment saw that she was crying.

'Don't worry' she said, and stroked his face. 'These are tears of joy.'

Leonidas arrived with the first delivery of explosives that weekend, and the bomb factory went into production immediately. In the first seven days, there were three attacks on targets inside Nicosia. Over the next three weeks, a total of twenty-seven explosions throughout the island. Elvides was careful to return to his hotel most nights, well before curfew: his practice was to move into the old city during the morning, always entering by a different gate, and to work in the bomb factory until the afternoon, when the whole city dozed off, drugged by the sun. The siesta hours he spent with Elli, talking, planning, making love. In the hour before curfew he met the bomb-layers and their drivers, and briefed them carefully on how and where and when to drop their deadly cargoes. Elli sometimes served as a driver, especially if the journey was a long one: even driver and bomb-layer together. A number of young British officers knew her well, and competition was keen to escort the beautiful, unattached American doctor to a dinner and dance whenever she was free, in one of the 'safe' hotels or restaurants. She went with Eoka's blessing, and rarely came back without some snippet of military information that was passed at once to Intelligence. She took enormous risks. One night she drove to the Ledra Palace with a time-bomb in the boot of her Ford. While she and her British Army escort sipped their brandy sours, Nicos and his guerrillas collected the bomb, stole through the streets with it like ghosts and placed it gently against the wall of the city's divisional police headquarters. It exploded fifteen minutes before Elli left for home, causing huge damage – and presenting her with the perfect alibi, if one were ever needed.

At the end of the first month she and Elvides and Nicos met to celebrate their unbroken run of success that all began with the bomb factory. And what a month. Four police stations damaged. A number of army lorries wrecked by mines. Two convoys ambushed, after their route had been blocked by electronically detonated charges. Defences breached at Nicosia airport, with one RAF plane destroyed and another seriously damaged, by incendiaries. Eoka men had set off bombs and mines from one end of the island to another, to leave a trail of havoc and terror behind them. By no means all the casualties were British, but the conspirators found consolation in the thought that at least some of the maimed Cypriots had been on the British pay-roll, as servants or municipal workers. Newspapers throughout the west gave the Eoka campaign major coverage and General Grivas issued a jubilant Order of the Day to his peasant army. 'You have struck a great blow for freedom. The justice of our cause is a talking point wherever men are free, and the final victory is assured. Eoka, the Leader: Dighenis.'

The three of them celebrated with dinner at Elli's house. Candles flickered on the table, wild orchids from the Karpas panhandle lit the room with brighter colours. She served mullet poached in wine, and moussaka rich with the smell of spices and aubergines and dressed overall in white bechamel sauce, with dips of homus on the side and plates of olives, tomatoes, cucumber, onions, lettuces and cheese. They drank a fine, dry Paphos wine and ended with toasts in Keo brandy.

'Dighenis,' said Nicos, loudly.

'Dighenis!'

'To Nicos and his gallant men,' said Elvides: but not entirely tongue-in-cheek.

'Nicos!'

'Paul Elvides.' Nicos was very flushed and unsteady on his feet. 'Paul Elvides, hammer of the British.'

'To Paul,' echoed Elli, loyally.

As he looked back now – more than twenty years later – Elvides could smile at their youth and foolishness then. But something strange undoubtedly happened to him that night, some rare alchemy of moonlight and wine and the scent of jasmine bewitched him so completely that he asked Elli to marry him as soon as they were alone together. He could recall every word of their conversation in that hot, shadow-filled room below the Paphos Gate. He felt strangely tongue-tied and clumsy: love was a word which had not appeared in his vocabulary since the day he was born.

'Elli.'

'Yes, darling.' She was drowsy, completely spent.

'The message from Grivas tonight. About final victory being assured. Do you go along with that?'

'M'mmm. Of course.'

'Then how long do *you* think it might be – before the British give in, I mean?'

'Oh Paul. I don't know, six months, a year, who can tell these things? Go to sleep, darling.'

'Elli. Listen to me.' He sat up in bed and lit a cigarette. 'When the war does end . . . I shall be going away.'

'Where?' She was awake now and holding him tight.

'I don't know.' It was impossible to tell her the truth. 'Wherever there's a struggle for freedom taking place, I suppose. It's – its how I earn my living, Elli. I'm not like you and Nicos and the others. You do what you do for love. I'm . . . I'm a professional.'

'I see.' Her voice was so faint he could barely hear her. 'And who sent you here, Paul?'

He was ready for that. 'A certain person in Athens. I can't tell you his name, but he's very high up, a very important politician. Like everyone else in the government, he wants Enosis to become a reality. Unlike the others, he's prepared to put his money where his mouth is.'

She accepted that at once, because love is blind. 'But why are you telling me this now, Paul?'

'Because . . .' he began, and stopped. This was irrational, it was against all his training to act in such an irresponsible manner. He was behaving like a callow youth, and yet he was unable to stop himself. 'Because I don't want to leave you, Elli. I want you to come with me.'

She clung to him and sobbed, as if he was on the point of

leaving already. Suddenly he found the words he had been trying to say all along.

'Look at me, Elli. I love you, kid. Will you marry me?'

To Elli, a wedding meant a church ceremony, and not a registrar's office. Nicos introduced them to a priest, a plump bearded figure in flowing black robes and a round black hat, and an insatiable thirst for the wine of independence. He was prepared to make any accommodation for this Greek bomb-maker and his bride-to-be: he himself had smuggled guns and sticks of gelignite beneath his holy vestments from time to time, to aid the sacred cause.

'Tell me when you wish to be married, my son,' he said, 'and it shall be done.'

Elvides had been working all morning in the bomb factory, and surveyed the unctuous cleric and his ornate, jewelled crucifix with a mixture of contempt and suspicion. To please Elli, he needed the help of the Church if they hoped to marry quickly, or indeed at all with no questions asked. But it went against the grain: as a communist, he despised religious teaching and as a radical he felt unable to reconcile the cloth and the gun. Nicos had told him before about this priest who worked for Eoka, had even suggested him for work with the bomb pyramid. But Elvides had rejected the offer, arguing that he did not see how the churchman and the British – who both professed to serve the same God – could fight on opposing sides in this war to the death. 'Our friend might find himself faced with a crisis of conscience one day,' said Elvides, 'which could cost you and me our lives. No thank you!'

However, carrying bombs beneath one's robes and conducting a wedding ceremony of convenience were two quite different things: he would therefore accept the offer yet somehow show his scorn for the religious mumbo-jumbo involved. He searched around in his mind for the best way to do it. 'I'll take you up on that offer,' he said with a laugh. 'How about this Saturday?'

No one laughed with him and the request was followed by a moment of shocked silence. 'No, my son,' replied the priest firmly. 'Not this Saturday, nor any other. I feel sure your lady would not wish it, nor any of your comrades.' He turned to Nicos in considerable embarrassment, and said in an aside,

'How sad to discover that any man such as this, who bravely risks his own life for our freedom, knows so little of our traditions.'

Elvides pretended not to hear him. Elli saw the shocked faces of her Cypriot friends and quickly explained 'Paul, darling, the wedding service is always held on a Sunday: any other day is considered terribly unlucky.' She shrugged her shoulders as if to tell him it was an unimportant trifle, but it was not: not to a devout Greek-Cypriot. Even to joke about marrying on a Saturday was held to be in bad taste and courting disaster, but she did not add that.

'All right,' said Elvides. 'Let's make it Sunday, then. This Sunday.' He looked directly at the minister. 'No point in delaying things, we could all be dead this time next week.'

There was no mistaking his hostility now. But the priest gave no indication of displeasure: he simply nodded assent, and made the sign of the Cross. It was already Wednesday. Clearly it meant foregoing all the old, traditional pre-nuptial ceremonies, but no matter: the insurrection had put paid to most of them, anyway. The time factor and obscure personal details could all be arranged. Elli had no father alive to bless the bride, but the matter of a dowry was surely unimportant in the circumstances. In any event, it would not be lack of money which decided how many best men and how many bridesmaids filled the church – it was more a question of finding enough volunteers from both sexes who were not on the official 'wanted' list. The signing of the ribbons could go by the board, if not the exchange of rings. Perhaps Elli herself could suggest some way round the bridesmaid problem: Nicos, thank God, was not yet known to the authorities and could act openly as principal best man. No tables would be allowed in the street after the wedding ceremony for the drinking and feasting after the hand-over of wedding presents – they were liable to hinder the progress of police and army patrols. The junketing would all have to take place inside, in spite of the heat. One of the bride's rooms could be cleared for dancing, no doubt, but there could be no band: the traditional music of accordions, drums and violins would have to be recorded if there was to be any music and dancing at all. And everything to be arranged in three days – in times of exceptional difficulty – thanks to this rude, ungrateful barbarian from Salonika! The priest burned with outrage and shame but kept his features bland, and impassive.

'This Sunday it shall be,' he agreed. 'Under what name, may I ask?'

Elvides held up his false passport. 'Elli will have to put up with being Mrs Parides until the war's over, I'm afraid. Nothing we can do about that: just see you don't call us Elvides, eh?'

The sherry was passed round, and the priest waited for his moment of revenge until someone jokingly brought up the age-old custom of the consummation. Before the insurrection, every self-respecting Greek Cypriot family would have paraded the bride's bloodstained sheet among the guests as the drinking and dancing continued into the night, or signalled completion of the joyous first act of physical union by firing shotguns out of a bedroom window: perhaps both together. However, in this case it was common knowledge that Elli and Elvides had been sleeping together for months, so that any maidenhead the good doctor may have possessed at the outset would have been ruptured long since anyway.

'In view of the emergency,' said the priest, 'quite clearly we shall have to dispense with the traditional firing of guns to celebrate the act of consummation.' He smiled slyly, and fluttered his dark, hooded eyes in the direction of Elvides. 'Perhaps it would be better to forgo the showing of the sheet as well, since the groom sets so little store by our local customs.'

On the orders of the Leader, every member of the wedding party – Paul and Elli included – were back in action against the British within twenty-four hours of the ceremony. But no wedding involving the beautiful and popular American doctor, yet attended by such notorious guests, could hope to pass unnoticed in the rumour-rife old city: and within those twenty-four hours a report had gone back to British Intelligence. There had been enough verbal indiscretions committed in drink that night to have everyone marched straight to the scaffold, and now the security services moved in swiftly to round them up. The priest was arrested in his church. Two of the minor best men were hauled from their beds, still drunk. A dozen guests were picked up for questioning. Elli had just driven her husband to the bomb-factory when the surgery door was broken down and the search teams stormed into her house. It was a simple matter to locate the missing Ford and as it began to grow dusk, troops moved stealthily into position round the old wooden house on the rise. There were two Eoka sentries on duty inside. One called softly to Elli, and pointed through the shutters to the alleyway below.

'Soldiers' he whispered, and slipped the catch on his Lee-Enfield. 'Go down and warn Paul and make your escape while you can, both of you.'

She tugged on the dark cloak she always carried with her at nights. 'You'd better come too, Markos,' she told him. 'Let's all run while there's time.'

'Our orders are to cover your escape.' His voice quavered a little, in spite of the brave-sounding words. He was nearly eighteen, and in command of the post. 'Hurry, Elli, I beg of you. They'll be here soon.'

'May God protect you both.' She embraced him and ran into the kitchen with Alex, the second guerrilla, at her heels. He put down his sten gun and helped her lift the trap-door, sweating with the weight of it. As they eased it back and he saw a way to save his own life, he burst into tears.

'Oh, Elli.'

'Goodbye, Alex.' She caressed his face for a moment with her finger-tips and then started to descend the ladder. As she did so she called out 'Paul! Paul, darling, the English are here! Save yourself, quickly!'

Elvides threw down the pliers and ran over to help her. The car-bomb he had been making sat unfinished on the work bench, obscene and menacing. Other devices stood nearby, all in various stages of construction: gelignite excepted, supplies still reached the peasant army in no more than a trickle through the tight British blockade.

'Don't waste time!' she screamed. The trap door slammed into place over her head. Almost at once, the first shots sounded. 'You go on, oh please Paul, hurry!' By the time she jumped down to the floor he had disappeared. Elli pulled the ladder away and let it fall with a crash: that would buy them a few minutes more. The cupboard waited ready to receive her. She pressed on the wall and lowered herself into the opening, trembling as the great stone slid home and the last shafts of light gave way to total darkness. Her heart was beating wildly as she started to inch her way down.

Elvides was already waiting in the Jew's house. Jakob had fled: only his cat stayed on, curled up in the warmth of the chair, ignoring the stranger who paced up and down so impatiently in her master's room. Time and again Elvides stopped to stare fretfully at the wall – what the hell was keeping her? It was more than a minute since he had come through, and soon this street, too, would be filled with soldiers.

'Elli!' he shouted, and pounded his fists on the stonework. 'Elli, for God's sake kid, come on!'

Elli could hear nothing at all. It was hot and cramped in the tunnel, without a single glimmer of light. She had always been afraid of the dark: she could remember waking up in the night as a child, screaming and weeping hysterically until her father brought a light to comfort her. But when he had dried her tears and returned to his own bed she would lie there trembling, afraid of the shadows dancing on the walls and praying for daylight to come to release her from the terror that always accompanied the night. She shook her head determinedly: she was grown woman now, a doctor – an Eoka fighter! – and would not allow herself to surrender to such foolish, unreasoning fears.

But that was easier said than done. Somehow, her cloak had snagged on the walls of the tunnel. And as she slid down so the cloth rode up, past her back and over her shoulders to drape itself in soft, clinging folds round her eyes and nose and mouth, adding to the heat and discomfort as well as her nagging fears. Suddenly she heard shouts, sounding faintly through the darkness. That must mean the British were down in the cellar. Soon they would discover the entrance – and capture her. With a tremendous effort Elli forced herself to lie still: then brought her arms up, one at a time, and dragged the cloak clear, over her head. She pushed it away and continued to back down the tunnel, sliding and bumping uncomfortably until at last she felt ground beneath her feet once more. Now she felt around her, first with one foot and then the other, trying to locate the stone that would set her free. *Just stick your foot in, push, and out you step,* said Paul – *easy!* But where was it? Where in God's name was the hollow? She felt the darkness closing in on her again, and drummed her heels against the ground in a frenzy of tears and frustration. But nothing moved, no air entered that confined space, no blessed ray of light appeared, no strong eager hands reached in to pluck her to safety. She was trapped.

Elli began to panic and hand-in-hand with panic came a desolate, suffocating wave of claustrophobia. She wept uncontrollably, she struggled and kicked and clawed at the stonework and knew what it felt like to be buried alive. She opened her mouth and screamed 'I surrender, I surrender!' at the top of her voice, but no one answered. A few moments later she screamed again, 'I surrender, do you hear me, I give myself up, *please*!' but still no one acknowledged. She screamed until her throat ran dry and her voice carried no further than the call of a frightened bird: no one heard her, no one shouted back. Later – a long, long time later – sanity was restored. She realised that Paul could not help her, while the British could not hear her: not down here, not at the bottom of this narrow stone tube. If she hoped to be rescued at all she would have to scramble back to the top and call for help through the stone guarding the entrance – guide her rescuers in, if need be. It would take time, it would call for every ounce of her strength and willpower, yet at the same time it would prove a benison. It would buy time for Paul to escape, dear beloved Paul, her husband of less than a day. She was under no illusions: if the soldiers ever laid hands on Paul he would hang, as surely as the sun came up each day over Mount Olympus. She herself would go to jail, of course, and perhaps for years, but that was nothing if it meant saving Paul's life.

Elli said her prayers, took a deep breath, and started to claw her way upwards.

As soon as the building had been secured, Lieutenant Ramage was ordered in to destroy any arms or ammunition found inside. At that time the house was believed to be no more than a refuge, a shelter for the street gangs who infested the old city. Then the bomb factory was uncovered, an Aladdin's Cave of explosives and precious bomb-making equipment. Radio reports back to Brigade suggested that the snap raid – based on an informant's tip about a wedding – might yet turn out to be the biggest single success in the war so far against Eoka, and further clarification was sought. An Intelligence officer arrived quickly on the scene and spoke to Ramage. He tapped his leg with a swagger cane and beamed with delight as he gazed about him. 'List everything you find,' he said. 'I'll send an official photographer to work with you. As soon as you're done, salvage whatever's required to back up our charge that help is reaching these people from outside – and then blow the rest up, house and all.'

'Right, sir.'

'A nice big bang, now: teach the swine a lesson. I'll have the infantry clear all the adjoining streets.'

The sticks of gelignite were old and sweating badly: it would have been dangerous to try to move them anyway. Ramage examined a number of part-finished devices, made sure they were safe, and sent them back for finger-printing along with the tools and electrical equipment. There was a cupboard in the cellar, full of dog-eared books and all printed in Greek. He threw some on the floor and left the rest where they were. He paid out a drum of wire back to the command post and then went into the cellar with an infantry sergeant, for a final check round.

'Everyone out of the building, sergeant?'

'All clear, sir.'

Ramage plunged a detonator into the heart of the gelignite and wired up the business end of a huge, crude bomb. The sergeant waited by the ladder. As Ramage straightened up and turned to join him, he suddenly stopped dead.

'Hear anything?'

The sergeant turned his head slowly, like a safe-breaker listening for the tumbling of a lock. 'No, sir.'

'Strange. I could have sworn I heard someone call out.'

The two of them were like statues, listening intently.

'Nothing down here, sir, except a few rats, maybe. In which case they're due for the surprise of their lives.'

'I was damned sure I heard something.' Ramage hesitated for a moment longer, then shrugged his shoulders. He had searched every inch of that bomb-factory personally. 'What the hell, I must have dreamt it.' As soon as they had climbed into the kitchen he wedged the trap-door down, tight. Then he followed the sergeant into the street and back up the rise, to the command post behind the sandbags. He connected up the wires to the exploder, and turned to the Colonel in charge.

'All set, sir?'

'Two minutes more, if you please. My chaps are still searching those houses, making sure no one's been left behind.'

Ramage wondered if he should mention the sound he had heard in the cellar – correction, the sound he *imagined* he had heard in the cellar. Then he thought no, the sergeant's right, those old buildings must be swarming with rats: the quicker he pressed the tit, the better.

Elvides swung round, gun in hand, as the door of the Jew's house burst open. It was Nicos, with two of his men, and all three close to panic.

'We'll have half the British Army on us soon, come on, time to go!' Their car stood in the street outside, doors open, engine ticking over. They were taking a hell of a chance in coming back for him, but Grivas had given strict orders that no matter who else was sacrificed, his bomb-maker was to be saved in the event of a raid.

'Elli's stuck inside the tunnel – quick, give me a hand to get her out!'

'There's no time, you fool, the soldiers will be here any minute.' Nicos grabbed hold of his shirt and tried to drag him out. 'She'll be all right, they won't harm a woman – come on, damn you!'

Elvides cuffed him off like a man swatting a fly. 'You yellow bastard,' he shouted. 'Touch me again and I'll kill you!'

Nicos nodded to one of his henchmen. A sandbag thudded down and Elvides went over like a skittle in a bowling alley. 'Get him in the car, quick.' Nicos ran ahead of them and climbed behind the wheel. The saloon was already bumping and lurching down the cobbled street as the last terrorist clambered on board. That stupid bitch, thought Nicos, she could have got us all hanged!

The infantry Colonel walked back from the radio car. 'All clear, Ramage.'

'Right, sir. Stand by.'

He pressed the plunger. The ground shook as if there was a ghost train rumbling by. There was an ear-splitting bang in the alleyway below and a plume of smoke spiralled into the night air, followed by a tinkling of glass as windowpanes dropped out of their frames into the street right down to the Paphos Gate. When the dust settled, the house had disappeared: like a tooth extracted by the dentist. There was no fire. The force of the explosion was concentrated underground, exactly as Ramage had intended. The walls of the bomb factory fell down, like the walls of Jericho at the sound of the trumpet, and the main force of the blast was sucked into the tunnel, reducing everything inside to dust: even the stones themselves.

Elvides astounded himself with the intensity of the pain he still felt when he thought of Elli: it was like a knife-wound. He had been unconscious when the bomb factory was blown up, and it was many hours before any reliable reports came in. But when he knew for certain she was dead he ran amok in the streets of the old city firing at anyone he encountered, women included. By great good fortune Nicos and his alley-cats found him before the British did. They clubbed him for the second time, threw him into the boot of a car and drove him to the Ktema monastery, two thousand feet up in the mountains.

He was mad with grief, and it was a long time before sanity returned. They kept him locked in a monk's cell, like a caged animal, for fourteen days and nights before they let him go again. To this day, Elvides could recall the inscriptions carved centuries earlier on the stone walls of his cell, beneath the religious frescoes. One was 'Many dogs have compassed Me, strong bulls have beset me round.' Of course it was all bunk, hogwash, any fool knew that: even so it was curious how apt the words were, in all the circumstances. The inscription over his bunk read 'Behold Him of whom I have spoken: He is coming, and will take you out of the bars of Hell.' And damned if it wasn't Grivas himself who came one night, stern faced, cold as an icicle, a little man without a spark of compassion in his body, to question him and finally agree to his release – on certain conditions.

Elvides swore to kill the Englishman who had murdered Elli, and Grivas accepted that. What he would not tolerate, he said, were any more 'mad-dog' killings. In fact Grivas – that sanctimonious, unemotional bastard – actually threatened to have him executed unless he took an oath to obey Eoka orders to the letter until the end of the campaign. 'Personal grief is a luxury we cannot afford,' he said in that pompous, pulpit tone of his. 'We are all soldiers, fighting for a common cause.'

That was Grivas's trouble, thought Elvides: he was too rigid and unbending in his outlook. A more flexible mind would have known from the beginning Elvides was no psychopath. On the contrary – once he had recovered from perfectly understandable emotional shock – he continued to do what he had always done, which was to kill to orders. Eoka was not the cause he served though, any more than was the P.L.O. later, or the IRA, or A.L. The cause was communism, now and always. And if there was any change at all in his attitude after Elli's death, it was merely that he set about his duties even more enthusiastically: there was a song in his heart as each bomb went off. The Muslims had the right word for it – they called it *jehad*, Holy War. That was exactly how he looked on his own role, as a fighter in a holy war, if a communist could be allowed to use such an expression. A *cause*.

Elvides honestly had no idea how many lives or how much money he had cost the western world since Elli's murder, but the most conservative estimate had to be several hundred lives and tens of millions of pounds. Some people might think that was an exaggeration, but they overlooked the destructive capability of the bomb. Every bomb – properly used – inflicted casualties and material damage out of all proportion to the size and cost involved. The IRA would tell you that one bomb alone in Ulster cost the British more than fifteen million pounds. Twenty men – or women – bombing in a series of disciplined terrorist operations could very nearly bring a nation to its knees – witness what A.L. was doing to Germany, rich all-powerful western Germany, at this very moment. The credit for that was his. Angela was the figurehead leader, but he, Paul Elvides, had taught it, drilled it and shaped it into the effective organisation it had become. Without him the Liberation Army commandos would have remained a bunch of vicious, blundering kids – dangerous certainly, but no more so than any other pack animals. It was only under his skilful manipulation that they had emerged as a genuine threat to the government of the day, as a force to be reckoned with. This setback over the ransom demand was the first they had suffered, and it was all the more galling to realise that the man responsible was – *Ramage*.

Ramage! That bastard had more lives than a cat, and that

was the truth. The gunmen in the ambulance should have accounted for him while he was still wet behind the ears, as he had so often told Grivas. They failed principally because they were inefficient and gutless, but no one could level any such charge against Paul Elvides – no, sir! For instance: Ramage's success in defusing the parcel-bomb was just one of those things. After all, the man was a bomb disposal expert – the operative word was *expert* – and you had to allow for an occasional technical setback, it was only to be expected. His survival from that ambush on the mountain road certainly rankled, but that was never inefficiency – that was luck, that was the million-to-one chance galloping home, if you like. Even now that he was in his fifties Elvides still prided himself on being able to score ten out of ten at 400 yards with the aid of a telescopic sight. And he had done everything right that day in laying the trap, setting up the ambush and timing it so perfectly: only to have Fate intervene, in the form of a stray goat. The damned thing came out of nowhere at the critical moment, dislodging enough stones to scare him into thinking it must be a British patrol sneaking up – with the result that he had pulled the trigger of the Lee-Enfield possibly one hundredth of a second too soon. Not that he realised it at the time, of course, in fact six years went by before he discovered the truth. When he saw Ramage go tumbling down the hillside that night with the blood pouring from his head, naturally enough he thought he had killed him.

Elvides recalled how they had celebrated afterwards: himself, Nicos, Leonidas, even big-mouth Tomazos and the rest, everyone got as drunk as a fiddler's bitch, and small wonder. The gratification in assuming Ramage's death was not just a personal one: they had all played some part in the conspiracy to murder the English anti-terrorist chief, and were as shocked as Elvides to learn that Ramage had foiled them at the eleventh hour. The thought that he at least was dead seemed sweet revenge at the time.

Few could deny that the attempt to assassinate Benchley was one of the most ambitious and audacious of the entire campaign, or that Paul Elvides' role in it was anything but courageous. In failure he succeeded in humiliating the British as they had rarely been humiliated before, and in so doing he had made Grivas eat dirt, too.

To this day he was unable to say which result gave him the greatest satisfaction.

As soon as he learned of General Benchley's appointment as H.A.T.O. Grivas summoned an emergency council of war to plan how best to meet it. He was continually on the run: his lair at the time was high on the Troodos massif. It consisted of a series of inter-linking natural caves screened by thick forest, and was as well fortified in its way as Benchley's own headquarters. As at Kyrenia, the trees had been thinned to provide maximum field of fire in the event of a surprise attack. Most tracks that led in were mined and booby-trapped. Trip wires through the bracken guarded the rest, while eagles kept watch overhead. The huge birds flew screaming into the air whenever man ventured too close, and were notorious for attacking the British helicopters: so much so that all pilots had orders to take avoiding action whenever they were threatened by that feathered, lethal, seven-foot wing span – and it was a constant source of joy to the Eoka rebels to know that their airborne watchdogs were *Imperial* eagles. Apart from the terrorists themselves, only the monks in nearby Ktema monastery knew of the hideout, and they were bound by vows of silence anyway: so that Grivas felt as secure in his eyrie as did Benchley in his villa if not quite as comfortable, and each general plotted ceaselessly in his chosen headquarters for the other's downfall.

'You will be wondering why I summoned you in such haste.' Grivas shivered in the raw mountain air and huddled inside his coat. 'The British have appointed a General named Benchley as the head of all anti-terrorist operations on the island. I have heard of him and he is good at his job. Therefore I want him taken out before he gets a chance to get started. Your suggestions, gentlemen, please.'

Their quarters were Spartan. Each man slept on rock. Goatskins served as blankets. No fires were permitted so that it was always freezing inside the caves, even in mid-summer. Like Grivas himself, all of them there lived permanently on the run. If it was harder for him than the others, none had yet heard him complain. He was like a sawn-off shotgun, small, hard and deadly. Yet he was nearing sixty. His face was gaunt and hollow-cheeked. His clothes hung from his skinny body. He moved his head in an odd, bird-like manner, jerking it sharply this way and that as he studied the faces of his lieutenants seated round the cave. All the time he sucked noisily on his moustache, and his dark, deep-set eyes burned with an unquenchable fire.

'Well, Markos. Let's hear from you first.'

'I count that an honour, Dighenis.' Grivas took his *nom de guerre* from the legendary Greek warrior, and the yokels loved him for it. 'I hear the new man has set up headquarters on the coast at Kyrenia. That means he has to drive through the pass every time he comes into Nicosia. Why not lay a culvert mine and blow him to smithereens?'

'We could explode a mine under the convoy easily enough' Grivas agreed. 'But could we guarantee to kill Benchley in the explosion, my friend? Clearly not: and if we attack this man and he lives, it will be the British who claim the victory, not us.'

The next man to speak came from Paphos. He had never fought in the north – indeed, had never travelled as far as Kyrenia in his life. 'I do not know the place he has chosen as his headquarters, you understand. But if I may offer a suggestion. Could we perhaps poison the water-supply?'

'We could, indeed.' Grivas shook his head in dissent, even so. 'But not without killing a lot of our own people in the process, I fancy. The British would make capital out of that in the United Nations, and label us barbarians. No.'

Kyriakis was a magnificent shot, one of the best in Eoka. 'I read about this British general, Dighenis. They say he's a keen swimmer. Let me hide up in a house overlooking the beach at Kyrenia, and I'll put a bullet through his head for you the first time he puts a toe in our clean Cyprus waters.'

The idea appealed greatly to Grivas, and it irked him to have to turn it down. 'This house he's living in has got its own private beach, Kyriakis. You could wait for a year and never get near him. And I want him killed *now*.'

There was silence in the cave for a while. Then Grivas said, 'No matter, let's eat first. Perhaps we shall find inspiration in food.'

There were nine present including himself and all had made a long and dangerous trek to reach the hideout: playing hide and seek with the Army patrols, always on the alert for the spies-in-the-sky, the helicopter pilots. Now all of them were starving hungry. With one exception, his lieutenants were all district leaders, each one responsible for a command of varying size and importance. Four were mountain districts, Kykko, Pitsillia, Paphos and Pentadactylos (or Kyrenia range), four fought a quite different war in the towns: Nicosia, Famagusta, Limassol and Larnaca. Young as he was, Nicos was senior as the Nicosia commander. All of them mingled like family, easily and intimately; and ate as family, with Grivas as the father-figure. The brothers Payanides, who were the Leader's personal bodyguard, also acted as his manservants, making up his poor bed, fetching water, cooking for him, running errands. As soon as he gave the signal they started to serve the piping hot *klephtiko* – goat meat baked in bay leaves – cooked in an underground oven, over the only fire allowed in the eyrie. They were bright and cheerful as clowns, as well as killers in their own right.

Christofou handed round the eathenware bowls with a little joke for each district leader. Two days earlier, he had executed a woman traitor as she haggled over the price of lemons in a street market. His elder brother Isychios, who achieved notoriety early in the campaign by shooting three young British servicemen in the back while they were out shopping, carried in the steaming dish and called 'Lunch is served, Dighenis!' just like a real butler, much to everyone's amusement. As well as meat there was bread, oven fresh from the monastery bakehouse, with a green salad and bowls of olives. There were two gourds on the rock floor of the cave. One held water, as cold as the snows on Mount Olympus, the other brandy. Each man helped himself in turn, according to taste: Grivas himself made it a rule to drink only water in the field.

'Delicious,' he said, and pushed his bowl away. He ate sparingly, like a little bird. 'Isychios, I hereby appoint you Director of the National Academy of Cooking, the appointment to take effect as soon as independence has been won. Such rare skills must not go unrewarded.' It was as near as he would ever get to cracking a joke, or showing affection for anyone. Isychios beamed, as his companions mocked him gently. 'If only he could fight as well as he cooks, the war might be won already.'

The odd man out at the meeting was Paul Elvides. He had no district command. His role was technical adviser to Eoka, although the duties he performed went much wider than the title suggested. He ran the entire bomb pyramid. As well as making bombs, he taught others and organised the supply lines. He was also a fine strategist, always offering ideas on how to escalate the war against the British, not always with the approval of Grivas. It was noticeable how he remained aloof from the others in the cave, and they from him.

There were a number of reasons for this, the most important being that he was the only non-Cypriot present. Grivas might have lived for years on the mainland and served in the Greek army, but he was born at Trikomo, near Famagusta: a more loyal son of Cyprus never breathed. All his district leaders were born and raised in the areas they now commanded as guerrilla leaders. But Elvides was an outsider. He came from Salonika, and had been accepted into the organisation only after the strongest representation by certain influential persons in Athens – people big enough to put pressure not only on Grivas, but on Makarios, too.

Another reason was plain, old-fashioned jealousy. Their peasant minds seemed to find it difficult to accept that his specialist skills made him irreplaceable. They resented the fact that he refused to take orders from anyone except Grivas himself, as if he were Number Two in the organisation. The fact was that no matter where he was born, he arrived on the island with an established reputation as hard-line terrorist and expert bomb-maker, whereas his Eoka colleagues – with the exception of Grivas, of course – still had to win their spurs, in their case against an enemy who was superior in numbers, training, experience and equipment. And when they failed – as they were bound to do at times – they resented even more the comments he made, and the advice he offered so freely. Grivas was aware of the friction, but powerless to do much about it. Apart from having influential friends on the mainland, Elvides carried out his duties with skill and efficiency: that much at least was undeniable. Likewise he had suffered enough at the hands of the common enemy to guarantee his loyalty. For all those reasons Grivas and his Eoka lieutenants, with the possible exception of Nicos, tolerated the outsider while secretly loathing his guts. There was no point in blinking at the facts after all these years, thought Elvides. He could remember as if it was yesterday how Grivas turned to him with that cold smile the moment he finished eating.

'Time to get back to General Benchley,' he said abruptly. 'I'm sure you'll have ideas on how to deal with him, Elvides – as you have on everything else. Very well, let's hear them.' It was the royal command and the rest of the group fell silent.

He was in his early thirties then: in his prime. Elvides was not as tall as some – five feet ten in his bare feet – but he towered over little Grivas, a bull-necked, powerful man with muscular thighs and forearms. He had a sprinkling of silver in that dark hair and lines like scars etched round the eyes, legacies not only of the strain they all endured but also of his recent bereavement. He was heavily bearded, as most of them were. Like his hair, his beard was turning badger grey. The leather jerkin he wore was unbuttoned, to show the Smith & Wesson riding in his waistband. He stank like a polecat of earth and sweat and goat-flesh swimming in garlic, and his hands were split and calloused.

'You can assassinate any man, given time. Presidents, governors, generals, it doesn't matter a damn what they are, they all have to offer their bodies sooner or later as a target. And no matter how long it took to kill Benchley – the head of the entire anti-terrorist network – it would rank as a feather in our cap. If you want it done quickly, there is only one way: we'll have to go in and get him. And to kill such a man in his own headquarters, with a bomb – the ultimate in terrorist premeditation – now *that* would demonstrate an Intelligence and strike capability of the very highest order.'

He rolled himself a cigarette and blew a smoke ring in the air. 'Is that not so, Dighenis?'

'That was the whole purpose of this meeting,' fumed Grivas. 'To demonstrate the power of Eoka to the world.' It was quite intolerable, the way this fellow tried to upstage him.

'Of course. It presents us with a considerable challenge, just the same. As you yourself acknowledged when you asked us all for suggestions.' He was careful to smile as he teased him, just the same. 'From what I hear, Benchley's house is more tightly guarded than the Kremlin itself. You want a selective killing, an execution, with no one else hurt?'

'Yes. To carry the greatest possible impact.'

'Ah. In that case, we must consider all the things he does alone. Shaving. Washing. Emptying his bowels. Things like that.'

Grivas shrugged his shoulders. But he was intrigued, none the less. They all were.

'There will always be his bodyguards close by, except in such intimate moments.' Elvides paused for a moment. 'Do we know if he sleeps alone?'

'Yes.' Grivas could speak with authority there. His district leader from Kyrenia had brought with him a complete dossier that morning on Benchley's household arrangements. 'He is unmarried, and has no woman with him.'

'Splendid. Then that's how we'll do it, with a bomb in his bed. A thing of technical perfection, a sweet-dreams bomb, a device that cannot explode until it feels the weight of his head on the pillow.'

Tomazos, the Kyrenia district leader, laughed aloud at that and poured himself a brandy. 'You'll have a job, my friend. Benchley is one of those keep-fit maniacs, sleeps naked on top of a bare mattress, winter and summer. Where the devil would you hide such a bomb?'

'You needn't concern yourself with technical matters, they're my department.' He took the gourd from Tomazos and cradled it on his elbow, taking a long drink himself. 'But tell me more. You seem to know an awful lot about General Benchley's personal habits?'

Tomazos winked at the others. '*Nothing* happens in the Pentadactylos I don't know about. Ask Dighenis here.'

'I don't need to. You have an informant inside the villa, obviously.' Ideas were buzzing inside his mind now. 'Do you mean to tell me Benchley's kept on Cypriot staff?'

Tomazos looked towards Grivas for permission to disclose the secrets in the dossier. 'Yes. Four of them. The British police leaned on them pretty heavily – but so did I. And I think it's fair to say I won.'

'Good. Then that's the way in.'

'Perhaps.' Tomazos sounded doubtful. 'Security is the strictest we've ever encountered. And that's saying something, believe me.'

'Is there a woman among them?'

'Yes. Loulla Eliades. Cook-cum-housekeeper.'

'Tell me, does she get a body search every time she goes in and out?'

'They certainly run their hands over her. I don't know about stripping her down to the buff. Dammit, the poor old cow's in her sixties.'

'She's our bomb carrier,' said Elvides instantly. 'I'll feed it to her a few bits at a time. She can hide them all in the kitchen until they're needed. The whole lot won't need to weigh more than three or four pounds all told.'

'But you still have to get inside and put it together.'

'Not me, Tomazos. That's somebody else's problem. I'm the only competent bomb-maker you've got on the island, and must not be put at risk.' He turned to Grivas. 'There's no question of me having cold feet, you understand. All I'm thinking about is my importance to the organisation.'

'Of course,' said Grivas, with that death's head smile.

'So, who's going to put the bomb together?' demanded Tomazos. 'Old Loulla? Don't make me laugh, she'd shit herself if she looked too closely at a detonator, never mind anything else.'

'All right then, someone else,' snapped Elvides irritably. 'It's not so hard. I can give a man a few simple lessons, and draw the sketches he needs. It's been done before.'

'No.' Grivas ended the argument personally. 'Loulla can carry the parts in, that's obviously the best way to get them past the guards. But we can't risk any slip-up afterwards. I want *you* to put the thing together, Elvides. It's a job for an expert, not for some half-baked family servant.'

Elvides stared at him in astonishment. 'But – '

'I want Benchley dead. Therefore I'm ordering you to enter the house and carry out the assignment – personally.'

'But that's madness!' Elvides was shouting now. 'You could never replace me if I got picked up by the British, and you know it! Surely I don't have to spell out elementary things like that to you people – '

Grivas was deathly pale. 'Watch your tongue, you pig's dropping,' he said, 'or I'll have it cut out from your head. You appear to regard yourself as indispensable to this organisation, I can't think why. I have a half dozen young men ready and willing to step into your shoes should you be caught and hanged, Elvides. Oh, not as clever as you, of course: but clever enough. They'll learn to make bombs, given time. As you did, when you began.'

Tomazos took out a hunting knife and began to pare his nails. No one else moved.

'You took the oath,' Grivas continued, 'when I freed you from Ktema. The penalty for refusing to obey my orders is death.' He sucked noisily at his moustache. 'For the last time: will you go into the villa, or not?'

'I have no choice.' Elvides was shaking with rage. 'I think the order is unwise, but I am no coward.' He put the obvious question. 'Loulla won't be able to carry me under her skirts. How do you propose I get in?'

'Tomazos has been very thorough. He knows a way.' Grivas smiled at his lieutenant. 'Tell our bomb-maker about the furniture.'

'According to the valet,' said Tomazos, 'they're expecting a shipment of furniture for the general any day now. We shall get a message from Famagusta as soon as it arrives. It will come ashore by lighter and be held overnight – perhaps longer – for Customs check, before it goes on to Nicosia or wherever it is in convoy. We've got friends in the Customs and we'll have a crate of our own there ready to join the others. With airholes drilled in the top, and Paul Elvides packed inside, like a sardine. Simple.'

Elvides reached for the brandy, and held his tongue.

Loulla Eliades was as nervous as a cow in a slaughterhouse and screamed abuse at the Military Police guards each time they went through the motions of searching her. 'Keep your filthy paws off me' she shouted, at the top of her voice. 'I'll have you know I'm a respectable widow woman. No man puts his hands up my skirts. I won't have it!'

'Hold your tongue, Mrs Eliades,' the sergeant rebuked her. He was genuinely embarrassed by the accusation. 'You know very well my men would do no such thing.'

He waved her away in disgust. She scuttled off to the toilet and relieved herself of the stick of gelignite secreted inside her body. She was not afraid of the British soldiers: it was her own people, especially that terrible man Tomazos, whom she really feared. She dried her tears and made her way into the kitchen. Within a week, Elvides had enough components stored in the tins of flour and sugar there to build his bomb.

Two floors above, Antonis the valet looked anxiously up and down the corridor before he knocked on the door of his own room, and entered. It was a small and neatly furnished apartment, with a distant view of the sea. A shower and toilet led off the bedroom, and his self-contained flat formed the end of the wing in the servant's quarters. Along the corridor and round the corner, only a few yards away, were General Benchley's own sleeping quarters. Antonis called out, very softly, 'It's me, Antonis. I've brought the food you wanted.'

The toilet door opened crack wide and Elvides peered out. 'You took your time, I'm starving.' He chewed ravenously at the sandwiches, and washed them down with water from the bathroom tap. 'Can't you get me something hot now and again?'

'It's not easy to get you anything at all, Mr Elvides. Those soldiers swarm round the kitchen like flies, always making cups of tea.' The valet was a pleasant looking man in his late fifties, and he enjoyed the cheerful banter of the troops. Until a few years ago he had been in the service of one British family or another most of his life, and he had no quarrel with any of them. But he walked in dread of the Eoka gangs. Especially the man Tomazos, who had stopped him on his way home from church a fortnight ago and threatened to burn him alive if he failed to carry out Dighenis's orders.

'When's the General coming back?' asked Elvides.

'I'm not sure yet. But he'll be stopping in Limassol tonight, so it will be quite safe for you to work on his bedroom for as long as you need.' He fumbled in his pocket. 'Here's a spare key. Don't go in there under any circumstances until you hear the helicopter take off.'

'Right. Warn me if there's any change of plan. Now get out.'

As soon as the door was closed he packed the components into a rucksack, and settled down patiently. Later he heard the roar of the helicopter taking off from the roof, and watched from the window until it disappeared from sight. Then he slipped on the rucksack and moved into the corridor. The door squeaked behind him and he felt naked as he quit the safety of the valet's room. It was only ten paces to the end of the corridor, but there was no cover: if anyone saw him now he was halfway to the scaffold already. Suddenly he heard voices, shouting urgently in English. He stopped where he was, gun in hand, rucksack on his back, and the sweat poured off him until somewhere in the distance a door slammed and the shouting ceased as abruptly as it had begun. Elvides swallowed hard: for a moment there he had felt the hangman's rope around his neck. He willed his legs to move again, and turned the corner.

The landing covered three of the four sides of the house, and opened into a staircase on the fourth. All the windows were curtained against the sun, so that the interior of the villa seemed very still, and cool. He could just see down into the hall. The front doors were kept locked: inside them stood a trestle table covered with an Army blanket. A military police sergeant sat there with his back to Elvides, writing in an incident book. Across the hallway were two more doors. One bore the legend H.A.T.O., and led into the operations room. The other was marked 'Private' and opened on to the living quarters, ante-room, dining-room, lounge and the gardens beyond. A second military policeman, a corporal in red cap and white webbing, stood at ease between the two doors, facing the stairs. His line of vision extended only to the landing: as long as Elvides crawled on his stomach, he could not be seen.

When he got to the apartment he reached up with the key, inserted it gently and turned it in the lock. At once the door flew away and hit against an inner wall with a bang, loud enough for both the sergeant and the corporal to look up inquiringly. Elvides jammed his face into the carpet and lay still. Minutes passed, and nothing happened: both guards assumed the noise had been made by a servant and thought no more about it. Scarcely able to believe his luck, Elvides dragged the rucksack after him and crawled inside. It had taken him more than fifteen minutes to cover the short distance from the valet's room. When his pulse had returned to normal he set to work.

The apartment consisted of dressing-room, bedroom, and a huge, high-ceilinged bathroom with a toilet at the far end. This was where he would work. He put down the rucksack and took off his shoes: then he padded out into the bedroom. It was a large room, simply furnished. Full length windows opened on to the balcony. Both were closed in the General's absence and shuttered with wooden-slatted Turkish blinds against the sun. The floor area in front of them was kept clear of furniture so that the General could perform his 100 press-ups on wakening, and breathe in the pure mountain air before it was tainted by the heat of the day. Pinewood cupboards and two enormous chests-of-drawers held the General's uniforms. Apart from the bed, a single rug was the only other item of furniture.

Elvides frowned as he examined the bed. It was no more than a narrow cot, better suited to a monk's cell, a wooden frame fitted with bed-boards and covered by a flock mattress perhaps six inches thick. Tomazos had been right when he forecast problems in hiding a bomb there. The mattress felt as hard as a rock. A solitary pillow, likewise filled with flock, nestled inside a spotless white slip. There was a thin sheet over the mattress: nothing else. The chest-of-drawers nearest to the bed would have to serve as his work-bench.

First he took out the explosive, two pounds of commercial blasting gelignite stolen from the Troodos mine Ramage had raided a few weeks earlier. It was malleable and came in the form of eight-ounce cartridges: each about the size and shape of a banana and each wrapped in the stiff, waxed paper old Loulla had discovered earlier, much to her discomfort and shame. There was no question of placing them in that thin, hard mattress in their present shape: they had to be flattened. Elvides searched through the bathroom until he found General Benchley's shampoo, a green liquid in a round glass bottle. He laid the cartridges on the chest-of-drawers and proceeded to beat them flat, using the shampoo bottle as a rolling pin. He shaped them until they were oblong and less than three-quarters of an inch thick, taking care to keep their paper skins intact. Then he took a large brown paper envelope from the rucksack and slid the cartridges inside, so that they lay side by side, and touching: this was his main charge. Before he sealed down the envelope to hold them in position he took a pencil and drove a hole in one end to a depth of two inches, through the paper. That was to take the detonator, later on. He left the pencil in position, and placed the package to one side: like all good bomb-makers, he was a meticulous man.

He decided to allow himself fifteen minutes to get clear of the room before the bomb became armed, and ready to explode. To make the delayed arming device was simple enough: he took his makeshift tool kit of bezel, pliers and battery operated soldering iron from the rucksack, together with the cheap wrist-watch he had bought on his return from the mountains, and removed the hour hand. Next he soldered a twelve-inch length of wire to the outer casing, took the bezel, and drilled a hole in the clock-face, at six o'clock. Then he inserted a drawing-pin into the hole to prevent the timing wheel from rotating and advanced the minute hand to three o'clock, taking care not to wind the watch in the process. He soldered another length of wire to the head of the drawing-pin, and all was ready. He now had his fifteen minute time-gap between minute hand and drawing-pin. All he had to do to set the watch in motion – and thereby arm the device – would be to tug gently on the wire he had soldered to the drawing-pin, and lift it out of the hole he had drilled in the clock-face. That would be his final act before quitting the bedroom.

His next step was to make the switch which would detonate the bomb under the pressure of the General's head on the pillow. He selected three strips of tin from the rucksack, each measuring two inches by one-eighth wide, and one-sixteenth in thickness. He separated each from the other by inserting a strip of insulating mica, held them together with his fingers and glued them. When the adhesive had set he soldered a piece of wire to each end of the metal block, and repeated the process by soldering two more pieces of wire to the top and bottom of a flat, two-inch battery. All these he placed in separate, smaller envelopes and sealed them down, so that he now had four packages: the main charge, to go inside the mattress, and the switch, the battery to arm it, and the delayed action device, to be placed inside the pillow. He felt enormously weary now: his limbs ached with the strain of working under so much tension. He longed for a cigarette, but dared not smoke. He would have given 10,000 mils for a single brandy, but there was none. He licked his lips and carried on: later.

He fumbled in the rucksack for the last time and took out his Stanley knife, plus a needle and thread. First he slit open the mattress, cutting a square just big enough to take the main charge, removing the loose flock a little at a time and heaping it carefully on a handkerchief spread on the floor. He would get rid of it later. Then he took a detonator, slid it home in the cavity prepared by the pencil, and pressed the envelope into the mattress as tenderly as a mother laying her baby to rest in its crib. He threaded the wires under the mattress along the cot to the pillow and connected switch to detonator, detonator back to battery and so on. As he began to tidy the apartment he suddenly heard a faint rattling of the door handle. For a second he almost gave way to panic: his heart missed a beat, the jet-black hair rose on his scalp and the gun appeared in his hand as he swung round. Then he realised it had to be Antonis, and with the realisation fear flowed out of him as quickly, like air from a punctured tyre. He turned the key softly in the lock and beckoned the valet inside.

'What the hell do you want?'

'You've got to get out quickly, the General's coming back.' He was gibbering with fright. 'The soldiers just took a radio message.'

'How long have we got?'

'Only a few minutes.' They were talking in whispers, as if General Benchley was already mounting the stairs. 'The helicopter's on its way now.'

'I'm almost through.' Elvides went to the bed, tugged gently at the wire he had soldered to the drawing-pin, raised it, and started the watch movement. That meant the bomb would be armed in another fifteen minutes. He laid the under blanket on the mattress, tucked in the sheet and stood back: perfect! No one would suspect the bed had been disturbed.

Behind him, Antonis was haggard with fear. 'Hurry. For God's sake, please hurry.'

Elvides remembered just in time to bend down and retrieve the handkerchief filled with flock. As he went to empty it into the rucksack Antonis stumbled into him and most of it spilled on to the floor. The bomb-maker had no time to see to it now. Instead, he gripped the valet's arm and pointed with his free hand at the fragments.

'I want this lot cleared up. Every last fragment: it's important, d'you hear?'

Antonis began to whimper a protest, and Elvides shook him like a dog shaking a rat. 'Calm down you old fool, and listen to me! No one's going to think it strange if they find *you* here, tidying up your master's room. Clean it carefully, lock the door behind you, and then leave the building in the normal way – have you got that?'

'Yes, yes, don't worry. Just get out before those soldiers find you – please!'

Elvides took the rucksack, peered up and down the corridor, and vanished. Immediately, Antonis got down on his knees and began to gather up the tiny pieces of flock. They were enough to hang him and he was so frightened he could hardly breathe. When he had them all in his hands, he stood up. In the same second, he heard voices on the stairs. Without waiting to see who was coming he gave a little moan of terror, ran into the bathroom, and flushed the tell-tale grey wisps down the toilet.

It never occurred to him they might float, as he tried so desperately to explain before Elvides shot him, next morning.

Eoka leaflets ordering the ceasefire appeared on the streets of Nicosia on 9 March, 1959. Elvides came out of hiding two months later, when it was clear there would be no treachery, and caught the plane to Beirut. Before summer was out he had begun his next assignment, as head of the bomb pyramid and technical adviser to the emergent Palestinian terror groups. Years later, when one of his pupils told him Ramage was still alive, Elvides insisted he must be mistaken.

It was 1966 and Russian arms and money were pouring secretly into the Yemen to equip and train the tribesmen further south who were already mustering to drive the British from the vital Red Sea base at Aden. Elvides flew in with letters of introduction from Arab friends in the P.L.O. and offered his specialist services to the rebels. They were brave enough, and blessed with a prodigious appetite for treachery. He taught them how to lay mines, rig booby traps, make incendiary devices, car-bombs and parcel-bombs. Nor did he forget to impress on them the importance of blackmailing the police and civil service, and using every convert to pass on information and set up targets for assassination.

The British Prime Minister was a guest in Moscow at the time. Even as the terror classes went ahead, the Kremlin solemnly warned its men in the area to do nothing – overtly – that would upset the diplomatic applecart. So Elvides posed once again as a mercenary, and studiously avoided all contact with the Russian embassy and its satellites in Taiz. He in turn was given specific orders not to enter the Aden Protectorate personally, as originally planned, for fear of arrest and interrogation by the security services. He would never have dreamed of disobeying them in the normal way. But one morning a group of NLF terrorists arrived in Sa'ana, bringing with them photographs stolen from the Special Branch files in Aden identifying the top security experts in the colony. Elvides looked through them before they were passed on to the Russians and offered his usual forthright advice.

'I know of that one. Formerly senior interrogator at Camp K in Cyprus. Ged rid of him as soon as you can.' Or 'He's an S.A.S. man, and very, very dangerous. You'll have a job to get near him, though. Try setting up an ambush, with a sniper waiting to pick him off.'

He spent a long time over one picture: it had been taken at a distance and the eye-patch worried him, but there was something ominously familiar about the big blond figure in khaki shown on the right of a group.

'Who can identify the soldier?' He held the photograph aloft and pointed with his finger, but in his heart of hearts he knew the answer before anyone spoke.

'His name is Ramage, effendi.' The tribesman from Lahej was a deserter from the South Arabian Army who had attended briefings on land-mines and booby-traps before. 'That is Major Ramage, the head of bomb disposal in Aden. I have heard him speak many times.'

He had not died in the ambush, then. Shock and disappointment were gradually replaced by another sensation quite foreign to Elvides: one almost of dread. Now he knew how Sisyphus felt, the Underworld figure who was condemned by the Gods to spend all his time rolling a huge boulder uphill, only to see it bound back again to the bottom. *To hell with the orders,* he told himself. This time I'm going to take the bastard out before he knows I'm within a thousand miles of him.

'When are you men crossing back into the Protectorate?'

'At the new moon. We have orders to attack Sheik Othman.' Sheik Othman was a key Arab township in the colony.

'I'll come with you' said Elvides. 'No doubt you could use a bomb-maker. And I have some unfinished business to attend to.'

God knows the murder in Aden was superbly planned: it deserved success, if patience, skill and surprise counted for anything at all. He travelled down from Yemen with the rebels.

through Dhala and Lahej across the State boundary line into Sheik Othman and lived in the township for weeks fighting the British. He built mortars to pound the detention barracks at Mansoura. He led forays across the white graveyard of the Salt Pans at night, to strike at the RAF base at Khormaksar; he sowed land-mines on every road used by the army convoys and even established a thriving bomb-factory, with parcel-bombs being delivered regularly to the top Civil Servants in the colony. But all the time the NLF terrorists were working for *him*, tailing Ramage home, timing the movements of Mrs Ramage and the children, blackmailing the servants into preparing the way for the bomb that was to end the duel, once and for all.

The Ramages lived in an apartment off the Maalla Road. In those days it was considered a 'safe' area but Ramage himself was cautious: he left at different times each morning and drove by different routes, always under strong escort. However the oldest child – a girl – went to Army school, and that meant a domestic routine. It was Mrs Ramage's daily practice to leave at 11.30 a.m. with the baby and collect her daughter from school, and then drive to the Officers' Club at Tarshine where her husband joined them at the pool, sometime between noon and one o'clock. At 1.30 p.m. they returned to their own apartment for a snack lunch, while the baby slept.

With the co-operation of one of the servants, Elvides smuggled a bomb into the apartment as soon as Mrs Ramage had left one morning. It was a highly sophisticated light-sensitive device, hidden inside the refrigerator and set to explode automatically as the door opened, and the light came on. Elvides left as soon as it was wired up. The servant made an excuse to go shopping, and – as instructed – left the house-key with neighbours, as a security precaution. That was at 1.20 p.m. It seemed that there was nothing that could go wrong.

Elvides could have wept at what happened next. The neighbour ran out of ice and sent his servant round with the key to take some from the Major's refrigerator. The bomb went off, killing the unfortunate servant and wrecking the apartment – while Ramage was still 200 yards away! There was no answer to that kind of luck, reflected Elvides: the Arabs told him it was the will of Allah, and maybe it was. He himself was back in Yemen before he found out what had happened, and was never given another chance to kill the bastard. He spent the next four years in Lebanon, on Russian orders. In 1971 the Eleventh Department of the First Chief Directorate of the KGB summoned him back to Moscow for talks. It was the same Ivan Aleksandrovich Gruchev who met the plane from Damascus, escorted him personally to his hotel and dined him later.

Gruchev was now Head of Liaison (Terrorism) for Western Europe, a little fatter, a lot greyer, and much more affable. 'You've done well, Elvides.' He beamed at the Greek, noting his tanned face and lean figure. 'I had certain reservations when we first took you on, I don't mind admitting it now. But you've done everything we could have asked a man since you left Chkalov, and more. I'm proud of you. Come on, drink up.'

They were sharing a table in the Aragvi, the Georgian restaurant in Gorky Street. Shashlik and kupaty followed caviare and vodka, washed down with bottles of a vintage kvanch-kara. Gruchev had prospered greatly since his early days in Diversion and Terror, thought Elvides. His suits came from West Berlin, his ties from Paris, his underclothes (sh!) from the Jewish manufacturers, Marks and Spencer of Great Britain. He was a V.I.P. now, a full colonel in the KGB.

'You've completed fifteen years in the Middle East for us now, Elvides, d'you realise that?'

'Not only do I realise it, comrade Gruchev, I've got a few scars to show for it,' he growled. He was no longer a frightened boy who needed to lie to gain admission to Soviet Russia, he thought: he was one of the most able operatives in the service, and to hell with this patronising, desk-bound warrior.

'What is it you want of me now?' he asked.

If he noticed the surliness of his guest's tone, Gruchev gave no sign. Still smiling affably, he took a notebook from his pocket and consulted it. 'We felt it might be time to give you a change of scenery. A chance to unwind and relax in quieter surroundings. The Jews seem to have given you a pretty hard ride recently.'

'They're tough bastards. And a damned sight meaner than the British.'

'Ah, yes. The British.' A pudgy finger smoothed down a page in the notebook. 'You were married in Cyprus, I see. We didn't know about the wedding – or your wife's unfortunate death, come to that – for a long time afterwards.' Back came the smile on his face. 'Or we'd have sent our condolences.'

'I didn't think you'd be interested.'

'We're interested in everything our operatives do. Not that there would have been any objection to your marriage to the lady concerned, even though she was an American citizen by her former marriage. We would have looked upon any such arrangement as the ideal cover for you, all things considered. Of course, we would have checked her out very thoroughly first. Had you told us about her, I mean.'

Elvides drained his glass, but refrained from comment. A tiny pulse began to tick in his throat as Gruchev continued.

More pages flicked open. 'I see there are one or two skeletons in the cupboard. Ah well, hardly surprising I suppose, considering you've had such a long spell away.'

Elvides let that go by, too.

'You were very nearly recalled and disciplined by us five years ago, did you realise that, my friend?'

The Greek frowned in disbelief. That would be 1966. How the hell was a man supposed to remember everything that happened five years ago, for God's sake? 'I'm not even sure where I was that year,' he said. 'Yemen, was it?'

'That's what we *thought*. You had orders to remain in Taiz. But you disappeared for some weeks, to try to settle an argument with a British Army officer in Aden. A man called Ramage.'

'That's right.' Elvides smiled at him, but without humour. 'I blew his apartment to bits. Just missed him, unfortunately. He's the bastard who killed Elli.'

'That may be.' Gruchev waved a hand impatiently, as though it were an irrevelance. 'However, if you had been picked up, there might have been unfortunate consequences for my Department. The British have persuaded better men than you to turn double.'

'You have to be out of your mind, Gruchev.' Elvides reached across the table and poured himself another drink. 'Listen, I just told you, Ramage is the offal who killed my wife. The NLF man from Aden presented me with a whole dossier on his movements. What would you have done – blown him a kiss?'

'You are impertinent.' The notebook closed with a snap. What is expected – no, *demanded* from every operative – is unquestioning discipline at all times. No one is too big to go unpunished once they step out of line. On both these occasions, your marriage to the American and your unauthorised journey to Aden, your actions were overlooked because of previous good service. Next time you may not find me so accommodating.'

'You armchair heroes amuse me,' sneered Elvides. The bottle was empty and without reference to his host he signalled for a replacement. 'You sit on your fat arses in Moscow, and imagine it's you who's fighting the war. Let me tell you something, comrade. I face death and torture every day of the week over there, and the Jews are absolute bloody experts at it, take my word for it. D'you really think you can frighten me with all this horseshit about bringing me back to *discipline* me? You know what, I'd love it, it would be like a holiday on the beach at Sochi after what I've been through out there.' He raised his glass contemptuously. 'Up yours, Gruchev, as the Americans say.'

Gruchev regarded him steadily for a moment. And then, without looking round, he snapped his fingers. 'Waiter!'

'Yes, comrade-colonel.' He bowed obsequiously.

'Ask my assistant to hand you my briefcase.' The waiter scurried away to a table by the door and spoke to the two big men who sat there. One of them reached under his chair and passed over a leather briefcase immediately. Elvides looked just a little worried as he sat and waited.

'You were saying something about holidays at Sochi, I believe.' Colonel Gruchev unzipped the case and took out a slim blue folder. Stamped in yellow on the cover were two words, WAR CRIMES. He held it up just long enough for Elvides to catch a glimpse of them and then began to read. 'Elvides, Paul. Born Salonika, on or about 13 May 1922 . . .' he mouthed the words of the criminal offence and prison sentence softly, as if he was speaking to himself . . . 'ah yes, here we are: *volunteered* for the Todt Organisation, 27 May 1941 – my word, you didn't waste much time, did you? – see affidavit sworn by Tassos Matsis, photostat copies attached herewith.'

He smiled genuinely now: he was enjoying himself.

'Matsis was a real Greek hero. He fought the Nazis all through the occupation of your country; perhaps he was the man you mixed up with your "father" when you made that sworn statement to me back in 1946, remember? Comrade Matsis was an exceedingly thorough man and a good communist, also from Salonika. He drew up a list of all known traitors and fifth columnists, and hid it safely shortly before he was sent to a concentration camp. He dug it up when he came back and sent it to us shortly before he was killed fighting for ELAS in the civil war.'

Elvides felt it difficult to stop his hand shaking when he picked up his glass this time.

'Because of the incompetence of my predecessor that report was pigeon-holed for a number of years,' Gruchev continued. 'Once it reached me it was a different story. I knew all about you before you landed in Cyprus, my friend, that you were a real Greek bastard, that you never knew your parents, that you never were a Party member, that you were nothing but a criminal and a collaborator. We had positive identification, signed statements, – why, we even traced a number of old ladies now living in East Germany who remembered you *very* fondly – so don't ask me to shed any crocodile tears over your late, dear, departed Elli Marvin, please.'

It was his turn to fill his glass now, and he offered none to his guest.

'I let you carry on in Cyprus for a number of reasons, Elvides. It was a Right-Wing insurrection, and we didn't care if it succeeded or failed, just as long as it embarrassed the British and drained their resources even further. We only had to let Grivas know you were one of ours – and we had a hundred ways of doing so – and his guerrillas would have castrated you, hung your balls out for eaglemeat. Another reason I let you carry on was that you were efficient at your job: although we always, but *always* kept watch on you in case you were ever tempted to go double.'

He accepted a Cuban cigar from the waiter and lit up appreciatively.

'You had the effrontery just now to call me an armchair hero, you pig's bladder. Tell me, do you think any Russian of my generation doesn't know the smell of gunpowder, eh? I was fighting Germans at Stalingrad in thirty below while you were exercising yourself under the blankets with their women in Wroclaw: and I mean *fighting*, not putting bombs in airliners to kill little babies and clapped-out old Jews who somehow managed to survive the concentration camps.' He tapped the blue folder that lay between them. 'We've gone soft in

Russia today, that's our trouble, we don't hang people from meathooks any longer. But what's written here will still bring you a minimum of thirty years in one of our Siberian health resorts, and you may take it from me it would prove very, very different to lying on the beach at Sochi. I know some camps where you would pray for the cold to put you out of your misery come winter, Elvides.'

Elvides seemed to be ageing as he listened.

'But it hasn't happened yet,' said Gruchev, 'and there's no reason why it ever should – as long as you watch your behaviour in the presence of your superiors in future. Speak when you're spoken to and mind your P's and Q's, that's what the British say, isn't it?' He summoned the waiter once more. 'Brandy for my friend here, he's looking a little pale. Now then, Elvides, as long as we understand each other, and you don't start getting too big for your breeches again, I'm prepared to offer you a new assignment. Are you interested?'

'Yes,' He read the message in Gruchev's face, and hastily added 'comrade-colonel.'

'Good, good. Now in my department we're planners, you understand: dreamers, if you prefer the word, we're always thinking up something new. And as we see it, the kind of terrorist campaign you've been running in the Lebanon is already on the way out, becoming obsolete. Oh, these Arabs will keep it going for years yet, and it plays a useful part in the general programme, certainly. None the less it's as dead as the dodo, Elvides. No more attacks from the outside: from now on, we strike from within. And the target needs to be changed. Not too drastically, merely a slight variation of course.'

His eyes were like a toad's, soft and dark and unwinking.

'I mean, look, these Jew-boys are tough. Three wars and still the Arabs have got nowhere, quite aside from losing a few thousand billion roubles worth of our equipment into the bargain. Add ten years of high-pressure terrorist activity on top of that – financed by Russia – and where has it got us all, eh, tell me that? You're right, nowhere. The objective remains, though, that never alters: destruction of the capitalist society. So, let the P.L.O. continue to bang its head against the Jewish brick wall, it will serve to keep them both occupied, even if it changes nothing. Meantime we'll graze in pastures new. *Germany.*'

He belched, loudly.

'I can see you're asking yourself, did I hear him correctly, did he say *Germany*? Oh, I agree: on the face of it, an even tougher nut to crack. A strong economy – fantastic how resilient the Germans are, you'd think it would take a hundred years to recover from the drubbing we gave them in the last lot – a sincere attempt to introduce a democratic form of government, a fat, contented working class, the best fed, best paid and best disciplined in all Europe: you name it, these Germans appear to have it going for them. But in spite of all that I say it's where we can win our greatest victory since we marched into Berlin thirty years ago – because it's all a veneer, a curtain hiding some enormous problems inside. There are a lot of rotten apples in the German barrel, my friend, and they're where you'd least expect to find them, among the sons and daughters of the prosperous *middle-class*. The German nation was compelled to go respectable after Hitler, to wash the stench of the concentration camps out of the nostrils of the rest of the world. Now the chickens have come home to roost: the kids have grown up, and they're sick and tired of so much dull respectability, they want to challenge everything the State and their parents stand for. They're hell bent on revolution, and we're going to help them bring it about.'

He raised his glass to Elvides.

'That's where you come in. A new terrorist group, with new targets to aim at. This time you're not going to teach your pupils to strike at *the people*, as you did in Israel: this time you're going to attack the whole fabric of law and order – the police, the judges, the courts, the State officials – and by your successes, to undermine the very foundations of national confidence. You will kidnap leading politicians and wealthy industrialists – the same privileged classes from which these young revolutionaries themselves have sprung – and make them suffer agonies of public humiliation before setting them free: and then only on terms which will erode future confidence in the authority of the State. You will make the high and mighty shiver in their shoes at the very mention of the name of your organisation, because you will demonstrate over and over again that the State is powerless to protect them against you.

The more police they assign to destroy you, the more police you will kill. If they arrest any of your commandos, and put them on trial, you will blow up the courtroom. The harsher the methods of punishment introduced by the authorities, the harsher still your treatment of your victims. You will introduce a reign of terror such as Germany has never known, not by hounding millions of helpless people, as Hitler did, but by persecuting the few rich and privileged, the governing class, for being what they are and all that they represent.'

Elvides was genuinely impressed. 'Brilliant,' he said.

Gruchev preened himself on the compliment. 'Thank you. It happens to be *my* thinking. Now then, organisation. The leader of your group needs to be one of these young firebrands from the universities: we'll pick one, and steer you his way. We're faced with an embarrassment of riches to choose from, incidentally. We've made a close study of the German scene recently, and according to the best available estimates there are something like a *hundred thousand* extremist students – on the Left and Right – in the country at the present time. We'll go for quality. There's a young fellow there called Baader making quite a name for himself already. That's the type we're after.'

'Why don't I contact him?'

'Use your head, man. If we set up a rival terrorist group that does bigger and better things than his own, it should spur him on to even greater efforts. The more the merrier, Elvides.'

'But of course.'

'You will appear on the scene and present yourself to our candidate as a stateless person: jetsam from World War Two with decided revolutionary tendencies – and enormous experience. You've served everywhere. Speciality explosives, all authentic stuff; except that you forget to mention us. And you'll be a teacher, not a leader. We want this to be a young people's organisation. But once the kids accept you, you begin to feed them ideas, the same ideas that I've given you this morning. Then you help them take it from there: helping only, never leading. They've got to imagine it's their show.'

'Brilliant. Really brilliant.'

'The name of the game is terror at the top. I want the whole *Bundesrepublik* to quake every time it opens its morning newspaper, wondering what the devil you've done this time. Go for the politicians, the judges, the capitalists, the top policemen, the Federal prosecutors and make them rue the day they were born. The sky's the limit in ruthlessness. Any member of the group who shows the slightest hesitation in carrying out orders must be dealt with.'

'Don't worry about that.'

'Now then. I want you back at Chkalov for a few months' refresher course before you leave for Germany. Not on explosives, that goes without saying: I daresay you can teach our people a thing or two there. But there are some new developments these days, some quite excellent nerve gases and so forth: you'll find it time very well spent. Also you'll need a crash course in the language.'

'I already speak German.' Elvides could have cut out his tongue as he said it.

'So you do,' said Gruchev slyly, 'so you do. I'm forgetting, you spent your formative years in the Reich.' He paused, as if trying to make up his mind. 'Look, since we're back on that subject, I feel I may have been a bit hard on you earlier today. We all made mistakes when we were young, eh? When I said at the outset that you'd done brilliantly in the Middle East, I meant it. Let's forget the other business.'

Elvides waited for the verbal kick in the groin, but none came.

'All I seek from you is an undertaking to toe the line in future. An agent who strays can find himself in all kinds of compromising situations.' He handed Elvides the slim blue folder. 'Here, take it, it's yours. You've earned it over the past twenty years.'

It was a considerable gesture, coming from whom it did. For one exhilarating moment Elvides felt exactly as he did on leaving Chkalov all those years ago: consumed by love for the cause. 'Thank you, comrade-colonel,' he said, and now his tone was genuinely respectful. 'I won't forget that in a hurry. As you yourself said, many people do things in their youth they later regret. Well, sometimes I feel sick to my stomach when I think of myself as a kid, working for the Nazis. The fact that I didn't know any better doesn't make it any easier. I don't say that to try to impress you. I don't even expect anyone to believe me. But it's true, none the less.'

'Forget it ever happened.' Gruchev flicked his lighter and

held the flame to the incriminating document. When it had disappeared into ash, he raised his glass. 'To hell with the past. Here's to the future – and your return to Germany. Under the right colours.'

'To the future.'

Colonel Gruchev felt no sense of shame in the knowledge that he had a photostat copy of the offending file in his office. The information it contained would never be levelled against the bomb-maker officially: he was far too valuable to the KGB. But you had to keep a stick of some kind to beat a man with, just to remind him who was boss.

It took nearly two years to recruit the right people and then lick the Liberation Army into shape. After that Paul Elvides simply made the bombs – and a few suggestions – while Angela Schless led her commandos into war against authority. It was the smallest, most compact terrorist group operating anywhere in western Europe, only a dozen strong: and what made it remarkable was that eight of its members were women, young, well-educated, intelligent women nearly all of whom were born with the proverbial silver spoon in the mouths. Elvides remembered them now with genuine pride and pleasure, all except Gudrun, that is.

Angela Schless herself might have been hard put to define precisely what it was that transformed her from privileged little rich girl into a gun-carrying revolutionary and finally, hardened killer: but there was no denying that she was an ideal choice for terrorist leader. She was fearless, quick-witted, ruthless almost to the edge of madness and utterly dedicated to the overthrow of the whole democratic system in Germany. Yet she had enjoyed a head-and-shoulders start in life over most of her contemporaries with a secure home, wealthy and adoring parents, good health, startling physical beauty, and all the benefits of the most exclusive education and upbringing that money could buy. The whole of her youth was sheltered. She attended convent school, then boarding school in Switzerland, and – for a brief period – university at Hamburg. There was no unhappy love affair to twist her outlook, she had never been tempted by drugs or sex orgies, and until she arrived at university she had never seen at close quarters, far less taken part in, a violent public demonstration: on any count she was a model daughter and perfectly normal seeming young woman, with rational feelings and views. In her twentieth year, this normal world of Angela Schless suddenly fell apart. She was walking behind a Vietnam protest march feeling rather self-conscious and silly – she had only come along to be with her friend Veronika – when suddenly the fists and the stones and the police batons began to fly, a student was killed, and she found herself fighting like a wildcat alongside boys and girls she did not know, and might never have spoken to in her life, but for the brutal half-hour which ended the rally. When she got back to the campus that night she was shell-shocked, outraged at the harshness shown by the police, and – although she could not have realised it at the time – committed. When she woke up next morning she found herself in bed with a total stranger, a lean and bearded youth who preached armed revolution and sexual licence with equal fervour and conviction. Instead of saying 'Hello' or 'Who the hell are you' or falsely, 'I love you' he just said 'All policemen are Fascist pigs' as soon as he opened his eyes, and mounted her again.

To her astonishment Angela found that she enjoyed the whole experience, mentally as much as physically: it was as if a door had suddenly opened on to a room which hitherto had been kept locked, on parental orders, all her life. She had taken a leading part in a violent public demonstration. She had kicked and fought policemen, she had been hit by a truncheon, she had got herself completely drunk and she had gone to bed with a total stranger, all within the space of a few incredible hours. And what a stranger! He was physically dirty, he used the most appalling language, he treated her as if she was a whore. And yet she felt that she wanted to give him everything she had, her body, her money, her mind and her time, because of what he represented: the cause. He *believed*: not in religion, as she had been taught to do, but in revolution. Until yesterday she had never really cared about other people very much: worldly things had always been far too easy to come by. Yet this drop-out who had gatecrashed her life seemed to have plenty to live for, something that was sparked off by the plight of his fellow creatures everywhere. He wanted to turn the whole world upside down, and after listening to him, she found the idea crazily exciting and wholly unarguable.

It could not be right that she had so much while millions

of others round the world had nothing. It could not be right that full bellies and warm clothing should be the prerogative of the rich – or the rich nations. It could not be right that the Americans should be allowed to bomb and burn Vietnamese peasants with napalm, *for any reason*. The regime they sought to prop up was visibly corrupt. Therefore to condone the American intervention was corrupt. Logically then, her own country – which supported American foreign policy and was in alliance with her – was corrupt: even men like her own father, who paid large sums annually to help maintain the present ruling Party in office, were therefore corrupt. The whole capitalist western *world* was corrupt, argued this rude stranger with the whiplash tongue – and the only way in which justice and truth would ever prevail was through armed revolution.

Even a bog Irishman with a dozen porters inside him would have recognised the argument as blarney, but Angela – still shell-shocked from the rioting of the day before – was deeply impressed. To this day, all she knew about this first man she ever slept with was that his name was Ralf: but no other man, before or since, had ever had such a mesmeric effect upon her. By the time he had emptied the contents of her handbag and moved on to the next demonstration, Angela Schless was on the road to becoming Europe's most feared terrorist leader.

On the morning that she was sent down and was packing her bags for home, another stranger knocked on her door. This time it was a young woman, and like herself, a former religious bluestocking turned revolutionary: although somewhat longer in the tooth. She was a dark-haired, passionate temptress who led the bewildered Angela even further into the ways of temptation. 'My name is Ulrike Meinhof,' she said. 'I greatly admired what you did yesterday: I saw you, and fought with you. I think it is quite disgusting and typical of this cringing capitalist society of ours that you should be treated in this way.' She put her hands on the red-head's shoulders and kissed her, in a compassionate, comradely way. 'You have the makings of a true revolutionary,' she went on. 'And I say to you, don't go home, don't give up now, at the very beginning. Come with me and help fight for the cause.'

For the next two years Angela served her apprenticeship with the Red Army Faction. She was quickly blooded in gun battles with the police, in kidnapping, bank robbery and extortion, and within a few months of turning her back on university and home had won a quite remarkable reputation for ruthlessness, together with the newspaper label of 'Red Angela'. In those early days she sent a stream of letters to the media, announcing the coming revolution with all the fire of a Hot Gospeller warning of the Wrath to come. She split with Ulrike and the Red Army Faction because of their increasing domination by the brash newcomer, Andreas Baader: a young man she cordially detested. She believed that because of him the group was beginning to lose its political purity – and with it, its irresistible appeal to the young – as the violence and attendant publicity escalated. As she saw it, the RAF was moving further and further away from the basic revolutionary truths in pursuit of self-glorification, a kind of group personality cult, and she wanted no part of it.

Her aim was quite simply to cause such damage to the capitalist system by acts of terrorism as to hasten its collapse, and inevitable replacement by Marxist Leninism. The trouble was, that she could hardly wait for it to happen: she was too young and inexperienced to comprehend that no fledgling terrorist group could hope to survive for long – far less succeed in its aims – on faith alone. It had to have money and muscle, and that entailed the employment of much more than a few believers armed with popguns. The Liberation Army group which she formed with such high hopes was getting nowhere fast: the answer for such a small organisation lay, among other things, in the intelligent employment of explosive devices, and the timely appearance of an expert such as Paul Elvides on the scene seemed to her to be little short of miraculous.

He was enormously experienced. There was no device he could not build to order. He was as dedicated to the revolutionary cause as she was herself. He was as brave as anyone she had met in the Red Army Faction, but infinitely more intelligent and calculating. Yet he had no ambition to be leader, or even share the leadership: he was content to serve. Which was as well, she thought, because it would have been grotesque to have a man of his age as leader of such a youthful organisation. However, if he was old in years he was young in his ways, and undeniably attractive. Physically, she found him entirely satisfactory. They went to bed together frequently and contentedly, although – and this was important too – he was in no way sentimental, or possessive. Total sexual freedom was an unwritten rule in A.L. The kind of life they lived, the strain of killing and being hunted afterwards, left them all emotionally supercharged: so that each turned to the other indiscriminately and like animals for instant reassurance and fulfilment. The rules of normal society could not apply to them, who were beyond the pale: one day they floated on Cloud Nine, the next they were in the agonies of spiritual withdrawal symptoms. There had to be times when she could reach out for Helmut or Kurt or Ralf, as she chose, without comment by the others. Equally, Paul was at liberty to climb into bed with Kristina or Ilse or Gisele Mittel, or simply lie up on his own and get quietly drunk, which he frequently did – and no one minded, no one cared, no one gave a damn for any of the old conventions any more. This was the terrorist world, the *revolutionary* world, man: you just took what you wanted in life.

On one thing, though, they were all agreed, that Paul Elvides, the sly, tough old Fox from God knows where, had the best tactical brain in the entire terrorist business. It was he who first proposed war on the whole legal system. It was he who argued that they should attack the middle class only, and leave the working class severely alone. We shall need them one day, he said: our job now is to impress them with our power, and frighten them into looking the other way. It was he who pointed the way to the overthrow of the capitalist system with such classic realism: on the same day that the words 'law and order' become a mockery, he said, we shall have won. It was also Elvides who named Hans Kohl as their next kidnap victim.

Even Angela whistled at that. Kohl was Minister of the Interior and about as closely guarded as the Berlin Wall. Armed police camped in his garden. An armoured car stood watch among the roses. Dobermann pinschers, as black as sin, prowled the lawns. A helicopter shadowed his police convoy to work each day. He lived his whole life like a knight in armour.

The Kohl fortune had been made out of steel and had survived two world wars, two defeats, two allied occupations, plus the witch hunts that inevitably attended such disasters. The main reason for its survival intact was that the Kohls were able, tough, unscrupulous, intelligent – and as tenacious as weeds. Nothing could keep them down for long. Hans Kohl came bouncing back after the nightmare of 1945 – and a long and profitable association with the Nazis – by moving boldly and conspicuously into the anti-Russian camp when the Cold War had scarcely begun. By the time the Berlin Airlift began in 1948 he was on the way, and American investment was already healing the wounds inflicted by Allied bombs on the Kohl steelworks. When he relinquished the controlling interest – to his brother – and entered politics, he had ready-made friends in Washington to promote his advance. But even without their help, he was good. He was one of the original architects of the Economic Community, and down-and-out Germany hailed him as a new Messiah when the country began to take those first, seven-league strides towards recovery, and eventual prosperity. Everything he touched turned to gold. Ten years after Germany surrendered the Kohls were richer and more powerful than ever before, and he himself was tipped as a future Chancellor.

As a politician, he was quick to appreciate the threat that came from the terror groups that spread like warts across the face of the Bundesrepublik. No voice was louder than his in urging that the full resources of the State must be marshalled to smash the Red revolution before it could gain momentum. 'It's them or us,' he insisted. 'Those bombs you hear are aimed at the very foundations of the State.' His suggestion – years ago – of the creation of an élite anti-terrorist force controlled by the central Government, was now a reality in the shape of the Antiterrorismus-abteilung. Others took the credit, but he was the first advocate. Now as Minister of the Interior he was its battle commander and he used it relentlessly to smoke out the revolutionaries wherever they could be found. There could be no more prestigious target than Hans Kohl in all Germany.

'What a brilliant idea,' said Gudrun, mockingly. She was new to A.L. and had not met Elvides before. 'Let's kidnap Kohl in the morning, and the Chancellor in the afternoon. Just like that.'

'We can do it,' insisted Elvides. 'I've got an idea all worked out.' He turned to Angela Schless. 'May I go on?'

'Of course.' He had pleased her last night. 'Gather round, the rest of you, and listen to the Fox.'

Elivdes unrolled a map of the suburbs and pinned it to the

table top. Then he opened two match boxes and tipped out a collection of pins mounted with coloured paper flags: green for the police, red for A.L. He stuck the first green flag into a residential area on the furthest outskirts of the city.

'Kohl's house,' he said simply. 'He leaves for work each morning between six and eight, varying the time each day for security reasons. Let's see what he's got going for him when he comes out.' He consulted his notebook. 'One police car containing four plain-clothes men, driving ahead of his Mercedes. Kohl has a personal bodyguard with him, plus a driver and presumably both armed. Also there's a helicopter flying overhead all the way into town.'

He looked round at his companions. 'We don't stand a chance of kidnapping Kohl while that helicopter's around. So – we strike on a morning when it's grounded by the weather.' He checked his notebook again. 'I've done my homework on that already. The helicopter has been grounded twice this month: on neither occasion was Kohl given any additional motorised escort. Obviously, something like that has to be a snap decision: but the chances are there will only be the single escort car, even in the event of bad weather. It's only a seven mile journey, after all.'

They all accepted that.

'Now, routes into town. Like his time of departure, they chop and change for security reasons. But the cars have to come over the cross-roads *here* sooner or later, to get to the autobahn. All right, that's where we take him.' In went the first red flag. 'We'll need two cars, plus a commando unit on the ground. If those on foot wait at the bus-stop with their guns hidden inside shopping bags, no one will give them a second glance. And that's important, since we have no way of knowing his timetable in advance.'

Next, he scattered a handful of pellets on the table top. Each was about the same size as the head of a match, and made of plastic. 'That's nerve gas, stolen from the British army camp at Celle a few weeks ago. I've been experimenting, fitting these pellets into ordinary 9mm bullets. The gas expands at the rate of about fifty thousand to one on contact with oxygen. So anyone who is not killed in those police cars will be knocked out simultaneously by gas, for up to six hours. Be careful only to aim at the front of Kohl's car. It doesn't matter how many live or die in the escort vehicle, of course.'

He consulted his notes again.

'Now, timing. Kohl's escort will be in constant touch with H.Q. by radio, of course. And even without that helicopter shadowing us, I doubt if we'll get more than five minutes start before the road-blocks begin going up. So as soon as we grab him, we head straight into the city with the prisoner: those five minutes will give the driver time to be on the outskirts, and in the main stream of traffic by then. That's the essence of my plan, to take Kohl *into* the city and hole up with him there. But I'll come back to that in a moment.'

He lit a cigarette. 'Next, cars. We'll have a decoy car waiting at the scene of the ambush, with tailors' dummies in the back dressed to look like people. All we do is supply a driver. As soon as we've got Kohl, he will drive with the dummies like a bat out of hell for the frontier at Aachen. Of course, the police will be waiting for him there, but he'll pull off the autobahn on this side of the border and continue to draw the hounds for as long as he can. The police won't dare open fire as long as they think Kohl is one of those dummies in the back of his car. With a souped-up engine, he ought to be able to lead them quite a dance. Of course, he's going to get caught eventually, his job is simply to buy time for the rest of us. We can always persuade them to set him free afterwards. All right so far, Angela?'

She waved at him to carry on.

'As well as that decoy car we've got a laundry van waiting at the ambush site. There's a firm called Alpine Clean who do the round of the big hotels every morning, picking up the dirty linen. We'll borrow one of their vans, bring it here, and pop Kohl into a linen basket. As soon as we've got him inside the city, we'll have a car waiting at the Park Hotel and transfer Kohl while the normal pick-up goes on. And the car will deliver him into the apartment here, while the chase is still going on round Aachen.'

He turned to Angela with a confident smile.

'I know we can do it, I feel it in my bones. Once you take that helicopter out of the reckoning, it's just one more police car with four bored men, doing the same old routine day after day. They won't give us any trouble, Angela. And with Kohl in the bag, you can really have some fun.'

'I think you're right,' she said. Then she looked at the others. 'I don't have to *order* anyone to do the decoy job: who's going to volunteer?'

Everyone held up their hands. 'The honour's yours, Kurt. Don't worry, we'll see they let you go soon enough, even if we have to cut Kohl's prick off.'

It was a morning when everything conspired to aid the terrorists. Once he learned that his helicopter was grounded by snowstorms, Kohl decided to leave immediately. He refused the offer of a second escort car and the two vehicles arrived at the road junction at 7.40 in drifting snow and poor visibility. Elvides roared in from the right, at speed and without lights, to ram Kohl's car and force it off the road. As the police escort started its skid turn to try to get back to the Minister's Mercedes, Angela and her girl commandos came out of the shelter and opened up on both cars at point blank range with their sub-machine-guns. It was all over within seconds, with Kohl taken unharmed. By a freak of weather conditions, radio contact between the convoy and police headquarters had been poor since the journey started. Now no one worried unduly until there had been no signal for ten minutes. By that time the van was inside the city, and Kurt was able to turn back off the Aachen road without sighting a single pursuer. Germany was stunned by the news: what next?

On Elvides' advice, the terrorists took their time before presenting their first demands, although responsibility was claimed at once in the name of A.L. And then, as the public outcry grew over the failure of the police to protect the Minister of the Interior and speculation mounted over his safety, Angela telephoned a newspaper office.

'*Achtung!* The Liberation Army commandos who captured the Nazi sympathiser Hans Kohl on December 5 are to place him on trial for war crimes. If the German government wishes to seek representation for the accused, it must: 1. Release all prisoners now serving sentence for alleged acts of terrorism, irrespective of the organisation to which they belong. 2. Pay the sum of ten million Deutschmarks to the Palestine Liberation Organisation headquarters in Tripoli, Libya. 3. Place an aircraft on standby ready to take the freed commandos to a country of their choice. All conditions must be met within forty-eight hours from receipt of this message, signed, Leader of the Liberation Army, Schless.'

War crimes was Elvides' idea: his meal in the Aragvi had not been entirely wasted. And it was at his suggestion that Angela put her name to the directive. 'It's not a question of any personality cult,' he assured her. 'It's a gesture to show your contempt for the authorities. You're issuing an implicit challenge and saying "I kidnapped Hans Kohl, and what can you do about it?" '

In an address to the nation, the German Chancellor went on television and firmly rejected all demands. Another ten days passed without word. Then on Christmas Eve, a video-tape recording showing Kohl in the Liberation Army dock was delivered to a TV studio. A written text of his 'plea to the court' was also sent to the newspapers, to ensure maximum publicity, and copies of both tape and text posted to the media in Paris, Rome and Amsterdam. There was no possibility of suppressing them all, and publication went ahead in all countries.

Kohl's appearance was shocking, although he was paraded naked first to demonstrate that there was not a mark or a bruise on his body. There had in fact been no physical brutality: maltreatment was confined strictly to degradation. His captors had removed his false teeth, and refused him permission to wash or shave throughout his confinement. He had been compelled to wear the same clothing day and night: to sleep on bare floorboards, like a dog, and eat his food from a bowl like one, kneeling down with his hands bound behind him. For some days Kohl refused to eat in this manner. No attempt had been made to make him. In the end, sheer hunger won and by the time he appeared on television he would have barked like a dog too, if ordered, so hungry was he. All he was given was one meal of scraps each day, followed by water.

He had lost a great deal of weight, and his clothes hung from him. There was no heating in his room, so that he suffered continually from the cold. He slept little, mostly from fear but partly from the nagging cold and hunger, and physical discomfort of sleeping on bare boards at the age of sixty-one: and also because the terrorists called him, every hour of the night and day to answer questions. He had to answer them all, on pain of forgoing his solitary meal next day. He was not allowed to see out of the window, which was shuttered:

the faint traffic noises he could hear from time to time made him yearn inexpressibly to awake from his living nightmare, step into his familiar chauffeur-driven limousine and be restored to the bosom of his family. He was not allowed to know the time or the date, and forbidden to make any mark on the walls or floors which might help him keep a rough calendar. He was denied tobacco, which he craved, as well as newspapers, radio and television. For the first week he believed that sheer strength of character would see him through. For the next few days he quietly despaired. Now he was becoming increasingly afraid, although still no one had laid a finger on him.

His coat and cardigan were taken from him, as well as his tie, collar, belt and shoes, for his brief appearance before the cameras. He wore a cardboard label round his neck which read 'Hans Erich Kohl, War Criminal, arrested by the Liberation Army on December 5.' He wept as they led him into the brightly lit room, not from pain or self-pity, but for the sheer joy of feeling warm again under the TV lights. He clutched his trouser band with one hand, and walked unaided to the chair set aside for him: he had already been told he would not be fed that day unless he behaved satisfactorily.

He would be asked a number of questions, they said. What he had to say in reply would be held up on a board in front of him, out of sight of the cameras. All he could think of as he headed for the chair was 'God in heaven, what will Mutti think of me when she sees me like this?' He stank, he was dirty, his body ached from the agony of the floorboards, his beard and hair were unkempt, he itched, he felt ashamed to be seen without his teeth, he was hungry, he was afraid and so very, very weary. The questions were put by a woman, a young one by the sound of her, but he was unable to make out her face clearly because the lights were so dazzling. It was all he could do to read the answer-board, and he screwed up his face and concentrated fiercely, determined that nothing in this world was going to make him miss his solitary meal of the day. Never in all his life had he imagined hunger like this.

'Have you been beaten or tortured by any member of A.L. since your capture?'

'No. No one has laid a finger on me.'

'Or forced to say anything at this trial that you do not wish to say voluntarily?'

'Nothing.'

'Do you swear that?'

'I do. So help me God.'

'Now, do you admit to paying funds secretly to the Nazi Party before the war?'

'I do.'

'How much?'

'Three million Deutschmarks altogether.'

'On the dates set out in the papers before this court?'

'Yes.'

'You co-operated with the Nazis willingly throughout the war, and used slave labour in your factories and mines?'

'I did.'

'And lied to the Occupying Powers afterwards?'

'In so far as I could.'

'What is the estimate of the personal fortune you paid into your numbered Swiss banking account over those war years?'

'I'm not sure because of the interest. It now stands at twenty-three million Swiss marks.'

'That was money made from forced labour?'

'Yes.'

'Are you aware that your colleagues in the government have refused to make certain concessions which in turn might have been taken into account when the sentence of this court is passed upon you?'

'Yes, I know. I hope they sleep well tonight.'

'You stand convicted of corruption out of your own mouth. Is there anything you wish to say in your own defence?'

'No. I am guilty as charged and unfitted to hold office. I ask Germany to forgive me.'

The film was cut there: the sentence was announced later, after he had been led back to his room. As soon as he got there Kohl begged his tormentors 'There, I've done everything you ordered. Please may I have some food now?'

'Tie him up,' laughed Angela, 'and give him his present for being a good dog.' Elvides kicked the bowl across the floor and they all watched as he knelt, and ate. It was his last meal. On Christmas Day Juliane shot him and left the body outside the offices of the Ministry of the Interior. This time the label tied round his neck said 'Hans Kohl, convicted of war crimes, and executed by the Liberation Army on December 25. By order of The Leader, Schless.'

Over the next six months A.L. ran up a number of spectacular successes in the war against law and order. British and American military installations in Germany were attacked and secret NATO papers stolen. These were subsequently sent to Communist newspapers through Europe, for publication. The top security jail at Stammheim was penetrated by its commandos who distributed radio sets, small arms and explosives among certain prisoners. News of the cache was then deliberately leaked, to the huge embarrassment of the authorities. Two of the nation's top industrialists and a high court judge were kidnapped, and released unharmed – on payment of ransom. No arrests were made afterwards because all three victims steadfastly declined to make any statement, or file any kind of complaint. Neither the Antiterrorismus-abteilung nor the Militärische Abwehrdienst – military Intelligence, popularly known as MAD – nor the Bundesnachrichtendienst – the secret service, or BND – were able to hit back with a single arrest in all that time and the forces of law and order were fast becoming a national laughing stock.

Soon, 'A.L.' was on the lips of everyone at some time or another each day, in private homes, offices, hotels, clubs and bars, planes and trains – wherever Germans gathered together. If a total stranger struck up a conversation with the question 'Heard what they've done now?' you knew automatically that 'they' were the Liberation Army terrorists. Every student with a grievance, real or imagined, carried the letters 'A.L.' in his mind, and the mindless crept out at night under cover of darkness and daubed them on the walls of Germany in bright, red paint. Wealth and position no longer carried its former automatic guarantee of privilege, and protection. Fewer and fewer people were willing to come forward as witness to any crime, lest those crimes had been committed by A.L. Without the support of the public at large, the police and the security services became increasingly hamstrung in their efforts to find, and punish, offenders. At the end of those six months of unbroken terrorist success, the cracks in the foundations of State were already beginning to show.

Gudrun, the new girl, kept pestering Angela to inflate the

A.L. reputation even further, by staging a prestige operation outside Germany. They were flexing their muscles in those days and the mood of invincibility was infectious. Against his better judgment, Elvides allowed himself to be talked into putting up suggestions: and a paragraph in the newspapers duly inspired the Honeymoon Jumbo attack. They all knew that the German security services were under intense pressure to produce some kind of results against the Liberation Army terrorists: on that basis alone it seemed prudent to turn elsewhere for targets, at least for the time being. Angela immediately approved Elvides' suggestion and gave orders for the group to leave Germany temporarily. She and Helmut left for Paris to make contact with French Left-Wing extremists. Kurt and Gudrun were sent to London to set up the administrative network required for Operation Jumbo: Elvides himself was to follow later as bomb-maker and commando leader. Gisele Mittel and the others went to Italy, with instructions to forge links with the fast rising Red Brigade. Contact between them was maintained by placing coded messages in the Personal columns of selected newspapers.

Elvides poured himself a last drink and was surprised to see the bottle empty. For a few more moments he sat there, brooding. The Honeymoon Jumbo had looked a soft enough target, he thought: instead he had met with a crushing reverse, and would have a lot of explaining to do when he caught up with the others. There could be trouble, and he would need to be watchful – he himself had taught Angela to deal ruthlessly with failure. From the window he saw Kurt's car arrive. He drained the glass, picked up his bag and made his way down to the street. I'll be back, he vowed. And next time – Gruchev or no Gruchev – I'll settle the score with Ramage, no matter what it takes.

The flight home from New York was uneventful. Their children met them at London airport and travelled with them to the cottage in Cornwall for the rest of the summer holiday. Ramage rang Scotland Yard and spoke to Commander Evans as soon as they were settled in.

'Any news of Elvides, Commander?'

'None, sir.' It was more than three weeks since he had escaped from the flat. 'I think we can assume he's back in

Germany by now, in spite of all our precautions.'

'So what about us? Will you tell the local police to call off the watch on my house, or shall I?'

'Neither of us. We won't have it called off, for the time being.' He made reassuring sounds over the telephone, but he was adamant. 'No special reason, Colonel. It's just that I believe in being on the safe side, with a slippery cove like that.'

It was past midnight and at the hideout in Picardy they had chosen as their base for operations in France, an A.L. kangaroo court was about to try Paul Elvides for his failure in London. No one mentioned the word 'trial', nor were there any formalities involved: at first glance it might have seemed more like a party. The women wore kaftans and jewelled sandals: the young men were like peacocks, with flared jeans and silk shirts unbuttoned to the waist, high-heeled boots, pendants of gold and silver hanging from each neck and gorgeous bandanas, drenched in perfume, bound round their foreheads. Only Elvides wore his normal clothes, dark leather jacket, dark woollen jersey, dark trousers. His face was inscrutable. Drink flowed like a river in spate, the air was thick with the pungent, sweet-sour scent of marijuana. But it was a court hearing for all that and if the verdict went against Elvides, there could only be one penalty. Aptly enough, they met in an old shooting lodge.

Angela Schless presided as judge and jury and there would be no appeal against her findings or sentence. She was drunk, and in one of her regal moods: there was no way of knowing which way she would turn when trouble started. Helmut sat next to her, red as a turkey-cock, sweating profusely. He was to be prosecutor and he was drunk too. Gisele, Veronika and Ilse, all recalled from Rome with Hans and Rudi to witness proceedings against the old Greek fox, awaited developments with all the expectancy of the crones who sat knitting at the steps of the guillotine. They drank continually and passed the time whispering and laughing, ostensibly admiring the shipment of new automatic weapons whose delivery had been made the official reason for the full group meeting tonight. Blonde-haired Juliane, Kohl's executioner, had been detailed to carry out sentence again tonight if Angela so decided. No one doubted her ability, for she was fast and very accurate with a gun. Finally, as the only survivor of the abortive London raid – apart from the man in the dock – Kurt was present as an independent witness.

Elvides had driven from Orly that afternoon happily enough, expecting to meet Angela alone or, at worst, Angela with the stud Helmut. Now the number here tonight surprised and worried him more than he cared to admit: they were all armed, they were all high, they were all drinking hard and they had been out of action just long enough to crave excitement. He sat apart from the others, although he was one of them, and gazed round the room continually, trying to read their faces, working out his plan of campaign. He guessed they were looking for a scapegoat for London: he would have to tread carefully with Angela. Kurt would stand by him, but apart from him, he would be on his own. He poured himself a huge brandy and settled down to wait for Helmut to lead the attack.

The auberge had once been a headquarters for the Maquis during Hitler's war, and the *patron* and his wife had learned long ago to walk about with eyes averted and mouths shut. It stood alone on the outskirts of a hamlet less than an hour's drive from Amiens, timbered and sleepy, off the beaten track. Visitors were rare at this time of year and business normally poor, so that the arrival of the young men and women of the Liberation Army had come like manna from heaven. The German red-headed lady – young and pretty but, my word! so very businesslike – had appeared one day out of the blue to offer quite sensational terms for the exclusive hire of all six bedrooms in the auberge, plus use of the shooting lodge, for the season: cash in advance. When the inevitable, polite questions followed she explained that she belonged to an ornithological society anxious to film the life of the mallard, and if the old patron found that a little hard to credit in one so young and sexually provocative, what did it matter? Two hundred acres of bleak Somme marshland went with the inn, good for nothing except for duck flighting in to herald a hard winter ahead, and a few big pike, lying in ambush for roach and frogs among the reeds. In his father's day there had been no difficulty in letting the shoot. Nowadays the lodge was rarely booked, not only because of the prohibitive cost but also because of the general decline in blood sports everywhere. As a result, the patron relied more and more on the tourist trade for his income and kept the shooting lodge for himself and a few friends, to fill the pot. However, better by far, and infinitely more profitable, to let it to the fräulein and her hippie friends.

They were a rum lot, there was no doubt about that. But whether they used his lodge to film wild ducks or wild orgies (as his wife believed, after seeing some of the change-of-partners routine that went on in the bedrooms) was of no real consequence. Money talked, and they gave him no trouble there. With the rent paid in advance, the German lady arranged to settle all food and drink bills at the end of each month and so far the arrangement had worked admirably. Tonight there was a house-full, ten rather secretive German youngsters plus a middle-aged man, and all had gone to the lodge immediately after dinner to work out a script for their film – or so they said. The patron believed none of it, but continued to mind his own business. Why worry, as long as the money rolled in?

Elvides saw Helmut glance his way and nod his blond head confidently in reply to a question from Angela: it would be any minute now. He felt he could almost reach out and touch the hostility that surrounded him, so complete was his sense of isolation. Suddenly Angela signalled to Juliane, who went behind the bar and turned off the transistor. By chance, there was a machine pistol on the counter beside her: Elvides also knew there was a Colt .45 somewhere under the bar, always kept loaded in case of emergency – he had heard Veronika discussing it earlier. The whole room fell silent, leaving the floor to Helmut. As he lumbered to his feet his head struck the lamp-shade, to send shadows flickering crazily over every wall.

'Perhaps you'd like to tell us what happened in London, Paul?' he blurted out. He was a bear of a man, six feet four and weighing perhaps 300 pounds, but running to fat around the belly and the back of the neck. Enormous hands hung at his sides, flexing and unflexing. Great thighs filled his cotton jeans so full that the stitches threatened to burst as he moved. He wore a fancy hunting knife at his waist. Elvides gazed at his pendant and the ludicrous, perfumed bandana and thought: he's like a hog in a ladies' powder-room. Now he spoke in an overloud voice. 'I think you owe us an explanation for such a shambles.'

'You're drunk, Helmut,' said Elvides steadily. 'And there's no need to shout if you want to say something to me. I can hear you fine – everybody can, you've got such a big mouth.' He set his glass down carefully. 'All right, what's eating you?'

Helmut growled at that and walked closer, putting a finger as big as a banana under the Greek's chin and tilting it up. 'You screwed things up in London, that's what's eating me. And all the rest of us: four members of the group shot dead, and a fortune lost in ransom money. It's also the first time any of us have seen you in weeks. I think you've got quite a lot of explaining to do, one way and another – old man.' He said the words not in the British way, but as a jibe, a sneer at the Greek's age. 'And it had better be good. For your sake.'

Elvides sat still, and measured the distance between the end of his right shoe and Helmut's bulging crotch. 'The reason you haven't seen me,' he said calmly, 'is because I've had half the police forces in Europe looking for me ever since I left London. But Kurt here knew where I was: any one of you could have flown out and talked to me, any time you wanted. But you didn't. Especially you, Helmut. You didn't even put your face outside those Paris whore houses. So don't give me any of that crap about not having seen me for weeks. Sit down and behave, before you get hurt.'

Helmut accepted the challenge and telegraphed his intentions by bunching an enormous fist and drawing it back to his shoulder. Elvides gripped the struts of his chair and kicked up, hard, driving the hard leather toe of his shoe into the German's groin. Then, as Helmut screamed and doubled over, he dropped on the floor and rolled away, fast. But not quite fast enough: a massive pink hand grabbed his hair and hauled him bodily to his feet. Helmut held him out, an arm's length away, drew back one of those tree-trunk legs and let fly. His shoe caught Elvides in the base of the spine, and for a second the bomb-maker felt as if his back had caught fire. He bit through his lip to silence a groan, and flew through the air to crash against the wall, five feet away. As he went down he overturned a table full of drinks: a bottle rolled off the edge, and Elvides grabbed it by the neck as it came down on top of him. He smashed it against the wall as he climbed to his feet and moved forward, stabbing the glass shards in front of him, aiming for the eyes.. Helmut backed away, fumbling for his hunting knife, as the broken bottle flashed dangerously close. 'What's the matter, *Junge*, afraid of the old man, eh?'

Juliane leaned on the bar, waiting for the signal, but none came. Angela flattened herself against the wall with the others, clutching her drink, her eyes glittering with excitement as she watched the duel. The end came very quickly. As Elvides feinted with the bottle, Helmut stumbled back, tripped over a rug and fell with a crash that shook the room. His head hit the edge of the hearth with the thunk of an axe biting into a tree. Elvides leapt in and kicked him with every ounce of strength left in his body, driving his shoe deep into the kidneys. Helmut felt nothing: he was already unconscious. After a few seconds, a thin trickle of blood ran from one of his ears. His face was pale and he appeared to have trouble breathing.

For a little while no one spoke, no one moved. Then Elvides made for the bar, weaving like a drunk. His back was numb with pain. He took the first bottle he found, pulled out the cork with his teeth, put his head back and drank. Then he became aware that someone was talking to him.

'Have you killed him?' asked Angela.

'Killed Helmut?' He eased himself round and stared at the hulk on the floor. 'Never. You couldn't break that skull with a crowbar.' But it was his chance to get off the hook, and he took it gratefully. 'What the hell got into him, Angela?'

'It's what he said, he wanted to know what went wrong in London. We all did. And when you took such a long time to get back' – she hesitated for a moment – 'some of us got the wrong idea.' Her eyes were shining as she spoke to him. It had been like watching two gladiators fighting to the death: beautiful!

'What I said just now was the truth. If I'd stayed in Athens, or tried to cross back into Germany too soon, the Antiterrorismus would have had me for sure. So I went to the one place where I knew I'd be safe – back with my friends in the P.L.O.'

The look on Angela's face was unmistakable. Elvides reached out a hand and pulled her to him. 'In one way I'm glad this all happened. At least, everything's out in the open now. You had every right to demand an explanation, Angela, you're the Leader. But I've got nothing to hide. Ask Kurt, he was in London with me.'

Helmut was slowly beginning to stir, like a bear coming out of hibernation.

'There was nothing wrong with the plan,' continued Elvides.

'Our problem began *after* we hid the bomb on the plane. By a million to one chance, we drew a bomb disposal expert among the passengers, you must have read about that. It was incredibly bad luck: he was actually booked on another flight, but they put him on the Honeymoon Jumbo because of a strike at the airport. Every bomb that's ever been made can be defused by an expert, there's no defeat in that, no disgrace, I've explained that a thousand times before now: it's a fact of life.' He took a long drink from the bottle. 'And, just to make our day – it wasn't just *any* bomb disposal expert, it was one who knew me from years ago, in Cyprus and the Middle East. If it had been anybody else but him, the police would never have got a smell of us. But this man was as good as a finger-print expert, he took one look inside that bomb and knew who'd made it. He radioed my name and description back to London and the police had my picture beamed on every TV screen while we were still talking money to Schumacher. They were on to us even before I put the phone down.'

Helmut was crawling slowly across the floor, shaking his head like a drunk coming round after a lost weekend. Elvides watched him carefully as he went on.

'It was Gudrun, Angela: she was the one who betrayed us. Don't take my word for it, ask Kurt here. She had half the male population of London banging on her door every night within a week of her arrival – and the gall to introduce me as her fiancé when I flew in to take over. Jesus, no wonder they all laughed, no wonder everyone remembered us when those pictures were shown on the TV screen! I'm telling you, it was a massacre. We didn't have a chance.'

'That's right,' Kurt kept saying. 'That's right.'

'That stinking bitch,' said Elvides savagely. 'I'd have killed her myself if the cops hadn't.' Helmut was clinging to the bar now, desperately trying to haul himself to his feet. Elvides hit him in the neck with a vicious, overhand blow that sent him skidding back against the wall. This time he was careful to lay still. Only his eyes moved, rolling in fear like a dog's after a whipping.

'*You* were the one who recruited her, big mouth. You brought her into A.L., you put her up for the London job.' The gun appeared in Elvides' hand as smoothly as an ace from the bottom of the deck. 'And you still have the effrontery to ask *me* what went wrong. You big dumb bastard, I've half a mind to shoot *you*.'

But he let Angela restrain him easily enough: reflecting that it was his job to keep the Liberation Army together, not to destroy it. 'Don't worry, I'll leave it to you to deal with him. You're the boss.'

She purred like a cat. 'Leave him alone, he's had enough.' She staggered across the room and poured a jug of water over the stricken Helmut. The others laughed with her, and the tension evaporated as quickly as it had built up earlier. 'To hell with the past, let's think about the future. I say it's too risky to start up again yet in Bonn. On the other hand, France looks wide open. What do you say to that?'

'Well: with respect.' Gruchev would have him killed if he allowed the Liberation Army to lose sight of its main objective. 'Don't think I'm querying your judgement, Angela, on the contrary I'm reinforcing it, in a way. I mean, the reason why it's so tough in Germany right now is because you took us so close to success, so very close. And the longer you leave it the harder it's going to be to get back in.'

He poured her another drink.

'I'm only thinking of priorities, you know? I feel Germany has to be the number one target: France will keep. After Germany, it has to be England. We've got to make an example of this man Ramage, for a start. And the airline must be made to pay in full. Plenty there to keep us busy for a while.'

Heads nodded in agreement all round the table.

'My suggestion would be for a kind of Operation Prestige to start as soon as possible. The main strike in Bonn, to signal your return to the German theatre. A commando raid on England, to deal with Ramage, and perhaps another in New York to put pressure on the airline. But whatever you decide, I think it ought to be done quickly.'

'What about the lodge here?'

'Keep it by all means: it's the perfect base. It won't need more than one of us to act as caretaker while the rest are away.'

Angela nodded enthusiastically. 'Yes, that makes sense. All right, I'll take the main group back to Germany myself. Hans and Ilse, you go to New York. Keep clear of the airports, they'll be on maximum alert after the Jumbo bomb scare. Go after

Schumacher instead. You heard Paul say earlier what a weak character he is. Turn the screws on the airline through him.'

She smiled at Elvides. 'You can leave for London as soon as you like: that's what you want, isn't it? Take Kurt and Gisele with you. I look to you to make an example of this man Ramage and show everyone what to expect if they cross our path in future. If you find an opportunity to put pressure on Atlantic Airways at the same time – take it. The harder we squeeze them, the better.'

She turned to Juliane. 'I want you to stay here as watch-dog. Sorry. But it won't be for long.'

Lastly, she stared down at the recumbent Helmut. 'And I'll give you a chance to redeem yourself,' she said. 'Get back to Bonn with Rudi and prepare a list of prestigious targets to celebrate our return to the Fatherland. You'll need to tread carefully, those Antiterrorismus boys will be swarming round like flies. I'll decide on which target we hit when we join up with you later.' She gazed slowly round the room, and raised her glass. 'I think that takes care of everything. Prosit!'

Helmut tried in vain to get to his feet but slumped back on the floor.

'Well, perhaps not *everything*,' said Angela maliciously. As Helmut watched, she gave Elvides a lingering kiss and led him to the door. She paused as they passed Helmut and bent down to slap her discarded favourite's bruised face.

'Wake up, I don't think you heard me,' she told him. 'You've got work to do in Bonn: on your way, *liebchen*.'

Part Three

THE DUEL RESUMED

Ramage had no income beyond his Army pension and started job-hunting as soon as the holiday ended. He had only a vague idea of what he hoped to do: he was forty-eight, and knew nothing but soldiering. In the event, it turned out to be easier than hc thought. He found he had moved into a world where his skills still counted for something – all the newspapers were predicting a renewed IRA campaign, while his achievement in beating the bomb-in-the-air had won enormous publicity. Men and women who hardly knew him stopped him in the street and shook him by the hand. On a wider scale, the response to his letters was quick in coming, and equally warm.

A firm that manufactured guided missiles invited him to come at once for an interview. 'Our headache,' said the chairman, 'is that should one of our weapons fall into the wrong hands, the country could find itself facing a crisis of terrifying proportions. We've got a large security force, that goes without saying. How competent it may be is another matter. We're looking for an expert terrorist-fighter to teach it to shape up to this permanent threat of hijack and sabotage, and see that it stays that way. I feel we can work out a satisfactory salary for the right man.' He beamed at Ramage. 'How soon can you start?'

It was hard work, and entailed a great deal of travelling. He arrived home one Sunday morning after driving overnight from Wales to find a note from Laura waiting for him. 'Commander Evans from Scotland Yard rang last night and said he would appreciate a call from you. L.' Ramage looked at the clock and decided to find out what it was all about before the family were awake. He telephoned the Yard and was put through to the Commander's home at once.

'Hello there. This is Ramage. What can I do for you?'

'Seen the Sunday papers?' asked the policeman.

'Not yet. I've just walked into the house. Why?'

'One of the colour magazines is carrying the story of the bomb in the Jumbo. The've tied it in with a general article on terrorism in Europe today – starting with A.L., moving on to the Red Brigade in Italy, and ending up with the IRA. A comprehensive piece, and very well done.'

'I see.' Ramage was completely nonplussed. 'Well, if there's anything in it you don't like – something I'm supposed to have said on the plane, for instance – I'll have to ask you to suspend judgment until I've had a chance to read it for myself.'

'It's nothing like that, sir.' There was the hint of reproof in his tone, just the same. 'It's just that, well, we were a little surprised to see that you've given these people your home address, Colonel. Particularly after our warning about Elvides.'

Ramage cast his mind back to the interviews on the plane, and at Kennedy airport. 'Commander, I haven't given my address for publication at any time to anyone, period. For the most elementary reasons.'

'It's probably nothing to worry about,' said the policeman cautiously. 'I noticed it because of my personal interest in the case – we still don't know where Elvides might be. However, I thought it only right to raise it with you.'

'I think I can guess what's happened,' replied Gordon. He told the Commander about the photographer on the plane who persuaded him to pose for one last picture. 'He asked me if I'd like a copy as a souvenir and promised to bring it round to my home address. Now we know why.'

'Ah.'

'He also took my daughter out for a drink and pumped her for information. While we were still in America.'

'That explains everything, sir. One or two of the photographs they've used could only come from your family album. Mrs Ramage and yourself on your wedding day, your boy in his school uniform. That kind of thing.'

'I'll sue them. Damned if I'll let them get away with it.'

'You haven't got a leg to stand on, sir,' said the commander gently. 'Quite clearly, your daughter must have given him the photographs. And the man was only doing his job. The bomb on the Honeymoon Jumbo made you an international hero: you can hardly blame the Press for showing a continuing interest.'

'They've got no right to publish without my permission.'

'These things happen, sir. Incidentally, I think I ought to point out they haven't identified the street you live in, merely the town.'

'It's not a town, it's a village. And we've only got half a dozen streets in the whole bloody place.'

'I see. Well, on the credit side Colonel, we haven't heard a whisper about Elvides since the siege. There was just that one phone call telling us where to find the boy – alive and unharmed, much to our surprise. Since then, silence.'

'No word from Germany?'

'Nothing. I spoke to a man called Wüst last night – this is between ourselves, sir – after I'd read the magazine story. Wüst is the head of the Federal Department in Cologne that directs the activities of the Antiterrorismus-abteilung, you know? Well, he told me he's examining the possibility that the Liberation Army may have broken up, following that bloody nose we gave them here in London. He's getting reports that some members of the gang have been seen as far away as France and Italy, whereas there hasn't been a squeak out of anyone in Germany now for weeks past.'

'That doesn't mean anything.'

'Perhaps not. He describes it as nothing more than a possibility. I specifically asked him about Elvides, by the way. The answer is he seems to have dropped right out of the picture. Wüst says it's conceivable even that the gang may have executed him for the failure in London.'

'Let's hope he's right. Tell me, Commander, what's the circulation of this magazine?'

'Copies will turn up all over the world in due course, sir. As you know better than anyone, terrorism is news from here to Tokyo. The chances of it being seen by Elvides are very remote, none the less. If he's still alive, that is.'

The magazine appeared on the Paris bookstands the same morning. At lunchtime, Angela Schless picked up an Englishman in the bar of the Crillon, and steered the subject round to the copy in her hand. 'This man Ramage. He must be very brave?'

'My word, yes. He's got the G.C., you know.'

'The G.C.?'

'The George Cross. It's a medal, darling, you wouldn't know about things like that. Another drink?'

'Thank you.' She continued to turn the pages as he gave their order. 'The poor child! This son of the G.C. man, I mean. Look at the ridiculous clothes they make him wear. They're – they're medieval.'

'That's just his school uniform, m'dear. One has to wear it, you know: tradition, and that sort of thing.'

'Every schoolboy in Britain has to wear such clothes?'

'Good Lord, no. Only at that particular school. It's called Hinton, after a town in Dorset. One of the best schools in the country, actually. After Eton and Harrow, of course.'

'How clever of you to know these things.' Angela dazzled her informant with a smile. 'And how interesting.'

It was a time when Ramage was needed at head office daily and his movements were routine. He left the house soon after eight to drive to London, and returned each night at about half past seven. His son John was back at school, his daughter spending the week with her fiancé's parents. Winter was setting in and after the long holiday in America and Cornwall, it felt good to be home by the fire in the evenings.

He knew better than most there was no guarantee of safety where terrorists were concerned: all anyone could do was remain alert and take sensible precautions, and this he tried to do without scaring his family. He had a burglar alarm installed, which was commonplace enough. He obtained a permit to carry a gun, a Walther PP 7.65 mm and explained to Laura he was obliged to do so because of the confidential nature of the papers he carried. Whether she believed him or not was impossible to say. However, under the laws of the land he was not allowed to carry it loaded – only one British civilian, a former commissioner of police, has that privilege – but comforted himself with the thought that he was a trained soldier, and it was only the work of a second or two to slam a magazine home. He made a habit of checking all outbuildings regularly, and kept watch on any parcels or packages that were delivered to the house. His telephone number remained ex-directory and he took good care that his name no longer appeared in any newspaper. By arrangement with Commander Evans, a local police patrol car continued to keep watch on the house at irregular intervals. It seemed enough in all conscience for a family living in the village peace of the Home Counties, and being human even Ramage began to relax as day succeeded day without incident of any kind.

Elvides and Gisele found it unbelievably easy to keep track of his movements. They took it in turns to shadow him to London, and to follow Laura whenever she left the house. Kurt telephoned them each night to report progress at his end.

'Ready when you are,' he announced on the fifth day.

'Good, then it's tomorrow. We've got it made to measure, Kurt. Our friend Ramage has gone soft in retirement, even follows a set routine – how about that? He gets home every night about seven-thirty, perhaps a minute or two later. His garage lies at the end of a driveway and has no outside light. There are no neighbours to hear us, and no police guard on the premises. We'll be all through by eight.'

'Right.'

'So time your own arrival for eight o'clock, Kurt, and get back to the rendezvous as fast as possible. Gisele should be in the London apartment by nine. Ring her as soon after that as you can.'

'Very well. And what time will you join me?'

'By midnight at the latest. After that, we'll all play it by ear. I don't honestly expect any money from the airline – we're just carrying out Angela's orders and stepping up the pressure.'

'Of course. See you at midnight, Paul. I'll have the scotch ready to celebrate.'

Kurt checked his watch, for the fiftieth time. When he first called the police they assured him a car would be on its way immediately. But that had been more than forty minutes ago and it was now almost seven: he was cutting things fine. The rain had turned to sleet now and the Dorset hedgerows were turning as white as an old man's hair while he waited. Suddenly he saw lights in the distance, and after a little while heard the drone of an approaching car. He shone his torch into the darkness: his own vehicle looked convincing enough, lying in the ditch with a dent in its side and glass scattered on the verge. As the police car picked him out in its headlights Kurt hurried towards it, waving it down with his left hand. His shooting hand stayed warm and snug in his pocket.

'You the gentleman that phoned, sir?'

'Yes.' Kurt peered inside and relaxed immediately. One man only, a middle-aged country bumpkin in uniform: easy! 'There's my car over there. Come and see the state it's in.'

'Whoa there, just a minute, sir. Headquarters are waiting for me to call in. You're all right, no injuries I mean?'

'Just shaken up, that's all.'

'Thank the Lord for small mercies, anyway.' He unhooked the microphone and made his call, still speaking to Kurt as he waited for a reply. 'Did you manage to get a look at this hit-and-run driver, sir? Get his number, or anything?'

'It all happened too quickly, I'm afraid. A glare of the headlights, a bang and he was gone.'

'That's what I don't understand.' The policeman frowned. 'If he came this way I don't see how I could have missed him. I waited in the lay-by back there for a good twenty minutes, but I didn't see anyone.'

Kurt could have kicked himself for the oversight. The country bumpkin was not as simple as he looked.

'This is Panda Four. I've found the gentleman who called in, by Deacon Hill. Weather's closing in and there's no sign of the other vehicle. I propose to try and tow him back on the road: if I can't, I'll send a breakdown first thing in the morning.' He listened for a while and said, 'Right. I'll escort him back to the station either way, to make a statement. Over and out.'

Kurt fidgeted impatiently as the policeman made ready to step out of the Panda car. He took his time, tapping his pockets to make sure he had all he needed, searching through the glove compartment for a torch, all the while keeping up a pointed but gentle interrogation.

'You must have had a fair old walk to find a telephone in these parts, sir?'

'Yes.'

'Two or three mile, I shouldn't wonder.'

'Something like that.'

'Still, you got back here in amazing time. I expect you were running on account of the cold.' Kurt made no attempt to answer that one. 'Well now, let's have a look and see if we can't get you back on the road.'

Whatever else he may have suspected – drink perhaps, or a false insurance claim – it was never murder. And as he bent down to examine the wrecked vehicle Kurt raised the gun slowly and shot him, through the back of the skull. There was the gentlest of sounds, as soft and discreet as the pop of a cork being drawn in a bar after hours. Grayston's cap flew off and disappeared into the night. The rest of him collapsed, and toppled into the ditch. Kurt splashed after him, hunting through his pockets. As soon as he found what he wanted he opened the boot of his car and lifted out a suitcase. It contained the police uniform he had rented from a theatrical agency, and he blessed Elvides for his forethought – Grayston had been twice his size. He ran back to the Panda and changed, twisting and turning awkwardly in the cramped space as he tugged on the unaccustomed clothing. It was nearly half-past seven before he was done and he set off like the wind, for Hinton and John Ramage's school.

Elvides and Gisele backed their cars into the lane so that they were facing the main road. It was snowing hard. A little way away, a light from Ramage's house stared into the night like a yellow eye. All else was darkness, and silence. Each of them carried a bulky canvas grip in one hand. They stopped under a hedge and whispered like lovers saying goodnight before they disappeared into the shadows of the garden.

'Remember: stay absolutely still as his car turns into the drive. If you move, he'll see you. I'll take him the moment he comes out of the garage.'

'Yes, Paul.'

'Then I want you in and out of that house like a dose of salts. Don't look for me, don't wait for anything, just get out – *fast*.'

'I'll remember.'

'See that you do. One against one is different, you need to think ahead, all the time.'

'I will.'

'As soon as you hear from Kurt, ring the news agency. Then stay put in the apartment until I get in touch with you.'

Laura moved busily round the kitchen, putting the final touches to the meal. A glance at the clock told her that Gordon would soon be home. Merely to know that, and be sure of it, held incredible pleasure for her. She was happier than she had been for years, since he had joined the Army if the truth were known: and certainly far happier than at any time since he had gone into Bomb Disposal. Those years had been purgatory, never knowing from one day to the next if her man was going to come back alive.

They had been childhood sweethearts, and it had all been so different at the beginning. They first met when she went to Cornwall on holiday soon after the end of World War II, when he was a country boy and she was a schoolgirl. They continued to meet and write and visit every year after that until he was called up by the Army. They were very much in love by that time. Both their families took it for granted that they would marry one day, and it made no difference to Laura when Gordon wrote to say that he liked the Army and wanted to make it his career.

They were married in 1954, soon after he was commissioned. The war in Korea had ended and for the first time in years the British Army was fighting nowhere abroad. The wedding took place in Tremeneth on the day that food rationing finally came to an end in Britain – after fifteen long years – and Gordon's friends and neighbours celebrated both occasions in grand style. All sixty odd men, women and children from the Hamlet-on-the-Hill attended the service, having first filled the ancient church with flowers from their gardens. As there was no single building in the entire parish big enough to seat them all together at the wedding breakfast or to serve as a refreshment centre for the fête to follow, the problem was solved by hiring a marquee and setting it up in the cricket field behind the local pub.

There was a whole sheep for roasting, potatoes by the sackful, cucumbers, tomatoes, cress, lettuces and parsley. More than two hundred pasties had been baked in the village overnight. The nationwide shortage of whisky was overcome by Gordon's fellow officers in Germany who sent a case of Haig. Tremeneth provided gorse wine, blackberry wine, parsnip and elderberry wines, home made ginger beer and lemonade. Trestle tables in the marquee sagged under the weight of saffron cake, seed cake, tarts and fruit pies. Young women of Laura's age had seen nothing like it before in their lives, because of the long years of rationing. Gordon's father, old Will Ramage, said all there was to say in a simple speech on behalf of both families.

'If you look up the books in our church here,' he began, 'you'll find there have been Ramages in Tremeneth for 500 years. The first one arrived like a drowned rat, so they say: a sailor off a wreck, a ship's carpenter from Brittany. *Ramarge*, he called himself. And it took a heck of a long time before the locals stopped calling us foreigners and began to think of us *Rammidges* as Cornish, too. It only happened because we were carpenters, and Tremeneth couldn't do without us. I doubt if there's a single house in the village hasn't got beams put in by us Ramages, or a table and chairs made by our hands. Which brings me to the point of this here speech, namely, that there won't be any more: on account of me growing old and my boy deciding to quit the family business and be a soldier instead. However, the ties between us Ramages and Tremeneth will always remain. My son and his lovely bride Laura, who Mother and me welcome in the family with hearts filled with joy, have promised us that our house will never be sold to strangers, no matter where his Army work takes him. And it will be handed on to their children on the same binding condition, that it will always remain in the family – this Cornish family of ours, the Ramages.'

The honeymoon had been spent in the cottage: Will and Elizabeth Ramage had given them the keys, while they went off to stay with friends. Bride and groom slipped away unnoticed as the drinking and dancing went on till late at night, and made their way down the street hand-in-hand. No amount of tidying could ever make the front rooms habitable: planks of wood leaned against the walls, the tools lay in their boxes, the air was heady with the smells of wood and saw-dust and glue. But a fire burned in the kitchen stove, and Gordon's mother had lit an oil lamp, turned down low.

'Your bed is made ready,' said the note. 'God bless you both.' The door of his parents' room lay open for them. Snowy sheets and pillow cases shone from the bed Gordon's grandfather had made for his own wedding night, in another century. Her cases stood against the far wall. It was a bigger room than Laura remembered. Both of them were virgin, and not a little afraid. Gordon waited downstairs, until she called him.

'Here.' The curtains were drawn when he entered, the cottage bathed in moonlight. Her hair spread like a dark cloud on the pillow as she reached out a hand to welcome him. Her mother had told her the first time would bring pain, but she felt none: only joy. He drew her close and began to kiss her: on the mouth, the face, the neck, the shoulder, the breast. He could wait no longer and mounted her, urgently and clumsily. She spread her legs wide and helped him, guided him into her, and rose to meet him: slowly at first, then faster and faster as they both neared the climax. Laura had called his name and clasped him to her, pulling him down, down, down. Within minutes, they were both fast asleep.

Yes, the beginning had been good: and the year that followed. Being Gordon's wife was everything she wanted. Being an Army wife was an adventure, too, especially the travelling abroad: she had never been out of England before. And then somehow it had all gone wrong in the tragedy of Cyprus itself, beginning with the day when he had come home and told her he had been transferred to Bomb Disposal – it was a long time before she found out he had volunteered – and ending in the nightmare period of those successive, vicious attempts on his life. Neither of them realised that she was not equipped emotionally to cope with such a situation. At first both he and she had made light of it, but it was true: she was the one who felt the fear, and the pain even, so acutely that she was the one who broke down following that dreadful evening when he was almost blinded. Gordon recovered quickly enough – or so it seemed – while she had to undergo more than two years of psychiatric treatment, two terrible years for the whole family as well as herself.

She used to beg him to quit the Army, but he would not. 'What can I do back in England?' he used to say. 'We've got no money, I've no other training – and there's no work in Cornwall, anyway.' And she would gaze at the hideous scars on his face, and see the red, puckered flesh of his empty eye socket and weep, not only because she was afraid for him but also because there was no way she could explain adequately the effect that his wounds had on *her*. She lived with fear all through his thirty years in the Army – fear for her husband, fear for herself and the children – and the better he did and more fame that he won, the more she resented it. The marriage had survived for many reasons, principally the love that they felt for each other and their children, but she had never managed to cross the divide that separated the two of them as long as he remained a soldier. She knew very little about Elvides and even less about what motivated such a man: all that mattered to her was that he wanted to murder her husband and she never ceased in her efforts to persuade Gordon to leave the Army. And when he finally did so – on medical grounds, with the loss of one eye proving more and more of a burden – the cruel irony of finding themselves travelling on holiday with a bomb in the plane had done no more than confirm in her own mind the correctness of his decision. That bomb was a throwback to a past that was over and done with for ever. Her husband was finished with danger now, finished for good. He was a civilian like other men: a man who drove home at regular hours, dug the garden at weekends and slept in his own bed at nights. It was all that she asked for, and she was blissfully happy. She looked at the clock and thought, he'll be here in five minutes.

Headlights gleamed as Ramage's car swung into the drive, and snowflakes danced in the beams like plastic flakes trapped in a paperweight. Tyres crunched over the gravel, and as he drove into the garage Ramage gave a single toot on the horn to tell his wife he was home.

Elvides took the machine-pistol out of the canvas grip and crooked it in his forearm, finger on the trigger. This time he was going to kill his adversary, and end the duel: at this range, with the element of surprise and a 9 millimetre automatic weapon in his hand there was no possibility that he could fail. Gisele had marvelled at his apparent composure, even likened him to a hangman waiting to pull the trap, but it was not like that at all: a fierce joy glowed like a fire inside his breast, so that he remained warm even as the snow settled on his cap and brushed his cheek and melted inside his collar to run in icy streams down his back. He listened serenely as the engine sighed into silence, the hand-brake creaked on, the car door slammed and footsteps echoed along the concrete floor. Come on, you bastard, he thought: I've waited so long, so very long.

Thirty feet away Gisele Mittel shivered as she crouched in the shadows, and not only from the cold. Elvides had been right – he was right in everything, that damned old fox – when he said this one-against-one killing would prove harder than anything she had ever done before. Oh, she had taken part in an ambush in Germany, but that had been different: when four of them, all women, burst out of hiding before it was light one winter's morning and opened fire on a passing car. They had killed everyone inside, true, but it was different in this sense, namely that not one of them actually *saw* the policemen's faces. Tonight she had been standing in the snow for fifteen, maybe twenty, minutes not just wet and cold and hungry but also curiously sad and melancholy, staring through a chink in the curtains at the woman she was about to murder. And that was something else, my God it was, that gave you time to think about lots of things you would far rather not remember at all.

For instance, that smell of cooking floating out on the cold night air and the glimpse of those cheerful lights burning inside the house as the snowflakes fell reminded her in a poignant, heart-tugging way of her own home in the Harz and the family she had not spoken to or seen for three years now. The music on the radio evoked old memories, too. How many times in her student days at Gottingen had she heard a choir sing the *Liebeslieder Walze*? But worst of all was to watch the Ramage woman's face as she sang in time with the music while she prepared dinner: that sweet, contented face and dark hair reminded Gisele far too much of her own mother. She tried desperately to shut her mind to that. Terrorists could not afford the luxury of sentiment, Elvides had told them that a hundred times since he joined the ranks of the Liberation Army.

'Come on, damn you!' she whispered in the darkness: 'for Christ's sake open fire, before I go out of my mind!'

Elvides curled his finger round the trigger as the metal door of the garage rumbled down into place and in the same instant that Ramage crossed in front of him, a shadowy outline only fractionally darker than the night sky behind him, the Greek opened fire. The noise was deafening, the automatic jumped in his hands like a living thing. He sprayed the bullets like a gardener wielding a hose, swinging the barrel from left to right and back again. Ramage was all of three yards away. There was no way Elvides could miss him and the bullets hurtled into his adversary's body with pulverising force. Ramage's feet shot from under him and he was thrown back into the rockery as if by some giant hand. He uttered one sound only, like a loud sigh and lay still. No need for anyone to look and see if he was dead: not at that range. Elvides was blinded by the flashes. The darkness stank of cordite. Suddenly, away to his right, Elvides heard a new burst of gunfire, and screams, as Gisele stormed into the house after Laura Ramage. It was time to go. The Greek hurled his machine-pistol as far from him as he could and ran through the snow, into the lane. As he went by more shooting sounded from inside the house, and more screams. He thought, I hope to Christ Gisele keeps her head. It was pandemonium. Someone, somewhere was bound to hear the shooting and ring the police. He jumped in the car and switched on. It fired immediately and he pulled away, fast, skidding in the snow. He remembered to keep all lights off until he turned into the main road. Then he switched on and drove steadily west. It was exactly eight o'clock.

At the same moment the Panda turned into the driveway of John's school at Hinton Magna. Kurt tugged his sergeant's jacket into place, tugged down the peak of his cap and rang a bell marked 'Inquiries'. Lights shone from a dozen windows: this was the junior staff quarters. A young priest came to the door and looked out.

'Hello. I'm Father Knight, the sports master here. What can we do for you, sergeant?'

'Sorry to have to disturb you, sir. I want to speak to the headmaster, please.' He was a natural mimic, it might have been Grayston speaking. 'It's a matter of urgency, sir.'

'I'll take you to him. He lives in a house in the grounds. Hold on while I get a coat, it's a miserable night.' A few minutes later the sports master had been dismissed and Kurt stood in the head's living-room with his cap tucked under his left arm and his boots standing to attention, the archetypal picture of the lower orders reporting to authority. He fumbled in his breast pocket and held out the warrant card he had stolen earlier from the murdered sergeant, taking care to show nothing more than the embossed gold lettering giving the name of the county Force.

'Sergeant Grayston' he said, and buttoned the warrant card back in his tunic.

'How do you do' replied the headmaster affably. He had

seen warrant cards before and had no doubt that his caller was all he pretended to be. He was a grey-haired man in dog collar and clerical grey. 'May I offer you something to warm you on this very cold night, a glass of sherry perhaps?'

'Thank you all the same, sir, not when I'm driving.' He smiled a refusal and added, 'I've come about young Ramage, headmaster.'

'Oh?' The Head took off his glasses and polished them anxiously. 'I do hope there's no further trouble. Involving his parents, I mean.'

'I'm afraid there is, sir, the very worst. There was an attempt to kill the Colonel as he arrived home from work tonight. We have reason to believe it was the work of the same gang who hid the bomb on the plane. Seeking revenge, most likely.'

'Oh, how terrible.' He put the glasses back on and stared at his caller. 'You said there was an *attempt* to murder Colonel Ramage. Does that mean he's still alive?'

'He's very badly hurt, sir: I don't know how badly, the doctors haven't operated yet. But between you and me it looks pretty bad. His family are with him and my orders are to take the boy to join them as fast as possible.'

'Of course. Had you telephoned first, we could have prepared John for the journey,' replied the headmaster mildly. As he went to the house phone, he asked, 'Which hospital is the Colonel in?'

'The City, I believe,' said Kurt easily: most hospitals in England seemed to have that kind of name. 'I'm afraid the attack was so recent we don't know all the details ourselves yet.' As an afterthought he said, 'I expect that's why nobody phoned you, sir.'

'Yes, how stupid of me.' The headmaster rang through and sent for the boy. 'Will he need any clothing, sergeant?'

'I shouldn't think so, sir.' Kurt was desperate to get away before the phone rang. 'His mother will be there to look after him. She's insisting he travels under police guard, which is why I'm here. But it's a matter of life and death, and as long as he's got a coat – '

'Quite. Ah, they're at the door now. How much shall I tell the boy?'

'Not much point in hiding anything, sir. He's got to know soon enough.'

'I shall pray for him. And his parents.' The old man slipped an arm round the boy's shoulder as he entered the room. 'John this is Sergeant Grayston. I want you to be very, very brave and listen to what he has to say to you.'

John Ramage was a tall, sturdy boy who looked older than his twelve years. Under the gaberdine raincoat Kurt could see the school uniform that had first betrayed him: a long blue woollen habit, black shoes, orange stockings and starched white cravat. Hair as yellow as his father's tumbled over his wide forehead. He took it well as he listened to the bogus sergeant.

'Where was Dad when this happened? In the house?'

'No. I understand they were waiting for him when he arrived home. They ran off after they shot at him.'

'What about my mother?'

'I told you, she's at the hospital with your father. And she wants you there as soon as possible. I've got a car outside, all ready to take you.'

The headmaster took the hint and led the boy gently into the hall. 'Have you eaten supper, Ramage?' he asked.

'Thank you, sir, yes.'

'Then you must hurry, it's a long journey ahead of you. Perhaps you would ask your mother to telephone me when ... when things are more settled, h'm? Bless you, my boy. May you have good news awaiting you on arrival at the hospital.'

'We've got to pull up' said Kurt to the boy. They had been driving less than twenty minutes. 'Trouble with one of the rear wheels, by the feel of it. Won't be a minute.'

He went to the boot of the car, soaked the sponge thoroughly with chloroform and went back to the near side door. 'Would you mind giving me a hand, young fellow?' he said. 'I need someone to hold the light while I change this tyre.'

'Of course,' said the boy, politely.

As soon as his head came through the door Kurt clamped the sponge tight over his mouth and held him in a bear-hug. John wriggled like an eel, holding his breath for as long as he could and kicking out hard with those heavy school shoes. But the man was too strong, and soon he lost consiousness. 'You little swine,' said Kurt, softly; the kid had hurt him. He bound his hands and ankles and threw him on the back seat, pulling a blanket over the body. He switched on the radio as he climbed back into the driving seat and listened to the police broadcasts.

'Come in Panda Four. Hello Panda Four: come in, please.' Kurt nodded in relief as the calls went on. Clearly, there was no word yet from the school, no alarm out for the missing Grayston. He jammed his foot down hard on the accelerator, and drove on.

One hundred and fifty miles away, on the other side of England, a policeman called his local station on Gordon Ramage's house phone. 'Hello, sarge,' he said breathlessly, 'Colman here. I'm inside the house and it's a bloody shambles, no kidding. Looks like a machine-gun attack, judging by the number of bullet holes everywhere, and the extent of the damage. Mrs Ramage is dead in one of the bedrooms upstairs. There's no sign of the Colonel: either they've kidnapped the poor sod, or he's lying out there somewhere in the snow. I haven't had a chance to look much beyond the back door yet. It's dark and snowing hard, and there's a lot of garden: we'll need lights to carry out a proper search.'

'The Inspector's on his way,' said the sergeant. 'And a doctor. Do what you can till they arrive. I'll send a van with proper search equipment as soon as I speak to headquarters.'

'I could do with some company' said the young bobby thoughtfully. He swung a truncheon in his hand as he spoke. 'The nearest neighbours must be a quarter of a mile away. Who called in?'

'A couple of teenagers out skylarking in the snow ran home when they heard the shooting. Thank God their parents phoned us right away. We've got road blocks going up all over the county and if this weather holds, we might strike lucky.'

'Tell the boys to be mighty careful, sarge. This lot mean business.'

Ramage came round in a hospital bed. Someone was trying to split his skull with an axe. The ward was spinning like a Frisby. A kindly red face appeared from nowhere and spoke to him.

'Feeling better, sir?'

'Agh.' He remembered now, but the suddenness of the attack, coming out of the night and the snow in his own back yard, had left him mentally sandbagged. Ramage fumbled for words like a drunk. 'Burp gun. Caught me as I walked out of the garage.' His hands moved up and explored the bruising on his chest. 'Quite a test for the L.B.A.'

'The L.B.A., sir?'

'Lightweight Body Armour.' He was still dazed. 'Lightweight Body Armour Limited. Name of the firm who made my bullet-proof waistcoat, God bless them.' He felt the bandages round his head. 'Did he hit me with that damned gun, too?'

'You stopped a burst of 9 mm automatic at point blank range, Colonel. The sheer force of the bullets knocked you off your feet and you split your skull on a rock. You'd been out for twenty minutes or more when we found you.'

'Where's Laura? What about my wife?' He began to vomit.

A doctor hurried in and administered a tot of white, cloudy liquid. 'Here, drink this.' He turned to the Inspector. 'I told you, this man has twenty stitches on his head. He's badly concussed and he's got to rest.'

'Just one question. Did you see anyone, Colonel? Can you give me a description?'

'What happened to Laura, damn you?' The room was spinning round again, faster and faster. The lights in the ward became a blur and the blur turned into a soft white bed and as soon as Ramage climbed on it he was fast asleep.

Elvides reached the house soon after midnight. The gates waited open for him, the trees lining the drive were dressed in white. It was the perfect hiding place, an old rectory standing in six acres of ground, unoccupied since the death of the last incumbent. The village he had served was dying too, and there would be no new minister to take his place: the house awaited the auctioneer's hammer, in brooding silence. It stood in splendid isolation, way off the beaten track yet within comfortable reach of the coast, or the road that led back to Salisbury and London. Kurt had done well to find it.

Inside he had chosen as John Ramage's prison a garret that once housed the boot-black: a bare, high ceilinged box shut off by a corridor from the stairs. Its door was made of oak, as they all were in the rectory. For the boy's benefit, this one had been fitted with a padlock and hasp and furnished by a mean mind. A weary, iron-sprung bed sagged against the far wall, covered by a biscuit-thin mattress and a single blanket. There was a wash-basin plumbed in nearby. There were no carpets or chairs or table or ornaments, no mirror or picture-frame, nothing anywhere that could conceivably be used as a weapon, even by a twelve year old boy. The only light came from a window set high in the wall: high but not inaccessible, for the terrorists took the view that if their prisoner wanted to climb out and jump to freedom, he was welcome to try. The cobbled yard that waited to receive him stood more than seventy feet below.

Kurt's hijacked Panda hid alongside Elvides' rented car in an outhouse big enough to take a fleet of buses. The men themselves camped in the kitchen and lived almost as frugally as their captive. Their beds were sleeping bags on a stone floor. Their supplies – whisky, tinned food and butane gas stove – looked as lost in the big bare room as mice on a skating rink. There were no curtains at the windows, which meant no light except torchlight. It was too risky to light a fire. But as a prison it was ideal, and Elvides had no complaints.

'Did you get through to Gisele?'

'No.' Kurt lit a cigarette, carefully shielding the flame. 'I went out and phoned twice from the village, but there was no answer. Think she's all right?'

'Damn' well ought to be.' Elvides opened a bottle and drank deep. 'One unarmed woman to deal with, and not a policeman in sight? Christ, it was child's play.' He crossed to the window and stared out at the snow. 'The roads are bad, we'll give it a few more hours yet. If there's no answer by morning we'll be on our way.'

'And the boy?'

'No problem. We just booby-trap the house and leave him.'

The walls of the ward stayed still this time as Ramage opened his eyes. There was another man sitting by his bedside now, an older man with an iron-grey moustache and hooded eyes. He smelled of pipe tobacco. 'You've slept for more than six hours,' he remarked pleasantly. 'That's good.'

Ramage sat up and touched the bandages. The wound at the back of his head throbbed unbearably. 'Christ, that hurts,' he said.

'Some people are never satisfied.' The policeman smiled as

he said it, though. 'It might have been a lot worse, Colonel. The body armour saved your life.'

They were doing everything bar talk about the weather.

'Yes. We took delivery of a sample vest yesterday, for the security people at the factory,' Ramage explained. 'It's a new one on me, made by a fellow called Macgill. Only weighs 2½ pounds, so I wore it home in the car to try it for comfort. By God, no need now to test it for anything else. It's fantastic.'

'My word, yes. Fantastic.' Neither of them spoke again for a time.

'All right' said Ramage finally. 'Don't treat me like a child. She's dead, isn't she?'

'I'm afraid so, sir.' The policeman was having trouble in finding his pipe. He had all of two pockets to search through. He stumbled across it, took it out, looked at it and put it back again. 'I'm deeply sorry for you.'

'Elvides.' Ramage growled the name, like a dog hearing distant footsteps. 'I'll kill him for it, if it's the last thing I do. Oh, the bastard!'

His visitor stopped him there. 'My name's Evans, sir. We've spoken often enough on the telephone. Commander Evans, of New Scotland Yard.'

'I recognised your voice as soon as you spoke to me. I'm still going to kill him when I catch up with him.'

'That's why I came to talk to you, Colonel. We've got the terrorist who murdered your wife. It's a woman.'

Ramage stared at him disbelievingly.

'We don't know much about her yet. Only a kid, twenty, twenty-one maybe. Clothes made in Rome. Refuses to say a word. She was picked up only because she panicked and tried to run for it when she was questioned at a road block.'

'She had the gun with her?'

'No, thank God. Our two chaps were unarmed. If she'd behaved normally, they'd have had to let her through. My guess is it was her first job. There has to be a first time, even for terrorists.'

'How do we know she did it?'

'Two automatic weapons were found in your garden. One had killed Mrs Ramage. And it has her prints all over it.'

'Then the other one belonged to Elvides.'

'I don't doubt it for a moment. But there's nothing to prove that. She'll have to tell us who it belonged to.'

'Let me have five minutes with the bitch. I guarantee to make her talk.'

'I don't think you would.' The Commander shook his head. 'I've been trying too, Colonel. I may be wrong but I think we've got a fanatic here: a red-hot, dyed-in-the-wool revolutionary, you know? I believe this one would die rather than talk – *under duress.* The only way she'll respond is to political argument, not the third degree.'

'You talk as if I'm some kind of greenhorn, Commander. Fanatics who wouldn't talk came ten a penny in Cyprus, and Aden. We managed to persuade quite a few of them to change their minds without too much trouble.'

'No, sir. I'm handing this one over to Intelligence. I honestly believe it's the only way to get her to talk.'

'Talk?' sneered Ramage. '*Talk*? You've already got her prints on the gun that killed Laura. A babe in arms could tell you who fired the other one. What's left to talk about, for Christ's sake – except where to find Elvides?'

The Commander filled his pipe now and lit it, in defiance of the health warnings on every wall. 'I've been trying to find a way of breaking it to you gently,' he said, 'but you're not making it easy, Colonel. It wasn't only you and Mrs Ramage they were after last night.' His voice was full of compassion. 'They've kidnapped your son, too.'

Ramage flinched, as if he had been struck. 'What?'

'The boy was kidnapped at the same time they tried to murder you. Another one of the gang called at the school, dressed as a policeman and carrying a warrant card: he'd already murdered a police driver, and hijacked his car. He told the headmaster you'd been wounded in a new assassination attempt and said he had orders to escort the lad to hospital here, to be with the rest of the family.'

'When did you find this out?'

'An hour or two ago. We knew a police driver had been killed, of course, but there seemed no reason at the time to connect it with the attack on you. Then a man phoned the Press Association early this morning to say you and Mrs Ramage had been "executed" – that's the word he used, sir – and your son kidnapped by the Liberation Army. We hadn't released details of the shooting for a variety of reasons, and quite properly, the agency checked back with us before releasing the story.'

'But what the hell did they hope to achieve by kidnapping John?'

'I'm not altogether sure, sir. They're demanding five million pounds for his safe return – the same as they wanted for the Honeymoon Jumbo, and from the same airline.'

'But that's insane! Atlantic Airways will never pay that kind of money for my son's release – no one would, whatever the circumstances.'

'The terrorists know that, sir. Equally, there'll be no profit in it for them once the boy is killed.'

'Elvides is an animal. All he wants is revenge.'

'I think you're only partly right there, Colonel. To my mind, the kidnapping was subsidiary to the assassination attempt. I don't see revenge as the motive there. More likely, it was an insurance policy in case anything went wrong during the attack on the house – in which case they'll certainly want to use him now to bargain for the girl's release. And all the time they've got him they're putting pressure on the airline.'

'Who cares about that?'

'Atlantic Airways might. The pressure on them will be enormous now. You're the man who saved 450 lives on their Honeymoon Jumbo a few weeks ago – not to mention a twenty million dollar aircraft in the process. The public won't allow them to forget that. There'll be an outcry if it looks as if they won't lift a finger to help save your son: who'll want to fly with people like that? I think it's a hell of a clever move.'

'Isn't there a time limit on the ransom demand?'

'Yes, forty-eight hours. But when they announced it, they didn't know for sure we had the girl. They do now. And she's our ace-in-the-hole.'

'I hope you're right about this, Commander,' said Ramage grimly. 'This is my son we're talking about.'

'I know exactly how you must feel, sir. Please, trust me.' Ramage made no reply. 'There's still one member of your family we haven't accounted for, incidentally. Your daughter.'

'Fortunately, she's staying in Sussex with her fiancé's family.' She would have been killed too, he reflected, if she had been at home overnight.

'If you'll give me the address, I'd like to put an armed guard on the house. I'll sleep better, if nothing else.' Ramage gave him the details without argument, 'I'm also leaving an armed man on duty outside the ward here, sir.'

'I've got a better idea,' said Ramage. 'Let me come back to the Yard with you.'

'They won't allow it. The doctors spent half the night stitching your head together: they won't let you out of here.'

'To hell with the doctors. I'm not going to lie in bed while you and your men are out searching for my son. I want to be at the centre of things, ready to help or advise in any way that may be needed.'

The Commander took pity on him.

'Very well, sir. I'll tell them to bring your clothes.'

Elvides kicked the door open, scowling. Kurt had returned to say there was still no answer from the apartment or any sign of Gisele. 'Get up.' He threw a pen and paper on the bed. 'You're going to write a little letter for me, boy.'

'I won't.' John jumped down and tried to run past the burly figure blocking the way to the stairs, and freedom. Elvides grabbed him by the scruff of the neck and held him at arm's length as he kicked and struggled. Then he slapped his face, hard, and flung him back on the bed.

'Try that again and I'll kill you. Like I killed your father last night.'

John sat on the bed, hating him with his eyes.

'Now.' Elvides handed him a typewritten sheet of paper. 'Copy what I've written there, and sign your name on the bottom. I'll give you five minutes.'

The note said 'To the directors of Atlantic Airways. I am a prisoner of A.L. and unless you pay the money they are going to kill me. Tell the BBC to read this message over the radio and to show my picture every day on television until the money is paid, otherwise I won't get any food. Please help me. John Ramage.'

'They won't pay you anything,' said the boy defiantly. 'They don't even know me.'

'They knew your father and they owe him a favour. Now get on with it or I'll give you a beating you'll never forget.'

'No.'

Elvides hit him so hard he screamed. 'Do as I tell you!'

John slumped down on the floor, weeping, and began to write. As he did so Kurt came into the room and took a polaroid picture. He examined the print and showed it to Elvides, who nodded approval.

'Great.' He turned back to the boy, and took the note. 'We're going now,' he said. 'Shout and scream all you like, there's no one to hear you. And you'd better hope these friends of your father pay up soon. Otherwise you're going to starve to death.'

He and Kurt left the room and padlocked the door behind them. John heard them moving about for some time afterwards, apparently working on the stairs. He pressed his head against the door and listened carefully, but could not tell what they were doing. He climbed back on the bed and wrapped the blanket round him: eventually, he fell asleep in spite of his fears. When he awoke the house was still, and they had gone. He took off one of his shoes, stood on the bed and reached up to smash the window pane. Then he filled his lungs and started shouting for help.

Byron Schumacher addressed a full Atlantic Airways board meeting in New York next day about the Ramage affair. The General had made no physical improvement since he suffered the stroke, and his son-in-law continued to run the company.

'You've all seen this story of the attack on Colonel Ramage and his family, gentlemen. On your behalf this morning I sent him a message of condolence on the tragic death of Mrs Ramage, a lady of whom we all have the fondest memories.'

Heads nodded expectantly as they waited for him to raise the jackpot question, and he did not disappoint them.

'I've been snowed under with calls from the media asking me what we're going to do about this ransom demand for the boy. My answer to them has been that we're studying the matter, with all its implications. That will also be your answer, should anyone approach you. The fact is that we are not going – and could not afford – to pay eight or nine million dollars to any terrorist gang for any reason whatever, and that's final.'

No one dissented. What else was there to say?

'I gather there is speculation in the London papers already that the gang might extend that forty-eight hour ultimatum as they start to bargain for the release of the captured woman.

Whatever happens it is going to be to our advantage to delay a statement as long as possible and keep the terrorists guessing about our intentions. With due respect to Colonel Ramage and his son our first concern in this matter has to be our own security, when all is said and done. The moment it becomes known we are not going to pay, we can expect those Liberation Army hoodlums to try to cause us maximum damage – by putting bombs on our planes, or by bluffing us with a crippling series of hoax calls, perhaps even mounting an attack on the ground. And that in turn means we've got to use every minute at our disposal *now* to forestall them.'

There was silence in the room as he continued.

'While every Atlantic Airways plane and overseas office and installation must be considered at risk, I myself believe the risk will be greatest at three particular airports: here in New York, for reasons of prestige, in London where the first attempt to blackmail us failed and the second is now being mounted, and on A.L's home ground, in Frankfurt, Germany. I think responsibility for putting each of those particular houses in order should therefore be delegated to senior members of this Board. I myself will supervise security here in New York, assisted by Sam Northeim. I want Bill Rogers to move temporarily to Frankfurt and Arnold Schuster to London, as a matter of urgency. Meantime, everyone here must look to his own safety at all times because the threat of assassination is a very real one.'

He spoke to Sam Northeim for a moment now.

'You will take over New York right away, Sam: I'll be in London for a few days.' He turned back to the others. 'Although I don't intend us to give in to these blackmailers, I also feel it's very important from the public relations angle how we put that across. I mean, we have to say no – with decorum. I don't anticipate any difficulty with Ramage. He's a soldier and a realist, dammit: I don't think he could fairly expect anyone to pay that kind of money to save his child. The general public may take a very different line, however, especially as the time for his son's execution draws near. And if we expect to stay in the business of selling airline tickets, we'll need to show a warm and sympathetic attitude throughout. Above all, we'll need to be publicly associated with Colonel Ramage in his hour of trial.'

His colleagues on the board thought of their own families, and avoided his eye: Jesus, did the man have to be so damned clinical about it?

'This is why I am going to London personally, as acting president of the company. I want to talk to Ramage, and explain our position. I shall also attend Mrs Ramage's funeral, so that no one will be in any doubt about our feelings of grief and outrage: it's certain to be given maximum coverage by the media. I'm going to demonstrate that we're all in this *together*, that all of us live under the constant threat of attack too. Now then, does anyone have any questions? Or any suggestions? No? Very well, gentlemen, let's move on to the main item on our agenda: airline security.'

John Ramage's hands were raw and bleeding. Ever since he had woken he had been trying to dismantle his iron bedstead, in the hope he could fashion some weapon to help him batter down the door leading to the kitchen. Fortunately, he had failed to loosen so much as a single spring: now he was obliged to look for another way of escape. He accepted that Elvides and the other man would never return – that he had been left here to starve if no ransom money was forthcoming. Certainly no one was going to hear his cries for help. He had shouted so loud and long already that his voice was down to a croak, and all he had succeeded in doing was scatter the rooks. But what else was there to do? There were only two ways out of his prison cell, through the door or the window. The door was like the Keep at the Tower of London: immovable. Yet no matter how longingly or how often he gazed out of the window, he could not bring himself to jump. That was certain death.

It had stopped snowing while he slept. A pale blue sky mocked him now, the sparrows cheeped at this house-bound fledgling as they sported in the bright sunshine and freedom above the rooftops. Suddenly the idea came to him, *the roof*. Instead of going down, why not try up and across? He turned the bed and stood it on end so that he could perch on the top and look out. He used a shoe to tap out the remaining shards of glass, folded the blanket over the frame, twisted his head round and stared up. The guttering was five feet above the sill. If he could crawl out, stand on that three-inch wide ledge and somehow keep his balance as he reached up over that terrifying, seventy-foot drop he would be able to take hold of the guttering easily enough. Whether it would prove strong enough to take his weight was another matter, but he was young enough not to dwell on that too long: there was only one way to find out and the alternative was to stay in the room, and almost certainly die anyway. John Ramage had no illusions about the payment of the ransom. His father had had nothing beyond an Army pension, the family had no rich friends, the airline officials did not know him.

He craned his neck a little further. If he managed to climb to the roof safely, what then? His eyes followed the guttering to a drainpipe at the corner of the rectory roof. That was it. Drainpipes led to the ground. That was the escape route. Quickly, he dropped back into the room and examined his clothing. The woollen habit would have to come off: the skirt would surely hamper him as he clawed his way from window sill to roof and felt desperately for a toe-hold en route. A toe hold! He thought about that too, and looked at his shoes. They would have to go: they were too long and too wide to permit any kind of purchase on that narrow window sill. However, he would need both the shoes and the habit once he reached the ground, for it was colder than ever now that it had stopped snowing. He stripped down to his underclothes and climbed back on top of the bed. He could reach out of the window easily enough, so easily that it made him careless. The shoes went first, tied together by their laces. The sound carried dully as they went through the covering of snow and hit the cobbles below. Too late he realised he should have wrapped them in the habit. He rolled it into a ball, and hurled it after the shoes. A capricious wind met it halfway and draped it over a cornice, to leave it flapping like a sail thirty feet above the yard.

Now it was his turn. He climbed through, holding on to the sash frame for dear life, literally, as he placed one knee and then the other on the sill as he turned to face the wall. It took an age to complete this simple gymnastic manoeuvre: his fingers grew numb with the cold, the sill felt as slippery as a frozen pond, it cost him a fearful effort not to glance down at the drop yawning beneath him. Then he let go the sash, raised his hands with infinite care and pressed them against the wall to steady himself as he gradually eased himself upright. He was conscious that the drop was directly behind him now and his supple young body went rigid with fear. Cramp seized every muscle and it required a tremendous effort of will-power not to surrender, and fall back into space.

He ordered his hands to reach on upwards until they found the guttering. As he began to pull himself up, the guttering creaked under his weight and started to buckle. John panicked as he felt it give and screamed, scrabbling with his feet for any kind of hold. One foot touched a protruding knob of stone, and he thrust down on it with all his might. The next second he was up and over, sprawled full length on the rectory roof with his nose touching the grey, icy slates. His lungs heaved as if he had run a fast mile, his nerve ends tingled, his legs bled where he had scraped them raw: but he was free at last, and he laughed and cried together in joyous relief.

In a little while he got up and walked along the edge of the roof, steadfastly refusing to look down at the snow-filled yard below. A skylight to his left offered him a safe way back into the building. For a few seconds he was tempted. In the end he decided against it, lest the doors leading from it were locked too: there was no point in climbing out of the frying pan to drop straight back in the fire. He determined to stick to his original plan, and shin down the drainpipe. He tested it as soon as he reached the corner of the roof, tugging and pulling at it to see if it would hold. Then he took a deep breath, hooked one leg over the coping, and began the long descent.

It was the woollen habit that betrayed him, for the second time. The drainpipe seemed firm enough, with each retaining bracket bolted into the mortar. In fact it felt so secure that John reached out with one hand as he passed the habit and tried to tug it free. It flapped awkwardly, giving a little, declining to come clean away. The harder he pulled the more it resisted. Exasperated, he took a fresh grip on the cloth, put one foot against the wall and heaved. This time it came free – so fast that it fairly flew towards him, causing the boy to lose his balance. The hand that clutched the drainpipe surrendered its precarious hold and he toppled backwards with a shriek. His hip struck the stonework halfway to the ground, causing him to cry out with the pain, turning him over with the force of the impact. A moment later he thudded into the yard, and lay still.

It was like watching the re-run of an old film. Both the London evening papers carried a photograph of Gisele Mittel on their front page, and the headlines were disquietingly similar. 'TERROR ATTACKS – GERMANS SEND HELP' said the *Evening Standard*, and Kurt and Elvides read the news story with mounting anxiety.

'Scotland Yard last night confirmed that a high-ranking officer from Germany's crack Antiterrorismus-abteilung (anti-terrorist) unit was flying to London to assist inquiries into the murder of Mrs Laura Ramage on Thursday. Mrs Ramage, 46, was machine-gunned to death at her home in Surrey, and a young woman later detained for questioning. Colonel Gordon Ramage, G.C., husband of the murdered woman – Britain's foremost bomb disposal expert, and reckoned to be the main target for the attackers – escaped serious injury but his only son John, aged 12, was kidnapped from boarding school and is still missing. Responsibility for the whole outrage was claimed in the name of A.L., the German terrorist organisation, and a huge ransom demanded for the boy's safe return.'

The newspaper then recounted the story of the Honeymoon Jumbo, highlighting Ramage's role in saving the 448 passengers and crew and Elvides' subsequent escape from the Kensington siege.

'Fingerprints taken from the arrested woman were circulated by Interpol and unconfirmed reports from Bonn say they match those of Gisele Mittel, prison escapee and one of the most notorious members of the Liberation Army gang. Meantime, a vast manhunt is in operation throughout southern England for two men known to have been with her on the night of the attack. One is thought to be Elvides. The other is sought for questioning in connection with the killing of Sergeant Grayston, the Dorset Panda car driver whose stolen vehicle was used in the kidnap of John Ramage. The search for both men is being concentrated in the West End of London, where Elvides is known to have stayed on previous occasions – almost certainly, say the Yard, in a self-service apartment.'

'It's only a question of time, Paul,' said Kurt. 'Let's get out while we can. The boy will keep. So will his father.'

'I still don't know how that bastard did it.' Elvides shook his head in disbelief. 'I tell you, Kurt, it was all of three metres range. With a whole stick of bullets. I saw him go down.'

'To hell with Ramage. They've got Gisele and I can't see her holding out much longer.'

'It says in this paper the funeral's in three days' time. We could take him then.'

'There'll be police crawling all over the place, like lice.' He poured Elvides a drink. 'Leave him for the time being. We know where he works now. You can fly in, wire a bomb to his car one night and zap! be back in Germany before the dust settles. But not now, it's crazy, wait till the heat's off.'

'You're right.' He hurled the glass in the fireplace. 'But it sticks in my craw, just the same.'

'They'll be watching the airports, Paul. Which way do we go?'

'You travel via Dublin. Lie low for a week before you move on.'

'And you?'

'I'll go the long way, through Damascus. See you in Bonn in ten days' time.'

Byron Schumacher landed at ten o'clock at Heathrow, and Johnson, the London manager, hurried aboard to meet him. 'Grand news, sir,' he said. 'The Ramage boy is free. We've just heard. Isn't it splendid?'

'Incredible.' Schumacher gaped at him. 'Don't tell me someone paid the ransom?'

'No sir. The lad escaped. Climbed out of a window and jumped for it, so I gather. According to the reporters here he suffered some pretty bad injuries in the process, but crawled through the snow and lay in the road till he was spotted by a passing car. A chip off the old block, if you ask me, Mr Schumacher. A very, very brave boy.'

'When did this happen?'

'He got away during the afternoon, but wasn't found until tonight. About an hour ago, I believe.'

'So the Colonel's with him?'

'They say so. Flew to the scene in a police helicopter, apparently.' He led Schumacher off the plane and escorted him to immigration and customs, smoothing his passage through. 'Will you still want to talk to the Press, sir?' Johnson had leaked the news of his acting president's arrival, in accordance with instructions received earlier.

'Sure.' There would be no need now to raise false hopes about payment of the ransom. 'Where are they?'

'Over here, sir.'

They plied him with questions. 'Would your airline have paid the ransom to save him?'

'Hey, now. If I say "yes" the terrorists may try again. If I say "no", they might want to attack my aircraft. Let's make it "No comment", uh?'

'But what was the purpose of your visit tonight? Did you plan to meet Colonel Ramage?'

'Obviously. When I took off from New York today, the boy was still a prisoner with a price on his head. I planned to meet Colonel Ramage as the other interested party in the ransom demand, and talk to him personally about this hideous problem we were both facing. In Atlantic Airways none of us can forget the very great debt we owe him, gentlemen. We were all appalled and horrified to hear of Mrs Ramage's murder, and his son's kidnapping.'

'Mr Schumacher. You didn't come all this way merely to tell him the airline wouldn't pay, surely?'

'Look, please don't go jumping to any conclusions, I am not going to be drawn on this question of payment of the ransom. There were other reasons for my visit. One was to raise this whole matter of airport security with the authorities here.' He paused. 'And I had another reason, a private one.'

They waited confidently for him to tell them, and were not disappointed.

'It was to attend Mrs Ramage's funeral, gentlemen. I had the pleasure of entertaining her in New York not so long ago, after her husband had saved the Honeymoon Jumbo. She was a most gracious lady, and I came back to London to pay my final respects. You won't print that, I hope. And now, if you'll excuse me, I have work to do.'

He invited Ramage to lunch, shortly after the funeral. No one else was present. Over the brandy and cigars Schumacher said, 'I'd like to talk awhile about A.L., Colonel, if you'll allow me.'

'Of course. Go ahead.'

'It's not over yet. You know that, don't you?'

'I'm not absolutely sure I follow you, Mr Schumacher.'

'Those monsters killed your wife and kidnapped your son

as an act of revenge, simply because you defused the Honeymoon Jumbo bomb.' He watched Ramage closely. 'But above all they wanted to kill *you*. You cheated them. And they'll be back, just as sure as the world is round.'

'Elvides might.' Ramage shrugged his shoulders helplessly. 'That's a possibility I have to live with. Just as I have for the past twenty years.'

'He knows where to find you, now. And the children.' Schumacher smoothed a finger along the tablecloth. 'And don't kid yourself, Colonel – it isn't just Elvides any more. He's a member of A.L. You've made the whole organisation eat dirt, for the second time. They've all got a score to settle with you now.'

Ramage frowned, but made no reply.

'Not only with you, either. They aren't finished with Atlantic Airways yet. Or me.'

'It's a terrible thing to have to admit, but all rich companies and most rich men face that kind of possibility nowadays, Mr Schumacher. Terrorism is a symptom of the times, the new western disease.'

'Maybe it is. But this is a little more personal, Colonel. I've been getting phone calls again. Not here – in New York.'

'Threats to murder you?'

'Just frighteners, so far. Like "You owe us nine million dollars, Schumacher." And "We found out where you live easy enough, one of these days you're going to arrive home and find your wife dead." That kind of dirt. Myra's had calls too.'

'I'm sorry to hear that, sincerely. Fortunately, it doesn't automatically follow that such calls are coming from members of the Liberation Army.'

'But I've got proof.' Schumacher took an envelope from his pocket. 'My bodyguards, Colonel. They're all former FBI men. It wasn't too hard to trace the employee who sold these people my private number, the goddam bitch.'

'And not hard to deal with her, I imagine.'

'I fired her, of course. But I didn't go to the police. I preferred to avoid the publicity, and did a deal with her instead.' He opened the envelope and took out two artist's sketches, of a young man and a girl. They looked to be in their early twenties – like Gisele Mittel, thought Ramage. 'We never found the couple, but these were drawn to her description. I had copies sent to Germany, to see if they were known to the authorities. They are. Their names are Hans Albrecht and Ilse Glenz. They're both known members of A.L.'

Ramage stared at their faces, imprinting them on his mind.

'I'm telling you, Colonel. This gang is out to get the pair of us – and our families. Our paths crossed on that Honeymoon Jumbo flight and we're stuck with each other, for as long as those bastards stay alive.'

'What is it you're trying to say, Mr Schumacher?'

'Answer me a question first. Are you going to sit on your ass and wait for these hoodlums to come gunning for your family a second time – or are you going to do something about it before they get the chance?'

'Like what?' He knew the answer before he spoke.

'Like taking the law into your own hands, maybe. Hell, you're an explosives expert, Colonel: an eye for an eye. Do I have to spell it out?'

He must not listen. 'I wouldn't even know where to start looking for them.'

'Someone has to know where these people can be found. Maybe you need to beat the information out of them, maybe it's for sale – at the right price. Either way I want this Liberation Army off my back for good, and I'm willing to pay whatever it costs for the privilege.'

Ramage eyed him bleakly. 'If I killed Elvides, it wouldn't be for money.'

'Hold on, now. I'm not trying to buy you. I'm talking about a partnership. It costs money to take on an organisation like A.L.: money to pay informers, money to buy arms and explosives, money to get out of a country in a hurry. You don't fight any outfit like that – and win – without money.'

In his mind's eye, Ramage watched his wife run screaming through the house pursued from room to room by a girl killer firing a machine-gun. He saw his son John crawling through the snow with broken limbs after falling from a lonely, booby-trapped makeshift cell. He did not like to think what Elvides might do to his daughter if ever he kidnapped her.

His heart said yes, his head said no.

'You do the fighting, I'll do the financing. Between us we'd be doing society a favour,' urged Schumacher. He held out a hand as Ramage still wavered. 'Is it a deal, Colonel? Do we declare war on the Liberation Army – or do we run and hide for the rest of our days?'

'I guess fighting is all I've ever done,' said Ramage, slowly. He took the American's hand. 'All right. War it is.'

Talking was easy. Everything else for the law-abiding citizen was uphill. He had a licence to carry a gun – so long as he kept it unloaded. To break into a quarry might be simple enough – but where was he going to use the explosives? He maintained daily contact with Commander Evans, but learned nothing that would help him carry the fight to the enemy. 'Our intelligence people have got nothing worthwhile out of the girl yet' said the Yard man. 'And there's no sign of your friend. It's beginning to look as if he's given us the slip once again.'

Ramage decided there was only one place to pick up the scent: in Germany. He was unafraid, but there was a terrible finality about everything that he did now. He asked his employers for extended leave, put his house on the market, rewrote his will and then drove down to Sussex to call on his daughter.

'The firm want me to work in Europe for a while,' he told her. 'I think it's a good idea, in all the circumstances. I shall visit John when I leave here and explain the situation to him.' He slipped an arm round her shoulder. 'I'd like you to keep in touch with the hospital and as soon as he's fit to travel, to drive your brother down to Tremeneth. Keep the police informed of your movements and do exactly as they tell you. They may insist on keeping a man in the cottage with you both till I get back, but don't worry: you'll be quite safe there.'

'Of course, Dad. How long will you be gone?'

'A week or two, possibly. It depends really on how I get on.' He smiled at her. 'Incidentally, I've put the house in Surrey up for sale. You'll be getting married soon, while young John has got a few more years at school ahead of him. And frankly, I never want to set foot in the place again. Not now.'

'I think that's the best thing.' She too had dreaded the thought of going back. 'When are you off?'

'First thing in the morning.' He kissed her, shook hands with her fiancé and his family and climbed back in the car. 'I'll phone each day. See you soon.'

As soon as he landed in Dusseldorf Ramage hired a self drive car and headed for München Gladbach, headquarters town for the British Army of the Rhine. It was after dark when he arrived at the house.

'Ramage! Good to see you again, come on in.' Brigadier William Torrance was deputy head of Intelligence and a friend from Cyprus days. A log fire burned in the study, a bottle of whisky stood on the table. 'Take the weight off your feet and tell me what it is you want.'

Like everyone else in the Army he knew of Laura's murder and the boy's kidnapping. If he guessed what was to come he gave no sign: Ramage himself had been very guarded on the phone.

'Information, Will. I need to be steered in the right direction.' He sipped the whisky. 'I want to find Paul Elvides. No need for anyone else to get involved.'

'It's madness, you know that?'

'These people aren't playing games. Laura's already dead and it's only a matter of time before they come back for the rest of us. I don't intend to sit back and wait for that to happen.'

'Leave it to the authorities. Don't be a bloody fool.'

'They've had twenty years to get him. Now I'm going to have a go.'

'God knows, you've got all my sympathy. But even if I wanted to help you, I couldn't. Nobody in Germany knows where to find Elvides. Or anyone else in the Liberation Army. They've vanished. Gone to earth in pastures new – England, maybe. There hasn't been a single incident involving them in this country for months now.'

'The hunt for them must be going on, just the same. Don't tell me the anti-terrorist unit hasn't got a whole list of people and places under observation, I won't believe it.'

'Maybe it has. But the Antiterrorismus-abteilung hasn't been able to smash the Liberation Army in almost two years, my friend. What chance do you think you've got?'

'Sometimes one man is better. The element of surprise.'

'Of course, I'd overlooked that.' Torrance surveyed the

scarred face, the eye-patch, the shock of blond hair. 'You must be the least noticeable man in the country. What's more, hardly anyone knows you're here. Apart from the police, that is. It'll be in the papers next. Why don't you make it really hard for A.L., like wearing a red nose and a clown's outfit?'

Ramage flushed. 'All right. But I'm not leaving Germany till I've found Elvides – or at least had a damned good try. It might not be such a bad idea to ask the Press for help, at that.'

Do that and you're dead, thought Torrance. Aloud he said 'Anyone in England know you came here?'

'No. The kids think I'm on a legitimate business trip. I was careful not to say exactly where.'

'Well: you haven't done anything so far except ask for information which I've been unable to give you. No reason to report that to the authorities: any fool can see you're overwrought.'

Ramage made no reply, and waited.

'It's too late for you to look for a hotel tonight. So you'll stay here – my dear chap, my wife's away, only too glad of the company.' He took his chin between thumb and forefinger and rubbed it thoughtfully. 'I was thinking of asking one or two people round for drinks tomorrow, incidentally. Stay and meet them. You may find it interesting.'

'I'll do that. Thanks, Will.'

'I'm not sure if I ought to be thanked – or fired.' He refilled their glasses. 'You're armed, of course?'

'In England now I carry a gun all the time. Legally,' he added. 'But I didn't bring it with me – deliberately. Guns attract too many questions as soon as they show up on the airport metal detector. Simpler to buy one on arrival.'

'Not so simple here any more,' warned Torrance. 'Thanks to Paul Elvides and company, even the black market is becoming gun-shy these days.' He crossed to his desk and opened a drawer. 'Well, there's a coincidence for you. I've had that Smith & Wesson in there since Nicosia, and the morning the Man from Whitehall flew in to warn us about Paul Elvides. Beautiful little job, that. So light and short-barrelled you could wear it in your button-hole and no one would notice. Not like the old Army issue Colts, eh?'

'No.'

'I really shouldn't keep it lying around like that. Nothing's safe, with all these terrorists about.'

'No' said Ramage. 'I don't suppose it is.'

Torrance called him over to meet a thin, grey-haired man as the party was beginning to get noisy. 'I don't think you two have met. Kurt, this is Colonel Ramage, a very old friend of mine. Gordon, let me introduce Kurt Wüst from the Bundesverfassungsschutz – the Federal Office for the Defence of the State. We're very honoured to have him here, Herr Wüst is a very busy man these days.' A voice called his name, even as he made the introductions. 'You'll have to excuse me, more guests arriving – back in a moment,' he said, and left them standing together.

'Ramage,' said Wüst slowly, letting the name lie on his tongue. His eyes were dark and shining, like coal newly washed by the sea. His face was lined. When he spoke his Adam's apple bobbed up and down in an overbig collar, like an apple in a tub at Hallowe'en. 'I feel as if we know each other already, Herr Colonel. We have so many interests in common, *nicht wahr?*'

Ramage watched him over his whisky, and waited.

'One of the duties of my Department is to direct the activities of the Antiterrorismus-abteilung, as you are possibly aware. It so happens that I was in London recently.' He studied the big man opposite and made no attempt to offer condolences. 'My task was to identify a wildcat known as Gisele Mittel.'

'Ah. I was speaking to a friend about her before I left England yesterday. Still unrepentant and uncooperative, I gather.' Ramage's one blue eye held a baleful gleam. 'I recommended a much more vigorous approach.'

'There are many people here in Germany who would subscribe to that point of view.' Wüst nodded sympathetically. 'However, our good friend Sydenham won't hear of it. I must say he seems confident enough.'

'He would.' Commander Evans had been careful not to name the Intelligence man who was conducting the Mittel interrogation, but as it happened Ramage knew him – from Ulster days. Before he could draw his man out, Wüst had changed the subject.

'May I ask what brings you to Germany, Herr Colonel?'

'I'm glad you did, Herr Wüst.' To hell with this polite fencing, thought Ramage: *he knows*. 'I'm looking for Paul Elvides.'

'So. Two huntsmen after the same fox.' He chuckled, as if at some private joke. 'I guessed it, long before Herr Torrance introduced us – at eight o'clock last night, to be precise, when the immigration controller rang me from the airport to say you had arrived.'

The tip must have come from Evans, thought Ramage. The Special Branch had seen him leave Heathrow. They had phoned Evans, and Evans had phoned Wüst. This strange affinity of policemen: not a blood tie, so much as one of mentality. His face remained expressionless.

'I'd hate to spoil the scent. Perhaps we could hunt this particular fox together?'

'I fear that would be impossible.' Wüst sounded sympathetic but firm. 'The way we hunt in my Department is prescribed by the law. So is the treatment of the fox when we catch him. And we permit no exceptions.'

This time he could not resist it. 'You sound exactly like my friend at Scotland Yard.'

'I'm speaking as a friend, never doubt it. The Department has not been informed – officially – of your arrival in Germany, nor does it know the purpose of your visit. As far as I am concerned there is no reason why it should. In so far as Paul Elvides is concerned, if he should meet with some dire accident in the near future no one in authority in West Germany would lose any sleep. On the contrary, we'd all sleep sounder than at any time in the past two years.'

'I see.'

'On the other hand, if it transpired that he had been murdered the police would be duty bound to pursue normal inquiries. And if caught, his murderer would be punished – under the same law that guides all our actions.' The Adam's apple was working overtime. 'What a waste that would be, Herr Colonel. To spend the rest of one's days behind bars – merely for doing society a service by ridding it of vermin. A tragedy. Better by far to leave it to the pest control officers.'

'I am going to settle accounts with Paul Elvides. Before he kills the rest of my family.'

'As long as we understand each other.' It grieved him to have to talk down to a patently honest man: no one loathed and despised the Liberation Army more than Kurt Wüst. 'If you want to waste your time, no one can stop you. As a guest of this country and a man who has suffered grievously at the hands of these terrorists, it's only natural you should ask us how the search for them is progressing.' He felt in his wallet and took out a card. 'This is where to find me. I have very little to tell you, to be perfectly honest. Many officers in the Antiterrorismus-Abteilung believe the gang has left Germany for good, did you know that? One or two known members of A.L. have been seen as far afield as Paris and Rome recently.'

'London too,' said Ramage succinctly. 'Even New York. That doesn't mean the fox has left for good. Just gone to earth for a while.'

'Huntsmen get hurt, too. See that you don't fall at any of the fences.' Wüst held out a hand. 'I have to go now, but I shall be pleased to see you at any time – in my official capacity, you understand.'

Snow covered the street in the Altstadt like a fitted carpet. Neon signs painted the swirling flakes blue and red and green, making a fairground out of the winter's night. Car doors slammed in the darkness beyond as the customers began to arrive. You could smell the river. Ramage paid off the taxi and came out of the cold, hurrying down the steps to a hole in the wall labelled 'Mitzi'. The Mitzi was where Gisele Mittel had been arrested, before anyone in Germany had heard of the Liberation Army. The thick roll of Schumacher money burned a hole in his pocket, but an amateur detective had to start somewhere and Wüst had been as tight with meaningful clues as a miser with his money at a charity ball.

Ramage had spent a whole morning with him, to no avail. When he walked into the office in Cologne, the first thing he had seen was a wall-map decked with coloured flags and seemingly full of promise. Wüst had invited him to examine it, and all it represented was a chronicle of terror. A court-room blown up here. A multiple store burned down there. This judge murdered. That minister kidnapped. A police chief assassinated. Bank cashiers shot dead, robberies, blackmail, escapes from jail – these were the red flags pinned on the wall-map, and in abundance. The yellow ones showed the Antiterrorismus successes and were as rare as cuckoos in mid-winter. So Ramage had ended up at the Mitzi, on a trail that was two years cold.

'It's just another drinking club,' said Wüst. 'With a cabaret show that's looking tired these days but was a hit with the Left Wing when it first appeared. It's what you English call a skit, on the famous Munich beer-cellar – where it all began with Hitler and the Nazis, you know? Steins of beer, big buxom waitresses, fat Bavarians in lederhosen playing the squeeze-box: pure music-hall Germany. Only in the Mitzi beer cellar scene they all sing the Red Flag and salute each other with a clenched fist, and instead of violence erupting there's a love-in. It's a smut show with political overtones – I found it boring myself, but the young set, particularly the young Red set, lapped it up. We were tipped off there were some interesting types using the club, so we raided it. That's when we picked up Gisele Mittel. You know the rest.'

'Yes. Her arrest brought the others crawling out of the wood-work.'

'Correct. But we kept watch on the club for another year after that without finding any other member of the gang. In the end we gave up.' The cadaverous face melted into one of its rare smiles. 'It was costing the German government too much money.' Then he said, 'You should look in there, my friend. The cabaret goes on till midnight. After that it's the usual routine with drinks at millionaire prices, music loud enough to cause a man permanent injury, dancing on a floor the size of a postage stamp – and the world's sorriest collection of women. I can't think of a better place to discourage you from this foolish quest.'

'We'll see.'

Tonight was his fifth visit and he was beginning to appreciate the difficulties of the chase. In the Mitzi he spent more in one night than he had earned in a month as an army colonel. A single scotch cost more than a whole bottle in over-taxed England, champagne was prohibitively expensive. The hangers-on swarmed round like flies – and they all drank champagne. No waiter ever came near, no barman ever heard an order without an accompanying tip. And that was only the beginning. He had a service apartment in town now. Each day he wanted something new and his visits to the Dresdner Bank were becoming more and more frequent. And he had nothing to show for any of it.

He had changed his appearance: his hair was dyed black, and instead of the eye-patch he wore dark glasses. The scars still showed, but not so obviously. In the permanent twilight of the Mitzi, no one cared: only money counted. At two in the morning, one of the women sat down and joined him.

'Poor man, you look lonely. Would you like me to talk to you?'

'Please.' He signalled for the waiter. 'Drink?'

'Thank you. Perhaps a glass of champagne?' She made it sound as if the girls who worked the Mitzi were allowed a choice by the management, and listened as Ramage gave the order. 'You're an American?'

'No. English.'

'Ah.' Coloured lights spinning over the dance floor reached out to touch their table and she noticed the scars. 'From the army?'

'No. I'm a journalist.' That was Torrance's idea. 'On a special assignment.'

'If you can cover it from the Mitzi,' she said, and giggled at the thought, 'it must be a very special story indeed. Excuse me, I didn't mean to appear rude. But you're in here every night, isn't that so?'

'Yes.' He offered her a cigarette. 'The reason I come here is that I don't have anywhere else to start.' The waiter poured the drinks and vanished again into the night-club shadows. Ramage allowed him plenty of time to get clear. 'Perhaps you can help me. I'm willing to pay for information, naturally.'

'There are worse ways of earning money.' She was in her twenties, with hair as red as fire. She was dressed all in black: a fine cashmere sweater hugged her as close as an ardent lover, the ski pants fitted as if they had been painted over her rounded hips. A patent leather belt with a huge silver buckle circled her waist. She looked young and happy and attractive – until you came to the eyes. All the human frailties were mirrored in those green, hurt eyes. 'Tell me what it is you need to know.'

'I'm writing an article about the Liberation Army. One of them is under arrest in England now, the woman who was found in this club nearly two years ago – Gisele Mittel, Now I'm looking for anyone who knew her. Preferably someone who can introduce me to her terrorist friends.'

She cringed as he spoke. 'Please. No one in Germany will do that for you. It's dangerous even to talk about such things.'

'You see?' Ramage grinned at her. 'I told you it was a special story. I know it won't be easy – but I have to keep on asking till I find someone willing to help me. For that I will pay a lot of money.'

'Listen to me. Perhaps it's different in England, perhaps you don't have such awful people. But the men and women in A.L. don't speak to reporters, my God! no, they're wild animals. Step too close to them and they'll kill you.'

'Have you ever seen them? Or are you just saying the same things that everyone else says about them?'

'Yes, I've seen some of them.' He could just hear what she was saying. 'I was in here the night Gisele was picked up – I was arrested too, half the women in the club were. The police let us go once they knew who we were. But I spoke to Gisele in the cells, and I saw the men she came in with.'

'And have they been back since?'

'The Mitzi was full of policemen for nearly a year after they got Gisele.' Her fingers stroked the stem of her wineglass nervously. 'No one from A.L. came anywhere near, of course.'

'But when the police left?'

'I've seen one of them: a man. He used to fancy one of the girls who worked here, a girl called Gudrun. He was in here last about three or four months ago. A big man with fair hair, about my age. I haven't seen him lately.'

Ramage called for his bill and took out his wallet. It was bulging with notes. 'What's your name, little girl?'

'Jutte.'

'Well, think about what I said, Jutte. I know these people are dangerous and I give you my word I would never get you into any trouble with them.' He slid a thousand marks across the table and pressed them in her hand. 'That's a present, for what you've told me tonight. And here's my phone number. If ever you see that man again – or any of his friends – all you have to do is ring me. That's all, just ring me.'

'And for that you'll pay me?'

His mouth was smiling. She could not see through the glasses. 'For that I'll pay you – a king's ransom.'

She shivered. 'And your name?'

'Gordon.'

'Herr Gordon, take me home.'

She lived in the old town, only a mile from the club. It had stopped snowing now and a moon lit the way. Sharp-sloping roofs sparkled white as they passed and the ice that was forming crunched underfoot. Way out on the river the Rhine barges sounded a warning of dangers ahead.

'This is where I live.'

Once it had been a warehouse. Now it was an apartment building, concrete hutches stacked one on top of the other like a house of cards. Jutte lived at the top, on the fifth floor. She had three rooms, living room, bathroom and kitchen. A bed came down out of the wall to turn the living room into a workshop. She gave him a drink and made the bed expertly.

'Here.' She patted it invitingly. 'Make yourself comfortable while I get cleaned up.'

He passed the time examining the tiny porcelain figures that lined the tallboy shelf. Some bore the initials 'KPM' and marks that identified them as early eighteenth-century Meissen. Ramage whistled his admiration.

'You know about such things?'

Jutte was wearing a pale green dressing gown that matched the colour of her eyes. Red curls tumbled carelessly over her shoulders. Below the dressing-gown her feet disappeared into furlined mules. She had washed off the makeup and looked as young as his daughter back in England. It seemed a long time since he had said goodbye to his family.

'A little,' he said, and put the figurine down. 'Enough to know these are worth a lot of money.'

'They're my savings.' She gave him a bitter-sweet smile. 'But I'll never get back what they cost, believe me.' She filled his glass. 'It's started snowing again. Will you stay?'

He felt lonely and tired and it would have been the easiest thing in the world to say yes. 'Forgive me. We'll just stay friends, eh?'

'If you want.' She removed his glasses and touched the empty flesh, and silver scars. 'From the war? You were wounded?'

'Yes, I was wounded. A long time ago.'

They sat in silence for a while. 'This story you want to write. How long do you have?'

'It's difficult to say.' He rubbed his eye. 'A month, two months: longer if I thought there was a real chance of making contact.'

'I'm very frightened.' She looked directly at him. 'For you. If you're not what you pretend to be, they'll kill you, don't ever doubt it.'

'Don't you worry about that, Jutte. No one's going to harm either of us, I promise you. All you need to do is pick up the phone and tell me where to find him. I'll do the rest. For that you get 10,000 marks – guaranteed.'

'But supposing he won't talk to you?'

'I'll do my level best to persuade him.' He grinned as he said it. 'I never expected it to be easy. But you'll get paid however he reacts.'

'All right, I'll trust you.' She leaned over and kissed him on the mouth. 'But don't ever let him know it was me who called you.'

It was so cold the snow had turned into hail and gusts of sharp, ice-white stones tapped impatiently on the windscreen, urging him to hurry. Visibility was down to thirty paces. The Opel skidded from side to side as he hurtled through the frozen streets, like a toboggan on a fast run. Voices screamed abuse through the night as pedestrians jumped for their lives, lights flashed a different kind of obscenity as drivers got out of his way. But there was not a police car in sight and he made the Mitzi in twenty-one minutes flat.

Jutte had telephoned him just before midnight. He could barely hear what she was saying for the shouting in the background. 'What the hell's going on there?'

'Nothing, it's just the orchestra, the cabaret's just finishing.' She was hoarse with fear. 'Gordon. He's here. At the bar.'

'Keep him there if you can. If he tries to leave ask him back with you, anything you like, just don't let him out of your sight till I catch up with you.'

'I'll try. He's very drunk.'

'He's worth 10,000 marks to me, Jutte. Don't lose him.' Ramage slammed down the phone, felt for the Smith & Wesson in his shoulder holster and ran for his car.

They were not in the bar, nor on the dance floor. Ramage

masked his disappointment and gave the barman exactly the right tip with his drink, not too big, not too small: after all, he was asking the most casual of favours.

'Where's the red-head tonight?'

'You're too late, sir. She left with a friend.'

Ramage nodded, and drifted away to the tables. Five minutes later he got up and left unnoticed. This time he drove more carefully. As he turned into the cul-de-sac south of the river he switched off power and lights, and glided silently down to the apartment block. A number of lights were still on: Jutte's neighbours kept late hours. A car was parked in the courtyard, out in the snow. The engine was still warm. Ramage merged into the shadows, and waited. After half an hour his feet were numb while his hands and ears felt so cold that they burned. Fine hail powdered his newly-dyed hair. His eyebrows turned silver. The tiny hairs inside his nostrils froze against the flesh, his breath hung in the air like tobacco smoke. One by one the lights went out until they burned only on the fifth floor.

Suddenly Jutte's flat was plunged into darkness. Ramage crossed to the weather porch and peered through the windows, watching as the lift descended, leaking light. When it came to a halt on the ground floor the metal gates opened and closed again with a resounding crash. Whoever got out was a big man, bigger even than Ramage himself. The outer doors rattled impatiently as he fumbled for the lock to let himself out, into the weather porch. The time he had spent with Jutte had tired him. He was yawning, and his breath smelled as stale as yesterday's news. Ramage drew the Smith & Wesson and flattened himself against the wall. The doors clicked shut. As the big man went by Ramage brought the gun butt down, hard. It might have travelled ten inches. It landed on the back of the head and the big man keeled over instantly, like a heifer in a slaughter house. Ramage knelt over him and gagged him with his scarf. He took a coil of thin nylon rope from his overcoat pocket and tied him, hands first, with the strangler's loop running from the hands behind his back round the neck and down again to the ankles. He took hold of his hair and dragged him out into the snow. That was the easy part. Then he took a deep breath, swung the deadweight into the air and over his shoulders, and staggered like a drunk across the roadway to the Opel.

He got the boot open and poured the big man in. It was a

big boot but he filled it to overflowing. His head struck against the jack as he dived in. A sound of protest trumpeted through the gag and he kicked out viciously with pinioned feet. Ramage clubbed him again. This time the big man gave a loud groan and went as limp as a melted jelly. Ramage squeezed the unresisting body into whatever space he could find and forced down the lid. He looked at his watch. It was half-past three. It had taken him only four minutes from the moment the light went out in Jutte's apartment to capture his first Liberation Army prisoner. Half an hour later, he had him upstairs in his service flat, stripped and pegged out on the bed.

The big man was pale, but very much alive. Blood trickled from his nose, his bear-skin chest rose and fell frantically, as if he had been running a long way. Ramage slapped his face with roundhouse, stinging blows that sounded like a sail snapping taut in the breeze. Pale blue eyes opened uncertainly. They were very moist, as if their owner might be close to tears. Ramage slapped him again to make sure he was paying attention. Then he addressed him, in English.

'Reveille,' he said. 'Wakey wakey.' The big man was shivering. 'I'm going to ask you some questions, and you're going to tell me everything I want to know. Tell me any lies and you'll wish you'd never been born.'

Ramage loosened the gag and pulled his fingers away only just in time. 'Try and bite me again,' he warned softly, 'and I'll play dentists with you. Now then. Question number one. Who are you?'

There was no heating in the room and the big man's bare flesh was goose-pimpled with cold. He lifted his head and called Ramage an ugly, obscene name. Ramage got up. 'You're freezing,' he said. 'Perhaps you'd be a little more co-operative if I warmed you up.' He disappeared for a while into the kitchen. When he returned he was carrying a small gas-powered blow-lamp. He fitted a metal paint stripper into the nozzle, turned on gas and lit the flame. There was a steady roaring sound. As the big man watched, the paint-stripper changed colour. First it turned dark blue, then an angry red, like a drunkard's nose. The roaring sound of the flame burning under pressure filled the room. Ramage picked up the blow-lamp and held it over the little bedside table. He had bought it for bomb-making, to solder wires together.

'Watch.' He held the paint-stripper over the woodwork. Immediately the varnish swelled and bubbled and started to come away. Ramage took a Stanley knife and scraped the surface clean. 'That's how I'm going to use it on you' he said. 'The soles of your feet first, then we'll work our way up. Want to bet you tell me your name before I run out of gas?'

The big man writhed and twisted and screwed his eyes shut as Ramage bent over him. The flame was turned away from him, he was completely unmarked. But the pain he felt was real enough: that was already in the mind.

'Helmut,' he said quickly. 'Helmut Wehrner.'

'That's more like it.' The blow-lamp roared away on the table, close enough for Helmut to feel its hot breath on his face. A.L. treated its own prisoners with such brutality he was wild with fear of what might be in store. 'Next question. Where is Paul Elvides?'

Helmut had no intention of suffering pain to save the Greek's hide, and the answer came pat: perhaps too pat. 'In England. I don't know where exactly.'

'I'm hoping you can do better than that, Helmut.' Ramage felt sure he was lying. He made a gesture of reaching for the blow-lamp again while he kept his eye on the terrorist's face, trying to read his expression. As he did so his fingers brushed against the metal container and knocked it over. It rolled from the table on to the bed and under Helmut's naked, twisting back. He arched his body and screamed.

'Don't burn me! For God's sake, I'm telling the truth!'

The blond hair on his legs lay as thick as down in an eider's nest. His bonds prevented Helmut from avoiding the flame completely. Where it touched the hairs they turned brown and then black, and instantly shrivelled away. He struggled so violently it took Ramage several seconds to recover the blow-lamp and set it back on the table. By that time there were bright red marks down Helmut's inside thighs and buttocks. A blister as big as a bantam's egg puffed up on his scrotum. His eyes were shut, but not tight enough to stop the tears tickling down his face.

'Look at you,' jeered Ramage. 'A few iddy-biddy little burns and you go all to pieces. You're not tough, Helmut.' He slapped his face to stop him weeping. 'You Liberation Army people aren't tough at all – unless you're facing unarmed women with a machine-gun in your hand.' He slapped him again. 'Or kidnapping twelve-year-old schoolboys. Stop blubbering, damn you, and answer my questions. Lie to me once more and I'll burn your tongue out.'

He removed the gag altogether. There was no attempt to gnaw his fingers this time.

'Let's go back to question number two. Tell me all about Paul Elvides. Where he lives. Where he eats and drinks. Where his bomb factory is. Everything you know about it.'

He called a halt at seven in the morning. He was exhausted, Helmut was drained: the confessional does that to a sinner. Ramage went into the kitchen and drank scalding black coffee as he weighed it all in his mind. Parts of it rang true, even confirmed the police theories. Elvides was out of the country, last known whereabouts – England. There was an A.L. group in New York. Angela Schless and her other commandos were in France or Italy. Helmut carefully made no mention of the shooting lodge, or the fact that Rudi was with him in Germany. Ramage in turn accepted that anything Helmut told him under duress would be less than the whole truth: but it was a beginning, more than he had dared hope to achieve only twenty-four hours ago. On the credit side he knew where three A.L. apartments were. He also knew where the bomb factory was, and he was going to need explosives for the forthcoming battles. He put on an overcoat, and looked back in the bedroom at the hapless Helmut.

'I'm going to check on the things you've told me' he said. 'If you've been telling the truth I'll give you a blanket when I get back.' He checked the bonds and fastened the gag so tight Helmut winced. 'If I find you've been lying, I'll make toast out of you.'

He slipped Helmut's Luger into his pocket to back up the Smith & Wesson under his arm, spent some time in the living-room out of sight and then made his way down to the Opel.

Rudi Meitner was a late sleeper, and did not wake until after eleven. He put on dressing-gown and slippers and shuffled blearily into the kitchen to make coffee. When it was ready he called to his friend asleep in the far bedroom. 'Hey, Helmut! Come and get it!' His voice was soft and high-pitched, like a girl's. But there was nothing ladylike about his manners. He got up on a chair and pounded his fist on the wall. 'Helmut, you lazy bastard, time to get up!'

When there was still no reply he hurried out and threw the door open, frowning as he saw the untouched bed. A night's whoring was standard behaviour for the big fellow. Not to make contact with base at least once in twelve hours was unthinkable. Rudi went straight to the telephone and made a number of urgent calls. A few minutes later, one of the waiters from the Mitzi told him all he needed to know. He made no attempt to dial Jutte's number. An inner voice told him this might be a good time to call unannounced.

He shaved and took a shower, and made ready to leave in less than ten minutes. For all his haste he was something to see when he left the apartment. The black razor-cut hair lay flat to his scalp, glistening with brilliantine. He wore a suit of robin's-egg blue, with lapels as wide as a plank, and an hourglass waist. His trousers flared like a matelot's bell-bottoms and hid all but the toecaps of his Cuban-heeled leather boots. His eyebrows were plucked, there was rouge appling his cheeks and he smelled delicately of attar of roses. He had a knife strapped to his left wrist, above the love bangle. Rudi Meitner – *die puderquaste*, the powder-puff, the queer – was five feet five inches small and as pretty – and as deadly – as a coral snake. He zipped on a fur-lined parka, slid a Mauser into the pocket as his insurance premium, and rang for the lift to take him visiting.

Ramage left Jutte's flat about the same time. He had been to the bomb factory and did not like to leave the Opel unattended for long. She had aged since he saw her last and looked as if she had been in a prizefight. Powerful fingers had raised weals right across her pale face. Her eyes were red and swollen. The fire had been doused in that auburn hair: now it held grey, like ash. As soon as Ramage stepped inside the door she was in his arms, weeping bitterly. 'God, he was like an ape. I've never been hurt so much in my life.'

Ramage held her very close for a while, and then led her gently to a chair. Blood from her split lips stained his shirt. He poured two glasses of schnapps and sat down opposite her. 'Here. Straight back now, you'll feel better.' He felt in his pocket, took out an envelope and placed it in her lap. 'I wouldn't have asked you if there had been any other way. Forgive me.'

The envelope was fat and heavy, and she counted the money. 'But there's more than 20,000 marks in here!'

'I know. The rest is from Helmut. He's ashamed of what he did to you.'

'Who are you?' she sobbed. She began to tremble and the money spilled on the floor. 'They'll kill me for leading you to him.'

'You won't get any more trouble from Helmut, I can promise you that. It might not be a bad idea to leave town for a while.' He smiled at her. 'It's time you got out, anyway. The Mitzi is no place for a lovely woman like you.'

'Gordon, please come with me. They'll kill you too if you stay here.'

'I wish I could.' He emptied his glass and put it down. 'But I've got work to do.' He looked round the room and found it very vulnerable: one push and the lock would give. 'I should get out today, if I were you. Just to be on the safe side. You know where to find me if you need any help.'

Her face was awash with tears. Ramage went out into the corridor without another word and waited for the lift. One of Jutte's neighbours passed him on the landing with no more than a casual glance. After all, a girl had to live.

The traffic jam was one of the worst he had known. At first Ramage blamed it on the rush hour, that nightly hardening of the metropolitan arteries that reduces the flow of vehicles in every city in the world to snail's pace. But this was total stoppage, chaos. The Opel had not moved an inch in the past hour. He climbed out and peered through the whirling flakes, trying to make out what was holding them up so long. A pedestrian loomed up out of the night like a snowman, and shouted the news to all who could hear him.

'It's A.L.!' he cried. 'They've been bombing up there, and the police have got the whole area sealed off!'

Helmut was in the apartment, less than half a mile away. Ramage abandoned the car and started walking. Crowds had gathered at the inter-section, where policemen in camouflaged jackets forbade all further civilian movement. Some spoke urgently into walkie-talkies. All wore guns, swinging from their leather belts. Out-riders in black leather coats and gauntlets roared up on their motor-bikes, reported, and vanished again in the snow. Past the police barrier, standing by the windows of a brightly-lit multiple store, a tiny group of men in plain clothes were talking together. One of them was Wüst. Ramage tried to break through the cordon, calling his name. As a young policeman forced him back Wüst turned, and saw him. He came hurrying over, barking orders.

'Let that man through, I want to talk to him!'

He was hunched in a heavy overcoat, with a Cossack hat tugged down low on his forehead. His glasses were splashed with snow. He walked a few paces from the barrier, holding Ramage by the arm. There was a curious expression on his thin face. 'You are either the luckiest man in Germany,' he said, 'or an even bigger fool than I thought. I warned you to keep your nose clean.'

Ramage thought of all the crimes he had committed that day, and remembered the warning Wüst had given him at the party. He said nothing, and waited for him to go on.

'Where were you at four o'clock this afternoon?'

He had been in Elvides' apartment, booby-trapping it with ten pounds of gelignite. 'In a building off the Kaiser-strasse' he replied truthfully.

'Can you prove it?'

'I can prove I was there' said Ramage, and laughed. 'But I've no way of proving the time. Why?'

'Because the service flat you rented was blown up at exactly four o'clock, Herr Colonel. One man in it was killed, another was badly wounded. We thought the dead man was you. The other one is from A.L.'

Ramage said nothing to that.

'The wounded man is called Meitner. We've identified him by his finger prints. We assumed he was trying to kill you, and was hoist by his own petard in the process. Now we have to find out who the dead man was.'

'His name was Wehrner' said Ramage. 'Helmut Wehrner. Also a member of A.L. He came home with me last night and told me one or two things about the organisation. I last saw him around midday. He was in bed and fast asleep at the time. Very much alive.'

'Until we know better then,' Wüst told him, 'we'll leave

the theory of the explosion as it stands. That they went to the flat together to kill you – carrying explosives – and were caught in the subsequent blast themselves.'

'It's a sound enough theory,' said Ramage. 'The IRA in Ulster scored a lot of own goals too. It happens all the time when you start playing around with dynamite.'

'We know.' Wüst wiped the snow from his glasses. 'Tell me, what sort of information about A.L. did you get from Wehrner?'

'Not as much as I hoped. Where the bomb factory was. Where Elvides lived when he was here. That kind of thing.'

'Was he holding out?'

'Of course he was. I'd only had him a few hours.'

'As soon as we leave here, I'll take you down to the Federal Prosecutor's office. You can make a voluntary statement – before you leave the country.'

'Who says I'm leaving?'

'The Bundesverfassungsschutz. I told you that next time we met it would be in my official capacity.'

'And if I won't go?'

'You'll find yourself on a murder charge. The murder of a call girl you met at the Mitzi. Jutte Lahn.'

'I haven't touched her – and you know it.'

'I'm afraid I don't know any such thing, Herr Colonel. Do you deny you took her home from the club four nights ago?'

'No.'

'And spent some hours there?'

'I didn't sleep with her.'

'You were there the last time this morning, between eleven and twelve?'

'What the hell is this all about, Wüst?'

'Fräulein Lahn was found murdered, shortly after midday today. From the look of the room she was packing to leave, in a hurry. A neighbour coming back from shopping saw a man waiting for the lift on the fifth floor just before noon. A big man, more than six feet tall, with dark hair and wearing dark glasses. The police found a great many fingerprints in all the rooms – on drinking glasses, porcelain ornaments, everywhere. She was a woman who had lots of callers, of course. But it's only a question of elimination of suspects until they find the one most likely to have killed her.'

'She helped me find Wehrner. Why would I want to harm her?'

'It was a sex murder. That's reason enough, in itself. We haven't found the weapon but perhaps it's not so surprising, with a river nearby.'

Ramage stared at him, dumbfounded. 'What weapon?'

'A knife. It may not be too hard to find the killer, even without it. He mutilated the body. Jutte Lahn had the rarest of blood groups. Our man is almost certain to have some blood somewhere on his clothing.'

He felt the bloodstains on his shirt, burning the skin. 'I went there to pay her some money for putting me on to Wehrner. I gave her 10,000 marks and there was another 10,000 I took from Wehrner.'

'We found 100 marks in her purse. Nothing else.'

'Then he robbed her too.'

'No, robbery wasn't the motive here. There were some very rare porcelain figurines in the room, left untouched. This was a sex killing and we can't rule out anyone.' While they stood there talking the snow had coated his face like a mask. 'I think you'd be well advised to leave Germany while you can, Herr Colonel.'

'And if I refuse?'

'As soon as the police identify those prints they'll have more than enough evidence to charge you. And I wouldn't bet a pfennig on your chances of being acquitted in a court of law. I mean that.'

'All right,' said Ramage wearily. 'I'll go quietly. But I didn't touch the girl, and you know it. Helmut's Liberation Army chum must have done that. He arrived at the apartment just after I left, forced Jutte to tell him where to find me, and then murdered her to shut her mouth. The sexual attack was just a cover.'

'Perhaps. We'll question little Rudi if and when he recovers from his blast wounds. Meantime, you remain the number one suspect. Because I can tell you this, there are none of his fingerprints in the room.' Wüst signalled for his driver. 'You can come with me now and make that voluntary statement. We'll stop on the way and take a look at Elvides' apartment, and if there's anything in there that needs defusing you'd better do it fast – before any of my men get hurt, like Meitner. Then I'll have you escorted on to the first available plane. Please, take my advice and don't hurry back.'

'I'm going to keep on looking till I find Elvides. None of you are going to stop me.'

Sydenham had already signed him in. Ramage handed his coat and hat to one steward and followed another into the bar. There was no mistaking the figure right at the end, perched on his stool like a Toby Jug on a farmhouse shelf.

'Colonel.' They shook hands warily, like heavyweights before the fight. 'Good to see you after all this time. What's it to be?'

'I'll join you in a pink gin, if I may.'

They chinked glasses, murmured the conventional phrases and made their way to a distant table. Sydenham had not changed since Ramage had last seen him, on a soft Spring morning in Ulster. He was as big and round as a wine barrel, weighing more than 250 pounds. He stood five feet nine but sheer bulk made him appear smaller, squat, and no amount of skill on the part of his tailor could disguise that corpulent frame sufficiently. Other men walked across a room, Sydenham rolled. He was no oil painting, either. His skull shone in the artificial light as if it had been buffed and like the rest of the man, it was over-large, unseemly. But he was not just bald, he was hair-less. There were no eyebrows, merely a darker shade of pink where they would have grown if Nature had been more kind, and no eyelashes: their work was performed by a fold of skin, like a hood. He could boast two features only that rescued him from a surpassing ugliness. The most noticeable was his eyes. The whites were as clear as virgin snow, the irises set in them an Arctic blue. The combined effect was uncanny: as if they were lit from within. His mouth too was a revelation. It had the policeman's stamp, hard and unyielding, but there was humour too, with compassion and wisdom. Eyes and mouth together signposted the way to his character, at least to that side of his character he showed in dealing with men like Ramage. When you finished looking him over Sydenham was not ugly at all but strong, and intensely masculine.

Each man surveyed the other as they sat down at table, and thought their secret thoughts. Sydenham was an Intelligence man, the anti-terrorist coordinator. Now he was the first to break the silence.

'I was exceedingly sorry to hear about Mrs Ramage,' he said. 'I was abroad at the time or I would have written. About the boy. How is he?'

'He'll live. But he's having a hard time.'

'You don't seem to have had the best of luck since you left the Army.'

'That's precisely why I'm here, Sydenham.'

'I guessed as much when you rang.' Wüst had been on the phone beforehand, with much to say. 'What can I do for you?'

'Help me find Paul Elvides.'

'I wish to God I knew where he was.' He signalled for two more pink gins. 'The Fox has gone to earth again. But not in England, I fancy.'

'But you've got a head start on the rest of them. Aren't you still interrogating Gisele Mittel – the bitch who murdered Laura?'

'You seem well informed about my activities.' The pale blue eyes frosted over, then smiled again as quickly. 'Forgive me, no one has a better right to ask. Yes, I'm talking to her. Constantly.'

Ramage refused to beg. He just sat there, poker-faced, waiting.

'She was hostile enough at first: like a wild animal. But a week or two of total deprivation works miracles. Now she actually asks to see me, sometimes three and four times a day. There are times when I can't stop her talking.'

'In which case you ought to be able to find out where I can look for Elvides. That's all I want, Sydenham. A shove in the right direction.'

'Alas, we haven't got round to mundane things like that.' He offered Ramage a cigarette. 'Not yet, anyway. We argued the inevitability of the Marxist-Leninist victory until three this morning, for instance. The night before it was the works of Marcuse. There are times when I fall into bed punch-drunk on dogma.' Up went his finger for another round, like a signal to the mast-head. 'We'll get round to Elvides eventually, don't worry. But I daren't rush my fences. Softly, softly.'

'I don't have time to wait. That bastard's out to get me – and my family. And you know it.'

'I can't promise you a thing, Ramage. Sorry.'

'Sorry be damned. You owe me a favour. Now I've come to collect.'

He was referring to an afternoon in Ireland neither man would ever forget. An investiture was scheduled to be held on Ulster soil, with all VIPs landing by helicopter to beat the terrorists. Sydenham had been flown in from London to take charge of all security arrangements. The Royal party was due to be housed in a heavily guarded country house. As head of 'Felix' – the British Army bomb disposal unit – Ramage was called on to make a final, personal search of the building for hidden explosive devices. At the end of the day, he reported to Sydenham. 'It's clean,' he said. He made the statement with all the authority of the best man in the world at his job. Sydenham had never met him before then.

'Colonel,' he replied, 'neither of us will ever win promotion should your judgment be at fault. Forgive me for being a Doubting Thomas. Could anything at all have been overlooked? Or can I go nap on this?'

'The house is as clean as a whistle,' said Ramage doggedly. 'There are also forty acres of ground. I haven't searched them, obviously, in the time available. I can do so easily enough if you want.'

'There's no need for that. I've had my own people in here for a fortnight, with dogs. If there was anything in the grounds they'd have found it by now.'

And then, when the choppers were on their way the police got a call on the Confidential Line telling them there was a device buried beneath one of the flower beds. Working against the clock, Ramage dug under the tulips and found a sophisticated device designed to explode acoustically from the sound of the Royal helicopter touching down twenty paces away. It was a sleeper, buried by the terrorists weeks beforehand, when the news of the visit was no more than a brief announcement from Number 10. And it had remained unexploded, exactly as the IRA had gambled, because the official helipad was painted red, white and blue – and left covered against wind and rain – while all visiting security chiefs were obliged to land on a grass strip a hundred yards away. Ramage defused the bomb and identified it as Elvides' handiwork: the first he had seen since Aden.

He won another medal for his work that day – and Sydenham's undying gratitude. It was Sydenham who later reported Elvides' death, and caused the official search for him to be called off.

'We now know he first contacted the IRA when they sent some of their men arms shopping in Europe a year ago,' he said. 'Our information is they hired him for this one prestige assignment only. I've only myself to blame, but the fact is it would have worked if only he'd kept his nose clean. It seems however that he was drinking heavily and got involved with someone else's colleen, whereupon the jilted party tipped us off about his master bomb. The two men met afterwards, and shots were exchanged. Elvides has not been seen since and word has it he was killed in the fight, and buried in a nearby wood. I'm inclined to give it credence. My sources are very reliable.' Before he left Ireland he sent for Ramage. 'If ever I can repay you, Colonel,' he told him, 'just say the word. I mean that.'

The time was now. 'I don't care if you have to choke it out of that bitch,' said Ramage. 'Just get her to tell you where I can find the Liberation Army watering holes. I'll do the rest.'

'Let's think about it while we eat.' Nothing ever spoiled Sydenham's appetite. *Escargots à la chasseur* were followed by smoked breast of gosling. Then a leg of lamb *boulangère*, flanked by a Bordeaux with the Pauillac label. Calvados and Havanas arrived with the coffee. Ramage toyed with his meal while the fat man feasted and fired a barrage of questions throughout.

'Suppose it's Germany?'

'You heard about that?'

'Of course. Wüst and I are in daily contact. Over many matters.'

'If it's Germany then I go back, and to hell with Wüst.'

Sydenham nodded. 'But I wouldn't recommend it. He says you went about things with all the restraint of a bull in a china shop. Look, I'm not being funny. You're the best bomb disposal officer there was, and the bravest. But this kind of war is out of your depth. Leave it to the professionals.'

'No. I'm going to kill Elvides. You intelligence experts don't eliminate your enemies any more, you psycho-analyse them and then store them away in a nice, warm jail ready for barter.

I won't be able to sleep sound at nights until I know the Greek's dead.'

'I tell you, we're close to him: very close. If you screw things up now, you'll have a hell of a lot to answer for.' He had spoken to Wüst only this morning, and it had been an encouraging conversation.

('For God's sake keep that wild man away,' said Wüst. 'He doesn't know it, but he did us a great good turn when he built the bomb in his flat that killed Wehrner and wounded Meitner. Meitner's a queer, and a vain little *puderquaste* at that. I went down to the hospital today while the doctors were changing his bandages. I took a mirror with me and persuaded them to leave us alone for a moment. Then I showed Rudi how he looked without a nose. *Gruss Gott,* I haven't seen any man cry like that for a long time. So I said, "Listen, *junge*, you can't go through life with a face like that, what man is ever going to want to kiss you now?" Then I put it to him, I said, "Tell you what, Rudi, I'll do a little deal with you. Tell us where to find Angela and Paul and all the others, and I'll ask the plastic surgeons to build you a nice new nose." He was too upset at the time to say much, but I'm quietly confident. Whatever I get I'll pass it on to you, and you can try it out on Gisele. Between the two of us we ought to have A.L. in the bag before we're much older. But for God's sake don't tell Ramage. The man's a menace. We'd been watching that night-club girl *for two years* before Ramage appeared on the scene, and he got her killed within a week. I tell you, if he turns up in Germany before we've got this gang safely under lock and key we'll jail *him* – for as long as it takes.')

Aloud, Sydenham said, 'Use your head, Ramage. Stay out of this.'

'I can't. I owe that much to my kids.'

'All right.' Sydenham signed the bill and made ready to leave. 'Maybe it will be safer to guide you, at that. If I get any information out of Gisele Mittel, it's yours – for twenty-four hours only. After that I pass it on to the appropriate authorities for official action. That's the best I can offer you.'

'And all I ask. Thank you.'

•

Two nights later he arrived at Ramage's hotel, in the early

hours of the morning. Sydenham looked as if he had stepped out of the bath. Ramage was yawning, a massive unshaven Cyclops.

'You're still determined to go ahead with this one man campaign?'

'Yes.'

'Then you'll want to look into this.' He handed over a slip of paper with an address scribbled on it. 'I gather it's some kind of cache where A.L. keeps arms and ammunition. Burn that as soon as you've memorised it.'

Ramage lit a cigarette and put the match to the paper. 'Done.'

'I don't know if you'll find anyone there or not. Gisele wasn't too well tonight, so the doctor gave her a little injection.' Sydenham chewed his lower lip. 'You know how it is, it's not like a normal interrogation when they're like that. That's all we got out of her. All that's new, anyhow.'

'I understand.'

'Here, take this with you, you might find it useful.' He gave Ramage a tiny package. 'It's one of those laser-powered bugs, a long-range earwig. I expect it's simple enough for an electrical expert like you to understand how it works: I must say I find it quite remarkable. Effective up to 500 yards.'

'It could come in very handy.'

'Remember. That address is your private Tom Tiddler's ground for twenty-four hours only. After that I call the Deuxième Bureau. I daren't hold it any longer.'

'That's fine by me. Thank you, Sydenham.'

'You've got nothing to thank me for.' He was smiling, slyly. 'We haven't met since Ireland – remember?' They shook hands, and he was gone.

Ramage flew over the area first, in a private plane. The French pilot took the Comanche over the marshes at 600 feet. Lofty poplars lined the main road, pushing their green heads dangerously high. Broken cloud made visibility patchy and there was no room for error.

'There it is, m'sieu. The road to Amiens, on our left. And the village, in the valley. You see?'

He stared down, beyond the village. He wanted to see the terrain, and know where to hide. The lake sparkled like a jewel in the morning sun. Then he saw the hut, nestling in the reeds:

that had to be the shooting lodge. The track that led to it was perhaps half a mile long.

'One more pass, pilot – lower still, if you can. Then back to Amiens.'

He felt naked as he came to the village in his car a few hours later. Once again he had left England without his gun to avoid drawing any attention to his departure. But all he had been able to buy in Amiens was the shotgun he had in the boot, with a couple of boxes of cartridges: it was like going into the bull-ring armed with a toothpick. And this time he had to go in, and show himself. There was no other way to find out what he wanted to know.

The old *patron* was only too pleased to gossip. 'I much regret we can't offer you any sport' he said. 'The shooting here is let. In its entirety.'

'It must be good. I'm really disappointed.'

'On the contrary.' The old man laid a finger alongside his nose and tapped it, the international language that said he was about to reveal a confidence. 'I'd be cheating if I told you otherwise, m'sieu. I'm eighty years old, and I've never known the shooting to be worse. Not that it worries me any more, you understand.' He put his hands on his hips and cackled at the thought of it. 'I've let the lodge to a duck preservation society, they're paying me good money not to shoot anything, can you beat that?'

'Oh, that's rich,' said Ramage. 'Of course, these anti-blood sport cranks are multiplying all the time. Which lot is this, papa?'

'They call themselves The Friends of the Mallard.' He sniffed his contempt. 'Everyone knows you have to shoot some birds, or there won't be enough food to go round. But these foreigners never learn.'

'Oh, foreigners are they?'

'No offence to you, of course. Yes, these are Germans.'

'I've never heard of any society by that name. Is it a big one?'

'I doubt it. Certainly, we've never seen more than eight or ten of them here. Plenty of money, though.'

'That's the main thing.' Ramage bought them both another *pastis*. 'Any of them here now?'

'Just one. The pretty little girl over there, in the corner of the restaurant.' He shook his head. 'That's the craziest part about it, they continue to pay for the whole shoot – our rooms, the lodge, boats, lake, everything – whether they're here or not. Even when they're here they don't do any serious bird-watching. They don't seem to do anything much except eat, drink – and make love. When they're all here my wife says they're in and out of each other's beds like cuckoos in another bird's nest.'

'You can't blame them for that,' said Ramage, man to man. 'Not if the girls are all as pretty as that little one over there. What's her name?'

'Juliane. But you're wasting your time if you think you can chat her up, young fellow. She never speaks to men, never mixes.' His rheumy old eyes watched her wistfully as he dried the glasses. 'Not that I care about that kind of thing any more. Just as long as they pay me.'

'When are the others coming back, papa?'

'Who knows? They come and go as they please.'

'But you still can't let me have a room for the night?'

'I'm sorry. I'd like to have you here to talk to. But the rooms are let, I've told you.'

'In that case I'll just have lunch and be on my way.' He gave his order, and went out to the toilet. On the way back he wandered through the guest lounge, admiring the old shooting prints on the wall. It was the work of a few seconds to plant the bug Sydenham had given him. Then he went into the dining-room, and waited for his meal.

There was nothing to do but wait. Half of the twenty-four hours' grace allowed him had gone already, but he had learned a little patience in the past few weeks. Ramage had parked his car across the street from the auberge, in the village square. The rain beat down, drumming a tattoo on the roof of his rented Citroen. It was even colder than it had been in Germany, in a wet, melancholy way. The windows had steamed up, increasing the sense of isolation. He missed Laura and his family with a fierce longing. He had positioned the bug to intercept every phone call that came to the auberge: so far there had been none. He turned the dials of his portable radio and picked up the faint voice of a BBC announcer.

'News is just coming in from the West German capital,

Bonn, of a fierce gun battle in the city between men of the crack Antiterrorismus-abteilung unit and so-called commandos of the outlawed Liberation Army. First reports say that the terrorists, who had mounted an ambush on a bullion convoy carrying bars of gold bound for the Federal reserves, were flushed out of hiding by police helicopters and that in the ensuing chase at least three members of the gang were shot dead, two of them women. Six or seven others are said to have forced their way into a multi-story office block in the centre of the city where they are holding a number of workers hostage.

'There are no reports so far of any casualties among the security services although the sound of heavy firing is still coming from the area. Eye-witnesses say half-track vehicles packed with troops are moving into the surrounding streets, while unconfirmed sources claim that a contingent of paratroops is on its way to back up the Antiterrorismus-abteilung units. The BBC correspondent in Bonn says that this time all the indications are that the German authorities had been tipped off well in advance – almost certainly by an informer – about the threat of a new A.L. terrorists' strike, and had secretly moved up police and army combat teams ready to deal with any eventuality . . .'

Ramage switched off the radio, uncertain whether to cheer or weep. If what he had heard spelled the end of the Liberation Army, then it meant the long duel was over too. For that he had to be profoundly grateful. What left such a bitter-sweet taste in the mouth was the thought that he himself had been used and then shouldered aside at the moment of triumph, first by Wüst and then by Sydenham. What was it Sydenham had said to him over lunch at the club? 'I tell you we're close to him, very close: don't interfere now or you'll ruin everything.' Well, just how close they were had been revealed in the radio broadcast he had just heard. Someone in Germany – in all probability Meitner, the man who had been wounded by the booby-trap he himself had so carefully planted – had been pressured into giving the authorities a list of the new A.L. targets: and they had been waiting in strength for Elvides and company, lying in ambush for the ambushers themselves. Whether Elvides was alive and among the six or seven holed up in the office block still remained to be seen. Either way

Ramage was left to savour the unpalatable notion that he had been side-tracked here to the Somme valley while the terrorists he had so confidently sworn to kill were being rounded up hundreds of miles away: rounded up, moreover, largely as a result of the digging he himself had done, however clumsily and amateurishly. That hurt. By Christ, it hurt. Ramage sat in the car for a long, long time feeling angry and resentful and not a little foolish.

Then he looked again at the electronic apparatus he was using and wondered: what other conceivable motive could Sydenham have had in bringing him here? If the intention had been only to deceive, then it would have been easier to leave him in London, and when the news of the ambush in Bonn was announced simply to plead ignorance of the German plan. It would have been a lot kinder, and Sydenham was the type of man who would have thought of that. There would have been no way of disproving it. Instead, Sydenham – this man who owed him a favour, a man with a reputation for playing both ends against the middle – had sought him out on the eve of a top-secret operation to feed him with the location of the Liberation Army bolt-hole in Picardy. Certainly, he was protecting him. Yet one of the terrorist gang was in there still, Juliane, waiting for messages that could come only from one source now. And thanks to Sydenham, when they came he held the key – in the shape of the tiny laser bug that the Intelligence man had so thoughtfully supplied. He had even stressed that the information was Ramage's for twenty-four hours only. Of course! He would pass it on to the Deuxiéme Bureau within the next few hours because he was determined that no member of A.L. should slip through the net this time.

The fat man from Whitehall must have had it all worked out in his mind long before he came to the hotel last night. And he had contrived to pay the debt he owed a friend without betraying the far greater obligation, to his calling: a remarkable feat of tightrope walking.

The metal bug was no bigger than a flea and invisible in the afternoon shadows of the auberge. One end fed on the wall of the telephone booth inside the lounge, the other pointed to the window fronting on to the village street. Ramage adjusted the sight on his black box recorder, adjusted the clip-on audio device and settled down to wait. All the time the rain teemed down, the square was deserted, and it called for faith to keep hope alive. The call came late in the afternoon, when the light was beginning to fade.

'Auberge de Vasigny. Who is calling, please?' It was the *patron's* voice, followed by a woman's.

'Friends of the Mallard.' She was breathing hard, as if she had been running. 'I'd like to speak to Fräulein Schmidt.'

'One moment.' Electronic snuffles crackled down the line, then another woman's voice, a small, cautious one. 'Yes?'

'Juliane, is that you?'

'Yes. My God, Angela, I've been – '

'Guard your tongue, *mädchen*.' A pause. 'Tell me, how is everything with you? No shooting – to scare the ducks?'

'No. All quiet. As quiet as the grave.'

'That's good, that's good. You heard the news, of course. I'll be there about ten. Be ready to leave with me right away.'

'Of course. Angela. Are you hurt?'

'A little. Don't worry, I can drive well enough.' Another pause. 'I've been thinking. I can see your room from the courtyard. If the light's burning when I get there, I'll know everything is all right with you.'

'I'll see to it. Tell me, how many were wound – I mean who's coming with you?'

'Paul. Only Paul.'

'Oh no!'

'You don't understand, they were waiting for us, like farmers round a field waiting for rabbits when they cut the corn.' Ramage could have sworn she was weeping, but it must have been the static. 'We'll just have to rebuild, that's all, and teach them a lesson they will never *ever* forget.' The voice was growing weary, too. 'Listen, *mädchen*. Paul and I are travelling in separate cars. I can't tell you what time he'll get there, but I've told him to go straight to the lodge: to pick up the gear, you know?'

'I understand.'

'Use the time you've got to get things ready for him. He can catch up with us later. You be at the auberge before ten, and remember the light.'

'Yes. I'll remember, don't worry about anything here.'

She ran down the steps as if the devil was behind her. She wore a black beret and a pale blue raincoat and she looked slim and young and very beautiful. There was a canvas grip in her hand. The car was in the yard, behind the inn, out of sight. She drove out fast, with her headlights painting rainbows on the night air. Rain beat so hard on the roof of his Citroen Ramage could not hear her drive by. He gave her a half-mile start before he crept out on to the south-bound road. He was burning sidelights only. There was no need to hurry. He could see Juliane's car in the far distance, bumping its way down the track with the headlights pointing the way. He would take her in his own good time.

He pulled in off the road, and lifted the shotgun out of the boot. He slid a cartridge into each barrel and snapped them home, locking the twelve-bore with a loud click. Then he filled the pockets of his mackintosh with handfuls of spare ammunition, and set off for the lodge. It was dark now, as dark and lonely as Laura's grave, and as cold. It was so dark he was unable to see a foot in front of his face. The mud was so thick it was like walking through a sea of treacle. The rain lashed down. Within a minute of leaving the car he was wet to the skin, and numb with cold. Ramage felt none of it. Elvides was on his way here, and all he could feel was exhilaration.

It took him half an hour to cover those 800 yards to the lodge but then it was easy to take Juliane, as easy as stealing coppers from a blind man's can. He could have squelched down the track with a torch flickering while he whistled 'Rule Britannia', and it would still have been a piece of cake: she was a greenhorn, a novice, a simpleton, a pushover, a tenderfoot, a trusting little flower who had no right to be allowed out of the potting shed alone. He almost found time to feel sorry for her. Ramage crawled the last thirty yards through the mud on his belly, and then watched her through the slits that were cut in the walls of the shooting lodge, sited there long ago for the guns to spy on the equally unsuspecting mallard. Ramage reversed the process, and bided his time. He watched her fill the canvas grip with things he could not see, then stagger with it to the door. Then she began to drag some heavy boxes into the middle of the floor. Ramage opened the door slowly and silently and approached her as stealthily as a poacher stalking a hind. Then he swung the shotgun and hit her with the stock, not so hard that it would break her neck, hard enough to send her flying across the room to end up head-first against the bar.

Juliane crumpled into a heap, and lay quite still.

He took his time to look around for some cord, and bound her wrists. As an afterthought he tied her ankles, then dropped her back on the floor, like yesterday's shirt. He was much more interested in what the shooting lodge contained that was important enough to bring Elvides all the way from Bonn. Now he whistled aloud as he gazed about him.

A line of light automatics leaned against the wall, shining dully. He examined them closely. They were made in Czechoslovakia, exported by the Russians, and almost certainly brought into France via Libya and the hold of a tramp docking slyly at Marseilles. The hand grenades were from Italy. There were two anti-tank guns with armour piercing shot. These were British, most probably stolen from some Rhine Army depot, perhaps even sold and bought on the black market which once thrived so handsomely in Germany. There were a dozen heavy sporting guns, .357s, big enough to stop a charging rhino. The floor was heaped with pistols and revolvers and thousands of rounds of ammunition. That was just part of the A.L. armoury. The rest of the hide had been turned into a bomb factory. There were sticks of gelignite, tools galore, switches, detonators, tape and wire, and a series of sketches to show where the Fox had been holding class. He consulted his watch. It was a little after six. Four hours until Angela Schless arrived at the auberge. There was no telling when Elvides would come, but he faced the same journey as the woman. Ramage decided to make time to dump it all in the lake. The French police could recover it later, at their leisure.

He left the unconscious Juliane where she was and started carrying the weapons out to the landing stage. A handful of punts lay tied up alongside. It had stopped raining at last and the moon was trying to help him, through a break in the cloud. He paddled one load out to the middle of the lake, towing a second punt behind him. There were mallard darting in and out of the reeds, hunting for frogs. Ramage emptied his own punt, slowly: they were awkward craft and twice he nearly plunged in. It was taking too long. He pulled the unmanned craft alongside, smashed a hole in the bottom with one of the anti-tank guns, and watched it sink with a soft, gurgling rush. By eight he was almost through. He paddled back to the landing stage, hooked the painter round a wooden stake and went back into the lodge for the final load.

As he bent down to gather up the machine-guns Juliane untied the rope that bound her ankles and lunged at him with the first weapon that came to hand: Helmut's old bone-handled hunting knife. She was quick on her feet for a beginner who had taken so much punishment. Ramage was slow in turning. He dropped the guns with a clatter and took the point of the blade high in his shoulder, grunting with the pain. He backed away, stumbling through the litter of weapons. She caught him again as he reached down for one, cutting a deep line across his knuckles. He kicked out and tried to trip her, but she was too fast, too agile. This time the knife slashed down and opened his slacks from waist to knee, just missing the groin. He was a big, powerful man, a trained fighter, she was a slip of a kid, as green as they came, so green he had almost felt sorry for her: and now it looked as if she was going to kill him, even before Elvides arrived to help her. He was afraid that she would throw the knife at him. That way he would have no chance – if she was good enough. But she was loath to give up the weapon and made the mistake of coming in too close. His right hand closed on her wrist. He got his left hand under her elbow, straightened the arm and snapped it back, like the victor in a sword-fight snapping his opponent's blade. She screamed in agony, and fell. But she did not let go of the knife completely. She still held it, pointing up and as she went forward the blade came towards her and caught her under the rib-cage. The weight of her falling body did the rest. She was dead as soon as she hit the floor.

Ramage walked stiffly to the bar, sucking his knuckles. They were running with blood, so was the cut in his arm. He reached up with his left arm and took the first bottle he found: a five star cognac. He spat the cork out and took a long drink. He stripped quickly, and examined the wound in his right arm. The point had gone deep in the muscle and the whole limb was already stiffening. Ramage tore his shirt sleeve off, soaked the makeshift bandage in cognac and bound the wound tight, tying the knot with his left hand and his teeth. Now he looked at his left hand. The cut across the knuckles had laid the flesh open to the bone. He could use the hand, but it was going to slow him down and there was no way he was going to beat Elvides in a gunfight now unless he took him by surprise. He thought for a moment about that and pictured Elvides, the sly experienced old fox leaving Germany today by car. After the battle in Bonn and subsequent escape of the two A.L. ring-leaders the watch on the frontier would be doubled, trebled even in intensity, and Elvides was unlikely to risk arrest at the last fence by being caught with a weapon of any kind in his possession. So at least they would meet here on equal terms: Elvides without a gun, he himself unable to hold one properly.

In his search of the shooting lodge earlier, he had found a single gun hidden under the bar, a Colt .45 automatic fully loaded with seven rounds in the magazine. It sat on a shelf, within comfortable reach of the barman's hand but out of sight from the drinkers. It was obvious why it was there, as a standby in case of emergency. Elvides would know about it, thought Ramage: he was the kind of man who would make it his business to know where everything was in the hideout. He thought of Juliane, and the Colt under the bar, and knew what he had to do to outwit Elvides.

First he took the things he needed from the bomb store, bent over the girl's body and booby-trapped it. When he was done he carried the body out on to the track, connected up the bomb circuit and left it. It would not fool Elvides, far less kill him: but it would tell him that his enemy was here and would soften him up so that he was ready to take the bait that would finally land him, in the shape of the Colt .45. Ramage hurried back to the lodge and removed the seven rounds from the magazine. He took one and clamped it in the vice Elvides used in the bomb factory, removing the bullet first, and then the propellant charge. Next he placed the round back in the vice once more, and counter-bored it. Finally he inserted a cut-down detonator taken from the bomb store, and re-assembled the round. It was not a difficult task for an explosives expert, nor a lengthy one. He repeated the process with each round in turn and reloaded them in the magazine. When he had finished there was no way in which anyone could tell the ammunition had been tampered with – until they pulled the trigger. Ramage cocked the gun, put the safety catch on and slid the Colt back on to its shelf below the bar. He looked at his watch. It was almost ten o'clock. He had to hurry now, for there was still a final boat load to sink in the lake.

He carried everything else left in the arms cache out to the punt, the bomb-making tools, the detonators, the sticks of gelignite, every strand of wire. The hand-guns went last. He kept one for himself, a Mauser, and took care to load an empty magazine in case it fell into the wrong hands. Now there was nothing left to do but pray. He thought of Angela Schless. She was due at any moment and he had no way of knowing how she would react when she found no light on in Juliane's room – and no Juliane at the inn. Ramage decided he would cross that bridge when he got to it. Meantime, there was a duel to be fought to a finish.

With every mile he had covered since he crossed the frontier Elvides had felt increasingly naked without a gun. The Anti-terrorismus-abteilung had given them a real beating, killing all three in the leading car with their opening salvo: and the way they had surrounded that office block, the speed with which they had moved in and the sheer magnitude of the fire-power they assembled so quickly had soon convinced him that there was not going to be any deal this time, no negotiations, nothing except a long-drawn-out siege followed by the inevitable surrender and lifetime imprisonment. He had found himself alone with Angela and, after a fierce argument, had persuaded her to see reason and bolt for it with him. They had got away too, bluffed their way through the police lines in the snow-storm and made it to her 'safe' apartment, the one that no one else in the gang knew about, the one no informer could ever betray. There the two of them had changed their clothes and their appearance, after he had cut the bullet out of her leg and bound the wound. She had telephoned Juliane and told her to stand by: they were virtually home and dry. And then the stupid bitch had screwed it all up – fortunately, for herself only – by ignoring the advice he had given her and trying to smuggle a gun through the frontier. Thank God he had insisted on separate cars. She had hidden a tommygun in the false petrol tank and of course they had found it, within minutes. He could still hear her screaming and shouting abuse as they beat her up and handcuffed her, and took her away.

He had got through without any trouble. But the sheer stupidity and waste of her arrest had shaken him, and he had driven like the wind across Belgium and France, stopping only for fuel, counting the hours until he got to Vasigny and the shooting lodge. He could get a drink there, and hold a gun in his hand again. But he would not linger: it was only a matter of time before one of the gang started to blab to try to save his own skin. He would collect only the equipment he needed to make a fresh start, pick up Juliane at the inn – and disappear into the mountains of southern France till the hue and cry died down. Suddenly he saw the gates leading to the lodge loom up in the headlights. He ignored them and drove on, as if he was some passing motorist travelling south along the road. A mile further on he turned to the right and pulled up in a copse, switching off all the lights. Being a prudent man, he decided to walk down to the lodge and sniff round before committing himself finally with the car.

He took his time walking back along the road, hiding whenever a vehicle approached. No burglar breaking into a house ever made less sound than Paul Elvides as he picked his way down the track. Rain and cloud had given way now to a cold, clear moonlit night. He saw a light burning in the lodge and left the track abruptly, continuing to move forward through the field on his left. He had listened to Angela as she told Juliane to prepare everything for him, so that he could make a quick getaway: it was possible she took the order to mean she should leave a light on here, as well as in her bedroom, to indicate that all was well. Possible, even likely; but by no means certain. He decided to take no chances, and stayed off the track. It was a moment when he would have given £10,000 to have the feel of a gun in his hand, a weapon of any kind: he felt so naked. He kept on towards the lodge. He saw her when she was still thirty yards away, sprawled across the track. No one needed to tell him Juliane was dead. He dropped to the ground like a stone, and lay motionless. He lay there in the mud for perhaps half an hour, not moving a muscle. No one opened fire. No one challenged him. Nothing moved, except the rare cloud overhead. There was no sound. Only a single light burning, above the bar. He began to inch his way forward again.

As soon as he got close to the body, he knew immediately Ramage was waiting for him somewhere in the darkness. Juliane's mouth was wide open, crammed with plastic explosive. An electronic detonator caught the moonlight, glinting like some grotesque filling among her white teeth. The wire that led from it trailed across her stomach, peeped coyly into view through the muddied raincoat for a quarter of an inch or so, and then disappeared again between her legs. It had to be Ramage's handiwork. No one else in the world would have prepared a welcome for him like that, and comparatively few would have known how. It was a genuine bomb circuit, a classic example of the clothes-peg booby trap device. Ramage would have defused a great many like it in Aden and Ulster and had borrowed the technique to try to kill the Fox with it tonight. Not bad, thought Elvides grudgingly, not bad at all. Ramage had been a little unlucky with the weather, with the pitch dark and the rain giving way to bright moonlight. And he had done the best he could in the time available. He had obviously beaten up Juliane to make her tell him when he and Angela were due to arrive. But clearly that was all she had told him and Ramage hadn't been able to make up his mind where best to ambush them, at the shooting lodge or back at the auberge. He had been forced to make a decision – and he had wired up the dead Juliane to keep watch for him here while he waited back in the village. He forgot one thing, thought Elvides: he forgot he was up against the world's greatest bomb-maker, an expert who would spot the booby-trap a mile off, even in total darkness. I will now go into the lodge and take what I need, he said to himself and deal with the Englishman when I am good and ready.

He crept round the outside of the building, peering in through the slits to make certain there was no one inside. He could not see the floor and had no way of telling Ramage had stripped the cupboard bare. He stared round him when he finally went in, unable to believe his eyes. Everything had gone, guns, ammunition, grenades, bazookas, all the components and explosives from the bomb factory. One glance down at the muddy footmarks running across the floor told him where they had gone: into the lake. There was only one thing to do now – to run, while he could. But as he turned to go, he remembered. Helmut had always insisted they keep one gun hidden from sight in case of a sudden emergency: it was a Colt .45, a stopper, placed just within reach of a man's hand beneath the bar, on the shelf behind a row of glasses. Kurt had told him how they planned to use it on him on the night of the kangaroo court, until he had turned the tables on the big German by taking him apart with his bare hands. Elvides went behind the bar, bent down to look – and there it was. He checked the ammunition: the magazine was full. With this revolver in his hand he could knock Ramage down at fifteen paces, exactly the distance between him and the door. He was back in business.

There were bottles on the shelves behind him, too. He needed a drink almost as badly as he had coveted a weapon. He took the cork out of a bottle of Black Label and sniffed it, cautiously. The best blended whisky in the world, and it was unadulterated. Elvides left the cork on the counter, tilted the bottle to his lips and drank. Magnificent, nonpareil, life-saving, courage-restoring, uplifting whisky. He drank some more. Then some more. For the first time since the disasters of the morning he felt good again: invincible. He decided to take a last look outside before he left, and peered through one of the slits at the track. Moonlight made it almost as bright as day now. And there was a figure approaching, a tall bare-headed burly figure carrying a revolver in his hand. Elvides waited against the wall inside the door, and let him come in. Then he jammed the barrel of the .45 into the Englishman's back.

'Drop it,' he ordered. The gun clattered to the floor. Elvides kicked it aside. 'Hands on the wall,' he said, and searched him. He was unarmed.

'You can turn round now,' said Elvides. As Ramage turned to face him the Greek pistol-whipped him, raking the long barrel and raised foresight hard across the nose and mouth and cheekbone until he sank to his knees.

'You amateur,' said the Greek, contemptuously. 'Did you really think you could kill me – Paul Elvides – with that . . . that contraption you rigged up out there? I'm afraid you wasted your time booby-trapping little Juliane, my friend. Angela might have fallen for it, but not me. I graduated from that school more than twenty years ago. And Angela won't be coming at all. They picked her up at the border tonight. You killed Juliane for nothing.'

Ramage made no reply. Elvides hit him again and left him lying on the floor, dazed and bleeding. Then he went back to the bar, placed the .45 on the counter within reach of his right hand and took another drink. He stared at the eye patch, and nodded.

'Take it off. I want to see how badly I hurt you.' Ramage took off the black patch and stared back defiantly. 'That's good,' said Elvides. 'That's very good. It must have hurt like hell when I shot you.'

He was nothing like the man Ramage had expected. For twenty years he had seen in his mind's eye the Identikit drawing of a handsome young man with jet-black hair and film star looks. The terrorist standing by the bar could have been seventy years old. His hair was silver, so were his eyebrows. His clothes were shiny and old-fashioned and he wore a celluloid collar that dated back to pre-war days in Athens – and the heyday of the late Andreas Spiliotopoulis, his cover for leaving Germany with the Antiterrorismus-abteilung on his heels. Ramage had never thought of a disguise. He simply looked at him and wondered why he had ever been afraid.

'We're the same kind of people Ramage, did you ever think of that? Oh, I read all about you in the papers in England, after we kidnapped your son. It's strange, I always used to think of you as a rich man because you were an Army officer, but not a bit of it, you were born a poor boy, like me. And we both made our names in the world of explosives, you on one side, me on the other and we both got right to the top of the tree. And listen to something else – we're both colonels, did you know that? They made me a colonel in the KGB on the same day we shot your wife and kidnapped your son. Not for that, naturally: for past service to the Cause.'

Ramage watched him, saying nothing.

'I hope you're as brave as I am, too. Jesus, you should have heard those Liberation Army commandos of mine squeak when the soldiers caught up with us this morning. They cried their eyes out when the bullets started to whistle round *their* ears for a change, I can tell you. They were a rabble and I told Angela so. Gutless wonders. Yellow. You won't be like that when I shoot you tonight, I hope? No. I think not. You'll look at me with that ugly dead eye of yours and wait for me to get on with it, but you won't beg.'

Up went the bottle again and he took another long drink. He thought of something else, and he laughed. 'Your wife screamed loud enough, though, my word she did, before Gisele put her out of her misery. Don't look at me like that Ramage, there's nothing you can do about it, not a damned thing. You'll soon be joining her, anyway.' He drank again. 'I enjoyed hearing Mrs Ramage scream, I don't mind telling you. It was a kind of poetic justice ordering her to be shot – because you killed Elli, you bastard, didn't you? That's right, look surprised, I expect you've forgotten that: blowing up the bomb factory in Nicosia all those years ago and pretending you didn't know my wife was trapped inside. You must have known it though, yet you went ahead and blew the house up – and her with it. We'd been married one whole day. Oh, you bastard!'

He hurled the bottle at Ramage. It missed him and shattered against the wall. Ramage made no attempt to duck or turn away. He just sat there with the blood trickling down his face, watching the Greek, and spoke for the first time.

'I never realised why you wanted to kill me,' he said, 'until now. If your wife was in that house I never saw her. I was last man out, and I checked every room. Then I waited until the patrols had checked every house in the street to make sure no one was left inside before I blew up that factory. I don't kill women and children, Elvides. I leave that to scum like you.'

'Listen to the man,' jeered Elvides. 'What about Juliane?'

'She attacked me with a knife. I fought her off. She stumbled over a pile of your guns and killed herself.' Ramage had had enough, and started to get to his feet.

Elvides picked up the .45 and waited. 'I'm going back to your home after you're dead, Ramage, to kill the rest of the family. I'll shoot John first, your boy. I understand he hurt his legs and his back when he fell out of the window: well, don't worry, I won't let him grow up to be a cripple.' He smiled. 'And I shall enjoy meeting your daughter, very much. I've seen her picture in the papers. Such a pretty girl. I'll keep her with me for a long time before I kill her, you can be absolutely sure of that.'

Ramage had pulled himself upright now. He leaned against the wall with a curious expression on his face, one almost of impatience, and started to come towards Elvides, very slowly.

'So many times I should have killed you,' said Elvides wonderingly. 'When you lost that eye, when I shot you in your garden at point-blank range . . . tell me, are you wearing the bullet-proof vest again tonight, my friend, eh? It doesn't matter this time I'm going to make sure.' He raised the gun and held it with both hands, aiming the foresight between the good eye and the empty socket.

Still Ramage came on. The barrel of the gun was almost

touching his forehead. In the final moment of his victory Elvides searched his mind and found there was no thought of communism there, no sense of loyalty to anyone or anything, no trumpet sounding for the Cause: only a feeling of sadness, and payment deferred for a pretty girl choking to death in the old walled city of Nicosia.

'For you, Elli!' he shouted, and pulled the trigger.

The striker propelled by the metal spring travelled three millimetres in a thousandth part of a second, and impinged on the nickelled surface of the percussion cap below. The cap in its turn crushed against the tiny brass internal anvil, fired instantly, and the flash rushing through the firehole sought the charge of the propellant which should have awaited it. Instead it burned against the cut-down base of the detonator, which detonated instantaneously. At once, the build-up of pressure in a minute steel chamber designed to withstand a maximum of four tons to the square inch soared far beyond that figure. The locking lugs of the breech block tore from their seat and the steel block inside the Colt – propelled now by a force far greater than its designer ever anticipated – rocketed back along the slide, and into the face of the man who pulled the trigger, Paul Elvides.

The block measured one inch long and weighed perhaps one and a quarter ounces. It plucked out Elvides' right eye, killing him instantly.